BARRACUDA BAY

A Detective Emilia Cruz Novel

Carmen Amato

BARRACUDA BAY

Copyright © 2025 Carmen Amato. All rights reserved.

Published 2025 by Laurel & Croton
Trade Paperback Edition

Identifiers: ISBN: 979-8-9891403-7-4 (Print)
ISBN: 979-8-9891403-6-7 (Ebook)

Praise for Detective Emilia Cruz

CLIFF DIVER

"From the moment I started the first one, I couldn't put it down. . . Her work touches on important issues affecting Mexico in a real, human way and is exciting, fast paced and utterly gripping." – *Mexico Retold*

HAT DANCE

[Emilia] is a force to be reckoned with." – *Mystery Sequels*

DIABLO NIGHTS

"Amato brings her characters to life with her vivid writing style and sets them on the streets of a Mexico steeped in Catholicism and corruption." – *OnlineBookClub.org*

KING PESO

"Danger and betrayal never more than a few pages away." – *Kirkus Reviews*

PACIFIC REAPER

"Carmen Amato . . . out does many of the best crime authors out there." – *Artisan Book Reviews*

43 MISSING

"A fast-paced procedural . . . a real page-turner . . . a very original plot." – *The BookLife Prize*

Also by Carmen Amato

DETECTIVE EMILIA CRUZ SERIES

CLIFF DIVER
HAT DANCE
DIABLO NIGHTS
KING PESO
PACIFIC REAPER
43 MISSING
RUSSIAN MOJITO
NARCO NOIR
BARRACUDA BAY
MADE IN ACAPULCO
FELIZ NAVIDAD FROM ACAPULCO
THE LISTMAKER OF ACAPULCO

GALLIANO CLUB SERIES

ROAD TO THE GALLIANO CLUB
MURDER AT THE GALLIANO CLUB
BLACKMAIL AT THE GALLIANO CLUB
REVENGE AT THE GALLIANO CLUB

THRILLERS

AWAKENING MACBETH
THE HIDDEN LIGHT OF MEXICO CITY

Barracuda Bay is dedicated to the memory of my mother Jean.

Forever Emilia Cruz's biggest fan.

Regarding names and monetary conversion

Regarding Mexican names: It is the custom in Mexico to use two surnames. The first is from the father's family and is always used. The second surname is the name of the mother's father. The second is sometimes dropped in conversation and/or to shorten the name in keeping with American and European naming conventions.

Conversion rate: For the purposes of this novel, $US1.00 = 10 Mexican pesos.

Spanish words: A glossary of Spanish words and terms commonly used in the Detective Emilia Cruz series is included at the end of this book.

**I'm a fighter who can adapt
to my surroundings.**

Canelo Alvarez

PROLOGUE

He swaggered in like he owned the place. The diamond embedded in the gun's grip was tight against his hand.

His target scooted her chair away from the table. Eyes wide with fear. Made a little gasping sound. Hands up. Pink nail polish.

Bam, bam and it was done, pretty as a picture.

The woman sort of collapsed in on herself. Chin flopped onto her chest. Hands dropped into her lap, red and slick. Shoulders slumped. She slid down like a rag doll but didn't fall out of the chair.

A man was seated at the table, wearing a nice suit right out of a magazine. Nodded to say the deed was done.

They'd been having a party. Tablecloth and napkins and real china plates. High above, a fancy chandelier like in an opera house with somebody about to sing nonsense real loud. Not her, of course, unless she came back to life.

He imagined the video game. Screen all black until the assassin comes in, shoots the target, she turns into a zombie and he has to shoot her over and over to rack up the score.

It would be even better if the woman came back to life as a different person each time. Different enemies. Different targets.

Bam, bam. Bam, bam.

The crazy game idea collided with the adrenaline flooding his body. His vision went swimmy and he started to laugh uncontrollably. The gales of laughter sent him staggering, gun still in his hand like an extension of his body.

The man in the suit watched him.

Eventually the laughter ran out of fuel. He remembered that the clock was ticking and the instructions he'd been given.

Still holding the gun, he went over to the dead woman and used his elbow to shove her head against the back of the chair. There was a fancy sparkler on her left hand. It came off easily, her finger lubricated with blood.

"That's mine," the suit said.

CHAPTER 1

In the days to come, Emilia Cruz Encinos would remember that golden morning. If only she'd been able to bottle it, like a secret elixir of courage when she was on the run and alone and frightened.

Emilia had returned home last night from a 3-week assignment in Chilpancingo to the penthouse she shared with Kurt Rucker in the Palacio Real hotel, which he managed. They'd shut out the world and celebrated the way lovers do after too long apart.

While most of their reunion festivities took place in the bedroom and the shower, they had spared ten minutes to plan a Christmas trip to New York to break the news of their engagement to Kurt's parents. It would be Emilia's first trip out of Mexico.

Now it was noon and they were on the way downtown. The SUV sped along the Carretera Escénica toward central Acapulco and their appointment in the Colonia Progreso neighborhood on the other side of the bay.

As Kurt drove, the road unspooled like a gray ribbon, hugging the mountain that guarded the city. To the left, sunshine gilded the leading edges of the ocean waves lapping at the shore. A rim of deep blue indicated the horizon.

It was a view Emilia never tired of seeing.

Sunday traffic was light as they passed the sign for the Las Brisas resort, where lavender-pink jeeps ferried guests to their *casitas*. To make the day even more perfect, a favorite Maná song was playing on the car stereo.

Emilia pulled on her sunglasses, feeling sexy and elegant in a new midriff-baring top with skimpy straps that the salesgirl had called a bralette. She'd paired it with high heeled sandals and a flaring black and white skirt that fell to just above her ankles. The perfect outfit for a leisurely real estate tour followed by dinner at Acapulco's trendiest restaurant, a tapas bar called Madrid.

Her engagement ring caught the sun as she turned her hand to play with the ovals of light that bounced off the dashboard, reflecting the shape of the center stone. She never wore the ring to work, when on any given day she could be scraping dead gangbangers off the sidewalk in the El Roble neighborhood or wrestling drug-addled suspects into handcuffs in front of the Fuerte de San Diego fortress.

Today, the deep red ruby matched her lipstick.

As soon as they completed all the paperwork, hers for the police department and Kurt's for permanent expatriate resident status, they could get serious about planning the wedding.

Hopefully in May, seven months away, she would become Señora Emilia Cruz de Rucker, dropping her mother's name of Encinos, as was the custom.

Of course in the squadroom she'd still be Detective Emilia Cruz of the Acapulco police department.

Acapulco's sugary white skyline took shape in the distance, heralded by a phalanx of billboards advertising candidates for mayor on either side of the highway. Enormous faces loomed over cars traveling in both directions.

"When did all these billboards go up?" Emilia asked. "I don't recall there being so many."

"I heard this is the most expensive mayoral race in Acapulco's history." Sunshine caught Kurt's profile as he drove, turning blonde hair to spun gold and throwing shadows across the dark blue polo shirt hugging his toned torso. Sometimes, Emilia's heart clenched just to look at him.

"Where did you hear that?" she asked.

"Last hotel association meeting. No one has seen a campaign like this."

In addition to managing the Palacio Real hotel, Kurt was the current president of the Acapulco Hotel Association, an expert in high threat area hospitality, a dedicated triathlete and a reluctant member of the mayor's committee exploring the possibility of Acapulco hosting a Summer Olympics.

Although five candidates were running for mayor, the election was really between incumbent Carlota Montoya Perez and Nadio Vallejo Loy, a businessman who'd made a fortune putting up cell phone towers across the state of Guerrero. *The man for the job!* was his signature slogan. It was a dig at Acapulco's first female mayor as well as a reminder of the way violent crime had skyrocketed during Carlota's tenure.

Carlota was popular but Vallejo Loy had plenty of ammunition to throw at her re-election campaign, ammunition that no amount of recycling schemes or potential Olympic glory could blunt.

Elections were the reason why Emilia had been working non-stop for a month, the same as every other cop across the state of Guerrero. Voting for city officials had become a flashpoint for violence, with candidates murdered and their families terrorized by cartel gangs.

Things were so bad that municipal elections across the

state had been rescheduled. Instead of all localities going to the polls on the same day, elections in the state's major cities were staggered throughout the last half of an election year. The goal was to send flying squads of police officers from across the state to whichever city was holding elections. Emilia had been assigned to a squad on loan to the Chilpancingo police to manage elections there.

With that vote over, it was time to swing into high gear for the home team. Acapulco's vote was coming up in mid-November, just a few short weeks away.

They had just passed the southern end of the park bordering Playa Icacos when traffic ground to a halt. Four car lengths ahead, the statue of Diana the Huntress presided over the traffic circle poised like a referee between beach access and a maze of concentric half-circle streets.

Mexican flags and yellow banners came into sight, passing in front of the base of the statue, held high enough to be seen above the roofs of the stalled cars. Lively mariachi music poured in, along with the chants of many voices.

"Another rally for Carlota," Emilia said, recognizing the distinctive yellow color used by the mayor's campaign.

Dozens of teens in yellow tees and ball caps swarmed the line of stopped cars as a five piece mariachi band strolled down the center of the highway between the opposing lanes. The yellow tee shirts chanted the mayor's name as they slipped flyers under windshield wipers. *CAR-LOH-TAH, CAR-LOH-TAH!*

Kurt slid his window down, plucked the flyer off the glass, and handed it to Emilia.

Traffic started up again, the mariachi music gradually

fading. Emilia idly looked at the slickly produced brochure plastered with color photos of Carlota presiding over a meeting, making a speech, leaving a bottle in one of Acapulco's new recycling receptacles, and donating schoolbooks to a room full of children. Once upon a time, Emilia had voted for Carlota because she was the most exciting politician in Acapulco. But as the violence skyrocketed, Carlota's continued popularity felt false. The bid to host a Summer Olympics felt more like a gimmick to distract than a policy to lift the city out of trouble.

Perhaps Vallejo Loy was the more sensible choice. He wanted to reduce gang activity by keeping kids in school, improve training programs and offer tax incentives to revitalize Acapulco's business sector.

They passed the huge Parque Papagayo, turning right toward the Colonia Progreso neighborhood. The ocean was at their back now, slowly disappearing from view as they drove deeper into the residential area.

Colonia Progreso was a hilly mosaic of ochre, amber, and cherry stucco against the bright blue sky. Emilia liked this neighborhood with its undulating streets. Clustered closer together than in more modern parts of the city, houses were large and well-tended. Jacaranda trees bloomed blue and purple inside wrought iron gates. Pots of red geraniums and waxy lemon trees studded porches and patios.

While the tight architecture meant that Colonia Progreso lacked the airy spaciousness of the more famous Las Brisas neighborhood on the east side of the bay, the elevation gave most houses a rooftop view of the ocean.

"This is it," Emilia said as they approached a street corner dominated by massive gray walls topped with jagged shards of glass.

Casa de Plata.

House of Silver.

"Battleship meets Luis Barragán," Kurt observed.

They passed through open metal gates into an expansive courtyard. Two other vehicles were already there. Emilia recognized one as belonging to her former partner and current boss, Franco Silvio. The other was a sporty German model that was much newer and much, much more expensive than Silvio's battered official sedan.

Kurt cut the engine and leaned across the console. Emilia met his kiss halfway, her hand stroking the hard line of his jaw, regretting that they had to pop the private bubble of bliss they'd been in since last night.

"Hold onto that thought for later," Kurt said softly as they eased apart.

Her heart gave a happy flutter at the way he could read her mind.

They made their way across the courtyard to where Silvio and Emilia's best friend Mercedes Sandoval were waiting in front of Casa de Plata's massive two-story entrance. To Emilia's surprise, the ex-heavyweight boxer had shed his usual white tee and granite-jawed scowl for a black polo shirt and a pair of Ray-Ban sunglasses. Next to him, Mercedes glowed with happiness in a strapless pink sundress that swirled around her ankles in the breeze. Brown hair tumbled over one shoulder.

"You look gorgeous," Emilia murmured as she and Mercedes exchanged kisses. "Are you really ready to move in together?"

"I'm more than ready." Mercedes smiled and stepped back, holding Emilia at arm's length to admire the full skirt and skimpy bralette top. "You look very sexy, *chica*."

Before Emilia could reply, Silvio cut in and gave her a clumsy buss on the cheek. "*Rayos*, Cruz. Heard you didn't fuck up in Chilpancingo. Don't wear that shirt in the office."

"Nice to see you, too." Emilia couldn't help smiling as he caught Mercedes's hand in his big paw. Silvio drove Emilia *loco* most of the time, but he was finally in a good place after his wife's murder two years ago.

Kurt came to stand next to Emilia. His eyes roamed over the massive gray building's stained and cracked facade. "This place could be amazing, Franco. But you weren't kidding when you said it needed work."

Once a famous architectural gem in the style of famed Mexican architect Luis Barragán, Casa de Plata was a two-story monolith of horizontal lines edged with the remnants of a tile frieze depicting the *flota de plata,* the treasure ships hauling New World treasure to Spain. Housing four apartments, two up and two down, the building had been abandoned for years.

Most recently, a *federale* unit operating undercover as the police department's Financial Crimes unit had used the abandoned property for an operation targeting a drug distribution network run by fugitive druglord Diego Barrielos Luna. Emilia had played a small and unhappy role in the operation. She could do without encountering *federale* lieutenant Vicente Campos and his double-dealing fake accountants ever again.

Not much had changed since the *federale* operation. In front of the two-story entrance, a bronze galleon sailed over a giant cement fountain lined with bird droppings and scraps of dry palm fronds. Broken windows, crumbling stucco, and tears of rust cried out for repairs.

Despite its dilapidated state, Casa de Plata was a smart investment for someone who believed that Acapulco was still a good place to live. Properties in Colonia Progreso were holding value compared to other neighborhoods. Plus, the extra apartments offered not only rental potential but space for Mercedes to have a private dance studio.

Silvio could afford both the purchase price and the upgrades thanks to a duffel bag of money he had liberated from a crooked Russian diplomat, some of which had already provided Emilia with a new car and a home for her mother. He simply needed a cover story to avoid inevitable questions about buying and refurbishing a huge property in pricey Colonia Progreso on a police lieutenant's relatively modest salary.

That's how Emilia found herself, along with Kurt and Silvio and Mercedes, partners in a real estate scheme financed by Russian money and propped up by Kurt's undeniable affluence and unassailable standing in the expatriate community. With Kurt Rucker's name on the dotted line next to Silvio's, no one would question the purchase.

The front door opened and a stylishly slim man emerged, holding a sheaf of brochures. "Are we ready?" he asked.

Silvio made the introductions. Felipe Hernandez was from Metro Properties, the listing agent for the property. Shoulder-length hair waved back from a high forehead combined with skinny distressed jeans, blue shirt with an elongated collar and a plaid blazer to make him resemble a Zara shopper looking for the sale rack. Everything fit him like a coat of latex paint.

"I think you'll be very impressed." Hernandez eagerly distributed brochures featuring a computer-rendered image of Casa de Plata as a glorious mid-century showplace. Palm trees framed the building, blue water gushed out of the fountain and sun slanted across a paler shade of gray stucco. Tiny Spanish galleons sailed bravely across the bands of mosaic edging the roofline and balconies, carrying their loads of silver to captivated real estate shoppers. "Shall we start the tour?"

He ushered them in and flipped a switch.

Emilia nearly gasped at the dramatic change since she was there with the *federale* operation. Not only was there electricity, but the curtains of cobwebs and layers of dusty grime were gone. The place had been repainted and moldy furniture removed.

Two stories above, an enormous sputnik-style brass chandelier burst into life, casting a dazzling pattern against creamy walls. A massive stairway rose from the terrazzo floor and divided halfway to the second floor. Open circles of wrought iron created a unique banister that married mid-century modern design and traditional Mexican craftsmanship. The marble floor shone.

Silvio caught Emilia's eye; he'd been there before as well.

"This is amazing," Mercedes breathed.

The first apartment they toured was on the west side of the foyer. It was empty and clean, making the cracked stucco and broken windows even more obvious.

"The floors are still in good shape," Kurt remarked to Silvio as they passed through to the dining room.

Emilia trailed the group, seeing the empty rooms through the lens of the recent past. Would the upstairs be as clean?

That's where she'd found a packet of money intended for a snitch who worked for Rafa Gamboa, a deep cover *federale* agent.

And her brother.

"The two sides of Casa de Plata are mirror images of each other," Hernandez said as he relocked the apartment door and led them across the dramatic foyer to the apartment on the other side. The real estate agent had a habit of flicking his head so that the long hair stayed out of his eyes. "You'll see how this layout is exactly the same, only reversed, when we see the apartment on the other side."

He ushered them into a living room in the second apartment that was, as promised, a mirror image of the other layout.

"This is almost move-in ready," Mercedes marveled.

Emilia had to agree. Glass twinkled in the living room windows. The stucco had a few cracks, but nothing like the chipping and flaking in the other apartment.

Help me.

The sound was no more than a breathy vibration.

Help me.

"Did you hear that?" Emilia gasped.

"Hear what?" Kurt asked.

"I heard a voice." Emilia looked around, expecting to see someone else in the room besides their group.

With another twitch of his head to keep his hair in place, Hernandez held up his ring of keys. "No one else is here, I can assure you."

"Of course." Emilia gave herself a mental shake. If she was hearing things, it was because she was exhausted from the nonstop work in Chilpancingo and exuberant reunion with Kurt.

"Shall we continue?" Hernandez asked brightly and opened the door to the dining room, releasing a gust of foul air.

"Wait," Silvio said and kept Mercedes from following the realtor.

"A new water pump will--." Hernandez stopped talking. The brochures cascaded to the floor as his hands went to his mouth. He screamed, releasing a feral pitch that reverberated off the hard stucco.

Silvio pushed the realtor aside as the rest of the group came through the doorway.

"*Madre de Dios*," Emilia exclaimed.

Kurt said something in English that she didn't catch.

Mercedes gave a gasping cry.

"She's dead." Hernandez screamed again and again. His keening was primal and panicked. "She's dead. Do you see that? She's dead."

"Call it in," Silvio barked as he hustled both the realtor and Mercedes out of the room.

Emilia fumbled in her purse for her cell phone, unable to take her eyes off the gruesome scene in the dining room.

A halo of flies writhed around the body of a woman slumped in an armchair positioned several feet away from a massive mahogany table. The woman's eyes were closed, long lashes making a dark halo on high cheekbones as if she was asleep with her chin resting on one shoulder.

She looked to be in her late 20s, with glossy light brown hair pulled into a sleek ponytail, the same hairstyle as Emilia. Plum-colored lipstick and small gold earrings completed her ensemble.

The bodice of her silky blouse was soaked with blood. More stained both hands lying palms up in her lap. Blood had leached into the thighs of her cream colored trousers.

The smell of death was musty and acidic at the same time. The feasting flies made a hideous drone.

"I know her," Kurt said.

Emilia froze, cell phone in hand. "What?"

"I know her," Kurt repeated, making an obvious effort to control his voice. "I met her at the opening of the new consulate a few months ago."

"Who is she?"

"Her name is Monica Montoya," Kurt said. "She's Carlota's sister."

CHAPTER 2

Doctor Antonio Prade, the coroner who ran Acapulco's morgue, lifted the sheet shrouding the body on the examination table to expose the face and torso of the woman from Casa de Plata. She still wore the bloody clothing she'd died in.

In their finery, mayor Carlota Montoya Perez and her escort Victor Obregon, head of the police union for the state of Guerrero, were out of place in the morgue's examination room with its floor drains and banks of stainless steel body drawers. Apparently, the call had caught them as they were heading to some glamorous campaign fundraiser.

Beautifully ageless, Carlota wore a silver lame evening gown that was apparently held up by magic. Her jet-black hair was swept into a low chignon that showed off dangly diamond earrings that Emilia was sure were genuine. Obregon was in a tuxedo, the severe cut accentuating his hawk-like features and dark hooded eyes.

Emilia fought both nausea and a sense of claustrophobia.

The air was heavily scented with the morgue's signature miasma of intestinal offal, chemical preservatives and lavender Fabuloso cleaner. The noxious smells were exaggerated by the crush of too many bodies occupying too little space and trying very hard not to be sick.

Besides Emilia and Silvio, Carlota and Obregon and Prade, Chief of Police Rodrigo Salazar loomed over the proceedings to formally identify the body, knocking elbows with Enrique Santibañez, Carlota's chief of staff who was a testy, bossy man.

"Yes," Carlota said faintly, then again more strongly. "Yes. That is my half-sister, Monica Montoya Alvarez."

For a long moment, no one spoke. Carlota stayed rooted in place, a small silver purse dangling from her left wrist.

Emilia had to give Silvio credit for immediately calling Chief Salazar. Now that he was a lieutenant, the big ex-heavyweight champ often showed a surprising flash of political acuity. Of course, neither had any idea what would now happen to the plan to purchase Casa de Plata, which had just become the most politically sensitive crime scene in Acapulco history.

Carlota stayed motionless by the body. Shoulders slumped, head bowed, eyes closed, one hand on the sheet at her sister's waist as if saying a silent prayer.

Santibañez snapped her photo with a cell phone, then leaned to the side to capture a different angle. *Click, click, click.*

Emilia's blood boiled. The man was a ghoul.

"Please, I've seen enough." Carlota straightened and directed her attention to Prade. "What have you found out?"

Prade gestured to his assistant to cover the body. "Your sister was shot twice and would have died instantly. Moreover, she was holding her hands up like this." He held both hands at chest level, palms out. "Each bullet went through a hand before entering the chest."

"Shot through both hands?" Obregon asked skeptically.

"Yes, exactly."

"Let me see." The order was brusque. Obregon was a man accustomed to being obeyed.

The dead woman's body was revealed again.

Prade raised the right hand over her chest, palm out, holding it over a hole above her right breast. "It looks like she held out both hands in front of herself, six or seven inches from her chest. Two bullets, each one passing through a raised hand before entering the chest and killing her."

Positioned that way, the hole in the hand aligned perfectly with the hole in her chest, inches from an identical hole on her left side that would have stopped her heart.

Emilia and Silvio exchanged a look. She knew what he was thinking because she had the same thought. Was shooting through hands some sort of killer signature?

Prade gently lowered the hand and covered the body again. "She was shot at close range with both hands raised as if in defense," he said. "From the trajectory, I estimate she was seated and directly facing her killer."

"The crime scene tech teams are at the scene now, señora," Silvio said. "We'll have more information in a few hours."

Obregon opened the door and escorted Carlota into the hallway, Santibañez at her heels. Chief Salazar motioned to Emilia and Silvio to follow.

Once they were clustered outside the examination room, Chief Salazar cleared his throat. "Señora, the police department would like to offer condolences. I'm putting the homicide unit at your disposal."

The chief reminded Emilia of pictures of old Spanish dons: a narrow face, hawk-like nose, bald head like a shiny brown egg emerging from his ornate police uniform. He was not a fan of females in his department. Emilia's bralette top would be another mark in his book against her.

"Monica's mother needs to be told," Carlota said.

Obregon's hawk-like stare slid to Emilia and Silvio. "Lieutenant Silvio and Detective Cruz discovered the body.

Send them."

"*Por Dios*, that vampire Victoria will accuse me of disrespect." Carlota squared her shoulders but her eyes were suspiciously dewy. "Rodrigo, I'd like you to go. Take Hector Placido. As campaign manager he is . . . was Monica's boss."

"Of course," Salazar said.

Carlota turned to Santibañez. "Prepare a statement for the press. Send it out first thing in the morning. This will give us all a little time to cope. Let everyone know I'll be doing a press conference tomorrow afternoon."

"With her mother?"

"Absolutely not. No, just me. I'll do it from my office. Put a picture of Monica on the desk next to me. We'll dedicate our election victory to her."

Emilia watched Carlota rattle off decisions, both awed and repulsed by the swift transition from grief to public relations planning.

Santibañez bobbed his head. "Of course, señora. I'll get that arranged for tomorrow afternoon."

Carlota rounded on Salazar. "How long before you catch my sister's murderer?"

"Señora, I can hardly say now--."

"Who has the best record in your department?"

Salazar blinked. "Señora, be assured we will have--."

"Detective Cruz has an excellent record," Obregon interrupted silkily. "Given that she and Lieutenant Silvio discovered Monica's body, they probably have several leads already."

Carlota swung around as if noticing the two detectives for the first time. "Yes, excellent. I want you two handling this investigation. Find out who did this to my sister."

Before either Emilia or Silvio could speak, Salazar replied with a tight-lipped nod. "Of course, señora. If that's what you want."

Carlota stabbed a finger in the air at Salazar, anger finally breaking through her elegant facade. "I want to know what's going on each and every day until you arrest whoever is responsible. And I will be the first to know when you do."

"Daily briefings," Santibañez declared.

"The full resources of the police department, Rodrigo." Carlota's voice rose in volume and intensity. "Monica was my family. Do you understand? Family!"

She and Obregon swept out a minute later, Santibañez following like a tugboat bobbing in the wake of a luxury ocean liner.

As soon as they were gone, it was suddenly easier to breathe, although Chief Salazar pointed to Silvio. "Lieutenant, you're with me. We'll collect Placido on the way but I want the mother to see who's leading the investigation."

He gave Emilia's bralette top and full skirt a pointed look of disdain, then turned on his heel and marched toward the exit, skirting the trio of elderly women mopping the floor.

"Stay here for the autopsy," Silvio murmured to her. "Call Dispatch for a squad car back to the squadroom when you're done."

"I'll meet you there," Emilia said.

She watched him pass the row of big metal carts flanking one side of the corridor, black body bags stacked three high. The dead waiting to be processed.

Monica Montoya Alvarez had jumped to the head of the

line. Even dead, it paid to have connections.

Emilia donned one of Prade's threadbare lab coats over her cherished outfit and watched Prade poke and prod Monica Montoya's flaccid body.

"Shreds of pork fat and bits of almond are caught between Monica's back molars," Prade announced for the benefit of the recording equipment in the room. "Olive oil on the thumb and forefinger of the right hand. Blood smears interrupt the blood pattern on both the ring and pinky fingers of the left hand, suggesting contact with an object after the shooting."

Emilia looked away as he proceeded to open the body. Her stomach was empty but it still took force of will not to gag. It wasn't so much the smell, which was lessened by both her mask and the eye-watering smell of disinfectant, but the sounds. Ribs cracking. The buzz of Prade's electric saw. Slithering, goopy sounds of entrails being slopped into a bowl.

"Well, what have we here?" Prade sounded intrigued. "Emilia, you should see this. The stomach contents are completely undigested. I can smell the champagne. Death occurred within minutes of eating."

"Eating?" Emilia's stomach gave a lurch of protest at the mention of food in such a fetid atmosphere. "But there wasn't any food at the scene."

"I can only tell you what the body shows me, Emilia."

By the time the body was stitched back together and secured in a closed stainless steel drawer, the preliminary laboratory report was ready. Prade took Emilia into his office down the hall to review it.

Monica Montoya had eaten mushrooms, cheese, eggs, flour, lard, olives, potatoes, almonds, shrimp, and sausage. The food was accompanied by champagne, but so recently that the alcohol wasn't yet in her bloodstream. Time of death was estimated to be between nine o'clock and midnight of the day before.

"Tapas," Emilia muttered to herself. She glanced up from the tablet displaying the results. "Mushroom tarts. Potato and chorizo puffs. Spiced olives. That's how she got olive oil on her fingers." She mimed picking up an olive with thumb and forefinger.

This wasn't the first time she'd sat in Prade's cluttered office in the morgue, drinking tea and paging through autopsy reports. Over the years Emilia had come to know him fairly well, largely because he treated her as respectfully as he treated male detectives. Moreover, Prade knew about the list of missing women Emilia kept that she called *Las Perdidas*—The Lost Ones. He always let her know if an unidentified female passed through the morgue.

"Tapas," Prade repeated and removed his lab coat, revealing an equally threadbare pair of jeans and a plaid flannel shirt. "Yes, that makes sense."

Emilia put down the tablet, completely baffled. "Carlota's sister was eating tapas and drinking champagne in a locked and empty apartment building that's for sale. Someone comes in and shoots her. Then takes all the food away."

"You've solved cases with less," Prade pointed out.

"I don't think so," Emilia said.

CHAPTER 3

Emilia walked into the squadroom at midnight to find Macias and Sandor assembling the murder board. Partners both personally and professionally, the two were decent cops.

"*Oye,* Cruz." Macias stopped in the middle of taping a photo to the wall by the conference table to do an exaggerated double-take at her outfit. "Maybe you're a real girl after all."

Sandor gave a wolf whistle.

"Shut up," Emilia said. "Unless you've made coffee."

"Fresh pot." Sandor pointed toward the cabinet near the copier where the coffeemaker ruled over a mismatched collection of mugs. "Welcome home. Didn't expect to see you until Monday."

Emilia grinned tiredly at the two men. "It is Monday."

It was good to be back in the squadroom, she thought as she unlocked her desk. She liked working with Macias and Sandor, who'd been some of the first detectives in the squadroom to accept her as a peer. Emilia knew about their personal arrangement only because Silvio had inadvertently spilled the beans during a late-night stakeout. Not that it mattered.

She slung her purse into the desk drawer containing her big Las Perdidas binder. It currently held the records of 47 women missing from the greater Acapulco area, women everyone else had given up looking for.

Her favorite mug with the musicians of Maná looking tough yet soulful against white ceramic was in the drawer, too, where she'd placed it to prevent someone else, like the idiot team of Castro and Gomez from stealing it while she was away.

"Where's Silvio?" she asked as she poured a cup of fresh brew.

"He talked to that real estate guy, then headed out for food." Macias pinned another picture to the wall. "He said the victim is related to Carlota but not to expect help. Was he kidding?"

"Had to be." Emilia gulped down hot coffee as she crossed to the wall of photos. "Salazar was at the morgue when Carlota identified her sister's body. Gave her all sorts of promises."

The murder board was anchored by an enlargement of Monica Montoya's *cédula* identification card complete with the young woman looking directly at the camera and a home address in Las Brisas. Next to it, the crime scene was represented by an aspirational photo of Casa de Plata from Hernandez's brochure, along with the address.

Another dozen photos showed Monica's body as it was found in the Casa de Plata apartment. Emilia stared at the shot of Monica's hands, lax in her lap with gruesome holes like a martyr's stigmata.

The blood smear Prade had noted ran the length of the left ring finger. Elsewhere on both hands, the blood pattern was consistent with a spray effect from the impact of the bullet. The smear was an artificial interruption.

Emilia grabbed a card from the stack Macias had ready for case details and wrote down Est time of death: 10 pm-midnight. 2 shots, close range. Victim's hands held up at chest level. Rounds passed thru both into chest. Surprise? Defense? Blood smear on left ring finger post shooting.

Macias mimed typing at a keyboard. "We got a victim profile together already."

"That was fast." Emilia sank wearily into her desk chair and toggled through screens to the library of case files and the new folder with an URGENT icon on it.

Apparently in record time, Macias and Sandor had assembled a comprehensive dossier on the victim pulled from local, state and national-level databases, as well as social media profiles. Monica Montoya Alvarez was 29 years old, the offspring of Victoria Alvarez de Montoya and the late Felix Montoya.

The Las Brisas address was also home to Victoria Alvarez de Montoya and Belinda Alvarez de Hoya. Information from the national *cédula* ID database gave their ages as 52 and 41, respectively. Neither had police or employment records. Victoria was listed as the homeowner.

Monica owned a late model Toyota sedan. The annual taxes on it were paid. She had no outstanding tickets, liens, or loans. She had never been arrested.

Monica was a graduate of an elite private Catholic high school in Acapulco and had earned a bachelor's degree from New York University. Upon graduation, she returned to Acapulco and worked for an events company, organizing charity tennis matches, music festivals and other marquee events. She had both a LinkedIn and Instagram account. According to the former, she'd been employed by Carlota's reelection campaign for nine months.

Silvio barreled in, preceded by the heavenly scent of cheese and pepperoni. He skirted the score of empty desks and dumped two pizza boxes and a case of beer on the conference table adjacent to his office door. "Gonna be a long night," he announced.

"Thanks, *jefe*," Sandor said appreciatively.

The four detectives gathered around the conference table and fell on the pizza. Two hours ago at the morgue, Emilia couldn't have eaten anything even if someone paid her to. Now she wolfed down two slices. So much for the fancy meal with Kurt at Madrid.

Silvio twisted the cap off a bottle of beer. "Okay, we've got about fourteen hours until Carlota's press conference. We need something solid to give her before then. Cruz, what did you get from the autopsy?"

In a few brief sentences, Emilia covered the most important aspects. "Monica had to have been eating in Casa de Plata," she wound up. "The food in her stomach was completely intact."

"A woman sitting in an empty apartment building, eating tapas," Silvio said slowly as if rolling a theory around in his head. "Alone?"

"Maybe not," Sandor jumped in. "Date night. She and her date are followed and robbed. She's killed, date gets away."

"No purse, no cell phone" Emilia reminded them, "which suggests a robbery. But who shoots a woman, takes her purse and cleans up the food?"

"Maybe the date ran off with the purse and food."

"The date was the shooter," Emilia theorized. "Lures her there, then shoots her."

Macias helped himself to another slice of pizza, the cheese stretching into a fragrant string before it pulled clear of the box. "Okay, Monica and her date. He's the shooter. And a good one, if he shot through her hands. But how did they get in? And why there?"

"Question number five thousand." Silvio leaned back in his chair and looked at the murder board. "Hernandez, the realtor, said his office holds all the keys to Casa de Plata. Anyone who wants to visit the property has to sign for them, but he's the only one authorized to use them. The last time he was there was five days ago, with a cleaning crew."

"What about him?" Macias asked. "Did he know the victim?"

"Maybe they were dating and things went sideways," Sandor added.

"He says he was at a party with friends," Silvio said. "Check his alibi but judging from his hysterics when he saw the body, he's at the bottom of our list of suspects."

"We'll need him to give us the names of everyone who's had access while Casa de Plata has been for sale," Emilia added. "And check with the seller, too."

Silvio cut his eyes to her. "Put that on your list."

Neither could reveal in front of Macias and Sandor that the seller was an undercover *federale* team disguised as the Acapulco police department's Financial Crimes unit.

"All right. We need to start building a timeline of our victim's last hours." Silvio pointed the neck of his beer bottle at Macias. "Where are we on the victim's car?"

"I spoke to security at the Las Brisas address. It's an apartment building. She had a reserved slot for her car. It's not there. I put an alert in the system. Every patrol car's got the *placa* number and description."

Sandor spoke up. "She's got Telmex cell service. I put in

the request to get her phone records. You need to approve and send it up the line. I got the request for a hotline going, too. Should be up and running in a few hours."

"Okay, we've covered the basics." Silvio indicated both men. "In the morning, I want the two of you hitting every house in a three block radius. Somebody heard something, saw something. Get there early, before people go to work."

"Got it, *jefe*."

Next, Silvio pointed the beer bottle at Emilia. "Cruz, I want you to question the family. The mother and aunt were in rough shape after getting the news, but they know someone will be there first thing in the morning. Did our victim have a boyfriend? Somebody who was angry with her? Talk to as many friends and family members as you can. Look at the access angle, too. What connection did she have to Casa de Plata? How the hell did she get in?"

Emilia nodded. Silvio was throwing her a bone. Monica Montoya's address in Las Brisas was no more than a ten minute drive from the Palacio Real. "What about you?"

"I'll hit the campaign. Question Hector Placido and her co-workers," Silvio said.

"Are we getting some more hands in here?" Macias asked. "We need hot line workers, warm bodies to knock on doors, the usual."

Silvio scowled. "I talked to Salazar. Until the elections are over, he can't spare anyone. Not even for Carlota's sister. The only thing he can give me is space. The rest of the unit will relocate upstairs on a temporary basis. We can spread out. Use the squadroom as the investigation hub."

As great as it was to hear that Castro and Gomez would be

out of the way, a major investigation needed more than the four sitting around the conference table. More people asking questions, more people collating data, more people digging into the victim's background and associates. More of everything.

"Wait a minute," Emilia exclaimed. "Salazar said right to Carlota's face that we'd get all available resources."

"You can sleep after the elections," Silvio told her. "Or when we catch a killer. Whichever comes first. Any current cases you're working on will go upstairs for the time being."

On that unhappy thought, they all went back to their desks. Emilia poured herself another cup of coffee and woke up her computer. The police intranet, burdened by so many internal firewalls and permission-only data enclaves, seemed to be even slower than it was an hour ago.

When the pixels finally stopped vibrating, she added her notes from the autopsy to the newly minted Montoya murder case folder. Prade's official report would take a few days to bounce through the system and land in the right folder, so her notes gave them a head start on any leads. Perhaps the tapas meal was actionable information. Emilia yawned as she scribbled herself a note. *How many tapas restaurants offer delivery service to the Colonia Progreso neighborhood?*

"Go home, Cruz," Silvio bellowed from his office. "There's a squad car waiting for you out back."

"Thanks," Emilia shouted back, still focused on the computer screen. She wanted to check her inbox before leaving.

Not surprisingly, she had 52 new messages. Most of the subject lines started with *Urgent: Campaign Activity.* They were all variations on warnings about upcoming events organized by either Carlota or her rival Vallejo Loy that were expected to cause violence and traffic disruptions.

One message stood out amid the clutter of similar subject lines. It was the message she'd waited weeks to see.

Re: Detective Rank Application for Permission to Marry

Fatigue fell away as Emilia clicked open the message. The first sentence took her breath away.

Officer's application is denied. No appeal will be considered.

CHAPTER 4

The air was cool at this elevation, where the Las Brisas neighborhood looked down on the rest of Acapulco from its lofty perch on the east side of the bay.

These were the houses of Old Acapulco money, ranging from Spanish colonial styles to modern glass and chrome. The apartment building where Monica Montoya had lived with her mother until Saturday night between the hours of ten and midnight was a frosted pink cake from a 1950s Hollywood production. She parked by a line of jacaranda trees laden with purple blooms. Against a cobalt sky, with the city spread out below, the intense colors made her task even more surreal.

A steady breeze played the length of Emilia's ponytail. Her white tank, skinny dark jeans, loafers and short linen jacket were a bit casual for Las Brisas but considering that she barely slept after that earth shattering email, it was a miracle she was dressed at all.

The building's bubble gum-colored stucco was crumbling. The lobby could have been an interior shot from a vintage Hollywood movie. The bubbly overhead amber glass pendants barely emitted light. Two long flowery sofas with no arms and overtired cushions faced each other across a chipped and discolored marble coffee table.

This was the oldest part of Las Brisas. Heritage and tradition, but empty pockets.

A white-haired doorman in a threadbare uniform sat behind a tall desk. He gave her a mournful nod when Emilia showed her badge, obviously having heard the news already.

The elevator was out of order.

Emilia took the stairs to the second floor. The apartment door was flung open immediately after her knock to reveal an elderly woman in a blue maid's uniform. Her eyes were watery and she clutched a damp handkerchief.

"Detective Emilia Cruz to see Señora Alvarez--." Emilia began.

"They're waiting for you," the maid interrupted. She led the way through the foyer into a spacious living room furnished with more people than furniture.

At least a dozen people rose as one as Emilia walked in; a jury of elders radiating distrust and anger. She had no idea which woman was Monica's mother.

"You're a detective? Prancing about in the newspapers?" The man who thrust his finger in Emilia's face was old enough to be her grandfather, with graying temples and a silk scarf tucked into the neck of his starched dress shirt. "Go tell Carlota that we're not going to let her make a mockery out of our Monica's death!"

Emilia stood her ground, refusing to be pushed backward by his hostility. "Señor, I assure you--."

"Look at this!" He thrust a copy of the *Jornada de Acapulco* newspaper at her. Spittle flew from the corners of his mouth. "Carlota put our Monica on display for the entire world to see!"

Carlota's sister and campaign worker murdered! the headline blared in giant letters. Below the red masthead, a picture of Carlota at the morgue, her hand on her dead sister's arm, was splashed across the entire front page. Monica's face and torso were clearly visible, as was one bloody hand with the hole in the palm. Worst of all, Emilia was in the background, wearing that skimpy bralette and staring at Carlota like an *estupida*.

If Emilia could wring Santibañez's skinny neck right now, she would.

The man holding the newspaper was shaking with rage. "Carlota doesn't care who killed Monica as long as she gets publicity. Go back to her. Say we don't need her help."

"Señor." Emilia forced herself to stay calm. "I'm Detective Emilia Cruz from the police department, not the mayor's office. I'm here to speak with Señora Alvarez."

"Leave her alone, Sergio." A trim woman with red, swollen eyes detached herself from the group and none-too-gently pushed the spitter aside. "I'm Victoria Alvarez de Montoya. Please excuse my brother. The newspaper coverage has made the . . . the situation even more horrible than it is."

The woman was quite beautiful with a honey-colored mane that went past her shoulders, the same color as her late daughter. She had delicate features with expressive eyes and accentuated these assets with slim black trousers, a gauzy black top, and impractical beaded slippers with kitten heels.

"I'm terribly sorry for your loss." It was the usual thing that cops said but was woefully inadequate. The woman's grief was palpable. "Is there somewhere we can speak in private?"

Victoria gestured to a woman hovering nearby, who looked remarkably similar. "Belinda, can you join us?"

Without waiting for an answer, Victoria brought Emilia into a spacious dining room and took a seat at a large mahogany table. The woman that followed was a younger version of

Victoria, similarly clad in skinny trousers and a flowing tunic. Belinda was obviously the aunt listed in the materials Macias and Sandor had assembled last night. She waited until Victoria and Emilia were seated at the large marble-topped table before unfolding accordion doors and closing off the living room.

"Belinda Alvarez de Hoya," the woman identified herself. "Monica's aunt. Victoria's younger sister."

"My condolences to you both," Emilia said. The Alvarez sisters were both attractive and well kept, the kind of women who had a regular schedule of hair and facial appointments and a weekly massage after tennis at the club. "I want to assure you that I had nothing to do with the picture in the newspaper. But yes, I was there as one of the police officers who discovered your daughter and now as the lead detective on the case, I will do everything possible to find who did this but I have to know more about Monica in order to do that."

"I don't know anyone who would do this to her," Victoria dabbed at her eyes with a handkerchief and fought for control. "Monica was a beautiful person. Full of life. And light. Truly."

"What do you need from us?" Belinda asked quietly.

Emilia began by verifying the basics. "How long have you both lived here with Monica?"

Belinda gave a thin smile and gently clasped her sister's hand resting on the table. "I've lived here with Victoria and Monica for almost ten years. I was widowed very early, as was Victoria."

Emilia would get to their respective backstories later. The essentials came first. "When was the last time you saw Monica?"

"Saturday morning around 11:00," Belinda answered for

both. "We all had coffee, then Victoria and I went to play bridge at the Claro Club. Lunch first, then duplicate bridge."

Emilia scribbled down the time in her notebook. "Did Monica say she was going out?"

Victoria put down her handkerchief. "She had some telephone calls to make for the campaign. Something about a golf tournament that Carlota's campaign was sponsoring."

"Was that a normal part of her job? Working on a Saturday?"

"She worked every day of the week," Belinda said. "The campaign sucked up almost every minute of her day."

"She loved it." Victoria plied her handkerchief again. "I wasn't sure that working for Carlota was a good idea but Monica loved the job. It was something new every day. And she was meeting people across the city and using her English. She was even invited to the opening of the new consulate."

"She went to college in El Norte, you know," Belinda said proudly. "New York University."

Victoria smiled through a fresh stream of tears. "She knew how important it was to do well in life. She played the violin, too, did you know that? And she never gave me a hard time growing up. Always came home on time and did her chores."

"And the dance lessons." Belinda stroked her sister's hand. "Do you remember all those recitals? Ballet and jazz."

"She looked like an angel in those costumes."

Emilia saw the pride on the faces of both women, as if Monica had had two mothers.

Belinda recovered first and took a deep breath. "You must have more questions, Detective."

"What did Monica plan to do after making those calls?"

"Shopping with Susana," Victoria said. "They were meeting at the Plaza Galerías Diana."

"Susana?" Emilia dove at the name like a shark after a sardine. "Who is Susana?"

"Susana Durán Diaz," Victoria said. "A lovely girl. She and Monica have been best friends for years. They were going to go shopping. She called me this morning and said that Monica had cancelled."

"Do you have Susan's contact details?"

"She's the assistant director of the mask museum." Belinda said.

"It would be very helpful if you have a personal number for her."

Belinda rose from the table and went through a swinging door. As it opened, Emilia glimpsed an old-fashioned kitchen on the other side, studded with blue and white tiles and chipped pine cabinetry. The maid was at the sink, head bowed in grief.

"Monica liked to go out," Victoria said softly, as if needing to fill the space until her sister came back. "She got that from my sister. Parties for the campaign. Concerts. Dancing. Tennis. Movies. She saw *Diamond Run* six times. Wanted a pair of sunglasses like the ones Alejandra Messi wore in the movie."

Emilia poised her pen over her notebook. "What about a relationship? Did Monica have a boyfriend?"

"You mean, Carlos?"

"Is he Monica's boyfriend?"

"Yes, Carlos, Carlos Lima."

Before the conversation went further, Belinda came back into the dining room with a leather-bound address book. She took her time paging through to find the contact information for Susana Durán Diaz.

"Susana has some personal issues," she said, and passed the address book to Emilia. "I always thought there was some jealousy there on her part."

"Jealous of Monica?" Emilia looked up from her notebook.

Belinda raised one shoulder in an elegant little shrug, as if to say judge for yourself.

Victoria gave her sister a frown of reproach. "Nonsense, Susana is a wonderful friend."

"Could you tell me more about Carlos Lima?" Emilia asked Victoria.

Belinda stiffened. "Carlos would never have done anything like this. He'd never hurt Monica."

"No, of course, not," Victoria told her sister.

"Carlos Lima is an investment banker." Belinda sat down, all her attention on Emilia. "Widely respected. An impeccable, unassailable reputation. He absolutely did not do this."

"He and Monica have . . . had . . . an understanding for quite some time." Victoria's face crumpled again.

"An understanding but not an engagement?" Emilia clarified. If anyone knew the difference, it was her.

"They were never engaged," Belinda answered swiftly as Victoria dabbed at her eyes again. "Monica was too focused on her career."

"Where would I find Señor Lima?" Emilia asked.

"Carlos works for Viejo Dorado, the big investment firm in El Centro."

Emilia's heart skipped a beat. "Does the company buy real estate?"

Belinda frowned. "I have no idea."

"Do you have his home address?"

As Emilia waited for Belinda to check the address book again, mutterings from the living room spilled into a heated argument. Words flew so fast it was hard to follow the logic thread, if indeed there was one, but money seemed to be at the heart of the matter.

Certainly the apartment looked as if the Alvarez family had fallen on hard times. From what Emilia could see of the living room, the furniture was reminiscent of the décor in the lobby, with worn velvet upholstery and deflated cushions. The dining room chairs and wallpaper had been in fashion thirty years ago and squares of brighter wallpaper showed where pictures used to hang. The brass chandelier was tarnished. The fake plastic candles holding the bulbs were scorched from decades of use.

Belinda finally found the entry for Carlos Lima and passed it over.

Emilia copied the details, trying not to show any excitement. Femicide in Mexico was all too common. Since Emilia started keeping track of such things, ninety percent of the women murdered in Acapulco were killed by a man the victim knew.

The perfect scenario flashed through her mind. Viejo Dorado planned to buy Casa de Plata. Lima knows it's empty. He lures Monica to the spot with a tapas picnic and kills her for refusing to marry him.

She put down her pen. "Did Monica ever mention a place in Colonia Progreso called Casa de Plata?"

"No." Victoria dabbed at her eyes with a handkerchief. "I

couldn't believe it when Hector Placido told us Monica had been found there."

"Did Monica know anyone who lives in Colonia Progreso?" Emilia paused. "Or was she interested in buying property there?"

Victoria blinked in confusion. "Monica was perfectly happy living here. Where would she get the money to buy property in Colonia Progreso?"

"What about a friend who wanted to buy property? Carlos Lima, perhaps?"

"No, of course not," Belinda said. "Carlos has a perfectly lovely house already."

The accordion doors juddered open, revealing brother Sergio still obviously in a bad mood. "Victoria," he barked. "You've wasted enough time with this girl. Has she told you anything useful? No?"

"Señor, we're in the very first stage of the investigation." Emilia rose from her seat. "I assure you--."

"Shut up," he barked. "Victoria, I'm calling Carlota's office and telling them to get a real investigator here to tell you what's going on. Not some *puta* trying to get famous in the papers."

"You must forgive our brother Sergio," Belinda murmured to Emilia. "He's taken the . . . the situation very hard."

"Don't make excuses for Carlota," he thundered at Belinda. "It's not enough what she did to Victoria, now it's Monica's turn."

"You're making everything worse, Sergio," Belinda shouted back at him. "Just go home. Be angry there. Monica will still be dead."

Victoria burst into tears.

"And what will you do?" Sergio was red-faced with rage. "Play nice so nothing disturbs your little nest? The nest you didn't pay one peso for?"

"What does it matter to you?" Belinda lunged over the table, shaking a finger at her brother. "You didn't get any of the Montoya money. Why should you? All these years, and you can't forgive her, can you? Go home. There's nothing for you here."

"You're a fool, Belinda. But then again, you always were." Her brother was nearly incandescent, a vein pulsing in his forehead, spittle flying from his lips again. "A fool and a freeloader."

"Get out!" Belinda shouted. "No one asked you to be here."

Sergio stomped out, pulling the accordion doors closed so hard that they nearly ripped off the hinges. A moment later, the front door banged open and footsteps thundered out. The door slammed shut.

A draft pummeled the dining room, adding to Emilia's sensation of having been in a fistfight.

"I hate him," Victoria sobbed. "I hate him. I don't want him here."

Belinda put her arms around her sister but looked at Emilia. "Our apologies for you landing in the middle of that, Detective. Our brother is angry at the world."

"I understand," Emilia murmured. "Your family has suffered a great loss. Emotions are running high."

Her thoughts were running, too. The talk of money and the obvious bad blood between Carlota and the Alvarez family was unexpected, especially given that Monica had worked for her half-sister's reelection campaign. Could family problems have led to Monica's murder? Emilia made a mental note to research the family backstory.

Victoria got herself under control. "It's kind of you to say so."

Emilia closed her notebook. "I need to look at Monica's room."

The maid took Emilia down the hall to Monica's bedroom, a tidy space decorated in tones of pale blue and cream. The bed boasted a matelassé coverlet and an artful stack of blue and white pillows. Subtly striped draperies flanked two large windows. Next to the bed, a round crewel rug in pastel shades softened Emilia's footsteps. Garden-inspired original watercolors hung on the walls.

A copy of *People en Español* waited on the bedside table next to a brass lamp. On the cover, movie star Alejandra Messi pouted to the world, those famous sunglasses perched halfway down that famous nose. Emilia stared at the image, recalling the few days when she'd doubled for the famous actress, caught up in the newest *federale* scheme orchestrated by Lieutenant Vicente Campos to nab fugitive druglord Diego Barrielos Luna. The cartel *jefe* was currently a fugitive after escaping from custody on the way to prison in El Norte.

Rafa Gamboa had been there as well, the lynchpin of the whole damn thing.

Emilia would never see another Alejandra Messi movie without thinking of that operation. The *federales* were underwriting a biopic written by Barrielos Luna himself called *A Misunderstood Man*, sure that he'd be lured out of hiding to see it. Somehow inveigled into working for the *federales*, Messi showed up in person to play the role of the man's late wife. The star was disappointingly rude, snapping at her assistant and immersed in her cell phone whenever the camera wasn't rolling.

Giving herself a mental shake, Emilia pulled on a pair of latex gloves and did a cursory search of the room, hoping to find something she could offer up to Silvio when the team reconvened. Like a note from the murderer signed *Carlos*.

Monica's closet was full of business suits, designer dresses and high heels. Leather purses were all stored with scented sachets inside so they didn't sag on the shelves and lose their shape. Emilia inhaled cedar and vanilla.

The adjoining bathroom was sparkling clean. The countertop boasted expensive lotions, makeup, and hair care products.

Emilia sat down at the desk and opened a small, sleek laptop. A code was required. She closed it and scrounged through the items on top of the desk. A tube of hand cream, a stack of sticky notes, a cup of pens, and the key fob to a car, which Emilia pocketed. No note with a line of digits to access the laptop.

The desk drawer came open with a hard tug, to reveal a silver frame lying face down amid a collection of office supplies, receipts, and monogrammed stationery. Emilia pulled it out but the frame was heavier than expected and she dropped it. The frame crashed to the tile floor.

Riddled with guilt, Emilia saw that the glass had cracked across a studio portrait of Monica and a handsome but unsmiling man. They were posed with him on the left, his hands resting lightly on her hips. Monica wore a clingy black dress with long sleeves.

"Carlos Lima, I presume," Emilia murmured.

"What's going on?" Belinda Alvarez stood in the doorway, face tight with anger.

Emilia turned. "My apologies, señora. I was startled--."

"You've broken the glass," Belinda said unnecessarily.

"Yes, my apologies." Emilia felt like a schoolgirl caught chewing gum by the teacher. "I'll pay to replace it of course."

"Perhaps my brother was right." Belinda held out her hand.

The woman's shift in attitude was due to something more than ten pesos worth of glass.

"We'll need this for the investigation," Emilia heard herself say.

Belinda's hand wavered. "I'm sure we can find you a better picture of Monica."

"This one will work fine." Emilia kept hold of the frame even as she knelt to collect bits of broken glass.

"The maid will do that," Belinda said sharply. Her tone made it clear that Emilia had overstayed her welcome. "I'm sure you have other things to do, Detective."

Emilia put the picture, laptop and key fob in evidence bags and followed Belinda down the hall to the main area of the apartment. The accordion doors between the living and dining rooms were open. Both spaces were empty. Apparently, the entire Alvarez clan was now nursing its anger elsewhere.

"Is your sister available?" Emilia asked Belinda. "I'd like to pay my respects to her before I go."

Belinda strode to the front door. "Victoria took a sleeping pill. I'm afraid she'll be unavailable for the rest of the day."

The other woman's sudden shift from helpful aunt to bouncer ejecting an unwelcome customer was disturbing. Was she really that upset over the broken glass?

"Here's my card." Emilia produced the plain white card with her cell phone number printed on it. "If either of you recall anything else about Monica's plans for Saturday, please call."

"Goodbye, Detective." Belinda was clearly in a rush to get Emilia out. "The sooner we get this scandal behind us, the better for everyone."

"A murder investigation is not a scandal, señora," Emilia said.

"It is if Carlota killed her," Belinda said. "I hope you are considering that possibility. My family certainly is."

She shut the door in Emilia's face.

CHAPTER 5

Emilia put the picture in its broken frame face down on the passenger seat, texted Silvio with the details about Carlos Lima. His response was brief.

Heading to alcaldía. Pick up info from Hernandez.

Emilia gave a silent groan. No doubt Silvio would be tied up at the mayor's office for hours.

Metro Properties occupied the ground floor of a classy Playa Condesa office building right on the wide boulevard that everyone referred to as la Costera. The sun beat down on the heavy midday traffic. Most of the vehicles were mini-vans covered in advertisements for tourist attractions. *Swim with the Dolphins! Paraglide over the bay! Outrigger Surf School First Lesson Free.*

The location was the perfect spot to reel in rich tourists ready to extend their stay or find investment opportunities. Brightly colored posters were affixed to the windows from the inside, showing off the real estate agency's listings of properties for sale. All prices were given in dollars.

A gaggle of tourists strolled by, leaving the aromas of coconut sunscreen and iced coffee in their wake as Emilia studied the listings posted in the window. Most were for apartments in high-rise buildings close to the water. Three bedrooms, three bathrooms, maid's quarters and a reserved parking space for the low price of $600,000. A cool million dollars for a penthouse overlooking Playa La Angosta on the west side of the bay. At least two million for a triplex in the

Torre Esmeralda near the Palacio Real or a double condo in the exclusive Club Playamar near the airport.

If Silvio hadn't known about Casa de Plata from the operation against Diego Barrielos Luna, he never would have known it was for sale. By listing with Metro Properties, the *federales* in the person of Lieutenant Campos could safely assume that any potential buyers wouldn't include Mexicans with a connection to the former safe house. Metro Properties would only market it to the usual pool of rich foreigners with more dollars than common sense.

Emilia opened the door to Metro Properties and stepped into a sensory blast of reflective surfaces. Blinding white walls, stainless steel divider panels and modern chandeliers made from loops of glowing chrome.

A receptionist wearing a headset offered a thin smile which broadcasted her doubt that Emilia was the type of buyer welcomed at Metro Properties.

"Detective Emilia Cruz," Emilia announced and held up her badge. "Here to speak with Felipe Hernandez."

The young woman's smile vanished. She murmured into the microphone attached to her headset, apparently heard the answer she wanted, and raised her eyes to Emilia again. "Please take a seat. He'll be with you momentarily."

Emilia stayed standing, still trying to get her bearings. Everything was shiny, including the highly polished terrazzo floor. The edgy atmosphere shouted prestige and success. She mentally congratulated Lieutenant Campos for picking a listing agency so far removed from anyone with a connection to Casa de Plata.

"Hello." Hernandez appeared, wearing a skinny plaid suit

that he'd probably ripped right off a store mannequin. The trousers were plastered to his body, revealing a bulge Emilia would rather not see. The pant legs stopped a good inch above his shoes, showing off magenta socks. "I'm Felipe Hernandez. How can I help you?"

"I'm Detective Emilia Cruz. We met yesterday at Casa de Plata."

He looked at her blankly. "Sorry?"

"I was with Franco Silvio," Emilia said, her bullshit meter sending out an alert.

Hernandez clapped a hand to his chest. "My apologies," he apologized. "I didn't recognize you."

"I'm here to pick up your file on Casa de Plata."

"Of course. I have it in my office."

He led her down a short hallway lined with colorful abstract prints reminiscent of the pretentious design magazines littered around the administrative offices of the Palacio Real.

His office was a glass-walled cubicle off the conference area, identical to four others arranged like spokes around a central hub. Hernandez sat behind the desk and waved Emilia into a leather chair in front of it.

"I apologize for forgetting that we'd already met," he said and pulled a file toward himself even as he did that annoying head tilt to keep his hair in place. "A man would have to be blind to forget a woman as beautiful as yourself. Has anyone ever told you that you look like Alejandra Messi?"

"All the time," Emilia said curtly.

Hernandez cleared his throat, obviously expecting a more appreciative response. "Well, the first thing we have here is a list of those who have expressed an interest in Casa de Plata and came to see it." He ceremoniously handed a sheet across the desk to Emilia.

Including Silvio, only four potential buyers had toured Casa de Plata. The last name on the list was definitely not Mexican.

"Who is Karen Chamberlain?" Emilia asked, unsure if she was pronouncing either name correctly.

"A woman from El Norte scouting potential locations for the new consulate," Hernandez said wistfully. "I was very disappointed. Buyers from El Norte are good for another ten or even twenty percent."

"No doubt," Emilia said dryly, tucking that information away to pass on to Kurt. "Why didn't she buy it?"

"Too many repairs."

"We need your entire file on Casa de Plata." Emilia pointed to the folder on the realtor's desk.

"It's a commercial sale." Hernandez reluctantly passed it across to Emilia. "Sol Directo is an estate management company selling off properties it has decided not to refurbish."

Emilia bit her tongue. Sol Directo was one of the fake companies that the fake Financial Crimes police unit maintained as a front for *federale* operations.

"We received a letter authorizing Metro Properties to act on behalf of the owner," Hernandez went on. "With a minimum acceptable price."

As Emilia leafed through the file, she saw Lieutenant Campos's invisible hand in every detail of the transaction giving Metro Properties the right to sell Casa de Plata on behalf of Sol Directo. A bank account for depositing funds from the sale was provided in a letter signed R. Diaz, a nicely anonymous name.

Metro Properties had replied by email, accepting the listing. At the bottom of a copy of the email, someone had scribbled that keys and gate access code were delivered by messenger.

The other papers in the folder included business cards from those who'd toured Casa de Plata. Karen Chamberlain's card was decorated with an eagle crest and a Washington DC address under tidy printing that said she was a Logistics Officer for the Department of State.

All the others were from property investment companies. Real ones, Emilia presumed, not fake like Sol Directo. She looked up. "How many other agents have access to Casa de Plata?"

"Only me." Hernandez smoothed his lapels. Under the plaid jacket, a sateen shirt stretched tightly across his chest, straining the buttons. "I'm the listing agent for the property. When it sells, I get the commission."

"So if someone wants to see it, they have to see you?"

"I can show it to them, yes."

"Are you the only one?"

Hernandez smiled knowingly, as if she should recognize that this exclusivity made him real estate royalty. "Yes."

"In addition to this list of people who expressed interest in buying the property, we need the list of everyone who works here and anyone you allowed on the property. Cleaners, landscapers, everyone."

Hernandez mimed turning pages. "It's all there. We keep very strict records."

Emilia found a sheet with the names of those employed by

the cleaning services and the landscape company Metro Properties had hired to tidy up Casa de Plata. Hernandez might wear his clothing too tight and need a haircut, but his tidy recordkeeping just made her life much easier.

She closed the folder and offered Hernandez her card. "If you recall anyone else who accessed the property, please let us know."

"Happy to answer questions." Hernandez exchanged her card for one of his own. "Maybe over dinner some time."

"Dinner?" Emilia stood up. "That wouldn't be appropriate, señor."

"Why not?" Hernandez came around the side of his desk. "I think you're very attractive, Detective."

"I'm engaged," Emilia managed, laughter bubbling up in her throat at his ludicrous attempt to flirt. "Besides that, I'm a police detective and you're a witness in a murder investigation. Best to keep things on a professional basis."

"I can wait until the investigation is over," Hernandez said.

In other circumstances, Emilia might have admired his nerve. Now amusement turned into irritation. "Goodbye, señor. Thank you for the information."

She left Hernandez in his office, blinking like a hurt puppy.

CHAPTER 6

Emilia found a parking spot on the far side of the pedestrian zone around the Fuerte de San Diego fortress on the corner of Morelos and Hornitos. She cut the engine, checked that the file folder from Metro Properties was secure in her shoulder bag and pulled out her phone. It had been pinging for the last five minutes.

Macias had sent a stream of texts. So far, the door-to-door effort in Colonia Progreso was a waste of time. No one had heard or seen anything. Sandor had taken over the interviews at Carlota's campaign headquarters, questioning Monica's co-workers and Hector Placido because Silvio was still at the mayor's office. The hotline was set up but there was no one to answer the phone but Macias himself and he was busy bickering with Telmex about Monica's phone records.

Emilia replied with a smiley face emoji and got out of the car.

Casa de Mascaras was the famous mask museum near the Fuerte de San Diego and a magnet for tourists. Emilia crossed the pedestrian zone, dodging tourists and pickpockets, feeling like minutes were ticking away.

Susana Durán Diaz was waiting for her in the reception area, clutching a slender book. Emilia showed her badge and asked if there was a quiet place to talk.

"My office is on the other side of the museum." Susana gave a thin smile. Her eyes were swollen and red, a sad counterpoint to her stylish cream linen shirtwaist dress, patent leather sandals, and armful of turquoise bracelets. "Have you been here before?"

"Not recently," Emilia admitted.

"We have a wonderful collection," Susana said. "From all around the country. Modern and antique. Put on a mask and you become someone else. Even a mythological being." She gave a strained laugh. "Of course, here we're focused on conservation and our cultural heritage. These masks are made from all sorts of materials and fibers, some quite delicate. They aren't for wearing but for learning."

As they walked past, Emilia resisted the temptation to linger in front of the displays like a tourist. The way the masks were mounted and lit, they appeared to be bursting through the stark white walls. Dark stripes bisected some of the brightness, providing a contrasting background for lighter toned masks.

The museum was busy. Tourists meandered through the beautifully designed displays, trading spaces with a second group of schoolchildren. Emilia could have spent the entire day there, captivated by the imagination and workmanship. Many of the masks sprouted horns or grotesquely exaggerated features. Dagger-like chins, bulbous, frowning brows, hooked noses. Winged masks, jaguar masks, and mournful elongated faces as tall as she was. Few of the painted wooden masks were designed to be worn, but were examples of fine handcrafted works of art.

Susana's office was a niche in one of the exhibit rooms. She led Emilia past a display of brown clay masks, more primitive than many of the others, and indicated two matching armchairs.

"Sorry to be such a mess." Susana produced a crumpled

tissue and dabbed at her eyes. "I don't even know why I came to work today, only that it was better than staying home and crying nonstop."

"Tell me about Monica," Emilia said.

"Best friends." Susana took a steadying breath. "We went to school together. When we graduated, she went to university in Washington and I went to UNAM in Mexico City. We both came home and it was as if we'd never been apart." She gulped. "I don't know what I'm going to do without her."

"Did she seem worried or stressed lately?"

"No, just the opposite. She was happy, crazy busy but happier than I've ever seen her."

"Happy with the job?"

"Ecstatic. She was doing great things for Carlota's campaign." Susana sniffed. "She and Carlota had talked about her taking a job in the *alcaldía* after the election. Public relations, something like that."

Before they went further, Emilia asked for a list of Monica's friends, which Susana willingly wrote out.

"Her mother said you met her on Saturday to go shopping," Emilia said, tucking the list into her shoulder bag.

"She canceled." Susana teared up. "I was at the mall, waiting and she texted and said she couldn't come. Something had come up. I assumed it was work."

"Has that ever happened before? Canceling at the last minute because of Carlota's campaign?"

"No, but I wasn't all that surprised. Monica is . . . was . . . in love with her job." Susana hesitated. "She really wanted to make a good impression on Carlota. Being sisters and all."

Belinda Alvarez's last words were lodged in the back of

Emilia's mind. "Why was that important for her?"

"History." Susana drew in a deep breath as tears trickled down her cheeks. "I can't stop thinking that she's still alive. You know, that she'll text me and apologize for not coming and say it was all a joke."

Emilia waited for the other woman to collect herself before asking her next question. "Did Monica ever mention Casa de Plata? It's an apartment building for sale in Colonia Progreso."

"I know, I saw the newspapers this morning." Susana shook her head. "I can't recall Monica ever talking about it."

Chattering voices preceded a dozen small children in school uniforms and three teachers in matching shirts emblazoned with authority. A tour guide bobbed her head at Susana before explaining to the group that the brown masks were made of clay, not wood like the devil and frog faces in the previous exhibit room. The children listened for a moment, then began to copy the wild expressions on the masks by crossing their eyes and sticking their tongues out. The teachers remonstrated quietly and the guide continued her lecture.

The distraction helped Emilia take the conversation in a different direction. "Her mother said that Monica was dating a man named Carlos Lima. Works for Viejo Dorado. Do you know him?"

"Carlos." It was subtle, but Susana actually flinched at the name.

It was an interesting reaction. "You don't like him?"

"No, not really," Susana said softly. "He's so full of himself."

"I gathered from Victoria Alvarez that he and Monica had an arrangement."

"The arrangement was mostly in Victoria's head." Susana's eyes filled with tears again and she angrily dashed them away. "Carlos has money. Not just any kind of money, either. Old Acapulco kind of money. His grandfather was buddies with Sinatra and Elizabeth Taylor and John Wayne. All those Hollywood people who came here in the 1950s stayed in hotels owned by the Lima family."

Emilia thought about the studio portrait stuffed unceremoniously in a drawer. "Did Monica talk about her feelings for him? Was she happy with the situation?"

Susana watched the children and their teacher for several moments before replying. When she spoke again, it was very deliberate, with carefully chosen words. "Monica was ready to move on."

"And Carlos?"

"I don't know."

The guide moved the gaggle of children in their direction, still talking about the wildly painted and fanciful masks. Susana left her chair. "Would you like a quick tour, Detective? Find a quieter spot?"

Emilia followed her into the next room, where a group of artists had set up easels and were sketching under the watchful eye of an instructor, and into a small room lined with a display of fanciful wooden masks. No one else was there.

As they settled into a nook with leather armchairs, Emilia recalled Belinda Alvarez making it a point to say that Susana had personal problems, as if the young museum curator was an unsound witness. But at least on the surface, Susana seemed smart and well-grounded. Someone Emilia might have as a friend.

"You should know something about Carlos," Susana said hesitantly.

"What's that?"

"He has a bad temper."

Emilia felt her pulse quicken. "Oh?"

"One time he got angry with Monica. She teased him because his shirt was buttoned wrong." Susana mimed misbuttoning a shirt. "Carlos flew into a rage and slapped her."

"Slapped her?" Emilia verified. "In front of you?"

"No, they were alone. She told me about it later." Susana leaned closer, tears threatening to spill over again. "I'm sure he hit her more than once."

"Did Monica have bruises after being with him?"

"Just once." Susana gestured to her own cheek. "She said that they argued over her quitting her job. He wanted her to quit and be a housewife so she'd never be more successful than him. But she loved working for Carlota's campaign and she was good at it, too."

"But I thought he was already quite successful as an investment banker."

"I honestly think Carlos saw Carlota as a rival for Monica." Susana shook her head. "Not romantic rivals, I mean, but for Monica's attention. He needs everything to be about him. He didn't care if Monica had a relationship with her sister or not, as long as she was always available for him and in this job, she wasn't. *Por Dios,* I'm already using the past tense talking about her."

"Monica told you all this?" Emilia asked. Her earlier fantasy of arresting Lima came into sharper focus.

"Victoria told you they were still together, right?"

Susana's lips trembled with the effort not to cry again. "Monica tried to break it off with him a few weeks ago, but she never told her mother. In some ways, I think Victoria and Belinda liked him more than Monica ever did."

"Do you know if Carlos owns a gun?" Emilia asked.

Susana shook her head even as her eyes grew wide.

CHAPTER 7

"Felix Montoya," Tía Lourdes repeated as she poured two cups of coffee and brought them to the battered table in her tiny kitchen. "Victoria Alvarez. Those are names I haven't heard in a long time."

Emilia picked up her fork, ready to dig into a steaming plate of *arroz con pollo*. "Felix was father to both Carlota and Monica Montoya, wasn't he? I heard he was involved in some scandal."

Not only was her aunt and uncle's apartment sort of on the way to the Financial Crimes building and a meeting with Lieutenant Campos, but Lourdes was a font of gossip from the past. In addition to a delicious free meal, Emilia knew that her aunt's memory and penchant for gloomy news was the fastest way to hear about the sins of Acapulco's wealthy. If they were in the tabloid newspapers or mocked in a *telenovela* any time within the last fifty years, Lourdes would know and save Emilia hours of online searching.

Lourdes gave Emilia a hard look. "Felix Montoya was an immoral man."

"Did he help launch Carlota's political career?" Emilia asked hastily before her aunt could commence a familiar sermon on the evils of men who took advantage of women, to include yellow-haired gringos who wanted free milk without buying the cow.

Seated across from Emilia in the tiny kitchen, Lourdes's eyes swiveled to the open doorway to the living room. From

Emilia's spot at the table, she couldn't see into the other room but she knew that the television was on and who was watching it.

A game show, judging from the slot machine clatter and audience cheers, not to mention the occasional gasps and clapping from the lone viewer. Emilia's mother Sophia had declined to join her daughter and sister-in-law, smiling vaguely at them before settling in front of the television.

"She said she didn't want to watch her program at home because Ernesto was taking a nap," Lourdes said.

Emilia made a mental note to check on her mother's husband later in the week. He was still frail after surviving a brutal kidnapping.

"Felix Montoya," she prompted and forked up more chicken and rice.

"He was such a big deal," Lourdes said and set her mug down. "He owned everything. Stores, airplanes, race cars. Hollywood people came to see him. Always in the society pages. Even in *HOLA!*"

"What about Carlota's mother?"

"Her family was rich, too. Beer, I think." Lourdes sighed. "Consuela Perez. She liked flashing her jewels. Felix and Consuela were always with the Hollywood people. On a yacht. Gambling in Monaco and Las Vegas."

"Before they had Carlota?"

"When Carlota came along, she was in the papers, too. A little copy of her mother." Lourdes got up to take away Emilia's empty plate and fetch coffee for both of them. "But Felix had a roving eye. He got another woman pregnant. *Oye*, I remember the scandal. He was famous, you know. All the money and attention."

"The other woman was Victoria Alvarez, wasn't it? Do you know how they met?"

"Montoya was in business with the Alvarez family."

This cleared up the mystery of the screaming argument between the Alvarez sisters and their brother Sergio. "Montoya and the Alvarez family were in business together? Doing what?"

Lourdes resettled herself with her cup of coffee, clearly trying not to enjoy sharing salacious gossip. "A bottling plant for *refrescos*. Sergio Alvarez was the principal partner. But Felix got the sister pregnant and everyone was angry. The business fell apart."

"The baby was Monica, wasn't it? Did he leave Consuela for Victoria?"

"Yes, Felix stayed with the Alvarez woman." Lourdes sighed. "Consuela killed herself, you know. The humiliation. Little Carlota went to live with her mother's people, the Perez family."

Emilia slumped against the back of her chair. This was an unwelcome angle to Monica Montoya's murder. Belinda Alvarez's words didn't sound so crazy now.

Her mouth felt dry and chalky from the coffee aftertaste. "How old was Carlota then?"

"Maybe ten or twelve."

"Did she ever see her father again?"

"She certainly used his name and money to get where she is." Lourdes rose and collected their empty mugs, clanking them together in a clear signal that the conversation was over. "Goodness, Emilia, go visit with your mother and don't talk about this nonsense with her."

"Why not?"

"We lost your father about the same time." Lourdes clattered the cups together in the sink. "Get along with you. Remind her that you're getting married. Finally."

"Hola, Mama." Emilia sat down next to Sophia. "Why don't you come have a cup of coffee with me and Lourdes?"

Sophia gave Emilia a distracted hug. "Don't you have school today?"

"I'm done with school, Mama. You know I have a job."

"That's right." Sophia gestured to the television. "Look, she could win a washing machine!"

Emilia watched the show for a few minutes, until she couldn't take it any more and her own family's secrets started to vie for attention with what she had learned about Monica Montoya's roots.

There was so much more to every family story, Emilia thought as she headed back to the station. Layers of sadness and scandal and things no one talked about until the very worst happened and then it all spilled out like poison.

Like finding out she had a brother called Rafa Gamboa whose birth name was Ernesto Cruz Encinos, Junior.

While undercover as a Santa Muerte folk saint worshipper to gather information about a cult leader called El Acólito, Emilia discovered that the cult concealed a human trafficking operation. She became one of El Acólito's victims, kidnapped, chained, drugged and raped by El Acólito himself.

DNA proved that the human trafficker was Emilia's sibling, exposing a family secret kept for nearly 30 years. Desperately digging for information, Emilia discovered that

Ernesto, Junior, was taken away from a widowed Sophia by her own sister, a woman named Karina Escobar de la Vega.

Emilia's family never saw Sophia's son again. No one spoke of him. It was as if the child never existed.

He was renamed Rafael Gamboa Escobar after Karina's first husband. As an actor, he used the name Rafa Gamboa and starred in a popular *telenovela*.

One of the few who had access to the El Acólito file, Lieutenant Campos contrived to push Emilia and Gamboa together again. The brutal encounter left them both bruised and bloody. It was then that Emilia learned that Gamboa was an undercover *federale* officer and that Campos was his control officer. The El Acólito persona had been an effort to get inside the powerful cartel run by Diego Barrielos Luna, otherwise known as the Barrel Bomber for his propensity for dissolving his enemies in acid.

Now that Barrielos Luna was a fugitive, the plan was to lure him out of hiding with *A Misunderstood Man*.

Emilia had met Barrielos Luna when he was in prison and she had survived the assault when his *sicarios* attacked the convoy taking him to prison in El Norte. He was the very personification of evil.

Campos and Gamboa were only slightly better. It didn't matter who was hurt, whose life was ruined. The operation was everything.

Campos never apologized for tricking her.

Gamboa never apologized for the rape she couldn't remember.

CHAPTER 8

A cash-strapped family nursing grudges, an abusive boyfriend resentful of her workaholic habits, and a friendship that weathered a last minute change of plans. Monica Montoya's personal life was coming into sharper focus. Yet the key issue remained. How had Monica gained entry to Casa de Plata and who was with her when she did?

With any luck, there was a link between Monica, Carlos Lima and the information from Metro Properties.

Juggling her shoulder bag, Monica's laptop, the framed photograph and the file from Hernandez, Emilia made it into the squadroom to find Macias there alone. He was slumped in front of the standalone computer that had the best connection to the internet.

Emilia dumped her load on the conference table near the door to Silvio's office. "What's up?"

Masias spoke over his shoulder. "Carlota's press conference is going to be on any minute."

She went to peer over the other detective's shoulder. The screen showed an empty podium decorated with the seal of Acapulco of a hand clutching stalks of wheat. The line of flagpoles stretched behind the podium alternated between the red, white and green flag of Mexico and the white banner of the state of Guerrero with its colorful central emblem.

"I thought Carlota was supposed to speak at one o'clock." Emilia checked the time on her watch.

Macias gave her a sickly grin. "Silvio had to go in uniform, too. Hat and medals and everything."

"*Madre de Dios*, I hope they haven't kept him waiting all this time." Emilia's heart sank. Despite the Carlos Lima lead, Silvio was going to be in a foul mood if he'd spent the better part of the day in the company of Enrique Santibañez, doing nothing useful to solve the case. Not only did it waste precious hours, Silvio wasn't going to be in a receptive mood to help her find a way to reverse Chief Salazar's decision against her marriage.

With a sigh, Emilia sat at the conference table, rummaged through her shoulder bag and pulled out her lunchbox.

A bonus of living with Kurt in the Palacio Real's penthouse was that healthy food magically appeared in the kitchen every day. Instead of the rice and fish dishes Emilia grew up on, most of the food were the high protein recipes that fueled Kurt's addiction to extreme sports, including triathlons. Thanks to the meals and workouts with him, Emilia had never been in such good shape. Her abs resembled a washboard and her arms and legs were sleek and well-muscled.

Today her lunch was mushroom risotto, orange glazed chicken and grilled vegetables, all beautifully arranged in separate compartments. The food was accompanied by a bottle of sparkling water, real flatware and a cloth napkin embroidered with the hotel's monogram.

"Here we go," Macias said and clicked on the volume icon.

Containers of food on her lap, Emilia scooted her chair across the room in time to watch Carlota, Obregon, Chief Salazar and Silvio file into view. Carlota went directly to the podium. The others arranged themselves on either side of the mayor in a grim-faced display of police resolve.

"I come to you today to share news that is devastating to me personally," Carlota began. "As well as to my campaign for re-election and to my extended family."

The mayor paused, staring directly at the camera, and pressed a tiny white handkerchief to one eye. As Emilia forked up risotto, she noticed that the mayor's nails were no longer the dark red of yesterday's dramatic evening look, but a subdued cream tone that went with today's severe black silk suit.

"My beloved sister Monica Montoya was the victim of murder." Carlota let the statement fall like a bombshell, although most of the reporters there already knew, thanks to Santibañez's leaked photo on the front page of *Jornada de Acapulco*. "I call on the deranged perpetrator of this crime to turn himself in. Otherwise, every resource of the city of Acapulco and the state of Guerrero and the nation of Mexico will be turned against you. Every day that goes by will only strengthen our will. Widen our hunt. Deepen your punishment."

Carlota told reporters in the room and viewers at home how devastated she was, somehow implying that she was one with the Alvarez family. Then Chief Salazar took her place at the podium and went on about the police dragnet which at that very moment was sweeping across Acapulco in search of Monica Montoya's murderer. Multiple leads were already being followed. He reeled off the number of the police hotline.

"Lieutenant Franco Silvio is chief of detectives," Chief Salazar gestured to Silvio to approach the podium. "He is in charge of the investigation. A seasoned homicide investigator with our full confidence."

Silvio actually looked good up there, Emilia admitted to

herself. Broad-shouldered, jut-jawed, steely-eyed. Muscles practically bursting out of his dress uniform. The crew cut said *don't fuck with me* and the grim expression said *you don't want to.* His voice was infused with a raspy menace that said that the killer could run but they'd only die tired.

Carlota came to stand next to Silvio when his short remarks ended and kept him from moving away from the microphone. "Lieutenant Silvio is ably assisted by his partner Detective Emilia Cruz," Carlota declared, one hand pressed dramatically to her heart. "She is the only female detective in the Acapulco police department, and the detective with the highest percentages of closed cases. I think it is destiny that brought her into my administration and destiny that my sister's killer will be caught by a woman. Detective Cruz was with me at the morgue last night and I drew great comfort from her presence. Of course, you understand why she could not be here with us today."

Emilia gagged on a bite of chicken and then proceeded to cough her lungs out.

The press conference continued with questions from the assembled reporters. From the start, the focus was on Monica's role in Carlota's re-election campaign. What was Monica Montoya's role? Would Carlota stop campaigning in deference to her sister's death?

In response, Hector Placido stepped up and described Monica's job as the campaign's outreach manager. And yes, the campaign would pause until after Monica's funeral and called on rival Nadio Vallejo Loy to pause his campaign as well "out of respect for the sanctity of the family."

With those preliminaries over, the questions went into

predictable territory in an attempt to link Monica's death to the city's escalating cartel violence. Was her sister's murder evidence that the mayor was being targeted by drug cartels? Was there a tie to fugitive druglord Diego Barrielos Luna who was known to operate with impunity across the state of Guerrero?

Curiously, Casa de Plata was never mentioned, as if the crime had taken place in the clouds.

Finally, as if planted by Carlota's re-election machine, someone asked if Carlota's campaign would pivot to talking about violent crime, like Vallejo Loy.

"I am the same as all of you," Carlota declared with just the slightest tremor in her voice. "We are all impacted by this evil. Our families are being torn apart. I call on the women of Acapulco to stand with me to fight. Men may have started this scourge of violence, but with the help of my sisters across the city and a lioness like Detective Cruz, we will stop the slaughter."

"*Madre de Dios*," Emilia murmured. *Lioness.* She was never going to hear the end of it.

"In about fifteen minutes, you're going to be more famous than Alejandra Messi," Macias observed as the press conference concluded. He closed the browser and skidded his chair backward. "Sorry, Lioness, those of us lesser creatures have work to do."

"Very funny." Emilia swiftly put away the remains of her meal and slapped the file from Metro Properties on his desk. "Look for any link to a *pendejo* named Carlos Lima. He's Monica's estranged boyfriend who has a mean streak. Investment banker for Viejo Dorado."

"You think this is a domestic?"

She took the photo out of the busted frame and tacked it to the murder board. "We need a dossier on this guy. According to Monica's best friend he was abusive. Hit her. She was afraid to break up with him. We need to know everything about this *pendejo* before we bring him in."

Macias let out a low whistle and began flipping through the file. Sandor came in and was quickly brought up to speed while bemoaning all the wasted time canvassing the neighborhood around Casa de Plata and the lack of anything useful from his interviews with Carlota's campaign.

No one, from Hector Placido on down, wanted to believe Monica's death was related to the election. Monica was popular, busy, ambitious and beloved. Still, an undercurrent of concern ran through all the conversations that other campaign workers might be targeted, but no leads regarding who might be responsible.

Emilia finished typing in her notes from the interviews with the Alvarez sisters and Susana Durán Diaz and decided to revisit the scene of the crime. Just to walk around, put herself in the dead woman's shoes. Maybe find a new angle.

If she solved Monica Montoya's murder in record time, Chief Salazar would have a hard time explaining to Carlota why he was firing a lioness.

CHAPTER 9

Casa de Plata looked just the same except for the yellow crime scene tape proclaiming PROHIBIDO EL PASO zigzagging across the massive front entrance. Emilia peeled it back on one side and unlocked the door.

The huge echoing foyer was the same as well. Emilia didn't bother to turn on the chandelier. She wasn't there to gaze upward.

The crime scene techs had come and gone but she combed the entire building, checking for door locks that looked to have been jimmied open and finding nothing. She even studied the balconies from all angles and concluded that the only way someone could have accessed a balcony from the outside would be to swing Tarzan-style over the razor-topped perimeter wall.

Each of the two ground floor apartments had a French door that opened to a patio running the full width of the rear of the building. In Casa de Plata's heyday, the doors would have allowed for a beautiful view of gracious living. Now all that remained were paving stones choked with weeds, shards of half a dozen terracotta planters, and an abandoned wrought iron table slowly turning into a heap of rust.

She went back inside and unlocked the door to the apartment where Monica had been killed. She stood in the silent dining room. The crime scene techs had taken the armchair away, presumably for forensic study, but Emilia was more interested in the faint streaks it left on the terrazzo floor.

"You were sitting here," Emilia muttered as she squatted

by the chair. Dust motes swirled gently in the air, illuminated by sunlight filtered through the grimy windows. "Eating all sorts of different tapas. There must have been lots of small plates or takeout boxes."

Certainly Monica had not been there by herself. No, someone else sat across from the woman, sharing an impromptu but elegant picnic complete with linens and champagne.

Until something spooked her. Monica pushed herself away from the table hard enough to leave skid marks on the floor. Raised her hands to ward off danger. The killer had faced her, with the table between them. Two shots, one through each hand.

She straightened up, looking at the clean tabletop and mute row of chairs on the other side. A tablecloth would have prevented fingerprints and made cleanup easy. No extra bullets that missed the target and hit the wall or chair. No wasted energy. The nerve to shoot a defenseless woman while staring straight at her.

"Her date was either lucky or a pro," Emilia said, thinking aloud. "He shoots her. Takes her purse and cell phone, then gathers up the tablecloth with all the leftovers and walks out."

Either way, the killer was someone Monica knew and trusted. Was comfortable eating and drinking with them.

But why here? Why Casa de Plata? Was there a *federale* angle to this? Lieutenant Campos rose up in her mind's eye. He was slick and trendy. Not at all the somber *federale* officer of public imagination.

Help me.

An invisible hand touched Emilia's cheek. She flinched so

hard that her feet went out from under her.

Her hip hit the floor first, then her right shoulder. Emilia twisted to keep her head from cracking like an egg against the terrazzo. She was instantly dazzled by sparks of pain shooting from thigh to neck.

Her phone rang. Breathing hard, Emilia managed to roll onto her stomach and extract it from the back pocket of her jeans.

"Where the hell are you?" Silvio thundered. He didn't wait for an answer. "Never mind. Meet me downtown. We found Monica Montoya's car."

CHAPTER 10

Café Romeo was an Italian restaurant catering to the sunburned tourist crowd. House wine in carafes, waiters in long aprons, clusters of plastic grapes dangling from equally plastic artificial wood beams. Dean Martin singing about pizza and the moon. It was a big, noisy tourist trap, the sort of place locals never went.

Monica Montoya's car was in the lot facing the front entrance. By the time Emilia arrived after a lightning dash back to the squadroom for the key fob she'd found in Monica Montoya's bedroom, Silvio was inside a perimeter of crime scene tape. The flashers on two squad cars sent circles of light revolving around the parking lot as uniformed cops stood around, talking in low tones but obviously excited to be part of a big murder investigation. The mayor's sister, no less.

The bomb squad arrived moments later, followed by the crime scene van. Silvio saw Emilia approach and lifted the crime scene tape so she could pass under the cordon.

"Here's the extra key fob." Emilia handed it to the bomb squad team leader.

She and Silvio watched as the car was searched for explosives before the techs were allowed to unlock the car. It was as good a time as any, so Emilia gave him a quick rundown on the Alvarez family and her suspicions about Carlos Lima. "I left Macias and Sandor working up on a profile on him," she finished. "She was supposed to meet her friend to go shopping and never showed. Maybe she stopped here for something and

Lima abducted her from the lot."

Silvio looked around, his gaze traveling past the techs swarming over the car and the gaggle of onlookers to the restaurant. "Tourist central. It's got to have a decent security set-up."

"You mean cameras?"

"Check out the grapes." Silvio jerked a thumb toward the main entrance where iron lanterns cast a warm glow. Artfully distressed green doors were set into a niche created from fake limestone blocks. A trellis dripping with plastic grapes provided camouflage for at least four wall-mounted cameras.

"We never get this lucky," Emilia replied. "The system will be broken or fake or something."

"Lieutenant!" The lead crime scene tech motioned to Silvio.

"Got something?"

"Not really." The tech unzipped his white coverall. "Car is clean as a whistle. We'll haul it to the yard and run the prints, but there's nothing else here."

It took the techs less than ten minutes to pack up, by which time the police wrecker truck was there. Emilia watched Monica's car get winched into the flatbed. No doubt she'd get stuck with the task of calling Victoria Alvarez to tell her how to pay the fee to retrieve her dead daughter's car. Murder came with all sorts of bills that the living never knew they'd have to pay.

"Let's see about those cameras," Silvio said as the wrecker left the parking lot.

Kurt had taken Emilia to Café Romeo not so long ago. He liked to check out new restaurants and clubs to assess the competition. After the meal, Kurt delivered a hilarious review of plastic ravioli and the equally artificial décor. They never went back.

The manager was a Canadian named Alex Brubaker, who had a lilting accent and a grim expression. No doubt having police cars in the parking lot was a deterrent to customers. In response to Silvio's question regarding security camera footage, he led them to a small office loaded with screens and introduced them to Jorge Maltez, the restaurant's security coordinator, an unsmiling man who was sharp-eyed enough to notice a car in the same parking space for three days. He'd phoned the hotline.

"We keep the digital files for 72 hours," Maltez explained as he clicked open a series of folders with dizzying speed. "Sixteen external cameras, four on each side of the building. What do you want to look at?"

"We want to see the front parking lot where the car was parked," Emilia said.

He explained how to toggle through the various folders to watch each hour of the archived videos from the four cameras in front of the building, then went back to monitoring real time camera feeds.

Silvio slumped in one of the swivel chairs in front of the double screens on the desk and crossed his arms.

"I guess you expect me to troll through all this footage?" Emilia clicked to start a video from Camera 1, beginning at 4:00 pm on Saturday.

"You're faster."

"Thanks for the compliment."

"Not a compliment. A fact."

Emilia didn't bother to reply. Camera 1 was focused on the restaurant's front doors, not the parking lot. She closed the video and selected the folder for Camera 2.

"This is it," she said as a new video played. This time the security footage showed a broad swath of the parking lot immediately in front of the restaurant. "Look. There's a white SUV parked in the space where Monica's sedan ended up."

"You sure it's the same spot?"

"Fourth from the end of the second row."

"What time was that taken?"

Emilia used the cursor to circle the time stamp at the bottom. "A little after four."

"*Rayos*," Silvio swore.

Emilia propped her head on her hand and yawned. The footage was good quality, for a security camera, but it wasn't like watching an action movie. She clicked to advance the feed but it was still boring. Cars occasionally drove by. People walked across the view. The timestamp counted the seconds.

Silvio rocked the swivel chair until the springs squealed in protest. "Did you catch the press conference?"

"You were okay." Emilia pulled out her phone and punched in Sandor's number. "Hey, what kind of car does Carlos Lima drive?"

Five seconds later she was scanning the feed for a late model Range Rover.

"Get ready for more." Silvio kept rocking, the springs squealing at regular intervals. "Her campaign is going to pivot. Use Monica's murder to show solidarity with the people of Acapulco. Carlota's in the same boat as everyone else. Her boat is just a little fancier. But no less full of tears and so on."

"Look." Emilia pointed to the screen. Two men climbed into the white SUV parked in the space that Monica's sedan would eventually occupy. After three minutes, the headlights flashed on. The vehicle slowly backed out and drove out of view.

"Okay, it's 4:43," Emilia said, noting the timestamp. "Monica's spot is empty."

A vintage Volkswagen Beetle slid into the space.

Silvio swore.

Monica's car finally appeared as the video display ticked past 8:00 pm. "There she is," Emilia said exultantly.

The car door opened. Monica Montoya stepped out, a monochromatic figure in the outfit she'd died in: pale trousers, silk blouse with the bow at the neck, and spike-heeled pumps. Her hair was in a ponytail.

Emilia leaned closer, absorbed by the sight of Monica Montoya alive and breathing and moving with athletic grace. She carried a handbag large enough to be an overnight case.

On the screen, Monica closed the car door. Her attention swiveled to something on her left, out of view. She turned in that direction and waved, her body language radiating excitement.

A moment later, carrying the handbag in her left hand, she walked toward whomever or whatever had captured her attention and passed out of the frame.

The video kept rolling. A couple walked past Monica's car and entered the restaurant. The shadow of an SUV passed over the hood of the car, evidence of another vehicle trolling for a parking spot. The digital counter in the bottom corner ticked the seconds away. Monica's car stayed put, a solid gray lump in the middle of the screen.

Emilia and Silvio kept at it, watching speeded-up video covering the hours until midnight, when Café Romeo closed. Monica never returned to her car. Nor did she go into the restaurant.

"Play the beginning again," Silvio said.

Emilia dragged the arrow along the bottom of the frame to the minute before Monica appeared. As before, the sedan nosed into the parking spot. It took a few seconds before Monica got out and shut the car door.

"Wait, this is wrong." Emilia stopped the video. "Everyone going in and out of the restaurant is wearing shorts and sunscreen. Except Monica. Look at what she's wearing. This outfit says special occasion, not fake Italian food in a noisy tourist trap."

"She never planned to go inside." Silvio caught her point immediately.

"Monica expected something really fancy." Emilia looked up at Silvio. "She canceled her shopping date for something special. I think Monica planned to meet somebody, leave her car and go somewhere in theirs. And for whatever reason, didn't want her friend Susana to know."

She restarted the video. Again, Monica waved happily and walked out of view.

In a few hours she'd be dead.

CHAPTER 11

"I told Salazar we could hang on for five days," Silvio said. "After that, if the Montoya case is still open, we have to either get help or cut the effort in half. In the meantime, Castro and Gomez have to manage incoming information. If you're expecting reports from Ballistics or whatever, let them know. Otherwise, don't expect to see the right stuff get into your case files."

Emilia didn't bother writing herself a reminder. Castro and Gomez, partners who liked to make her life a living hell, would screw up anything related to her open cases on purpose. No sense helping them along.

"Hell of a day." Silvio swept his arm across the conference table, shoving aside the empty pizza box. "We got the victim's car left at Café Romeo and her meeting somebody there. What else do we have now that we didn't have six hours ago?"

He pointed at Macias who swiped a paper napkin across his mouth. "Three neighbors in Colonia Progreso say that a loud vehicle was around Casa de Plata on Saturday night. Sports car or a motorcycle. Nobody saw anything, just heard it."

"What time?"

Macias consulted his notes. "Around 7:30, maybe a little after. Nobody was real sure. Just that it was loud and annoying."

"Stay on it," Silvio said to Macias. "Narrow it down. Find that driver."

"Sure thing, *jefe*," Macias said.

"That time is before Monica got to Café Romeo and met whoever," Emilia observed.

It was nearly 11:00 pm. The four detectives were all drooping with fatigue as they ate pizza for the second night in a row and tried to make sense of the murder board.

Monica Montoya's face stared blankly across the room from its spot crowning the murder board. The visual representation of the investigation had expanded with a photo of her car at Café Romeo, a series of stills from the security video feed and a section devoted to Carlos Lima, their prime—and so far only—suspect.

Lima's *cédula* picture boasted a dour expression and slightly longer hair than in the framed photo with Monica. The photo of him and Monica had been moved to the side, which Emilia took as an ironic reflection of their relationship.

Silvio snapped his fingers at the murder board. "Okay Cruz, what's the story on this Lima character?"

"Victim's boyfriend. Investment banker who works for Viejo Dorado. Monica's mother and aunt love him to bits, expecting they'd eventually get married. On the other hand, best friend claims he abused Monica. Slapped her around. Says she wanted to break up with him but was too scared to tell him."

"We dug up everything we could about the *pendejo*," Sandor chimed in. "Including the fact that the Lima family are big supporters of Nadio Vallejo Loy."

"You're fucking with me," Silvio exclaimed.

"They haven't been keeping it a secret." Sandor sifted through his notes and pulled out a spreadsheet. "Big donations to the campaign, plus Lima's parents hosted a dinner for the guy. Tickets were 20,000 pesos apiece."

Emilia's mouth fell open. She barely made that much in two months.

Silvio passed a hand over his mouth. "You're telling me that Carlota's sister, who was some sort of glad-hander for her re-election campaign, was stuck in a bad relationship with a guy funding the opposition candidate?"

"His parents are throwing money at Vallejo Loy," Sandor spoke carefully. "Not sure about Lima himself."

"*Oye*." Silvio raised a hand. "Let's keep an open mind. Could be a political motive, could be personal, could be something else. Right now, everything is on the table."

Emilia passed him a sheet of paper with information she'd swiftly dug up about Sergio Alvarez, following up on her aunt's helpful tip. "I don't know how this fits in, but our victim's family and Carlota aren't exactly on good terms."

"Yeah, I got that last night," Silvio said as he studied her notes.

Emilia nodded. "Monica's uncle Sergio Alvarez went into the hotel business with Felix Montoya, Carlota's father. Felix was already wealthy so Sergio was more of a junior partner. Not long after, Felix began his affair with Victoria Alvarez who got pregnant with Monica. Felix left his wife and little Carlota to shack up with Victoria and raise baby Monica. When Felix died, his money went to Carlota. He didn't leave Monica's mother much besides the apartment in La Brisas and enough to send Monica to college in El Norte. Victoria and her sister Belinda aren't complaining but Sergio is still mad."

Silvio slid the sheet back across the table to Emilia. "Is there a link between this uncle and Casa de Plata?"

"Not so far," she admitted. "But what I'm getting to is that Belinda Alvarez implied that Carlota had Monica killed."

Her words were met with guffaws of disbelief from Macias and Sandor. Silvio held up a hand for quiet. "She give you any reason for thinking that?"

"Nothing." Emilia slumped in her chair. "I got the feeling that something is going on in that household besides everyone being devastated by Monica's murder. But I have no idea what.'

"When your woman's intuition comes up with something concrete, let us know," Silvio said sarcastically. "Meanwhile, back to Lima. Maybe our victim met him at Café Romeo, finally got the courage to break it off and he offs her. He have any link to Casa de Plata. Potential buyer?"

"He's not in the file from Metro Properties." Emilia shrugged. "We've got a long list of cleaners and repairmen who had access to the place, plus everyone who saw the place with the realtor, including you and Mercedes."

"Okay, Cruz, I want you to stay on the access issue. Talk to stakeholders." Silvio fixed her with a meaningful stare. "Dig wherever you need to dig."

Stakeholders. Of course he meant Campos. Emilia knew that dealing with the *federales* was inevitable but her stomach clenched at the thought of shadow-boxing with the slippery man who was the agent handler for her brother's deep cover assignment.

"First thing in the morning," she made herself say. "But I want to sit in when you question Lima."

Silvio nodded. "Understood."

As he went on, parceling out assignments to Macias and

Sandor to grill Monica's co-workers at Carlota's campaign and follow up on the mysterious loud vehicle and run down any leads from the hotline, Emilia checked her phone. For the last hour, social media had been on fire with reports of a new rally to show support for Carlota. Vallejo Loy's campaign had put out a statement decrying violence in the city and announcing a pause in campaign activities until after Monica Montoya's funeral. The added attention would no doubt prompt more calls to the hotline.

Only sixteen calls had come in that afternoon after Carlota's press conference, including the one from Café Romeo. A few tips were sent off to Dispatch for uniform cops to investigate. The rest were proven to be false alarms.

But every call that came in meant that someone had to catalogue it, return the call, and follow up if the tip seemed legit.

"What about the tapas angle?" Sandor asked.

Silvio snorted. "We figure out how our victim got in, we'll find out who brought the food."

"What about delivery?" Macias started tapping on his own phone.

"I haven't had time," Emilia admitted. "But we should make a list of every restaurant that delivers to Colonia Progreso and start asking if anyone delivered tapas to Casa de Plata on Saturday night."

Sandor groaned. "Do you know how many that could be?"

"Put it on the list," Silvio said.

Emilia heard fatigue in every voice around the table. The lack of resources was like a thousand kilo weight they were each carrying.

As the three men continued to discuss the case, she abandoned her phone for the bulky evidence bag containing the items taken from Monica Montoya's car.

Obviously, the woman kept her vehicle tidier than Emilia's Suburban which customarily was strewn with takeout paper napkins, half-opened packs of gum, empty water bottles, her gym bag, post-workout towels, plus at least one pair of cross-trainers in case she ended up at the central police administration building which had an excellent gym.

The bag from Monica's car yielded the basics: car manual from the manufacturer, a Guia Roja spiral-bound map book for Acapulco and the state of Guerrero, the car's registration and tax documents and a dozen campaign flyers splashed with Carlota's famous smile.

"Look at this," Emilia exclaimed.

She held up a pink velvet covered box. It opened to reveal a creamy satin lining and interlocking hearts embossed in gold inside the lid. She held it out for the three men to see.

Understanding spread across Silvio's face. "Box for an engagement ring," he said.

Emilia set down the little pink cube, her skin crawling. "The autopsy showed that blood was smeared on the last two fingers of her left hand. Someone took the ring off her finger after she was dead."

"A robbery gone bad," Sandor said. "Maybe Lima's got nothing to do with it."

They argued for another hour, drinking cold coffee and finishing the last slices of pizza, theories growing more ridiculous as they grew progressively punchier. But in the end, the only workable theory was that Monica deliberately canceled her shopping date with a friend in order to put on an expensive outfit and an engagement ring and go meet someone in the parking lot at Café Romeo who might be an abusive boyfriend with ties to Carlota's rival for mayor.

All they had to do now was find out how she ended up dead in Casa de Plata.

CHAPTER 12

"Look," Emilia said, catching up to Silvio as he pushed open the door to the parking lot. "We need to talk."

She stayed on his heels until they were outside. It was very late and the parking lot was mostly empty. The big mercury lights topping the perimeter walls threw a pale bluish haze over the loops of razor wire crowning the cement.

The police station was far from the beach, in a nondescript central neighborhood buttoned up for the night. Just a few miles away tourists ate plastic pasta at Café Romeo. Homeowners enjoyed their rooftop view of the ocean before going to sleep in Colonia Progreso.

To the west, in La Quebrada, the cliff divers readied for their torchlight show at midnight. On the other side of the bay, tourists reveled in the noisy music blaring out of beachfront nightclubs along Playa Hornitos and Playa Guitarron. The late showing at the Cinepolis near the Diana monument was ending, spilling movie-goers into the street for a midnight meal at one of the outdoor restaurants in Acapulco's swankiest commercial district.

If Emilia was home, she'd be on the penthouse balcony with Kurt, enjoying their nightly ritual of sipping brandy and listening to the steel drum music drifting up to them from the hotel's Pasodoble Bar six stories below.

Instead she was hot and cranky and scuffing her feet against the dirty pavement outside the police station in the middle of the night, listening to the monotonous buzz of the mercury lights.

"Okay." Silvio leaned against the wall a few steps from the door and folded his arms. "I know what you're going to say. I was copied on Salazar's email."

At least he wasn't going to play coy. "Did you notice there was no explanation?"

"You don't have to resign right away." Silvio looked past her, as if the closed gate to the parking lot was of intense interest. "Find Monica Montoya's murderer, get a medal from Carlota and go out in a blaze of glory."

"I'm not resigning, you *pendejo*." As tired as Emilia was, his idiotic response injected new energy into her veins. "You're supposed to help me find a way to make Chief Salazar reverse his decision, not try to make this sound like the greatest fucking thing that ever happened to me."

Silvio shook his head and reluctantly turned his attention back to her. "Salazar is not going to change his mind, Emilia. You had to know this was coming."

"How would I know that?" Emilia countered but Silvio's use of her first name was a bad omen.

He gave her a look of absolute incredulity. "You're not stupid. Nobody else ever had to apply for permission to get married."

"I thought it was a formality," Emilia said slowly. She hadn't questioned the form, hadn't thought to ask if she was being singled out. "That everyone had to do it."

Silvio threw his arms out. "Really?"

Emilia felt anger rise like a storm tide. "How come you didn't mention this to me earlier? Like when you were signing the fucking form as my supervisor?"

"What good would it have done?" Silvio snapped back. "You wouldn't have believed me."

"Well, thanks. I'll just have to hope that the union does the right thing, seeing as you won't."

It was a harsh dig and Emilia saw that it had the intended effect. Once brothers-in-law, Silvio and Victor Obregon had been enemies for a long time.

"Don't take this to Obregon." Silvio's voice sounded as if he had a bone caught in his throat.

"That's what the union's for," Emilia shot back. "For recourse when the department cheats us out of what we're due."

"Obregon will want his pound of flesh." Silvio jabbed a finger at her. "Are you going to give it to him?"

Emilia simmered down, surprised at the expression on his face. For all his menace and bluster, Silvio had a strict moral center. "Do you really think I'd cheat on Kurt with Obregon so the union will give me permission to marry?"

"Rucker's a friend and a business partner. You cheat on him with Obregon and I'm going to have something to say about it."

"Thanks for the vote of confidence," Emilia snapped. "I just want the union to do what it's there for."

"Look." Silvio blew out his breath to the night sky. "Don't get in a rush. Let it ride while we wrap up this case. Find out who killed Carlota's sister and you'll be in a much better position to negotiate."

"With Obregon?"

He grimaced. "With Salazar."

The mercury lights droned on and on. The gate lifted and a patrol car drove in. The metal stanchion clanged as it fell back into place. The car engine cut. The driver ambled over to talk to the gate guard. Low male laughter floated through the night.

"Okay." Emilia stuck out her hand. "Deal."

Silvio shook hands without turning the moment into a test of strength. Then he stepped back. "Go home, Cruz. Stay safe."

"You, too." Emilia dug her keys out of her shoulder bag and pressed the fob. Three rows over, the Suburban's lights blinked on.

Silvio's sedan was across the lot but the big lieutenant didn't move. "You're talking to Campos tomorrow?"

"First thing," Emilia replied.

"About that." Silvio rubbed his chin with the back of his hand.

Emilia waited.

Silvio blew out his breath again. "Don't trust anything the bastard tells you."

CHAPTER 13

The modern office building that housed the Financial Crimes unit was eerily silent at 8:00 am, just like every other time Emilia had been there. Her footsteps reverberated against the terrazzo floor as she crossed the vast empty lobby. Doors sporting seemingly legitimate business logos branched off a central atrium but she knew there was nothing behind them. Every office suite was vacant.

In fact, except for the handful of *federale* officers posing as Financial Crimes on the second floor, the entire building was empty.

"Well, if it isn't Ester." Señora Mendez was the unit's secretary, seated in front of the hallway leading to the offices lining the second floor.

"I'm sticking with Emilia now." Ester was Emilia's cover name during the operation targeting Diego Barrielos Luna's distribution network. The secretary had been a logistical marvel then, handling everything from a special taxi license to renting a house in the fake name to support Emilia's cover story.

"Lieutenant Campos and Agent Ruiz are waiting for you in the lieutenant's office." Señora Mendez stood up.

"Don't bother. I remember where it is."

"Coffee's on the way." The secretary gave her a motherly smile and bustled off in the direction of the small kitchenette.

Seated at a small conference table, Lieutenant Campos was in earnest conversation with a second man Emilia didn't immediately recognize. Both shot to their feet when she tapped on the open office door.

"Emilia, how good to see you again." Campos extended his hand, exuding false good cheer. "It's been quite some time, hasn't it?"

He was just the same as when they'd worked together, a youthful forty-something dressed like a *norteamericano* college student in jeans, a pink polo shirt and glasses with trendy plastic turquoise frames. His shock of dark hair was worn a shade too long, but it suited him. If she didn't know what a lying bastard he was, Emilia would have thought him handsome.

"Do you remember Bruno Ruiz Ramirez?" Campos indicated the other man.

"No, I'm sorry I don't."

"No reason you would. I wasn't in the office much when you were with us." About the same age as Campos, Ruiz was a reedy man with closely cropped curly hair, his thinness accentuated by a navy blue collared shirt. He shook hands with Emilia. "No need to stand on ceremony. Call me Bruno."

Señora Mendez brought in coffee and a plate of small pastries. When she left, she closed the door behind her.

Campos's office was a large, windowless space. Besides the conference table and four chairs, it boasted a desk, two computers, an enormous printer and a safe the size of a refrigerator. Offsetting the industrial atmosphere was a credenza topped with framed pictures.

Most of the pictures featured a tall boy who was the spitting image of his father, with hipster glasses and the same shock of hair falling over a high forehead. Campos's wife was very attractive, possibly only a few years older than Emilia, suggesting that she'd become a mother at a very young age.

Emilia was welcomed with artificial heartiness and ushered into a seat at the table.

"Let me guess why you're here," Campos said, stirring sugar into his cup of coffee. "Casa de Plata."

"Yes." Emilia was relieved that they weren't going to play some cat-and-mouse game but could get down to business. "Your unit used the building where a woman was found dead last Sunday."

"Tragic," Ruiz murmured before biting into a flaky *orejas* pastry studded with rock sugar.

"Did you know her?" Emilia asked.

"The mayor's sister?" Campos sipped coffee. "We hardly run in the same circles as the Montoya family."

"Any idea how she got into Casa de Plata?"

"If you are wondering if Monica Montoya worked for us, the answer is no." Campos looked at Ruiz, who nodded as he chewed. "We were as shocked as anyone at the news."

"How do you suppose she got inside?"

"We've been asking each other the same question."

"And?"

"No idea." Campos leaned forward, the picture of bafflement. "As I'm sure you know by now, a full set of keys was given to Metro Properties, along with the agreement to act as the broker. Every exterior door, every apartment, every interior door."

"What about duplicates?"

Campos turned to Ruiz again, with a sly grin. "Didn't I tell you that our Ester was a sharp one?"

The reference to her cover name and his patronizing

attitude grated on Emilia's nerves. "You have extra keys," she said flatly.

"Locked in a safe in my office," Ruiz supplied. "When the place is sold, the buyer gets the extra set."

"I have to take them with me."

"Not a problem," Ruiz said. "Given the situation, better that you retain the keys rather than having them here."

Emilia was gratified by his easy attitude. "When was the last time anyone from this office was at Casa de Plata?"

"At Casa de Plata?" Campos frowned, brows coming together above the turquoise frames. "Months ago. Five, six maybe?"

Emilia stirred her coffee. "What about Sol Directo? Someone is running your cover story. What do they know about Casa de Plata? Do they have access?"

Campos chuckled. "Sol Directo is a folder on my laptop, Detective."

"What about Gamboa?" Emilia hated having to raise the specter of her brother but it had to be done. "Does he have a key?"

"Ah." Campos gave a little embarrassed laugh. "Yes, I suppose he does. I don't recall asking for it back."

"Any connection between him and Monica Montoya?"

Campos laughed. "Always willing to blame Señor Gamboa for your troubles. Well, let me tell you a secret. Rafa hasn't been in Acapulco in months. He certainly wasn't here last weekend."

Emilia stirred her coffee. "Who owned Casa de Plata before you?"

Campos blinked, the turquoise frames making him into a

modern owl. "*Oye*, now you've stumped me. Why?"

"What about the name Alvarez? Does that ring a bell?" It was just a vague hunch, but Emilia was curious to know if Casa de Plata had a role in the abortive business partnership between Felix Montoya and Sergio Alvarez.

"Is that your prime suspect?" Ruiz asked.

"We're working multiple angles, including the link between the victim and the location," Emilia said primly, unwilling to share too much. "The working theory is that she was brought there by someone she met at a restaurant near Playa Hornitos."

"Café Romeo," Ruiz supplied. "It's all over social media that's where her car was found. Carlota's campaign is holding a prayer rally there tonight."

"More coffee?" Campos poured her another cup.

He was clearly interested in prolonging the conversation, which Emilia found interesting in and of itself. She would play along, see where it led. "Have there been any inquiries about Casa de Plata that came to you and not Metro Properties?"

"No." Ruiz took another pastry. "Our cover story is solid. I doubt there's more than five people who know the connection between Casa de Plata and this office. Including you and your boss, Silvio."

Campos took off his glasses and made a show of polishing them on a napkin. "Frankly, the greater the distance between this office and the eventual buyer, the better. Safer for all concerned, including you and your brother."

Emilia wasn't sure if she'd just been delivered a veiled message or not.

Campos turned to Ruiz. "Bruno, could you get the extra

keys? I'm sure we've used up enough of the detective's time."

"Of course." Ruiz excused himself and left.

When the door shut with a soft snick, Campos leaned toward Emilia, creating a sense of intimacy. "Truly, Emilia, your visit is very timely. Saved me the trouble of arranging a quiet word."

"What about Casa de Plata aren't you telling me?"

"I admire your focus but put that aside for a moment." Campos held his glasses up to the light, then resumed polishing. "Rafa has been quite successful in his role as movie producer Manolo Bernal. He's sold the distribution rights to *A Misunderstood Man* to a big *nortemericano* movie studio. They're going to release it after some post-production work. Your scenes as Alejandra Messi's double are staying in."

Emilia gasped. "You can't be serious."

"Rafa says it's impossible to tell that you aren't Alejandro Messi. Camera angles, lighting, whatever. So you have nothing to worry about."

"Absolutely not," Emilia breathed. "I was promised that I would not appear in the movie and that the movie would never be released."

"Times change. Requirements change."

"What you mean is that promises change."

"Listen, Detective." Campos's tone was no longer amenable. "We have put blood, sweat and tears into this project. If this movie hits theaters, there's no way that Barrielos Luna won't show his face to see it. To claim that he wrote the screenplay and that he's the most famous *narco* Mexico ever produced. If that means you have to grit your teeth because sixty seconds of your life is on that screen disguised as the most famous movie star in the world, well, I think you can pull it off.'

"It's more than sixty seconds," Emilia argued.

"You're a dead ringer for Alejandra Messi, or so I'm told."

"What if this is a hit?" Emilia could not believe the conversation. "Anything with Alejandra Messi turns to gold."

"Then Barrielos Luna will be doubly tempted to come out of hiding and boast about it."

"Has Gamboa made a deal with him? A percentage of the profits? Maybe they're going to split it. I think Rafa double-crossed you. The hell with the *federales,* he's thinking, and the rest of us."

"Is that what you want, Detective? A share of ticket sales or however these things are calculated." Campos finally resettled his glasses on his nose. "That can be arranged."

"I want my face not to be in a movie about Diego Barrielos Luna that people actually see," Emilia said furiously.

The door handle made a springy metallic sound as it was depressed. Emilia sat back and forced herself to look composed. Campos gave her a nod of approval as Ruiz came back into the office.

For all he knew they'd been discussing new décor.

"Here you go," Ruiz said. "This is everything we have." He set down a cardboard box containing two oversized ziplock bags bulging with keys and tiny white labels.

"Good luck with the case," Campos said as he escorted her down the stairs. "I'm sorry we couldn't be more helpful."

Every word floated up to Señora Mendez and Ruiz standing on the mezzanine like sentries. Emilia understood that the conversation about Rafa Gamboa and the movie was effectively over.

Silvio had said not to trust anything Campos said. But in this case, she was sure that the bastard was telling the truth about Gamboa and that *maldita* movie.

CHAPTER 14

"Good cop, bad cop," Silvio said in the viewing corridor outside the interrogation room as they watched Carlos Lima drum long slim fingers on the scarred tabletop. He'd been waiting for two hours.

Emilia pretended to think. "Which one am I?"

"Funny, Cruz." Silvio yanked open the door and they went in.

From what Emilia knew about men's clothing, Carlos Lima had impeccable taste. Kurt would have approved of the slubby navy suit that had probably cost as much as a car. Underneath the tapered jacket he wore a starched white shirt, narrow striped tie, and heavy gold cufflinks that looked like Roman coins and dragged his shirt cuffs against the lining of the jacket sleeves.

"I hope you are here to apologize," Lima said belligerently as soon as Emilia and Silvio took their seats across the table and introduced themselves.

"Señor, you're here to answer questions related to a murder investigation," Silvio said dismissively. "I suggest you cooperate and don't waste our time."

Lima bristled but didn't offer an argument.

Emilia made a production out of turning on the audio and video feeds. Silvio identified himself and Emilia for the recording and gave the date and time.

"We are here to question Carlos Lima regarding his relationship with and knowledge of the late Monica Montoya

Alvarez," Silvio announced for the recording. "Señor Lima arrived for this interview directly from Viejo Dorado, his place of employment, and is here voluntarily."

Lima pressed his lips together in barely contained anger as Silvio intoned the company's address as well as Lima's home address. It was a subtle way of informing the man that he was under a microscope and Lima knew it.

"Now, then, señor," Silvio said. "When was the last time you saw Monica Montoya?"

"Six weeks ago," Lima said promptly. His body language was controlled, shoulders square, no twitches or foot tapping or refusal to make eye contact. "We had dinner at the resort at Playa Revolcadero."

The resort at Revolcadero was further east along the coast than the Palacio Real's location at the tip of Punta Diamante but it was nearly as prestigious, with prices to match.

She put the little pink ring box on the table between them. "Do you recognize this, señor?"

"No."

"It's for an engagement ring." Emilia opened the box to show him the little gold symbol. "Did you present Monica with an engagement ring at your dinner?"

"No," Lima said stiffly. "We agreed to part ways."

"Part ways?" Emilia frowned. "Monica's mother believes you and Monica had an arrangement. That you planned to get married."

"The relationship had run its course and we agreed to end it." Lima was a cool customer all right, radiating disapproval at having to answer questions posed by those beneath him in the social order. "I have no insight as to what Monica told her mother after that night."

"Basically, you broke up."

"A crude way to put it, but yes."

He strongly reminded Emilia of Rafa Gamboa when she encountered him not as El Acólito but as movie producer Manolo Bernal. Lima wasn't nearly as good looking but exuded the same air of personal entitlement. Others grubbed for what they had; Lima and Bernal simply took.

Silvio slapped a hand on the table. "Tell us about your connection to a Colonia Progreso property called Casa de Plata. Historic architecture."

Lima's lips twitched. "I've never been there."

"But you've heard of it," Silvio pressed.

"It was once a very important piece of architecture," Lima replied haughtily. "I probably learned about it in school."

Silvio didn't relent. "Did you ever take Monica Montoya there?"

"No, of course not. As far as I know, it's derelict."

"Then why would your girlfriend go there?"

"She was no longer my girlfriend. As to why she would go there, I have no idea."

"Did you ever use force against Monica?"

"Of course not." Lima looked from one detective to the other, eyes narrowed in suspicion. "I'm not a man of violence."

"That's not what we've heard," Silvio snarled. He leaned forward over the table, menace pouring out of him. "We've heard rumors that you struck Monica. More than once. Is that why she wanted out of the relationship?"

"Struck Monica?" Lima sat bolt upright, the greenish cast of the fluorescent lights stealing ten thousand pesos worth of value from his designer suit. "That's absurd."

"Do you deny it?" Emilia asked.

"I most certainly do."

Silvio snapped his fingers, making Lima swivel his head so fast the banker nearly fell off his chair. "Do you own a gun?"

"Certainly not."

"Where were you last Saturday night, starting around five o'clock?"

Lima steadied. "You're asking where I was the night Monica was killed."

"Shouldn't be hard to remember." Silvio rested meaty forearms on the table. "Where were you?"

"I'm not answering until I consult with a lawyer."

"Not a problem," Silvio said, in a surprisingly mild tone. "Go ahead and call. While we're waiting for your lawyer to arrive, we'll arrest you on suspicion of murder, refusing to cooperate with a police investigation, and trying to look down Detective Cruz's shirt. Always room for one more in the holding cells."

Lima ran a hand over his mouth, in what Emilia knew immediately was an uncharacteristic gesture. Men like him were too well-bred and restrained to show such a lack of composure unless they were under great pressure.

"I was working," he said finally.

"On a Saturday night?"

"Yes. It was a very important project."

"Tell us about it." Emilia smiled encouragingly.

"I doubt you'd find it interesting." Lima rubbed his mouth again, spidery finger restlessly pulling at the skin.

Emilia kept her good cop smile in place. "You work for

Viejo Dorado," she said. "I'm sure your clients appreciate the extra time you take on these types of investment projects."

"Yes," Lima said distantly. "I was in the office."

Silvio leaned forward, practically spitting in Lima's face. "We know where you work. It's a building with excellent security. Everyone has a badge to sign in and out, plus guards and cameras. I'm going to call the head of security there right now. It will take me less than two minutes to find out exactly when you were in that building Saturday and how long you stayed."

Lima's face twisted in anguish, his striped tie rising and falling so fast that Emilia wondered if he was having a heart attack.

"Señor?" she prompted.

"Can we end the recording for a minute?" Lima asked, his voice almost a whisper. Slender fingers kneaded each other in agitation.

Emilia raised her eyebrows at Silvio. He glowered, but knew as well as she did that it was time for the good cop to take over the interview. She went to the control panel and rolled her hand around the knob so that it looked like she turned off the audio recording and the feed to the speaker outside in the viewing corridor.

"All right, señor," Emilia said gently as she took her seat again. "What would you like to tell us?"

"I was at the Boulevard Hotel on Saturday. Stayed all night."

The Boulevard was one of the smaller hotels in the central downtown area with a private slice of beach overlooking Playa Redondo. Serviceable, not exceptional, as Kurt would say.

"Go on," she prompted.

Lima clasped his hands on the scarred table, obviously trying to conceal a tremor in one of those spidery forefingers. "The bank keeps a private suite for the senior staff. For private, discreet entertainment. It was my weekend to use it."

"You hired a hooker," Silvio said flatly. "For the entire night?"

"No, she left around two o'clock. I called for room service afterward. The waiter brought it up about half an hour later. After that I was alone."

Emilia sketched a quick timeline, then looked up. "What was the hooker's name?"

"She called herself Beso."

"Beso?" The word meant *kiss*. Of course it was a fake, no hooker who worked the downtown hotels gave a customer her real name. "How did you and Beso connect?"

"There's a man at the hotel who makes the arrangements."

"We need a name."

"No name. He just comes to the suite and takes the order." The confession had considerably dimmed Lima's snobby manner. "What kind of girl. How many and so forth."

Emilia kept her voice calm and soothing. "What time did the man come to the suite?"

"About 7:30," Lima said, now intently studying the ring bolt in the center of the table for those suspects who needed to be chained. "He had some pictures and I picked a girl and he said that was a good choice. I paid him, he left and she knocked on the door about fifteen minutes later."

"How much did she cost you?" Emilia demanded. The good cop act was over.

"Four thousand pesos."

"Okay." Silvio slapped the table, making Lima jump. "You say you checked into the Boulevard Saturday night and the fixer showed up. You ordered a girl, who said her name was Beso. Then it was just you and her until two in the morning. Does that sound about right?"

"Yes, but that can't become public. The suite is just for the executive staff. I'm taking a huge risk telling you."

"Sure," Silvio snorted. "You think this Beso is going to corroborate your alibi?"

"I just told you my alibi. That should be sufficient." Lima was going for both privileged and defiant.

Again Emilia was reminded of Rafa Gamboa.

"What about your support for Nadio Vallejo Loy?" Silvio said, turning the conversation in a different direction. "Your family has thrown big money at him."

Lima drew back in surprise. "Are you accusing me of meddling in politics?"

"No, just seems strange that your family are big supporters of Vallejo Loy, but you were dating his rival's sister. Who's now dead. And you've got the world's weakest alibi."

"It's the truth," Lima said indignantly.

"Believe it or not, people make up all kinds of shit," Silvio said. "Who else knew you were at the Boulevard?"

"It was my weekend to use the suite. I . . . I didn't have to tell anyone."

"Did you check in?"

"No, we have keys to the suite. Executive level staffers all have keys."

"Even the women?" Emilia couldn't resist asking.

"There are no women at that level at Viejo Dorado," Lima said.

"Did you drive there?" Emilia pressed. If the Boulevard's security cameras were as good as the array at Café Romeo, they might get footage of Lima driving in and a clear shot of his license plate. "Leave your car in the parking garage?"

"I took a taxi," Lima said, weakening his situation even further.

"Which *sitio*?" Licensed and registered *sitio* taxis operated from fixed locations. They were much safer than the *libre* taxis that cruised the streets looking for random fares. It would be easy enough to find and question the *sitio* driver who had taken Lima to the hotel.

Lima shook his head. "I took a *libre* taxi."

"In other words, you have no proof of anything." Silvio gave a laugh and slammed his notebook shut. "Your alibi hangs on a fixer and a hooker. You really didn't want anyone to know you were there Saturday night. I think that's because you weren't there at all."

"I was at the Boulevard all night in the company suite," Lima insisted, the spidery fingers kneading each other like bread dough. "I didn't kill Monica."

Emilia shook her head. "Señor, think about what you've just told us. There's a large block of time on Saturday evening when you have no proof that you were where you say you were. That's the exact block of time when not too far away from the Boulevard Hotel, your ex-girlfriend was shot and killed."

It was an all-too-common femicide scenario. Over a thousand women had been murdered in Mexico so far that year, almost all by a boyfriend or husband. That was only the ones they knew about. Many more went missing and were presumed dead. Their families never found out what happened or achieved any sense of closure.

The 47 women in her binder of Las Perdidas were just those missing from the Acapulco area. If Monica's body had not been found, she would have become number 48.

"Were you ever physical with Monica?" Silvio took up the thread. "Slapped her when she got out of hand?

"You asked me that before," Lima protested. "My answer is still the same. No, a thousand times, no."

Emilia stared straight at Lima, gratified to see him squirm.

Silvio raised his hands as if to say *what a liar.*

"I want to call my lawyer," Lima said.

CHAPTER 15

Twilight bathed the city in shades of purple and indigo as Emilia showed her badge to the guard at the Caseta de Cobro police station. He threw her a sloppy salute and raised the barrier. She drove into the lot, parked and presented her badge again, holding it up so the two cops waiting inside a thick bullet-proof glass enclosure could see it.

"Detective Emilia Cruz," she said into the speaker set into the glass. "I've got business with the shift supervisor."

A buzzer sounded. The door in front of Emilia clicked open and she was able to pass into the lobby of the police station.

There was more bullet-proof glass inside, a greenish-hued expanse stretching from the top of the counter all the way to the ceiling. If not for the lack of windows, scuffed tile floor, and official notices glued to the scratched green walls, the counter could have been a teller booth in a prosperous bank.

"Cruz, right?" The sergeant behind the glass was a jowly man who was probably younger than he looked, thanks to a few too many tortillas with every meal. "You've been here before."

"You've got a good memory, Sergeant."

"You make it easy." His eyes drifted to her chest. "Whatcha need today?"

"Pizza and a beer and a sergeant who can run ten meters without having a stroke." Emilia rapped on the glass and grinned when he drew back.

She left the lobby without waiting to hear him say

whatever crude thing he was sure to be sharing with the rest of the retired-in-place crew running the night shift.

The women's locker room was at the rear of the building. Half a dozen women were there, changing clothes, talking loudly, clanging locker doors. The air was charged with the familiar adrenaline high of cops who'd finished a shift without anything bad happening.

"I hear the shift supervisor is a real hard ass," Emilia said loudly.

The locker room went silent. Every face turned to look at her.

One of the women slammed her locker shut and stalked over to Emilia. She was a few years older. In jeans and a plain black blouse, with chestnut hair and broad shoulders, she wore no makeup, nor did she need any to accentuate chiseled cheekbones and perfect full lips.

She kept coming until she was practically nose to nose with Emilia. "She had a hard ass for a teacher, *puta*."

Emilia burst into laughter and pulled the other woman into a wild rocking hug that was returned with equal laughter and an embrace that threatened to crush Emilia's ribcage.

Rosalita Riva Diaz had been the last candidate to be hired during Emilia's reluctant stint as head of operations for an all-female police unit called Las Palomas, or The Doves. The entire project had been conceived and commissioned by Carlota. If Chief Salazar opposed it, he never let on.

In an attempt to burnish Acapulco's international image ahead of an Olympic delegation, Las Palomas were to bring peace to downtown streets by acting as police, tour guide and beauty pageant contestants all rolled into one.

Hiring a hooker was against Emilia's better judgment, but Rosalita met all the qualifications and then some. She was smart, she was fit, she spoke English and had no criminal record.

Yes, Rosalita was a hooker, but she'd never been on the street, luring customers with barely-there clothes and dulling the pain of existence with drugs. Rosalita was an "inside girl," a hooker who exclusively worked in the best hotels and by appointment only.

Still, it mystified Emilia as to why the glamorous woman would want to become a cop, even one with such a diluted law enforcement mission as Las Palomas, until Rosalita finally revealed her secret.

She was hunting for her teenage daughter.

The girl had disappeared without a trace. No one was willing to lift a finger to help a hooker so Rosalita took the opportunity that Las Palomas offered, in hopes of accessing information that would lead to her daughter's whereabouts.

The girl was still missing. She was an entry in Emilia's Las Perdidas binder.

"What are you doing here?" Rosalita asked after introducing Emilia to the other women in the locker room. They were all young, first assignment beat cops and more than a little in awe of Emilia having made it all the way up the ladder to the detective squadroom.

"I need a favor."

Rosalita frowned. "What kind of favor?"

"I need to pick your brain," Emilia said. "How about some food? I'm buying."

They ended up in a nearby open-air taqueria, sitting at a

white plastic table in white plastic chairs with bottles of beer and a dish of pickled vegetables to munch as they waited for their food. On the way there, the talk had been mainly gossip about the women of Las Palomas. Who was assigned to the airport and cruise ship port to reassure visitors that they were safe in Acapulco, who was patrolling downtown tourist spots, and if any of the unarmed Las Palomas officers were being assigned to help with election security.

When the small talk ran down, Rosalita fished out a slice of pickled carrot and pointed it at Emilia. "So what's going on?"

Despite the canny survival instincts that kept her alive as a hooker, Rosalita had always been the sort of person who liked to play it straight. Emilia rolled her beer bottle between both hands and decided to jump in the deep end. She took a deep breath. "I need to get in touch with the fixer at the Boulevard Hotel."

Rosalita dropped the carrot back into the dish and scrubbed vinegar off her hands with a paper napkin. "And you think I know who that is?"

"You're a cop now, and a good one," Emilia replied. "But a long time ago, I heard you talk about working the Boulevard."

Rosalita threw Emilia a murderous look, then lifted her chin and stared at the street.

Twilight was washing Acapulco in a purplish haze. They weren't close to the ocean, but in a neighborhood overshadowed by the mountains that ringed the city. The low cement buildings, most two or three stories, were softened by the fading light. At this time of the day, the advertisements for Tía Rosa snacks and Nescafé instant coffee painted on walls took on a cinematic quality. Even the lurid graffiti touting gangs and lovers splashed across the front of a mini-mart resembled art.

"A woman was murdered in an empty building in Colonia Progreso last Saturday night," Emilia said into the silence. "Her boyfriend, who says they broke up weeks ago, could be the killer. We've got reports that he hit her and that she was afraid of him."

"What's this got to do with me?"

"His alibi is that he was with a girl in a suite on the fifth floor of the Boulevard. The fixer set them up. I need to talk to the girl. She's the only person who can confirm his alibi."

Rosalita's glance came back to Emilia. "How long was the girl with him?"

"About six hours."

"Is he rich? Six hours is big money."

"His name is Carlos Lima." Part of Emilia hoped that Rosalita would recognize the name.

Rosalita shrugged, indicating that it meant nothing to her. "You said fifth floor?"

"His company keeps a suite up there. Viejo Dorado. Some sort of investment bank."

The conversation stalled as a sweaty cook in a stained apron slung down platters of rice, beans and grilled fish tacos. The food smelled like heaven but Emilia was too tense to enjoy the food. She hadn't considered that Rosalita would not want to be put on the spot and asked to recall a life she had worked so hard to put behind her.

But there was no sense in giving up now. Emilia picked up her fork. "The girl calls herself Beso."

Rosalita nodded. She shook some hot sauce onto the golden fried chunks of fish and folded the tortilla around them but didn't take a bite.

"Look, I'm sorry if this upset--."

"Edgar Arroyo," Rosalita said without meeting Emilia's eyes.

Emilia put down her fork. "How do I find him?"

"He hangs out in the bar on the fifth floor. Where the suites are. Men only. The only women who go up there work for him."

"Okay. Edgar Arroyo. Fifth floor bar. Do you--."

"What a piece of shit you are, Emilia Cruz," Rosalita whispered furiously. She threw down the taco and shoved her plate aside. "Don't you dare ask me to put on a red dress and sweet talk Arroyo into telling you what you want. I'm a cop now, same as you."

"I have no intention of asking you to do that," Emilia lied with all the vigor she could muster in the face of the other woman's fierce prescience. "I needed a name. That's all. Now I have it. Thank you. Let's eat." She busied herself with the fish tacos, folding the tortilla just right, then unwrapping it to add hot sauce and rearrange the chunks of fish.

A car went by, seeming to sweep away the last vestiges of twilight and leaving the street bathed in night. A couple went into the mini-mart, the woman holding a wailing child. Lights winked on above a hardware store where the owner probably lived.

A gust of cooking oil wafted through the *taqueria* when another batch of fish went into the fryer, sizzling and popping.

Rosalita blinked. "Okay. Sorry. I didn't mean to jump

down your throat. It's just that I'm never going back to that life. Not even for an hour."

"Nobody's asking you to." Emilia dredged up a smile. "You're a good cop, Rosalita."

The food tasted like the ashes of friendship.

CHAPTER 16

"I did a terrible thing today," Emilia said.

She rested her elbows on the waist-high wall encircling the penthouse balcony outside their bedroom. Far below, the Pacific was an inky expanse grasping endlessly at the shore. The ocean's restlessness matched her own.

Emilia watched two red dots rise and fall, the reflectors on the hotel's floating dock anchored so far away. Kurt liked to swim to the dock in the early morning as the sun came up. Emilia often joined him but it was hard to keep up with the competitive swimmer. The man slid through water like a blonde seal.

Kurt came through the French doors and handed her a small glass of brandy. "Did you rob a bank? Run over somebody's grandmother?"

"No." Emilia smiled in spite of herself. "But I'd feel better if I did."

Clad in an old tee and cotton boxers, the blonde hair just long enough to curl, Kurt leaned against the wall and warmed the brandy glass between his hands. Emilia inched closer so that her arm nudged his. Sometimes just being close to Kurt made things better.

"What happened?" he asked.

Emilia sighed. "Do you remember me telling you about Rosalita from Las Palomas?"

Kurt nodded. "The former hooker turned cop."

"I knew that she used to work the Boulevard Hotel."

Emilia took a fortifying sip of brandy as she replayed the meal with Rosalita in her mind. "Monica Montoya's boyfriend says he couldn't have killed her because he was with a hooker at the Boulevard that night."

"You thought Rosalita was the hooker?"

"No, no, she's never going back to that life." The brandy was beginning to work, oozing warm comfort into her veins. "I needed to know about the fixer who brings the girls to the company suites. Where he hangs out. It took some convincing but she finally gave me the name."

"What's the terrible part of this story?"

"Rosalita accused me of wanting her to pretend to be a hooker again and ask this Arroyo questions about my case. We both know Arroyo hasn't lasted this long by talking to cops. Of course, I lied and said something stupid like it never even crossed my mind to ask her. We both knew I was lying. She was really hurt."

"Ah."

Emilia shook her head. "I should have talked to her in the station. You know, cop to cop. Respected who she is now."

"Did it occur to you that Rosalita is really sensitive when it comes to who she was before? No matter how you broached the issue, she was bound to be upset."

"Great." Emilia felt her throat tighten and tears well up. "No matter what, I lose a friend. I don't have that many, you know."

"Come here." Kurt took the glass out of Emilia's hand and wrapped his arms around her.

She buried her face in his chest and breathed in a masculine mix of clean cotton, salty ocean and musky cologne. "What am

I going to do?" she mumbled into his tee shirt.

Kurt kissed the top of her head. "Write a memo to her supervisor citing her for helping a high-profile murder investigation."

"They'd want to know how."

"Franco has turned into a very capable bureaucrat. Make him write the citation. It'll be incoherent and therefore very impressive."

"That's not a bad idea," Emilia admitted.

"Here's an even better one." Kurt pulled back to see her face. "I know the manager of the Boulevard. Roger Boardman. Originally from Colorado."

Emilia's eyes flew wide in surprise. "Is he a member of the Acapulco Hotel Association?"

"No, but he came to a few meetings. Probably can't afford the dues. The Boulevard is a pretty small place. Extended stay suites. No restaurant, just an in-room catering service. My guess is that your target hangs out in the bar on the fifth floor."

"That's what Rosalita said. How do you know?"

"Boardman invited a couple of us gringos over there one night." In response to the question on her face, Kurt gave her a little jiggle, his arms still locked around her waist. "Long before I met you."

"Did you, uh, participate?"

"No, I didn't like the atmosphere and left. But I got the impression that Boardman knows what's going on up there."

"He takes a cut," Emilia theorized.

"I wouldn't be surprised."

"Can you introduce me to him tomorrow night? When Arroyo is there, too?" She remembered a conversation about an upcoming event at the Palacio Real right after she came home from Chilpancingo and they were still half-crazed with lust. "Tomorrow isn't Regatta Night, is it?"

"Not until the weekend." Kurt hugged her tight again. "Any other terrible things you want to tell me about?"

"No," she lied.

Later, lying in bed with Kurt sound asleep next to her, Emilia knew that if she told Kurt about Chief Salazar's denial of her request to marry, he would expect her to have already made a decision. The job or him.

Outside the open French doors, the sound of the ocean lulled her. She hoped that Silvio would keep up his end of their bargain. Help her find a way through this before she had to tell Kurt.

Before she had to choose.

CHAPTER 17

How Monica Montoya got into Casa de Plata was the million peso question no one could answer. If she had no direct connection to the old apartment building, then clearly, she knew someone who did. If it wasn't the person she met in the parking lot at Café Romeo, then who?

The missing ring was a wildcard, too. Emilia couldn't get the image of Monica out of her head. Left for dead in an empty echoing apartment. She could see Carlos Lima stripping an engagement ring from Monica's bloody hand.

Everything pointed to him, from femicide statistics to Susana's statement to Emilia's gut.

Monica tried to break up with him but weeks later when he wants her to meet him at Café Romeo, of course she has to go and pretend to be happy. She's terrified of him, who knows what he'd do if she refused.

The only snag was access to Casa de Plata. So far, nothing connected Lima to the place. Lima had never been in touch with Metro Properties. Viejo Dorado didn't invest in fixer upper property. It was highly unlikely that the banker had ties to Campos or Gamboa or *federale* counterdrug operations in general. No one on the list of friends from Susana Durán Diaz had a connection to the property, either.

Putting aside the issue of Carlos Lima's alibi until the evening when she and Kurt would go to the Boulevard Hotel, Emilia studied the file from the real estate agency. Sandor was running down the cleaners and landscapers who had been hired by the realty company to spruce the place up. It was up to Emilia to concentrate on the list of potential buyers.

Besides Silvio and Mercedes, half a dozen others had toured the property before last Sunday. If traffic wasn't bad, she would be able to talk to all of them in a single day.

The complicating factor was traffic. Downtown Acapulco was still being cleaned up after the prayer rally held by Carlota's supporters last night. Emilia had successfully avoided it by being so far north when she went to the Caseta de Cobre police station to find Rosalita. The news reports claimed that over ten thousand people had attended. A boxed meal was served to everyone who showed up, suggesting that whoever arranged the event had very deep pockets.

As she drove, Emilia passed at least a dozen street sweepers pushing carts made of oil drums, cleaning up the detritus. Candle stubs, prayer cards, empty water bottles and broken boxes littered both sides of la Costera, along with flyers bearing a black and white photo of Monica Montoya.

Seeing the woman's face in the gutter, creased and torn, felt like a sacrilege.

Emilia made short work of the first three potential buyers on her list. They were all property development companies, busy and competent but unwilling to make the needed investment to restore Casa de Plata. None had gone back to the property after their initial tour with Hernandez except for Silvio.

The fourth name on the list was Karen Chamberlain from the new United States consulate.

Emilia parked on the street in front, recalling that Kurt had met Monica Montoya at the opening. She wondered if the investigation would be any different if she'd accepted his invitation to go and met Monica, too. But work had kept her from going. It was always work that got in the way of her life.

So why was she so adamant about remaining a cop when the top of the department wanted her out?

Emilia pushed aside that question and reminded herself of the deal with Silvio. Find Monica's murderer, then tackle Chief Salazar. She got out of the Suburban.

The new consulate was housed in a sprawling building on the west side of the bay, not far from Colonia Progreso, a coincidence that wasn't lost on Emilia. The perimeter wall was newly whitewashed. Guards waited inside a Plexiglass enclosure next to twin iron gates that boasted bronze seals engraved with the words *United States Consulate*.

Between the two gates, each wide enough to fit a bus, red ginger and orange bird of paradise plants formed an inner hedge of spicy blooms and spiky leaves.

Emilia had made an appointment to speak with Katherine Singletary, the woman in charge, and was admitted through a pedestrian gate after presenting her identification. When making the appointment, she was told that under no circumstances was anyone with a gun allowed inside.

It didn't matter that inside the consulate's perimeter wall was probably one of the safest places in all Acapulco. Walking along the curving drive to the building, her loafers ringing on the tarmac, Emilia still felt uncomfortably naked without the familiar weight of her gun against her left side.

Her identification was checked again by a uniformed guard at the door. Emilia passed muster, was buzzed inside, and met by a young man who announced that he would take her upstairs.

Katherine Singletary turned out to be a motherly woman at least 20 years older than Emilia, with pale hair trying to show its gray roots and youthful pink lipstick that wasn't fooling anyone.

"Karen Chamberlain is a logistics officer," Singletary said primly and adjusted her glasses as she peered at the brochure for Casa de Plata. She spoke English and made no attempt at Spanish. "She is not assigned to the consulate, which is why your request is so irregular."

"I'd to speak with her," Emilia said. "She looked at properties for the consulate."

The name plate on Singletary's desk was very grand with engraved letters and an enamel eagle that looked as if it was flying right off the brass. *Katherine Singletary, United States Consul General, Acapulco.*

It wasn't as grand a job as being an ambassador, Emilia knew. Singletary was queen of a castle that issued visas in the name of the king.

Singletary refolded the brochure and pushed it to the edge of her desk with one finger. "When the State Department determines that a consulate is required, a team comes from Washington to assess security considerations and select a property. Karen Chamberlain was part of that team. Apparently, she saw the property you're concerned about and determined that it was unsuitable. There was no further action regarding it. Karen Chamberlain returned to Washington. As you can see, another property was selected that met our requirements."

"Yes, I see." Apparently, this was just another dead end,

just like all the other people who had looked at Casa de Plata, but there was something about Singletary's snotty attitude that made Emilia dig in her heels. "Considering that this is a murder investigation, I still need to speak with her."

"You're wasting your time, Detective."

Emilia gave a tight smile. "In addition, I'd like to get a copy of her report on the properties she looked at."

"Obviously, we can't provide you anything about this building." Singletary made a note on a slip of paper. "And I doubt there's anything significant about buildings not selected for an official U.S. presence."

"One other thing," Emilia said. "Did any member of the current consulate staff go with her?"

"If so, it will be in the report Ms. Chamberlain produced following her trip here to select an appropriate building for the consulate."

"When can I have that report?"

Singletary took off her wire-framed glasses and pointed them across her desk at Emilia. "Detective, I'm sure you need to be thorough, but time really is at a premium here. Every day we process over 300 visa requests. That means we're constantly shorthanded when it comes to supporting citizen services, which is our priority mission here in Acapulco. As soon as someone can check with Washington to find a copy of that report, someone will be in touch."

"I can wait." Emilia crossed her legs at the knee, suggesting that she'd be happy to stay right here in this nice sterile office with the giant enamel eagle flying off the brass nameplate.

"If you care to wait in the lobby, someone will check on

that for you." Singletary pinched the bridge of her nose before settling her eyeglasses in place.

"Thank you. I know the victim's sister will appreciate your cooperation." Emilia decided she wasn't above a little name dropping in order to get what she needed. "The victim was Monica Montoya, the mayor's sister."

"The mayor's sister?" Katherine Singletary sat up straighter. "I wasn't aware that the mayor had a sister."

Her interest was so sudden that Emilia wanted to laugh. "Yes, Monica worked for Carlota's re-election campaign reaching out to local businesses to build support. I believe she even attended the consulate's grand opening."

"You should have mentioned that before," Singleton said waspishly. "Of course the consulate is happy to assist the mayor in any way we can."

Dismissed by the queen, Emilia waited for someone to bring her Karen Chamberlain's report. She sat on a brand new sofa covered in scratchy fabric and used her phone to look up Carlos Lima. All she found was a press release from Viejo Dorado and the man's LinkedIn account.

"Detective Cruz?" The speaker was a well-built gringo with a square chin, wavy dark blonde hair, and round tortoiseshell glasses. He smiled and gave her hand a firm shake. "I'm William Gifford. When Katherine gave me your name, I thought that it sounded familiar."

"Oh?"

He held out a Mexican passport. "We'd just finished processing your visa."

"Thank you." Emilia took the passport and couldn't help flipping it open to see the visa. There it was, official emblem and all, proclaiming that she had the right to enter the United States of America, otherwise known as El Norte.

"Travel plans?" Gifford inquired.

"Going to New York at Christmas to visit my fiancé's parents." Emilia stowed the passport in her shoulder bag, trying not to look like an excited schoolgirl. "But that's not actually why I'm here."

"Katherine told me that you were looking for records pertaining to a property we'd considered for the consulate before finding this one."

"Yes, a place called Casa de Plata." Emilia told him. "Not too far away in Colonia Progreso."

"This is what we have." He passed her a folder stamped with a gold seal that matched the one on the iron gates in front of the consulate. Emilia flipped it open as they stood by the sandpapery sofa. It was full of architectural jargon referring to square footage, electrical conduits and plumbing requirements. Nothing about access to the property at all.

"You look disappointed," Gifford said.

"I don't know what I expected," Emilia confessed.

"May I buy you a cup of coffee?" Gifford asked. "Our canteen is small but makes an excellent latte. We have biscotti, too."

"Thank you." Emilia would take the coffee as payment for having to wait so long. "I accept."

In a neatly pressed blue check shirt and khaki pants cinched with a saddle-colored belt, Gifford was friendly and charming. Boyishly good-looking, too, with warm brown eyes behind the tortoiseshell glasses. Forty years old, Emilia guessed, but a forty that was still fit. Not as fit as a triathlete like Kurt, but still fit enough for a woman to take note.

The canteen turned out to be a cafeteria on the second floor. Gifford paid for coffee and pastries with American dollars, then indicated a table by the window overlooking the street.

"I'm sorry we kept you waiting so long, but I wanted to make sure we looked in every available place for Karen's notes," he said. "I finally just called her in Washington. She remembered the place because it needed so much work. Something about plumbing issues and repairs to the facade, although it did have a big courtyard that could be covered and turned into a visa pavilion. But that's basically it. The property was ruled out because it was too big of an investment, which in turn meant too big of a time investment. No one wanted to delay our timeline."

"I see."

"Karen found this location, and it really is perfect." Gifford made a vague gesture to the corridor behind the canteen. "Visa pavilion in the rear, big consular space, nice suite of offices upstairs. We even have a gym."

"May I ask what your job is here in the consulate?" Emilia thought he was a much more approachable representative of his government than the starchy Katherine Singletary.

"I'm head of the consular section." Gifford smiled ruefully as he stirred sugar into his coffee. "Forgive me, but a murder investigation is rather exciting to someone who spends all day processing visas. Who was the victim, if you don't mind me asking."

"Her name was Monica Montoya. She was our mayor's sister."

Gifford's eyes widened behind the classic glasses. "Oh, yes, now I know who you are talking about. The prayer rally was last night."

"Perhaps you met Monica. She was at the grand opening party for the consulate."

"Two hundred people attended the opening." Gifford sipped his coffee thoughtfully, then put down the cup. "Her name would be on the guest list. Everyone vetted by security, of course. I could check if you'd like."

"How does the consulate vet people? Meet them in person?" Emilia could not recall Kurt being investigated in any way before he attended the opening.

"It's more of a verification process," Gifford said. "Just confirming the person's personal information. Would you like me to check?"

"Any detail regarding Miss Montoya would be useful." Emilia took out one of the business cards with just her cell phone number and added her email address. "You can email or text me."

"Happy to help." Gifford tucked the card into his shirt pocket. "I'll check with security tomorrow. Is that soon enough?"

"Yes, thank you."

"Are you in charge of the investigation?"

"It's a high profile case," Emilia said. "Lieutenant Franco Silvio is in charge but it's all hands on deck."

"Of course." Gifford's boyish good looks were accentuated by frank curiosity. "Any leads?"

"I'm not at liberty to say."

"No, of course not." Gifford spread his hands. "Sorry, my

view of a murder investigation is from television. Glamorous detectives in New York City, swishing around in designer coats until the bad guy confesses."

"It's too hot in Acapulco for designer coats," Emilia heard herself say. 'But the rest of it is exactly what happens."

Gifford gave a burst of laughter and Emilia found herself grinning like an *idiota.*

"I wish you all the luck in the world," Gifford said, his humor fading into genuine warmth. "It's a tough job and I admire you immensely for doing it."

Emilia left the consulate quite buoyed by the brief exchange.

She was stuck behind a creeping street sweeper when it struck her that Gifford reminded her of Lieutenant Campos. Beyond the fact that they both wore glasses and were about the same age, they shared the quality of being an active listener, of being wholly present and attentive to the other person in a conversation.

The difference was that Vicente Campos was a *pendejo* whose solicitous attention was a mask for constant scheming while William Gifford was a genuinely nice man.

CHAPTER 18

Tracking down potential buyers of Casa de Plata had yielded exactly nothing besides caffeine and a cookie with William Gifford. Emilia was glad to get back to the squadroom without having wasted the entire day on a dead end.

In the afternoon, with the pink ring box perched on her desk, Emilia called the mask museum and spoke to Susana Durán Diaz. After a few awkward pleasantries, Emilia told Susana about finding the box in Monica's car and asked if she'd ever seen Monica wearing an engagement ring.

"No." Susana sounded stunned. "She would have told me. And her mother and Belinda."

It was the answer Emilia expected. She hovered her pen over the next name. "Did Monica ever mention a man named Vicente Campos?"

"No."

"Rafa Gamboa?" Emilia went on. "His full name is Rafael Gamboa Escobar."

"No."

"What about Manolo Bernal? Did Monica ever mention him? He's a movie producer."

"No," Susana repeated, with a catch in her voice. "Who are these people? Are they involved?"

"They're associated with the property where Monica was found," Emilia explained.

"Does Carlos Lima know any of them?" Susana asked.

"I'll be in touch if we have any more questions for you."

Emilia said. "But please call if you think of anything that could be significant. Anything at all."

Silvio leaned over her desk as she ended the call. "You get anything from the friend about the ring?"

"No, nothing." Emilia tapped on the list from Metro Properties. "She didn't know anyone on the realtor's list of people who'd been in Casa de Plata. I even asked her about Campos. And Gamboa."

Silvio's eyebrows shot up.

Emilia shook her head. "Nothing. She never heard of any of them. But what about Lima?"

"You think Lima's got a *federale* angle?" Silvio reached across her keyboard and stole a slice of roast chicken from the container on her desk. "Did you ask Campos about him?"

Emilia lowered her voice. "No, but I will."

"Give him a call. See if Lima's name shakes something loose. But make the Telmex records a priority."

Emilia sighed and held out a second container of pickled vegetables. "It's a huge spreadsheet. Monica Montoya must have spent her life on the phone."

Silvio swallowed a chunk of cauliflower. "Start with Lima's numbers, then people with access to Casa de Plata."

"What do we do if Campos's number comes up?"

"It won't." Silvio took another slice of chicken. "He's too clever for that."

Emilia actually didn't mind him wolfing her late lunch. "You look terrible. Like you haven't slept in a month."

Silvio growled something to the effect that if he had to speak to Carlota's chief of staff one more time he was going to shoot himself in the head. Before Emilia could reply he barreled back into his office.

Emilia finished what was left of her meal, then went over to the murder board, focusing on what was missing rather than what was there. *Whose phone number am I looking for, Monica?*

Monica's *cédula* photo didn't answer. Not even a breathy *Help me.*

Back at her desk, Emilia called the number for Financial Crimes. Señora Mendez put her through to Campos.

"Always nice to hear from you, Detective. What can I do for you?"

Emilia imagined Campos at his desk, eyes glittering behind those turquoise spectacles, hatching plans to ruin people's lives in the name of counter-drug operations.

"I won't take up too much of your time," she said. "Does the name Carlos Lima ring a bell?"

"Carlos Lima." Campos repeated the name without any hint of recognition. "Can you give me anything more than that?"

"An investment banker. Works for a private firm in El Centro called Viejo Dorado. Tall, good looking, snobby. Family supports Vallejo Loy for mayor."

"Are you asking me to stand in as big brother and bless your relationship or is this a person of official interest?"

His oblique reference to Rafa Gamboa made Emilia want to slam down the phone. "A person of interest," she said through gritted teeth. "Is he connected in any way to Casa de Plata?"

Campos didn't reply right away, his silence sending the message that she was talking about a cover situation on an open phone line. "Not everyone is, you know," he said finally. "The name means nothing."

"What about Rafa Gamboa? Are he and Lima linked in any way?"

"Not to my knowledge." Campos paused. "What's this about?"

"The Monica Montoya investigation. Anything you want to tell me?"

"Only that the Financial Crimes unit has no role to play in your investigation other than wishing you luck. Goodbye, Detective."

The connection abruptly cut out. Emilia was left with the receiver in her hand and steam coming out of her ears at the rebuke. Campos had gotten his message across that Emilia had breached classified protocol not only by mentioning a *federale* property on the phone but the true name of an undercover *federale* officer.

Emilia shook off the sting, made a fresh pot of coffee, and got down to business by opening the Telmex spreadsheet of Monica's cell phone communications. Even without any other applications open, the spreadsheet was so big that her system slowed to a crawl.

In six months, Monica had made or received over 94,000 calls or text messages. It was a staggering amount, more than 500 calls and messages a day. How had the woman dealt with that much communication?

The spreadsheet listed calls and text messages for each day, and whether they were incoming or outgoing. The duration of each call was given in a separate column. Text messages were measured by storage size.

That was it. No actual content or audio recordings. Nothing to help Emilia identify the owners of all the cell numbers slotted into the endless columns. Yet Monica's killer almost certainly was hiding in the clutter. Someone who had access to Casa de Plata.

Her screen kept stuttering, briefly causing the display to become pixelated or freeze up. Finally she was able to change the chronological order so that entries for Saturday, the day Monica died, were at the top of the screen. Seventeen outgoing calls, all made in the morning. Four incoming calls, along with twenty-nine text messages.

The last time Monica used her phone was for a brief text message sent to an unknown number. Emilia scribbled down the time of Monica's text and mentally compared it to the security footage from Café Romeo. She was almost positive that the timing meant that Monica had texted someone before she got out of the car and walked out of the camera view.

Combing through every entry for the day, Emilia found that the same number initiated a text to Monica six hours earlier. Immediately after that incoming message, Monica canceled the shopping date with Susana.

"Yes!" Emilia shouted at the screen.

"What's up, Cruz?" Macias turned from the murder board to stare at her.

"I found him!" she shouted.

Silvio came to his office door. "What the fuck?"

"Look at this!" Emilia jumped up from her chair, excitement coursing through her bloodstream. "I got a hit."

The next few minutes were thrilling. The entire squadroom crowded around her desk as Emilia explained the breakthrough.

All they had to do was find out whose cell phone was on the other end of the text messages.

Emilia, Macias and Sandor vibrated around the coffeemaker as Silvio called Telmex with an urgent request for a reverse lookup. It took an agonizing thirty minutes.

Silvio came out of his office shaking his head. "It's not a personal number. It's one of a bundle of cell numbers the *norteamericano* consulate bought when it opened."

"Well, shit." Emilia recalled Susan's insistence that even foreign consulates were constantly in touch with Monica as a conduit to Carlota. "Hold on. I know a guy."

Luckily, William Gifford was at his desk in the consulate. He quickly assured her that the phone was one of several that the consulate reserved for visitors from Washington DC. A group of public relations officers had recently passed through. Perhaps one of them had been in touch with Monica Montoya. He would check further into the phone's use, but was ninety-nine percent sure.

Emilia thanked him, hung up and shook her head. She could practically hear the excitement deflating, like air being let out of a balloon.

"*Rayos*," Silvio swore and stamped back to his office.

Everyone went back to work.

The break had apparently allowed the police intranet to top up on memory. The system stopped freezing. With the family out of the way, she started with Carlos Lima and typed his number into the search box.

Result: 17 matches.

Three were calls, the rest were incoming text messages from him. The most recent was three weeks ago, validating his claim that they were all but over. Yet Monica had not told her mother or aunt.

It was just one more question only the dead woman could answer. Emilia moved on.

She typed in the number for Hector Placido and waited for the spreadsheet gods.

Result: 1112 matches.

The result wasn't exactly a shock. The man was Monica's boss, after all. Placido's number was peppered throughout the six months covered by the spreadsheet.

Emilia was able to start eliminating numbers for those people connected to the case who had solid alibis. She already had accumulated more than 400 numbers of people associated with the case, including the Alvarez family, Susana Durán Diaz and Monica's other friends, everyone from the Metro properties list and Monica's co-workers at Carlota's re-election campaign.

It was a grueling process to type a number into the search bar, let the police intranet protest the use of digital resources, and finally see if the number matched one in the spreadsheet.

After three hours, Emilia had discovered that Monica called her mother every day during work hours, spoke to her aunt several times a week as well, and never called her argumentative uncle. Susana's number appeared frequently, verifying how close the two women had been.

That still left thousands of numbers unaccounted for; a dark ocean hiding the tiny drop that mattered.

CHAPTER 19

Whatever Kurt said to Roger Boardman worked. The two men came out of the manager's office at the Boulevard Hotel and Kurt introduced Emilia to the man. He apologized for the hotel security cameras being down. Unfortunately he had no footage from Saturday to show her. But he was happy to take them upstairs to the members only bar on the fifth floor.

Emilia assessed Boardman as they rode the elevator. Of course the *pendejo* was lying about his security cameras; her discerning eye didn't detect even the smallest lens trained on lobby activity. No doubt, Viejo Dorado's executives and other like-minded businessmen used the Boulevard for that very reason.

Boardman was in his fifties, at least, with a receding hairline the color of dirt and blotchy skin that suggested he spent much of his time away from the sun with a stiff drink in his hand. At least forty pounds overweight with a double chin, he made absolutely no pretense at the starched and monogrammed clothes Kurt wore during working hours as the face of the Palacio Real. But then again, Emilia guessed that Kurt and Boardman kept very different company.

"Here we are," Boardman said unnecessarily as they arrived on the fifth floor and the elevator doors parted.

Instead of a corridor lined with room doors, the elevator opened to a central lounge, complete with plush carpet that silenced their footsteps and curved black velvet sofas arranged in a ring. Five doors opened off it like spokes from a central hub, each labeled with a suite number.

The bar was tucked into a corner. The moody décor carried over from the lounge, with veined black marble floors, charcoal walls, cognac leather armchairs, and a large screen television silently showing a soccer match.

The bar hummed quietly with murmured conversations and canned instrumental music. Abstract paintings of nude women hung opposite a wall of windows overlooking downtown Acapulco. Men were seated at a scattering of tables, munching pretzels and watching the television screen.

Kurt caught her eye and Emilia immediately knew what he was silently transmitting. None of the patrons in the bar were there to drink or watch the match. They were all waiting for their turn in one of the suites. The hotel had no operable security cameras for good reason. Patrons here wanted privacy, even anonymity and were willing to pay for it.

Boardman said something to the bartender, a young man who was doing his best not to look surprised. He gave a nod toward the back of the bar.

Two seconds later, Emilia was in an armchair, staring at a mountain of a man.

Edgar Arroyo was encased in a tent-sized white guayabera shirt and baggy pink trousers and topped with a straw fedora with a gingham hatband. He smelled like sweat and a cloying floral perfume.

"Well, I'm honored," he wheezed after Boardman introduced Emilia and Kurt. "The Palacio Real! Are you looking to sponsor a modeling agency?"

A muscle jumped in Kurt's jaw. "No."

It was an open secret that prostitution was not allowed in

Acapulco's most luxurious hotel. Any Palacio Real employee that permitted, enabled or deliberately overlooked such activity was terminated immediately.

"I'd like to talk to you about one of your models," Emilia said. As helpful as Kurt had been, she wasn't sure how long she had before he exploded.

Arroyo's eyes, compressed into slits by the rolls of excess flesh, raked Emilia up and down. "You're a cop," he wheezed.

"Perhaps a fresh round of drinks," Boardman said brightly. "Edgar, your usual?"

Arroyo snapped his fingers at the bartender. The effort released a shockwave of body odor.

Lilies, Emilia thought. Wilted lilies. Funeral lilies.

The bartender brought four shots of tequila and a dish of lime wedges. Boardman mimed signing a check.

Arroyo carefully greased the rim of one narrow shot glass with a piece of lime. "Are we celebrating something, Roger? Or just lubricating a conversation with unexpected new friends?"

Emilia picked up shot glass, just to have something to hold. "I'm looking for one of your girls. She's a witness in a murder investigation."

"Well, well." Arroyo kept the lime circling the rim of the glass. "

"She calls herself Beso," Emilia continued. "You sent her to the Viejo Dorado suite Saturday night."

In response, Arroyo sucked down the shot of tequila in one gasping shudder, eyes closed as his pink tongue lapped at the lime flavor along the rim. Eventually he put down the empty glass, smacked his lips and opened his eyes. "Beso. My little

Beso."

"That's her real name?"

Arroyo eyed the last shot of tequila, which was ostensibly for Kurt. "As far as I know. Beso. Beso Sanchez."

"What does she look like?"

"A pretty little thing with kiss tattoos on her arm and her ass." Arroyo smacked his lips again.

"Tell me about Saturday. Tell me about the man who paid for her time."

Arroyo gave a belch. A wave of lime-scented bile floated across the table. "Nervous," he said. "In a hurry, too. Couldn't wait to get the girl inside the room. He's always like that. And he always picks the young ones."

"How young?"

"How would I know?"

Emilia felt her jaw clench and had to force herself to speak normally. "He's a regular?"

"Every six weeks or so. Viejo Dorado keeps a real regular rotation."

"Is this him?" Emilia presented her phone with Lima's picture filling the screen.

"Could be." Arroyo eyed Kurt who lifted his chin at the remaining shot of tequila, giving the fixer permission to take it. "What's he done?"

"Not your problem," Emilia said. "Where do I find Beso?"

Arroyo saturated the rim of the last shot with a fresh wedge of lime. "Don't know."

"You must know where she lives." Emilia was hard pressed not to show her impatience. It had been a long day and if she didn't lose it in the next five minutes, Kurt certainly would.

Arroyo gulped down the tequila and closed his eyes in bliss, then let out his breath in a long exhale that wafted nerve gas across the low table. "Don't know where she is. Disappeared."

Emilia's mouth went dry.

Arroyo put his second empty shot glass back on the tray. "I sent her up to the gentleman Saturday night. No one's seen the *maldita* girl since."

CHAPTER 20

Friday. Funeral day.

The cathedral was packed. Monica's casket, an ornate affair with brass and silver corners, was stationed in front of the altar. The Alvarez family, along with Carlos Lima, filled the first three pews on the right. Carlota, Hector Placido, Enrique Santibañez, and others from the re-election campaign were on the left side of the church.

It was warm inside, but Emilia could feel a glacial chill emanating from the front of the church. She was glad that Mercedes had come with her. No matter the circumstances, attending a funeral alone scraped a heart raw.

The funeral mass went on and on. Monica's killer was there, Emilia was sure. In the church or waiting outside to see the casket loaded into the hearse. Whoever it was, Emilia prayed they'd be rattled by the finality of their action, make a mistake, and reveal themselves. If not today, then later.

Her money was on Carlos Lima. He fit the profile of a man who'd commit femicide: entitled, angry, a previous history of violence, a user and abuser of women. The additional issue of his family's support for Carlota's main rival for mayor of Acapulco added to the compelling case against him, as did the lack of corroboration for his alibi.

But Emilia still couldn't connect him to Casa de Plata. Nor was the banker a pro shooter, as the bullet holes in Monica's hands suggested.

These disconnects were stones in her shoe that Emilia

couldn't shake out.

A lone guitar provided a spare and moving rendition of Adelita as the pallbearers hoisted the casket off its perch and slowly carried it down the aisle. Along with the entire congregation, Emilia and Mercedes stood as the little procession moved down the center aisle. Lima was one of the pallbearers, as was Monica's uncle and two men who had been on Susana's list of Monica's friends.

Mercedes gave her a nudge. "We can go now."

"Sorry, head in the clouds," she murmured to Mercedes as Carlota and her coterie followed the casket out the wide double doors at the rear of the cathedral.

Belinda and Victoria Alvarez came next, leading a sniffling contingent of relatives. Victoria's cheeks were wet with tears. Belinda was more stoic.

Grief had sharpened the sensual planes of both faces. Even in severe black dresses and adorned with simple gold crosses, the two sisters were more beautiful than before.

Emilia and Mercedes slipped out of their pew to join the mourners making their way out of the cathedral. They emerged into the midday sunshine to find an impromptu press conference taking place as reporters swarmed Carlota and her escorts.

Camera crews jockeyed for position, getting in the way of the pallbearers attempting to cross the plaza to the waiting hearse. Three different television broadcast trucks were parked in the way, generators grinding out electricity to power microphones and recording equipment.

With Mercedes in tow, Emilia threaded her way through the crowd to get close enough to hear what Carlota was saying as reporters thrust an assortment of cell phones, miniature recorders and microphones at the mayor.

"My family and my city are laying to rest another cherished life that ended too soon." Carlota raised both hands in the air as if channeling Evita Peron, emphasis added by the severe black dress and lace mantilla spilling over a sleek chignon hairstyle. "Too many of us have lost those we love to the violence caused by evil that seeks to overthrow civil authority across Mexico--."

"How dare you!" Tears still streaming down her face, Victoria Alvarez charged through the crowd, elbowing past Emilia without any sign of recognition. "How dare you make a mockery of my daughter's funeral?" she screamed at Carlota. "You've created a circus for the sake of attention and your damned election!"

Reporters gasped. Camera crews surged forward, the casket and hearse show abandoned for the promise of a juicy cat fight.

Carlota put a reassuring hand on the other woman's arm. "Victoria, together we--."

Victoria slapped Carlota, a stinging smack loud enough to be heard above the churn of the crowd and no doubt recorded by every microphone.

Carlota stumbled backward as her head snapped to the side, cheek bright red.

"Victoria, please." Belinda tried to intervene.

"How dare you turn my daughter's death into a media circus," Victoria sobbed. "That's all she is to you now. A convenient little drama to get yourself reelected."

"Stop, Victoria, please." Carlota was the picture of grief-stricken restraint, one hand on her reddened cheek, the other keeping her security detail from launching a counterattack. "We'll talk soon, I promise. But now is the time to mourn."

"She meant nothing to you," Victoria cried. "You use people, then throw them away."

"Please forgive my sister." Belinda managed to get between Victoria and Carlota. Carlos Lima was right beside her.

As if she had vented her very soul, Victoria swayed and almost collapsed. Carlos Lima caught her and helped the sisters move away from the circle of reporters in Carlota's orbit.

Hand still to her cheek, back straight, head high, Carlota was the picture of determination in the midst of chaos. The reporters jostled to get even closer as she looked directly into the cameras.

"Let the woman vent her grief on me if it helps. I mourn, I mourn, but I'm strong, strong in my grief, strong in keeping my sister's memory alive in my beating heart." The mayor raised her hands for calm as the reporters shouted questions. Santibañez and Hector Placido closed ranks behind her.

Emilia watched, torn between utter disgust at how easily Carlota turned the funeral into a re-election campaign event and grudging admiration for the way the woman bulldozed anything standing between herself and what she wanted.

As Carlota fielded questions, keeping to her themes of a city united in grief and identifying with families affected by cartel violence, Carlos Lima shepherded the Alvarez sisters to a waiting SUV with tinted windows. Victoria walked alone, but Belinda kept her hand in the crook of Lima's elbow.

CHAPTER 21

"What if Lima killed both Monica and Beso?" Emilia pressed.

Silvio blinked. "Who?"

"Beso, the missing hooker."

"Well, wouldn't Carlota love that." Silvio slurped coffee. His desk was piled with paperwork to the point that there was no place to rest the mug. "The Lima family would probably have to stop funding her political rival."

"Forget Carlota," Emilia said impatiently. "The girl never surfaced again after being sent to Lima Saturday night. What if he left the Boulevard, killed Monica and when he couldn't trust Beso to keep her mouth shut, he killed her, too?"

Silvio leaned back in his chair. "You really think Lima is our man?"

"I don't know." Emilia paced in front of his desk, too unsettled to stay seated. "We don't have any proof that he had access to Casa de Plata. Monica's phone records show that the last time they were in touch was weeks ago."

"Unless they connected face to face," Silvio pointed out. "Or he came to her office."

"Or the apartment in Las Brisas." Emilia stopped by the big poster advertising Silvio's last fight. Twenty-five years ago, he'd been a heavyweight champ. His boxing career had been on fire when his manager took a bribe. Silvio never fought again.

"Look, see what you can do about finding the girl, but be

back here by five. I want you to brief Carlota tonight."

"Me? She specifically asked you."

"You're her lioness."

"Am I supposed to referee between you and Santibañez?"

"Just be here," Silvio scowled.

Of course he'd never admit it, but Silvio needed her.

Emilia felt unexpectedly lighthearted as she jumped in the Suburban and headed for the Fuerte de San Diego, the ancient Spanish fort on the west side of the bay.

As expected, Chevo was near the entrance, startling tourists with today's choice of glittery tee shirt, baggy jeans, silver high-top sneakers and spill of beaded braids adorning a frame no more than four feet tall. Streetwise and connected, the dwarf was her best snitch.

Emilia snatched up one of his flyers. A doe-eyed girl with a sheer scarf around bare shoulders invited friends to meet Acapulco's finest models.

"I could arrest you for false advertising," Emilia said in disgust.

Chevo bristled with false indignation, braids swinging around his shoulders, the beads clacking together. "People just want to make an honest living. But no, we're subject to constant harassment by the police."

"Cry me an ocean." Emilia handed back the flyer along with a 200 peso note. "What do you know about a fixer named Edgar Arroyo? He works the Boulevard Hotel."

"Jabba the Hutt," Chevo slipped the money into a pocket as deftly as a magician. "Arroyo owns the Boulevard, if you know what I mean. Try to arrest him and you'll make some very, very important people very, very mad."

"People who reserve the suites on the fifth floor?" Emilia asked.

Chevo trotted toward two middle-aged gringos in shorts and straw hats. "Meet a Mexican model," he warbled. The startled men each took a flyer.

"Oye." Stooping, Emilia wrestled the stack out of Chevo's hands. "Pay attention."

"I am paying attention," he protested. "You want to go after Arroyo. What's in it for me?"

"One of his girls is missing. Her name is Beso."

"Who?" Chevo scanned the sidewalk for more tourists.

"Beso," Emilia said impatiently. "Beso Sanchez. Young, maybe 17 or so."

"Beso." Chevo tugged down his sunglasses again to peer over the rim at Emilia. "Got kiss tattoos on her arm?"

"Yes." Emilia gave herself a mental high five. "Where can I find her?"

"How should I know?" Chevo grabbed his flyers and pulled.

Emilia hung on for a moment, then let go.

Chevo stumbled back, clasping the precious papers to his chest, beaded braids swirling and clacking. "You're an evil woman," he protested.

"Tell me about Beso and I'm gone. Where does she live?"

"No idea." Chevo sniffed. "The only thing I know about the girl is that she's a big user. She's been around my patch a few times looking to score. Fentanyl patches, pills, whatever."

Emilia digested this fact, which wasn't so surprising. Apart from Rosalita, most hookers used something to blunt the trauma of their profession. "What about her supplier?"

Chevo threw his arms wide. "Take your pick, *corazón*."

From the Fuerte de San Diego, Emilia cast a wide net. She sought out other snitches who'd been helpful in the past. Taxi drivers from *sitios* near the fort and the Boulevard Hotel. Owners of corner grocery shops who sold pills and weed to those who knew how to ask.

It wasn't just the girl's pimp, Arroyo. No one had seen Beso Sanchez since the night she was sold for six hours to Carlos Lima.

Emilia went back to the office, created a Missing Persons report and put it in the binder with the other Las Perdidas.

Number 48.

CHAPTER 22

Sitting in the reception room outside Carlota's office, Emilia knew that she and Silvio weren't supposed to be hearing the argument.

Carlota's voice was loud and strident. Enrique Santibañez was more measured, but terse. The third voice had to belong to Hector Placido, whom they'd watched rush past the doorway and be swallowed up by the mayor's inner office. Placido's voice was gruff and forceful.

Apparently, the disagreement wasn't that the re-election campaign was running out of money for Placido's advertising plans, it was that money wasn't being spent fast enough.

"Stop mincing about, Hector," Carlota snapped. "We're budgeted for five hundred thousand pesos a week until the election. You're barely spending half that."

"Señora, there's only so many billboards and radio spots to be had," Placido countered.

"We are three percentage points ahead in the polls." Carlota sounded furious. "It. Is. Not. Enough."

"The new polls come out on Monday," Placido said. "Given the death of your sister, you'll get a huge sympathy bump. The press conference, the prayer rally and now the funeral will all provide a boost. Vallejo Loy won't be able to make it up between now and then. There's not enough time."

There was a crash of breaking glass. "I'm not depending on my sister's murder to win an election!"

"What about our list of influencers?" Santibañez said in a

mollifying tone, although Emilia wasn't sure which combatant he was trying to placate. "Have we really used it to best effect? What about more social media activity? A concert?"

Somewhat belatedly, someone slammed the office door shut.

"Did I hear right?" Emilia sputtered into the quiet. "Five hundred thousand a week?"

It was an absurd amount of money to spend on an election when over half the city lived below the poverty line.

Silvio rolled his shoulders, obviously uncomfortable on the antique settee. "If she's spending that much as the incumbent, think how much Vallejo Loy is throwing at his campaign."

"I can't, it's insane."

"Nice to be fucking rich," Silvio grumbled.

"You're rich," Emilia reminded him. "You just can't tell anyone."

Thirty minutes later, Carlota's office door opened. Santibañez took a step into the reception room and gestured to them. "Just the highlights," he said tersely. "It's been a difficult day."

No one invited them to sit. Carlota stayed seated behind her desk, sulkily toying with a gold pen. Emilia explained that they were mining Monica's phone records for information and examining potential points of access to Casa de Plata.

Two minutes later they were back in Silvio's car.

"That went well," Emilia said, loading the words with sarcasm.

"You want to get a beer?" Silvio asked.

"Now?" Emilia would rather just go back to the police

station, get the Suburban and go home.

"There's something we need to talk about."

Did he have news about her petition to marry? "Okay."

They drove in silence for a few more minutes. Silvio rapped the palm of his hand against the steering wheel, unusually fidgety. The feeling was contagious. Emilia thought of a dozen bad things besides the petition that he might tell her.

"Is this bad news?" she asked. "If it is, just tell me now."

"Good news, bad news. Depends on how you look at it."

"Are you breaking up with Mercedes?" Emilia demanded.

Silvio glanced at her and scowled. "No. Why would you say that?"

"Because it's the sort of *pendejo* thing you'd do right in the middle of a big investigation."

"*Rayos,* Cruz," he swore. "I've been offered a job. Chief of Special Assignments."

"Your old unit?"

"The job comes with a promotion to captain."

Special Assignments was a paramilitary unit. Members were recruited for size, strength and lack of interest in rules. Informally known as the Ball Busters, Special Assignments had a well-deserved reputation for mayhem. Most who served in the unit never moved out of it; Silvio's advancement through the detective ranks was a true rarity. To many in Special Assignments, he was a hero.

The news made Emilia feel oddly shipwrecked. Despite the ups and downs, she and Silvio had built a strong partnership. They'd put more criminals behind bars than any other detective team in Acapulco. Even now, with Silvio as her boss in charge of the entire squad of detectives, they still worked well together.

"Did you tell Mercedes?" she asked. "You'd really be on the front line in that job. What does she think?"

"I'm telling you first."

"Well, thanks. I guess." Their partnership counted for something after all.

"The job comes with strings attached." Silvio darted a look at her.

Special Assignments was a rough unit. "What kind of strings?"

"Salazar says you have to go before he'll give me the job."

Emilia blinked. "Go? To Special Assignments? Me?"

Silvio scowled. "No, go as in resign. Salazar has been trying to get rid of you forever. That's why he denied your request to get married. He wants you to quit."

"Wait." Emilia pressed fingers to her temples. "What about our deal?"

"That's why I wanted to get a beer."

"Let it ride, you said, until the investigation is over." Emilia's blood pressure rose so fast her vision blurred. "You said you'd help me get Salazar to change his mind."

"I said you'll be in a much better position to negotiate," Silvio parried. "That's all."

"You sold me out, you Judas. How could you do that?"

Silvio didn't look at her, but headed west on Avenida Independencia toward the intersection with Pie de la Cuesta which would take them north in the direction of the police station.

His silence was gasoline to her fire.

"You never had any intention of helping me stay in the

department," Emilia shouted, her voice amplified by the confines of the car's interior. "I fucking saved your life in the Maxitunel! Covered up for you when you got in trouble with that witness. Fuck all that, I introduced you to Mercedes!"

"Listen, Cruz--."

Emilia carried on, her tone scathing. "None of that counts for anything, does it? You never wanted to work with a woman. I should have believed you."

"I deserve this promotion," Silvio said tersely.

"You fucker!" Her fury ran out of words. Despite the restraint of the seat belt, Emilia launched a right cross over the console.

Her fist connected hard with Silvio's jaw. His whole torso twisted away and his head banged against the driver's side window and the car veered into the opposite lane. Emilia hit him again, bouncing that *maldita* crew cut off the glass.

Headlights of oncoming traffic on the busy boulevard bloomed in the windshield then shot away as Silvio muscled the car back into its own lane. Overcorrected so that the tires bit into the curb, rubber grinding against concrete and the sedan juddering with the impact.

Emilia's vision was a red film of anger as she hit Silvio again. He flailed out with his right arm, connecting with Emilia's shoulder as the car rocked and horns blared.

"You traitor," Emilia cried. She punched his arm and chest as hard as she could, the car veering wildly and keeping her from doing any real damage. "You fucking two-faced *pendejo*."

"Shut up!" Silvio found the collar of her jacket with his right hand and slammed her against the passenger side door.

Her forehead thudded against the window and Emilia saw stars.

She blindly kicked out, first catching him in the knee, then narrowly missing the steering wheel.

Silvio roared in pain. The car lurched into the other lane again. The shoulder harness bit into Emilia's torso as brilliant light lit up the car's interior like Christmas and the scream of braking tires filled the air.

Terror rose in Emilia's throat. The head-on collision was nearly upon them when the sedan slewed around a corner and came to a sudden stop that threw both of them at the windshield.

The safety harnesses held. The engine died.

"Are you insane?" Silvio roared.

"You made a deal with Salazar." Emilia's voice shook with rage. "After all we've been through together, you made a deal. Help him force me out of the police department and you get an overdue promotion to captain."

Silvio blew out his breath and looked up at the roof of the car. "Why can't you just get married?"

It took a tense moment of fumbling with agitated fingers before Emilia managed to unclip her seat belt, snatch up her shoulder bag and find some loose pesos in the bottom.

She wrenched open the car door. "Here you go, Judas. Thirty pieces of silver."

The car's overhead light went on, illuminating Silvio's expressionless face as the coins hit him.

CHAPTER 23

Seated in the back of a *sitio* taxi, Emilia took inventory. Her ponytail had escaped its elastic, her linen jacket was torn, a bruise was welling on her right shoulder and it hurt to breathe.

Emilia made the taxi drop her off at a *taqueria* not far from the police station. Maybe if she ate something, she'd stop shaking.

Only then would she go back to the police station and retrieve the Suburban. She could sneak in through the vehicle entrance and drive home. Like a frightened child running away.

At the *taqueria*, she ordered a beer and shrimp tacos. Her throat was so tight with tension that it was hard to get the first mouthfuls down. A sip of beer helped, but also made her feel like she might burst into tears at any moment.

Only a few tables were occupied at this hour of the evening. During the day, the *taqueria* was a popular place, known for cheap food and cold beer. Her first partner, the late Rico Portillo, had been a regular.

Madre de Dios, but she was missing Rico's honesty and sense of humor tonight. Rico never would have sold her out for a promotion. His highest ambition had been to find a third wife who was frugal enough so that he could keep paying alimony to the first two.

Emilia rolled the bottle of Pacifico beer against her cheek, condensation cooling her temper. In the wake of Rico's death, she and Silvio had gone from enemies to partners to something more. She'd saved his life and he'd saved hers. Introduced him to Mercedes. Watched him become genuine friends with Kurt. Was actually excited by the Casa de Plata real estate scheme.

Now she knew that none of that created any sense of loyalty. How had she been so stupid, so gullible?

As if she'd summoned the big lummox, Silvio walked into the *taqueria*.

The place was small, just eight tables. Although Emilia was seated farthest from the door, he still spotted her right away.

Emilia didn't react but kept chewing the bite of spiced shrimp and corn tortilla that now tasted like nothing at all.

He bought a beer at the counter and sat down at her table. Emilia choked down another mouthful. Silvio raised his beer bottle and drank down half.

Neither met the other's eye.

Laughter from a group of women at the next table washed over them. A few gave Silvio sideways glances, apparently admirers of traitors with big muscles. *Ranchera* music poured out of a tinny speaker mounted near the ceiling over the counter. An electric cord trailed down to a socket at eye level, the same socket that served a neon sign advertising Pacifico beer. Whoever had painted the melon-colored walls had sent the roller over both cords. The paint was flaking off the rubber, turning the cords into very skinny snakes shedding orange skins as they clung to the stucco.

The front of the *taqueria* was fully open to the street. A garage door would roll down when the place closed in the early hours of the morning. A ceiling fan turned lazily, producing just enough breeze to lift the edges of the vintage travel posters decorating the side walls and dilute the smells of frying fish and stale beer.

Silvio finished his beer. "Want another?" he asked and tipped the neck of his empty toward Emilia's bottle.

"No."

He got another at the counter and sat down at her table again. Took another healthy swallow.

Emilia picked a sliver of pickled radish off her plate. "Are you going to press charges?" she asked.

"No." Silvio put down his bottle and lifted his chin at her torn jacket. "You?"

"Probably not."

He ran his thumb through the condensation on the beer bottle. "You're no slouch in the figure-it-out department, I'll give you that."

Emilia saw a red welt along his hairline from hitting the window and a bruise rising on his cheekbone from her fist. "How did you know I was here?"

"Took a guess." He chugged a mouthful of beer. "Your car's still in the lot and you weren't in the office. This was the third place I tried."

"Why bother? You've said all that needs to be said."

"Look, Cruz. I didn't start this train moving. Salazar has been riding me for months to get you gone. I'm out of options."

"It was always an option to tell me."

"Why? Would that have done you any good? Salazar knows there's no grounds to get rid of you based on performance. You've got a high profile after breaking the Amistad 43 kidnapping case. What's more, Carlota likes you because you got Las Palomas off the ground and kept her from looking like a fool for hiring that Claudia woman to run it."

"So he's been biding his time?"

Silvio nodded. "The whole marriage permission thing was his chance to boot you out without pissing off Carlota."

"Offering you a promotion and a new job to make sure I go."

"Think about it, Cruz. Do you really want to keep working when you're married? It's not like you're going to need the money."

She answered Silvio's question with one of her own. "What about all those missing women in my binder? Women like that poor hooker Beso. Who's going to keep looking for them?"

"You've already done what you could."

"What about my pension? If I leave now, I get nothing."

"Maybe Salazar will negotiate."

"Sure he will. In hell." Emilia shoved her plate with the remaining tacos across the table. "Here."

"You don't want them?"

"If I eat any more I'm going to throw up. That's how crazy you make me."

She watched him fold the small taco and stuff half in his mouth, thinking *so this is how it will be from now on.* Ignore the chasm of distrust now open between them. Ignore the suspicion hanging over every conversation, every decision. Their working relationship was over.

Silvio wolfed the last bite and stood up. "I'm going back to the office. Are you coming?"

They walked to the police station in silence, the sounds of the city at night substituting for camaraderie. It wasn't even 9:00 pm yet traffic was light, the rumble of engines hardly making a dent in the laughter pealing out of neighborhood bars and clubs. The night was friendly, punctuated by the calls of an ice cream vendor, the chatter of families out for a late stroll, a giggling gaggle of teenagers. Overhead, the sky was clear and studded with stars. Even the air smelled happy, scented with vanilla cones and breezes stirred by the fronds of royal palms stirring overhead like toy helicopters.

Emilia wanted to cry.

CHAPTER 24

As soon as Emilia and Silvio walked into the squadroom, Macias held out a sheet of paper. "Hotline tip," he crowed. "A tapas restaurant made a delivery to Casa de Plata Saturday night."

"I'll go." Emilia snatched the paper out of his hand. If she went back to the Palacio Real now she'd dissolve into a puddle of tears and blab everything to Kurt.

Sandor swiveled his desk chair around. "What happened to you two?"

"Had to brake hard," Silvio said shortly. "Got tossed around in the car." He went into his office and slammed the door.

Emilia stalked out, not even bothering to check her email.

The restaurant in question was Madrid, the new and very upscale tapas restaurant that Kurt had wanted to try last Sunday. It seemed like a lifetime ago that Emilia was excited to be back from Chilpancingo, wearing a sexy outfit and looking forward to a fun day with Kurt and friends.

Friends. Hard to think she'd ever placed a certain former partner in that category.

An attractive man in his mid-forties with hair tied back in a ponytail, Juan Pedro Casillas was the owner of Madrid. His international culinary awards were splashed across the back wall of the restaurant, making an artistic display against stark white plaster and dark wood furnishings. The place was packed, but not especially noisy. Spicy, peppery, garlicky goodness wafted through the air, accompanied by the heady perfume of balsamic vinegar.

He'd been the one to call the hotline, Casillas explained, after looking through the order logbook for something else. Would she like a seat and some mineral water while he went to get it?

Emilia had exchanged her torn linen jacket for a sweatshirt from the gym bag she kept in the Suburban but even so, she probably looked as bad as she felt. Casillas had noticed, too. She accepted his offer and sat in a booth at the back of the restaurant near the swinging door that led to the kitchen.

Cheerful conversation and laughter came from the other side. Casillas obviously ran a happy kitchen. She wondered if his employees had to ask permission to get married.

A waiter brought her a glass, poured half a bottle of Aqua de Piedra into it and set down a dish of lime wedges before disappearing into the kitchen. The mineral water fizzed softly in the glass in front of her. Bubbles rose to the surface and popped with soft snicks of release. The pale green bottle with its antiqued label matched the historic-meets-modern ambiance of the restaurant.

"Here we are." Casillas came back to the booth with an ordinary binder and slid into the booth across from Emilia. A young man wearing a tee with the Madrid logo on the pocket came with him but remained standing. "This is my nephew, Luis, who delivered all our orders last weekend."

"Señora." Luis bobbed his head respectfully at Emilia.

Casillas opened the binder and swiveled it so that Emilia could see it was full of neatly typed spreadsheets. For each order, the restaurant knew when and how the order was taken, the food, if it was a pickup or an order to be delivered, payment, and when the order was completed.

"*Norteamericano* software," Casillas said by way of explanation.

Emilia ran a finger down the column headed DELIVERY, marveling at the chef's record-keeping.

Her finger stopped on an order with the name *Montoya* for the Signature Sampler Box. Payment of four thousand pesos cash was made at the time the order was placed, which was the Wednesday before Monica was killed. The delivery address matched that of Casa de Plata. The order was closed out at 7:30 pm on Saturday via the app on the driver's phone.

"This is exactly what we've been looking for," she said. "How many people does the Signature Sampler Box feed?"

Casillas considered. "Typically it would be for a group of six to eight."

Emilia stared at the spreadsheet entry, her brain digesting this new information. Had that many people been at Casa de Plata that night? If so, who else was there besides the killer and victim? This was potentially a fresh angle to the case.

"Do you recall this delivery?" she asked the nephew. "A house with very tall gray walls."

"*Si*, señora." Luis was clearly very impressed by her police badge on its lanyard. A first for everything. "It was a big order. I rode to the house and rang the bell."

"Rode?"

"We have a fleet of motorcycles for deliveries," Casillas supplied.

"Of course." Emilia recalled seeing five scooters, painted black with insulated boxes mounted over the rear wheel, decorated with the restaurant logo and parked in front of the restaurant like free advertising. This was the loud engine that several neighbors recalled hearing.

"I stopped the bike and pressed the intercom button next to the big gate," Luis said, nodding. "It took a long time before anything happened. I wondered if maybe the person who paid for the order forgot. Maybe they went away for the weekend, you know?"

"The light over the gate wasn't on?" Emilia distinctly recalled seeing a black carriage light set into the wall over the gate.

"No, it was all dark," Luis said. "I was almost ready to go when I heard someone on the other side of the gate."

"Go on."

"That's all," Luis said. "She opened the gate and took the box."

"She?" Emilia wanted to make sure. "A woman?"

"Yes."

"Young or old?"

Luis shrugged. "Like you. With her hair in a ponytail. Nice clothes, too."

Emilia called up a picture of Monica on her phone. "Was this her?"

"It was dark," Luis said doubtfully. "She didn't turn the light on so it's hard to be sure." He brightened. "But she gave me a nice *propina*."

They talked for a few more minutes, Emilia stunned to think that Monica Montoya herself had placed the order and was at Casa de Plata to accept the delivery of enough food for a party of eight. This meant that Monica had free access to the locked property, despite no evidence that she did.

Conversation over, Emilia sat in the Suburban and flipped through her notebook to the timeline she always made during a case. Comparing times, it appeared that Monica Montoya had been at Casa de Plata to accept the delivery from Madrid at 7:30 pm, then got to Cafe Romeo shortly afterward, where she met someone and went back to Casa de Plata in the other person's car. Given that time of death was between 9:00 pm and midnight, she didn't have much time to enjoy the food she'd ordered and paid for.

Who did she meet at Café Romeo? A party guest?

Was the party some sort of initiation ritual or creepy game gone wrong? What about Carlos Lima?

But above all, who gave Monica access to Casa de Plata multiple times? Who else besides Metro Properties and Financial Crimes had access?

Who was lying?

CHAPTER 25

Kurt expertly slid a mushroom omelet onto a plate and set it in front of Emilia. "This will make you feel better."

They were in the kitchen of the penthouse, a modern space that was all gleaming white enamel and polished stainless steel. Emilia was seated at the big island while Kurt made breakfast. Not only had she embellished Silvio's lie about getting banged up in the car with a fictional account of narrowly avoiding a fender bender, but she didn't say anything about the blowup with the big lieutenant.

Always in training for the next triathlon, Kurt had already worked out in the hotel's largest pool, showered and was dressed for work in khakis, loafers and a monogrammed white shirt.

Still in her sleep attire of tee shirt, topped by Kurt's old flannel shirt that she used as a robe, Emilia was off to a slow start. Her left shoulder ached only a little more than the rest of her, much of it from tension.

"Think you can still make it to the Regatta Night party tonight?" Kurt asked, coming to sit across from her with his own plate.

Emilia nodded. "Wouldn't miss it for the world."

"Eight o'clock," he reminded her. "Meet me at the marina."

"I'll be there."

Kurt took a sip of coffee. "What's your day looking like?"

He was really asking why she wasn't rushing off like

usual. Knowing how badly Salazar wanted her out had robbed her of any inclination to do anything. In fact, the last thing she wanted to do was listen to Silvio hand out assignments like nothing had changed.

If it wasn't for Monica Montoya whispering in her ear, Emilia would have gone back to bed and stayed there until it was time to put on her new dress and go to the Regatta Night event.

The click of flatware on china made her flinch. "What?"

Kurt had tapped on her plate with his fork. "You almost fell asleep."

"Just thinking about the Montoya case," Emilia fudged.

"Maybe the phone records will break the case wide open."

"What if I left the police department?" Emilia asked abruptly.

Kurt raised his perfect blonde eyebrows. "You mean take another job? Has someone offered you a position?"

"No, I mean, what if I didn't work when we get married?"

"It doesn't matter to me if you work or not, but I think you'd be bored out of your mind with nothing to do all day."

"I could take up painting. Or read books."

"Where is this coming from, Em?" Kurt put down his fork and reached across the table to take her hand. "You've faced tougher cases than the Montoya murder. You'll figure it out."

"You always know the right thing to say." And he always did, except now when he didn't know what he didn't know.

After reminding her again to meet him that evening at the marina, Kurt left for the hotel's management office suite on the first floor. Emilia finished her omelet, made another pot of coffee, and carried a cup outside to the balcony.

The sky was already a welcoming azure. The breeze carried a salty tang.

The Pacific stretched like a rippling sheet of glass to the horizon, the endless vista broken only by the hazy outline of the hotel's swimming dock anchored far off shore. On the beach below, the hotel staff raked sand, opened umbrellas and straightened lounge chairs. The Pasodoble Bar was already open, serving a continental breakfast buffet to guests who eschewed room service or the cantina on the second floor by the waterfall pool.

From her perch as high as an eagle's nest, Emilia couldn't see the marina, which was hidden by a bend in the shoreline. No doubt the staff there was readying for the usual day of ferrying guests on sightseeing cruises, fishing excursions and trips to the hotel's private island off Punta Diamante. The marina wouldn't be transformed for Regatta Night until later. Emilia had overheard enough of Kurt's conversations with his team of event managers to know how they operated with everything in readiness so that it only took a few hours to affect the most magical transformations.

Everything around her bore Kurt's stamp. His high standards. Quiet confidence. Persevering until he got it right. None of it came easy, she knew that now.

When they first met, she assumed that because he was a *gringo* and lived in an elegant hotel, that everything he had flowed to him effortlessly and that he was unquestionably entitled to all of it.

Only later did she learn how hard he worked. He'd been a warrior in his country's military and carried lessons in teamwork and training into jobs in the hotel industry. Kurt knew how to get things done.

He had taught Emilia many lessons, most rarely applied. The most useful was to consider all the angles, all the variables when confronted with a challenge. Not every problem needed the same solution. "When you're a hammer, every problem looks like a nail," he told her once.

Silvio and Salazar were both hammers.

Emilia decided she wasn't going to be anyone's nail.

At least not today.

The bruising on her face was minimal. Some carefully applied makeup took care of it. More time than usual was spent deciding what to wear. She finally chose an outfit from the big Zara in Mexico City, purchased during the Amistad 43 task force assignment. Skinny navy trousers and silk tank topped with a collarless mustard-colored jacket. Navy pumps with kitten heels. Discreet gold earrings, neutral lip gloss, and the ruby engagement ring.

Clothing was armor but a printout was ammunition. Her record spoke for itself. Emilia had a spreadsheet of statistics and closed cases to prove her point. She also had a citation from the Amistad 43 task force, letters from two high-ranking task force officials praising her performance, plus a letter of commendation from Lieutenant Campos on Financial Crimes stationery sent to her after shuttering the initial operation against druglord Diego Barrielos Luna.

She knew that Obregon was working out of his office in Chilpancingo until after the elections in Acapulco. Obviously, like everyone else who could, Obregon wanted to avoid the rallies, random street closures and unpredictable violence as the final countdown to the elections got underway. Chilpancingo was only about 65 miles away, as Emilia well knew, but the round trip to the state capital of Guerrero would eat up most of the day.

She swung onto the broad highway spur just beyond Puerto Marques, followed it around the east side of Acapulco then stayed to the right as it veered north toward Chilpancingo. Traffic moved fast on the highway which cut across the entire state and continued into Morelos and beyond.

The undulating landscape sped by in shades of gray and green, punctuated by villages and shacks and the occasional small herd of cows. This wasn't the coastal life she loved, but the poverty of Guerrero's interior, where the presence of law enforcement was thin, bordering on nonexistent. Despite the smooth road, highways were dangerous places lately. Carjackers and robbers set up impromptu roadblocks to stop vehicles. Those who tried to blow through the barrier were stopped with a hail of gunfire.

The further she traveled from the coast, the more vulnerable Emilia felt. Even during the weeks she worked in Chilpancingo and stayed in an apartment provided by the police department there, the uneasy feeling never dissipated. Chilpancingo had a great deal of Spanish colonial character, parks and pedestrian zones, but anger simmered below the surface and gang rivalries stoked political clashes. Violence during the elections had been kept to a low roar because of the influx of cops from across the state but no one knew what would happen now that they were all gone. The new mayor would be sworn in soon.

She took comfort in the bright daylight and the speed of the big Suburban.

Along the way, she mentally rehearsed the reasons why Obregon should challenge Chief Salazar's ruling about her marriage. Reason number one was that it was blatantly sexist. The union had an obligation to have all police officers treated fairly. This wasn't just about her; it was about professional standards applied equally throughout a department.

Second, how would police departments attract new recruits if standards were applied whimsically?

Third, she'd remind Obregon that he himself had declared that women were less corrupt than men. All well and good, but if they were victims of discriminatory practices, women would leave. Obregon would be stuck with more corruption-prone male police officers.

An awkward argument, and hardly based on ironclad facts, but Obregon had made that claim, not her. Emilia would just remind him of his own words.

She found the union offices, tucked into a yellow stucco building with a traditional terra cotta roof, presented her badge and had her name ticked off on an access list before being allowed to drive into a small courtyard.

Obregon's office on the top floor reflected the union chief's ego. The outer chamber was decorated with award plaques and photographs of Obregon accepting accolades or speaking at a podium. The flags of Mexico, the state of Guerrero and a union banner were in evidence, folded neatly around flagpoles as if waiting to be carried at the next parade.

The secretary was a clone of Señora Mendez from Financial Crimes, albeit without the mantle of kindness. She directed Emilia to a chair to wait. No magazines. Emilia had the choice of scrolling through her phone or studying

Obregon's self-congratulatory wall.

If she'd never met Kurt, never known a man with such a combination of decency, confidence, and physical attraction, she might have been tempted to spend a night with Obregon. Certainly the invitation had always been on the table for her to accept.

But even if real sparks had flown with the union chief, Obregon was always assessing her. Like a hawk, circling from above, waiting for her to show weakness so he could dig his talons into a tasty treat.

The way he did with Claudia Sanchez Rangel, a woman from the mayor's staff tapped by Carlota to run the Las Palomas all-female unit. Obregon seduced Claudia, who was wholly unprepared to run anything more challenging than an ice cream cart. Unprepared as well to handle a man like Victor Obregon who took what he wanted and ignored the consequences, Claudia got pregnant. The *idiota* was removed from her position shortly thereafter, which was a boon to Rosalita and the other women in the unit.

"El señor can see you now," the secretary said, breaking into Emilia's thoughts as she opened the inner office door.

"Detective Cruz." Obregon came around the side of his desk. As always, he was dressed in black, the better to accentuate his dark *indio* features; narrow blade of a nose and hair worn slicked straight back. "Welcome to Chilpancingo."

"Thank you."

He indicated a seating area. Two upholstered armchairs faced a gray linen sofa across a marble coffee table. As Obregon asked the secretary to bring coffee, Emilia perched on one of the armchairs and took the spreadsheets and letters out of her shoulder bag.

Obregon settled himself on the sofa and asked Emilia if she'd had a good drive.

"Fine," Emilia said, ready to launch into her spiel.

The secretary returned with a tray laden with a silver coffee pot, fine china cups and a plate of chocolate wafer cookies. She poured them each a cup and left, closing the door behind her.

"So, Detective, tell me why you're here." Obregon leaned back, cup and saucer in hand, the usual hawkish stare veiled with amusement. Not so much handsome as exotic looking.

Ignoring her own cup and saucer on the table, Emilia handed him the email denying her request to marry. "I'm making a formal request for the union to appeal this decision."

Obregon skimmed the message, a corner of his mouth twisted in amusement. "What grounds for appeal do you have?"

"On the grounds that it's discrimination against me as a female detective. No male detective ever had to apply to get married."

"Are you sure?"

"I'm quite sure I'm the only female detective."

"No, I mean, are you sure there's no other reason your application was denied?"

"I'm sure it was the only reason I had to apply in the first place. No male detective was ever asked to."

"I'm aware of this, Detective." Obregon let the printout slip to a corner of the coffee table. "You're engaged to Kurt Rucker, correct?"

"Yes." A small warning signal beeped in Emilia's head.

"He's a wealthy and prominent foreigner."

"Is that a problem?"

Obregon sipped coffee, his dark eyes assessing her reaction even as they radiated humor. "His demographic is one that is targeted by kidnap and extortion gangs. The risk of someone kidnapping him in order to gain influence over you would be unacceptably high."

It wasn't the reaction Emilia had expected at all. "That's a theoretical scenario."

"You'll be far too vulnerable to remain a police officer if you marry Señor Rucker."

Emilia clenched her fists in her lap. "Tell me where in the union regulations I can find the chart of acceptable incomes for marriage partners."

"Impertinence will not help you, Detective." Obregon leaned forward to set his coffee cup on top of her printout, effectively nailing it to the table. "Chief Salazar and I have discussed this. Señor Rucker presents a security threat and for that reason the union has no standing to appeal the decision."

"What if a male officer wants to marry someone with more than two pesos to her name?" Emilia told herself to stay calm, to remember all the points she'd carefully rehearsed but she was stuck on the basic unfairness of it all. "Just how much money constitutes a security risk?"

"Detective--."

"This is important information every police officer should know."

"This is a meaningless conversation." Obregon was no longer amused. "I'm a busy man."

"Too busy to appeal a clearly unfair ruling?"

"The union doesn't see it that way, Detective."

Silvio had warned her that Obregon would make her an offer. Negotiate her into his bed in return for the union's attention to her predicament. How wrong he was.

Obregon had no interest in her. He was indifferent. Giving her a cup of coffee was a show of good manners for the secretary, not an invitation to Emilia for a real conversation.

All the solve rates and spreadsheets and letters of commendation in the world wouldn't change his mind. There would be no negotiation.

Emilia had missed her opportunity.

If she had slept with Obregon, surrendered herself the way poor *estupida* Claudia did, then perhaps he'd be moved to help her. But she never did. As a result, Obregon owed her nothing and couldn't even summon the interest to watch her squirm.

Not that she would.

Emilia pushed Obregon's cup to the side, retrieved her printout and stood up. He remained seated, one arm resting on the back of the sofa, legs crossed at the knee, one polished black shoe hovering in the air.

"The union will watch your future endeavors with interest," Obregon drawled.

CHAPTER 26

The drive back to Acapulco was a blur. Emilia didn't bother stopping at the squadroom to talk to Judas, but went directly to the Palacio Real to get ready for the Regatta Night party.

At the appointed hour, Emilia was dressed in a figure-hugging strapless black dress, stiletto-heeled black sandals, a slash of red lipstick and her engagement ring. Her hair was pinned into a messy, sexy updo. She packed a silver clutch with her gun, badge, hotel keycard, and cash for tips.

The regatta party was being held in the hotel's private marina, sited on the water a short walk along a landscaped path from the main hotel. Emilia passed no less than three checkpoints staffed by helpful but serious members of the hotel's security team before the marina came into view, a long barrel-vaulted building sheltering close to the pier with berths for the hotel's fleet of motorboats. Tonight, it was ablaze with thousands of fairy lights

Music from a steel drum band filled the air, and more fairy lights formed a canopy stretching between the roofline to top of the mast of the enormous America's Cup yacht anchored beyond the pier. The yacht was lit with spotlights, too, that glinted off the surface of the water, creating a mirrored surface that rippled like molten glass.

The combined effect of brilliant building, bobbing boats, enormous yacht and play of light was breathtaking. Judging from the conversations of the party-goers milling on the pier, drinks in hand, Emilia wasn't the only one who was impressed.

The security situation was impressive, too. Probably half of the staff circulating in their signature blue and white floral shirts were armed guards. Emilia saw the hotel's chief of security, Ronaldo Olivas, passing through the crowd as well. All of these precautions, like the checkpoints and abundance of highly trained staff, were how Kurt managed to pull off these grand spectacles despite Acapulco's skyrocketing crime rate.

The three-sided interior of the vaulted marina building had been transformed into an upscale market, with stations for food, drinks, information about the upcoming regatta, the technology behind the America's Cup racing yachts, and displays showcasing sponsors running the gamut from Swiss watchmakers to local businesses. The place was thronged with people, voices competing with the music as well as gasps and laughter of those trying out virtual reality headsets that apparently were convincing women dripping with jewels to behave like drunken sailors on a tilting deck.

Emilia stayed on the edge of the action, positioned to feel the breeze rippling across the water and watch the gently bobbing yacht. A passing waiter offered a glass of champagne. It was ice cold and delicious.

"There you are." Kurt came up beside her, an earpiece in his ear as if he was a member of the security detail, which in a way he was. He was wearing the tan suit that was her favorite, the wool so fine that it draped over his shoulders like silk.

"I told you I'd be here."

Kurt kissed her then held her at arm's length. "If anyone has a heart attack tonight it's because you look that stunning."

"You look pretty good yourself." Emilia leaned in and

licked his bare ear. Another glass of champagne and she would start unbuttoning his shirt.

"Em." Kurt gave a laugh and slipped his arm through hers, steering them toward an enormous buffet table. "You should eat before Carlota gets here and the speeches start."

"What about you?"

One hand pressed to his earpiece, Kurt turned his head away from her. "On my way," he murmured, then gave her a rueful look and a swift kiss. "I've got to run. Will you be all right by yourself?"

"Of course." Emilia nearly burst with pride as she watched him stride off.

Another waiter came by with a tray of champagne flutes. Emilia gave him her empty and took another chilly, fizzy glass. The steel drum band kept up a lively rhythm.

Maybe Silvio was right and she should quit the police department. Spend her days by the pool drinking champagne as Kurt's señora. Glide through hotel events on his arm. Use Kurt's credit cards to buy more clothes like the strapless dress. Did she really need her police pension? It would be a pittance compared to what Kurt made.

She could give the binder of Las Perdidas to Rosalita.

Another glass of champagne helped her to remember what Kurt said about food. Emilia floated over to the buffet and was loading a plate with shrimp when the next person in line lightly touched her elbow.

"Detective Cruz?" It was William Gifford from the new consulate addressing her in English.

"Hello." Emilia gave him a bright smile. "Señor Gifford, wasn't it?"

"Please, call me Will."

"And I'm Emilia." She moved to the salads. "Are you here in an official capacity?"

"Yes, one of the less enjoyable aspects of the job."

With her clutch tucked under one arm, Emilia held out her plate and indicated her choices. The chef behind the buffet table added a leaf of stuffed endive and a wedge of grilled pineapple.

Gifford made the same choices.

"How could you not be having a good time?" Emilia indicated her plate, the buffet, the music, the steel drum band.

"I don't know anyone," Gifford confessed with that boyish grin.

"Well, you know me," Emilia said. She could relate. It was how she'd felt when she first moved into the Palacio Real with Kurt.

With a fresh glass of champagne in one hand and her plate in the other, she led him to a linen-covered table.

Gifford pulled out a chair for her. "Shall we pretend to have met under more exciting circumstances?" he asked before sitting.

"Such as?" Emilia dug into her food, washing it down with more cold bubbly.

"Let me see." Gifford pronged a shrimp as he pretended to think. "I rescued you from pirates. You were so grateful that you agreed to be my dinner companion."

Emilia laughed. The evening was taking on a charming rose-colored glow after the not-so-charming week. The man from the consulate was a charming companion. "Only if champagne is involved and you have completely banished the pirates."

"I believe that can be arranged." Gifford raised a hand. A waiter materialized with fresh flutes.

They made small talk about the regatta and the glamour attached to the America's Cup race world as they ate and watched the sails flutter on the yacht bobbing gently on the mirror-like water. Lively music and the buzz of hundreds of happy guests contributed to the effervescent atmosphere.

"This is the best food I've had in Mexico and that's saying something." Gifford bit into another shrimp and closed his eyes in rapture as he chewed. "Sweet and tangy at the same time, with a hint of apple. I've died and gone to heaven."

"I'll tell the chef," Emilia said, feeling quite light and untethered. Champagne was a wonderful invention. "But his ego is big enough as it is."

"You know the chef here?"

"Yes, he's French. Jacques Anatole."

"How do you know him?" Gifford raised his eyebrows above the tortoise shell glasses. He wore a navy jacket, a white shirt with no tie, and gray trousers. A *norteamericano* style that Kurt called "preppy."

"Through Kurt. He's the manager of the Palacio Real."

"Yes, of course, Kurt Rucker. I met him at the consulate's grand opening. Seems to be quite well-known here in Acapulco, head of the local hotel association and cozy with the mayor."

"I'm not sure cozy is the right word." Emilia flapped her hand like Carlota summoning Enrique Santibañez. "He's on her Olympic exploratory committee, but only under duress."

"Would you say that Rucker is a useful person for the consulate to cultivate?"

"Kurt's not the sort of person to be cultivated." Emilia made air quotes around the last word.

"Sounds like you know him well."

"We're engaged."

"You're engaged to Rucker?" Gifford's eyes darted to her left hand.

"Isn't my ring gorgeous?" Emilia fanned out her fingers. "It's a family heirloom. I love it."

Gifford gave her a genuinely apologetic smile. "When you said you were going to New York to meet your fiancée's family, well, um, I didn't realize Rucker was your fiancé."

Emilia tried not to giggle. "Don't worry. Most people have that reaction."

"Congratulations," Gifford said earnestly. "Although I confess this is a crushing blow to me personally."

"I'm sure there are many other women in Acapulco who need to be rescued from pirates." Emilia cut through the air, imaginary cutlass in hand. "Swashbuckling men with swords are in short supply."

"A toast," Gifford raised his glass, "To new friends."

"To new friends," Emilia echoed.

As if the chime of crystal on crystal was his cue, Kurt appeared at the table and put a possessive hand on Emilia's bare shoulder. "Emilia, please introduce us."

He sounded a bit jealous and she loved it. "Kurt Rucker, meet Will Gifford, from your very own *norteamericano* consulate."

Gifford stood. The two men exchanged a handshake and recalled meeting each other at the consulate's grand opening.

"Thank you for keeping my fiancée company while I've

been running the party," Kurt said.

"Not at all." Gifford beamed at Emilia. "You're a lucky man, Rucker."

"I'm reminded of that every day," Kurt said pointedly.

The waiter brought another round of champagne. Emilia nibbled her food as the two men chatted and then it was time for the speeches. Kurt gave her a kiss on the cheek and went to the podium. Gifford said something about the charity that was being supported by the silent auction.

Carlota was there in a silvery dress and made a short speech. Emilia didn't know if the topic was her dead sister or violence in Acapulco or the enormous sums of money being spent on her re-election campaign. She was floating happily above the proceedings, riding on a magic carpet of champagne.

Will Gifford said something. Emilia smiled. Her mouth felt loose and disconnected.

Both Will Giffords smiled back.

So charming.

CHAPTER 27

Emilia wished she was dead.

Despite two aspirin and a liter of orange juice, her mouth tasted like sand.

Kurt had said something about champagne hangovers being the worst of all, then laughed like a dump truck unloading gravel as she staggered out the door to go to the morgue.

Now she held a mask over her face as her stomach threatened to erupt like Mexico City's Popocatépetl volcano, along with the Monica Montoya murder investigation.

Beso Sanchez was a waxy doll with five puckered red lips marching the length of her skinny forearm. The girl was old enough to be hard-used for too long, young enough to have had a lifetime ahead.

"I've been looking for her." Emilia's knees were shaky enough to make her wobble past the body to lean against Prade's stainless steel work table. "She was a hooker who worked the Boulevard Hotel."

"One of your lost women?"

"Yes. But more than that, she was a witness in the Montoya murder case. You remember the mayor's sister, don't you?"

Prade gave her a look dripping with pity. "Hard night?"

"A party. I'll never drink champagne again."

"A terrible problem to have." Prade gestured to the body. "Do you need to see any more?"

Emilia reluctantly peeled herself away from the work table

and approached the body again. Apart from a few small bruises on her legs, the naked body was unblemished. "How did she die?"

"An overdose. Fentanyl."

"How long ago?"

"Several days ago."

"As long ago as a week?"

Prade nodded. "Possibly."

Emilia's brain groped past the iron curtain of her hangover. Yes, this could be an accidental overdose, but it could also be murder.

Lima said he tipped the girl some money but what if he lied and the *propina* wasn't cash but pills? Chevo had verified that Beso was a user. It would have been easy enough for Lima to give the girl an overdose and make it look accidental.

The drug angle could produce circumstantial evidence to tie Lima to both Monica's murder and Beso's death. If Lima provided pills to Beso to keep her from talking because he left the hotel during the time they were supposedly together, where did he get them?

The team needed to show Lima's picture to dealers. See if his upstanding colleagues at Viejo Dorado were buying pills and sharing. Go back to Roger Boardman at the Boulevard Hotel and find out who was selling pills there.

"Let me take a picture of her tattoos." Emilia dug out her phone. She wanted to stick Lima in an interrogation room again and watch his reaction when he saw pictures of the girl's body.

The heavy steel door to the exam room crashed open, making Emilia flinch and take an involuntary deep breath of the fetid air. A gurney topped with a body bag rolled in, pushed by two masked morgue attendants.

"Got a fresh one for you, Doc," one of them said cheerfully. "Unidentified male, not too old, big time blunt trauma. One of the roving crews picked him up. Found him in a parking lot next to a Jaguar."

Emilia pocketed her phone. Time to get going before the day's crop of dead bodies started rolling in. "All done. I'll let you get on."

The attendant recognized Emilia. "Hey, Detective, more work for you, I guess."

"How bad is it?" she asked.

"See for yourself," the attendant said.

Prade bustled into action, rolling Beso Sanchez's body into a drawer. "Well, let's see what we have." The doctor gestured at the body bag on the gurney, and the attendant unzipped it, then peeled the unwieldy stiff material away from its contents.

"Oh, yeah, this one's pretty bad," the attendant said to Prade.

Too curious to leave, Emilia watched as the body emerged from its black cocoon and was transferred to the examination table in the middle of the room.

This was the body of a man who'd lost a brutal fight. The face was all but gone, battered and bludgeoned beyond recognition. Shards of bone showed through tattered and dirty skin. Bits of pink tissue, rusty blood, and gray brain matter were scattered throughout the brown hair.

The crushed corpse, or what was left of it, was clad in khaki trousers and a pink polo short with a designer logo. The clothing was disfigured with tread marks as if run over by a truck. The hands were shredded. Where the skin was still intact, scrapes extended to the elbows on both bare forearms.

Something fell out of the body bag with a clatter on the tile floor. An arc of reflected light tilted across the floor.

Emilia used a tissue to pick up a broken pair of glasses with trendy turquoise frames. One lens was missing, the bridge was cracked, and an earpiece was badly bent.

The room tilted without warning.

Emilia vomited vile orange acid all over the polished cement floor. She doubled over, retching and gagging until there was nothing more to bring up.

"*Madre de Dios*," she croaked as Prade guided her to the stool at his work table. She was dimly aware of a team of ladies with mops who materialized out of thin air. They replaced the stink of bile with the bite of lavender Fabuloso.

Prade thrust a glass of water into her hand. "Do you recognize that man?" he asked.

Emilia couldn't stop looking at the wreckage. "His name is Campos," she said. "Lieutenant Vicente Campos."

CHAPTER 28

Emilia wasn't sure how long she sat in the Suburban, staring numbly at the rear entrance to the morgue. There was no question in her mind that the mangled body on Prade's slab was that of Lieutenant Vicente Campos. The only question was who had hated him enough to inflict such violence upon the man.

Campos was a devious schemer who used people and threw them away, but he was also a very effective operator. Had Diego Barrielos Luna discovered the *federale* plan to use the phony movie to reel him in? In that case, where was Rafa Gamboa?

A cold prick of latent anger pulled Emilia out of her own thoughts. Gamboa was the devil. Anything that happened to him was not her problem. Only the connection to Monica Montoya mattered.

Campos had used Casa de Plata in his ongoing operation. Monica was killed there. Now Campos was dead, too.

She'd been a cop too long to believe in coincidence.

Fifteen minutes later, she circled the block behind the Financial Crimes building and spied a line of yellow crime scene tape slicing the parking lot in half. Strung between orange traffic cones, *PROHIBIDO EL PASO* warned away nonexistent bystanders. A crime scene van was parked beyond the fluttering yellow perimeter. Two techs in white crime scene coveralls were engrossed in conversation, bulky metal suitcases full of gear waiting unopened beside them.

Emilia parked on the street and trotted over to the techs. She held out her badge on its lanyard around her neck. "Detective Cruz," she identified herself. "You done already?"

"Hey, Cruz." The taller tech pulled off his mask, revealing himself to be Jorge Allende, one of the better techs she'd worked with over the years. "We didn't even get a chance to start before getting a call to stand down."

His partner shucked off his white crime scene coverall.

"Stand down?" Emilia gestured to the area inside the tape. "This is a homicide situation."

"Don't tell me," Allende said. "I got eyes."

So did Emilia. This close to the scene, Emilia's empty stomach did a sickening flip. The dark pavement was blotched with blood stains that shone wetly in the morning sun, flecked here and there with bits of gray tissue. An irregular chalk outline showed where Campos's body had lain.

"I just came from the morgue," Emilia said. "The victim worked in the building over there. He was beaten and crushed."

Allende squinted at the pavement on the other side of the tape. "Just from the marks over there." He unzipped his own coverall before pointing to a streaky line that had its origin near the body outline. "I'd say your victim was run over. Well, mostly his head got run over. Brain literally got splattered in that direction."

The rumble of heavy vehicles made them both look toward the street. Three muddy green Army trucks bounced over the curb, chewed up the strip of grass separating the lot from the sidewalk, and stopped with fenders brushing the crime scene tape. Soldiers boiled out and began ripping down the tape and throwing the traffic cones into a pile.

"Stop! Stop!" Emilia shouted across the expanse of pavement. "You're contaminating a crime scene!"

"Who are you?" A burly soldier strode across the pavement, paying no attention to the blood stains he'd just compromised, and planted himself in front of her.

"Detective Emilia Cruz, Acapulco police." Emilia thrust her badge in his face. "You just walked through a homicide crime scene. Tell your men to leave that tape alone."

"Get out." The name tag on his uniform read Perera. The stripes on his sleeve said that he was a sergeant. "Take your people with you."

"The crew stays," Emilia exclaimed. "This is a homicide investigation."

Perera squinted at her. "Federal jurisdiction. Everybody out."

"There's been a mistake." Emilia held her ground, although she could hear Allende and his partner stowing their unopened cases in the van. "This is a major crime with a connection to the murder of the mayor's sister. I need my techs in here right now and don't need it contaminated by a bunch of army boots."

"Not my problem," Perrera said. "I got orders." He walked back across the crime scene, oblivious to the basic rules of crime scene preservation.

"See you around, Cruz," Allende called. "We got another call." He hopped into the passenger seat. The van sped off.

Emilia watched in impotent fury as Perera directed his soldiers to mark their own perimeter around the crime scene with metal bollards and spools of yellow tape with a different warning on it.

ESCENA DEL CRIMEN NO CRUZAR.

Crime scene. No crossing.

Emilia didn't know whether to laugh or cry.

CHAPTER 29

"Chief Salazar called." Silvio held up a hand to stop Emilia's protest. "The Campos murder isn't our case. The *federales* will manage the investigation. We can't even touch it."

"Did you tell Salazar that giving the case to the *federales* destroys Financial Crimes's cover?" Emilia paced his office, beyond despondent. For the last two hours, she'd basically done nothing except stare at the spreadsheet of phone records and try to rehydrate. The ghastly images of Campos's mangled body refused to fade.

To make things worse, the uniformed cops sent to pick up Carlos Lima reported that no one was home. Had the man fled Acapulco, knowing that his second victim had been found?

Silvio grimaced. "From what I could tell, nobody is giving Salazar a choice. The *federales*--."

A knock on the open door cut him off. Emilia turned, expecting to see Macias or Sandor. Instead, Bruno Ruiz Ramirez from Financial Crimes stood there, a rolled up manila envelope in one hand.

"Lieutenant, Detective." His eyes traveled between Silvio and Emilia. "Do you have a minute?"

"Sure." Silvio leaned over the desk to extend a hand. "We were just talking about what happened to Campos. Damn shame."

"My condolences," Emilia said.

Ruiz was on the brink of tears. "I'd like to speak to both of you."

Emilia exchanged a look with Silvio, eyebrows lifted in a silent question. He answered with a subtle shrug of one massive shoulder.

The habit of their longstanding partnership was hard to break. Emilia knew that Silvio also was wondering if Ruiz was there to ask them to pursue an unofficial investigation.

"Have a seat," Silvio said to Ruiz and indicated the chairs fronting his desk.

"Would you like a cup of coffee?" Emilia asked.

"Please." Ruiz gave her a look of gratitude that was almost painful. "Just black."

She found a clean mug in the cabinet below the coffeemaker, filled it and went back to Silvio's office. Both men were silent as she handed the mug to Ruiz. The man held it tightly in both hands as if his strength was all but gone.

"I found him, you know." Ruiz said after a swallow of coffee and a pathetic lie about its quality. "Sunday morning and all. I figured I would work a couple of hours. Make a dent in the paperwork."

"Of course," Emilia murmured.

Ruiz fortified himself with another gulp. "Campos's wife and son live in El Norte. Outside Washington. She works for some international do-gooder organization."

Emilia nodded in sympathy, recalling the photo of Campos and his wife and son in his office. He'd never mentioned that they lived apart.

"There's no way I can tell Laura in a phone call that he's dead," Ruiz went on "She deserves better than that. Vicente deserves better."

Silvio scowled. "Call our embassy. Have them send someone over."

"No." Ruiz nearly sobbed out the word. "They'll send some *estupido* who has no idea who Vicente was, what he did or how he lived."

Silvio made a noncommittal noise.

"I went to the new consulate already and asked how long it would take me to get a visa to tell Laura in person. They told me at least ten days." Ruiz's eyes darted from Silvio to Emilia. "They said you're the only local official with a current visa. You could go today. Break the news to Laura."

Emilia blinked. "What, me go to Washington to tell Campos's wife that he's dead?"

"Please, I can't leave it to strangers to tell her," Ruiz pleaded. "You worked with him. You knew him. You understand what it's like to live undercover."

Silvio rubbed a hand across his jaw. "How long would Cruz be gone?"

"Two or three days. Financial Crimes will pay for the trip, of course. Laura will need to make some decisions and having you there will help."

"Decisions?"

"Where to bury him, for a start."

"*Madre de Dios*," Emilia murmured.

Silvio blew out his breath. "What do you think, Cruz?"

Emilia was overwhelmed at the thought of dropping everything and flying to El Norte alone. "How soon would I need to go?"

"If you catch a flight out today, you'll be able to tell Laura before she finds out from social media that her husband is dead." Ruiz clutched the mug as if to keep his hands from shaking.

There was still so much to do. Find Carlos Lima. Follow up on the fentanyl angle from Beso Sanchez's death. Keep picking apart Monica Montoya's phone records. Dig further into the fleet of cleaners and landscapers who had access to Casa de Plata. Wonder if Campos had been telling the truth when he said that Rafa Gamboa couldn't possibly be involved, despite his past access to the property.

Tell Kurt she had decided to resign.

"We can handle the Montoya investigation for a couple of days without you," Silvio said into her silence.

Ruiz leaned forward, tense with grief and despair. "What if you were Laura, Detective? Living so far away, never knowing exactly what kind of danger your husband was in, always wondering if he was safe. Then one day you scroll through the news and read that he was beaten to death."

The thought of being in the other woman's shoes made the decision for her. How would she want to find out that Kurt had been killed if she was far away? A phone call from the Palacio Real concierge? On a television news program? Of course not.

"Okay," Emilia said. "I'll go."

The rest of the morning passed in a blur of emails, phone calls, and a trip to Financial Crimes where Señora Mendez gave her a pre-paid debit card, a pre-paid long-distance phone card, and a printout with flight and hotel reservations. The debit card was to purchase the return flight, scheduling subject to the needs of Campos's widow and son, and pay any other pressing costs including if they chose to bring his body to Washington for burial.

Ruiz produced a letter from the United States consulate for her to carry to smooth any bureaucratic wrinkles. The letter was addressed *To Whom It May Concern* and noted that Emilia was a Mexican law enforcement officer on official business and requested assistance as needed. It was signed by William Gifford.

There was just enough time before the afternoon flight for Emilia to race back to the Palacio Real, stow her gun, pack a bag and tell Kurt what she was doing. He arranged for one of the hotel drivers to take her to the airport.

The flight to Houston was uneventful and she had no issues going through passport control other than being amazed at the huge lines for both citizens and visitors. The uniformed Customs and Border Control officer duly studied her passport, glanced with interest at her police badge and identification, then stamped her passport and told her to have a nice visit.

It was her first time out of Mexico. Her first time in El Norte. Not the trip she and Kurt had planned, but a mission of mercy to tell a woman her husband was dead. Still, it was a little bit thrilling to be there.

She got herself a shockingly expensive burger in the Houston airport then settled in for the second flight to Dulles Airport outside Washington. The flight arrived close to midnight. Emilia picked up her small suitcase from the baggage carousel, breezed through the rental car process and found herself behind the wheel of a roomy silver sedan. The maps app on her phone gave directions to the hotel in Spanish as English-language road signs whizzed past in the dark. The roads were wide and the exits well marked. Perhaps it was because it was so late but *norteamericano* drivers were surprisingly timid compared to what she was used to in Acapulco. Plus, the rental car had power to spare. Emilia had a grim task to accomplish in El Norte but at least she'd have fun getting there.

The hotel was in Reston, Virginia, the same suburb as Laura Campos's address. To Emilia's surprise, the parking was free. Despite the late hour, the hotel staff offered her a selection of fruit and cookies and bottled water.

The room was pleasant enough and the bed was as big as the one she shared with Kurt in the penthouse. Still buzzing with adrenaline, Emilia texted Kurt to say she'd arrived, made herself a cup of tea from the tiny drinks station in the room and ate the cookies while scrolling through dozens of unfamiliar television channels.

Eventually, she crawled into bed and slept.

CHAPTER 30

Being made of something resembling corrugated iron, Emilia's reliable gray trouser suit had survived the trip with a minimum of wrinkles. She watched English-language news on television as she dressed and swiped on some mascara, pleased that she understood most of what was being said by the presenters. Traffic was bad, teachers wanted more money, and the Thanksgiving holiday was right around the corner.

Black loafers and a ponytail holder and she was done. It felt strange not to slip on her shoulder holster over her pink blouse before buttoning the jacket.

The hotel breakfast was heavy on cholesterol, but the coffee was excellent.

Before heading out, Emilia checked that she had Laura Campos's address, as well as the official letter signed by William Gifford and the cash that Kurt had pressed on her to buy a coat. As she walked outside to the rental car and freezing air played around her bare ankles, she sent up a mental prayer of thanks for his foresight. If she had to spend more than a day here helping Laura Campos, she'd need a coat. Socks and a hat, too.

The cold helped concentrate her thoughts as she started the engine. The windshield was covered in white rime. She'd never seen such a phenomenon before but Kurt had warned her about frost and that she'd have to wait for the car to warm up before it melted. She played with the dashboard buttons until warm air was blowing against the windshield. A small victory, although it was sad to see the frost melt away like the hopes and dreams of her police career.

While she waited for the car to defrost and to help forget that she was freezing, Emilia mentally rehearsed the conversation that would follow her knock on Laura Campos's door.

-Are you Laura Campos? I'm Detective Emilia Cruz from Acapulco.

-Hello.

-I regret to inform you that your husband Vicente was found dead yesterday under suspicious circumstances.

-Vicente? Dead? How did it happen?

-It appears that he was bludgeoned to death with a hunk of cinderblock and then run over by a car.

Perhaps she'd get Laura to sit down before telling her that last bit. Have a glass of cold water handy, too.

Her phone's map application directed her through heavy morning traffic, down boulevards called Sunset Hills Road and Reston Parkway, both bordered by trees and sidewalks and shiny commercial buildings, many with company names and logos prominently displayed. Overhead signs were big and green, proclaiming exits for Fairfax County Parkway and North Shore Drive. Drivers were more aggressive this morning, but still laughably timid compared to what she was used to.

A final left turn and she was on a residential street called Links Drive, cruising past clusters of narrow clapboard villas pressed *codo con codo*, or elbow to elbow as the expression went. Kurt had once referred to villas as townhouses so Emilia supposed that's what they were called here.

All were shades of red and beige with matching brown

roofs. The townhouses made a pretty tableau against so many trees wearing the ruddy tones of the *norteamericano* autumn season.

The house she was looking for was on the end of a row of nearly identical tan townhouses. The only distinguishing feature was how far back they were set from each other, creating a frontal zigzag effect. That and the number of pots of flowers by the front door; big mounds of purple, white or yellow flowers, all of the same variety. The people who lived there were trying to be individual, but not too much. She wondered if everyone looked alike or worked in the same place or simply wanted to fit some predetermined mold of sameness.

The row of townhouses was nestled in a woodsy enclave, far enough away from other townhouse clusters to create a feeling of privacy and exclusivity. Tall trees loomed behind them. Curving concrete walks spliced the deep grassy lawn in front of each set of porch steps.

Emilia swung into the parking area bordering the grass and parked neatly between white painted lines. She pulled her shoulder bag out of the car, stowed her phone, and looked around, clutching her blazer closed in a vain attempt to ward off the cold.

This wasn't an enclave that broadcasted wealth or prestige. The few cars parked in the lot were small SUVs or sedans, the kind of cars reserved for city commutes or taking children to dance classes and sports games. It made Emilia think that Laura Campos was practical and thrifty. Honest, too. Her husband hadn't paid for this from pocketing *federale* money or cartel bribes.

Or if he had, Campos had been smart enough not to invest

in a flashy piece of real estate.

Emilia had a good idea of what Laura Campos looked like from the family picture in the lieutenant's Financial Crimes office. Early forties, at least 10 years older than Emilia but about the same height. Dark hair, fine features. She'd be dressed for work, perhaps also wearing a trouser suit and silk blouse.

The sky was a mild blue, a mere afterthought of the hard cyan of Acapulco. Apart from a breeze rustling dry leaves and the distant sound of traffic, the neighborhood was quiet. The sense of emptiness, along with so few cars in the lot gave Emilia pause, slowing her footsteps as she approached the front door of the end unit.

What if she was late and Laura Campos had already left for work? Even worse, what if Laura was gone but the son was there alone? No one in Financial Crimes had considered the possibility of that.

Emilia would either have to tell him that his father was dead or ask him to call his mother to come home, then let him stare at her until Laura appeared.

Just some of the ways a ghastly task could get worse than it already was.

Once in front of the door, Emilia straightened her spine, hitched her shoulder bag a little higher and pressed the button for the doorbell. A circle of black glass above the button suggested that this was the kind of doorbell that sent a fisheye video to the householder's phone. Emilia tried to look official and caring.

A young man came out of the house next door. He was about her age, blonde and narrow-shouldered in a mossy green corduroy jacket. A reedy version of Kurt.

"Hello," he said, continuing past as she returned the greeting.

Emilia watched him get into a white SUV two spaces away from her rental sedan. After a moment, he drove out of the parking lot and turned right onto Links Drive.

The unmistakable *thunk* of a heavy deadbolt pulled her attention back to Laura Campos's townhouse. The door swung open.

Aqua polo and matching sweater vest with a little alligator on it. Khaki trousers. Wavy brown hair. Trendy glasses.

The frames were clear plastic this time instead of turquoise.

"You're supposed to be dead," Emilia faltered.

"I was until you showed up," Campos said and yanked her over the threshold.

CHAPTER 31

Campos poured water into the coffeemaker. "He was a *sicario* for hire. A contract killer. But I don't know who offered the contract."

Emilia was still trying to get over the shock of seeing the *federale* alive. "I saw the body in the morgue. So did Ruiz. We were sure it was you."

The townhouse had the uncertain feel of temporary accommodation. Coming into the townhouse, Emilia had passed through a bland beige living room outfitted with a bland beige sofa, a coffee table, and two armchairs upholstered in a tone-on-tone beige plaid. As if to keep all the beige from floating away into the land of utter colorlessness, the space was anchored by a fake red Persian rug. Two Picasso prints hung on the wall above the chairs, reflecting muted light seeping from around the vertical blinds covering the front window. The galley kitchen bisected the floor plan, creating a short hallway connecting the bland living room and a larger space at the back of the house.

Campos switched on the machine. A light glowed and a hiss signaled the start of the brew cycle. "Of course. I made it look like he had succeeded in spectacular fashion."

"Who was he?" It was a surreal experience to listen to a story that was both shocking and believable. Campos got the drop on his assailant, switched clothing and used the would-be killer's own truck to mangle the body and so fake his own death.

"He's me now." Campos took off his glasses and pinched the bridge of his nose as the coffeemaker gurgled. "It was sheer luck that he didn't have any tattoos so I could pass him off as me."

"And you have no idea who he was or why he was trying to kill you?"

"The obvious answer is that he was one of Diego Barrielos Luna's hired goons. I don't like the fact that he came to the Financial Crimes building. We've been compromised."

No kidding, Emilia wanted to say but it felt too flippant for a conversation with a dead man.

When each had a mug of dark steaming brew, Campos led her out of the kitchen to what was clearly the more well used portion of the house. Here the carpet was bottle green and the furniture was limited to a large workstation with three screens, a swivel chair, a television on a wooden stand and a large leather recliner. Emilia saw a bar-height box in the corner that might have been a safe. Upon closer inspection it was a wine cooler full of bottles, with a digital readout telling the temperature.

"You smashed him up pretty bad." Emilia sat in the recliner, directed by Campos's gesture of hospitality. She let her shoulder bag slip to the floor beside the chair. "The glasses were very convincing."

"I thought that would do the trick." Campos gave a harsh laugh and took the swivel chair. "Is the army investigating my murder?"

"Yes, they came in and immediately compromised the scene."

"Sergeant Perera?"

"You arranged for him to mess up the scene?"

"I couldn't have Lieutenant Silvio discovering that the dead man wasn't me, now could I?" Campos leaned forward, mug clasped in both hands. "Tell me again why you're here."

"Your office sent me. Ruiz thinks your wife lives here and he couldn't bear the thought of a stranger telling her that you were dead." Emilia slowly lowered the mug to a small table by the recliner. "Does she?"

"Does she what?"

"Live here."

"No, we're divorced. She and the boy live in Mexico City."

"Does Ruiz know that?"

"That's a very good question." Campos smiled. "I think your best bet is to go back home, tell Ruiz you broke the news to Laura and forget you ever saw me."

Emilia looked around at the oddly furnished room and its bare walls. She swiveled the recliner to look out the sliding glass door at an empty flagstone patio surrounded by a tall wooden privacy fence. A spot of red flickered by and alighted on top of a post.

"That's a cardinal," Campos said, tracking her gaze. "One of the few birds that stays in Virginia all winter."

"What is this place, then?" Emilia asked, spinning the chair back to face him.

"What do you think?"

"A hideaway. Someplace to go when overly ambitious *federale* operations go sideways." She paused. "Does Rafa Gamboa come here?"

"No, but he could. Reston is a good place to get lost in the shuffle. Lots of people constantly coming and going. Government types. Contractors who work in the Big Tech offices all around the area."

The desk behind him was cluttered with computer equipment including two keyboards, mousepads, and a tangle of cables. Three smartphones were off to the side, along with chargers plugged into a power strip.

Emilia decided that the townhouse was a command post of sorts.

Campos went into the kitchen. "Did you find out who killed that woman in Casa de Plata?" he asked over his shoulder.

"Maybe." Emilia narrowed her eyes. "Why, is she connected to all this?"

"Maybe." Campos brought the coffee carafe and topped up her mug.

"You told me you didn't know anything about her."

"A bit of truth stretching," Campos said jovially. He returned the carafe to the kitchen.

"I'm investigating the murder of Carlota Montoya Perez's sister and you're playing around with the truth?" Emilia couldn't believe the situation. Here she was drinking coffee with a man who'd been officially pronounced dead in Acapulco and he was still teasing her, as if everything was a harmless joke.

Campos eased into the desk chair again. "About a month ago, she made an appointment to speak to the person in charge of Financial Crimes. She wanted to discuss the signs of campaign finance misappropriation. I gathered that Carlota's campaign was contemplating charges against Vallejo Loy for campaign finance fraud."

Emilia's mouth fell open. This put an entirely new spin on the murder investigation.

Campos went on. "She specifically asked about using exchange rates to launder money. Dollars into pesos and so forth. I told her that if she had further concerns, she would have to take them up with the office of the attorney general for the state of Guerrero."

"Money laundering?" Emilia exclaimed. Obviously, this meant that Monica suspected that drug money was being funneled into Vallejo Loy's campaign. "Didn't it occur to you that this was relevant to my murder investigation?"

"What was relevant was that any connection between Financial Crimes and Casa de Plata be kept under wraps."

"And then she was murdered in a building you've been using? And someone attacks you?"

Campos spread his hands. "I'll agree that this doesn't look good."

A sick thought popped into Emilia's head. "Are you protecting someone? Rafa Gamboa perhaps?"

"Rafa's got nothing to do with the Montoya woman at all."

"How do you know?"

"I told you. Rafa's been here in El Norte for weeks, working on the Barrielos Luna movie project."

"Are you sure?"

"I'm meeting him tonight at the Willard Hotel bar. That's the reason I'm here. Otherwise you'd have come to an empty house."

"You'd planned to come here even before the attack?"

"Yes, of course. I can prove it, too. Mark Pardo, wine

importer and owner of this house, bought his ticket days ago."

"Mark Pardo." Emilia gave a little laugh.

Campos flicked a business card at her.

Mark Pardo
Importer, Fine Wines
Washington DC, Sevilla, Oporto, Marseille

Emilia had to admit that the *federales* had both imagination and resources that far outstripped the Acapulco police department. She handed back the card. "I'll bet Mark Pardo is best friends with Manolo Bernal, movie producer."

"I supply all the wine for his parties." Campos tapped the card against a thumbnail. "Rafa sent a backchannel message days ago, saying that he had something important he could only deliver in person. Hence the meeting at the Willard."

"If Barrielos Luna sent someone after you, what are the chances someone is after him, too?"

"Do I detect a note of concern for your brother?"

"Maybe I don't want to be caught in your mess any more than I already am."

Campos nodded. "You should just go home."

"Has it occurred to you that Rafa Gamboa set up the contract to kill you?" Emilia heard herself say. "That he sold you out and has thrown in with Barrielos Luna?"

Campos raised his eyebrows above the trendy eyeglass frames. "You don't know your brother very well. He didn't sell me out."

"He was El Acólito," Emilia retorted. "He has no conscience. He'll do anything."

"As I said, you don't know him very well."

Emilia knew that Campos considered himself the keeper of Gamboa's soul but she didn't have the man's confidence that Gamboa wouldn't turn against his fellow *federales*. In her view, Gamboa had been in the wind too long, had absorbed too many different dirty identities, and done too many heinous things to ever be trusted.

It was more than possible that Gamboa had been seduced by proximity to the money and power wielded by Barrielos Luna. With Campos gone, the last thread linking the deep cover *federale* to real life would be gone. A man who thrived on danger, Gamboa's new role would be as Barrielos Luna's lapdog and enabler of vanity projects like the ridiculous movie, *A Misunderstood Man*.

The doorbell rang, startling them both.

The screen of one of the cell phones on the desk woke up, displaying a black and white image. Campos snatched it up, stared at it briefly then set it back down. "Police are at the door. Stay here."

He selected a different phone and left the room with it in his hand.

Emilia went over to the desk and picked up the first phone. It was obviously connected to a video feed. The image was surprisingly good, showing two men in dark uniforms standing outside, their bodies slightly warped by the fisheye effect of the doorbell camera.

She watched as the door opened, the two men adjusting their stances to accommodate its swing. The two cops were virtually identical in dark uniform jackets, ball caps, heavy leather gun belts, and holstered weapons. Shield-shaped embroidered patches on the shoulders of their jackets identified them as police.

"Good morning, officers," Campos said in flawless English.

"Are you the homeowner here?" The police officer wore dark aviator sunglasses and a navy baseball cap. "Mr. Mark Pardo?"

"Yes, I am," Campos said. "How can I help you?"

One of them held out a sheet of paper. "We're looking for a missing person," he said. "Have you seen this person?"

"No." Campos shook his head.

"Anyone else here?" the cop asked.

The front door was still open, Campos still exuding friendliness. "My friend Ester was here," he said, "but she left."

Ester. It had been Emilia's undercover name during the difficult Financial Crimes assignment. Was Campos trying to tell her something?

"I smell coffee," one of the cops said. "Sure would be nice to have a cup."

Without warning, both men barreled into the house, forcing Campos to stumble backward. Emilia watched the sudden rush on the smartphone screen, confused as to what was going on. She heard the front door slam. The little screen went dark. The cops were in the house and there was nothing on the porch to keep the video rolling.

Campos said something. His garbled words were cut off by the unmistakable spit of a silenced gun.

Thwip, thwip. A sickening gurgle and something heavy thumped to the floor.

"Nice shooting," a voice said. "He's dead."

Emilia forced herself to move toward the sliding glass door, understanding in a primal way that she had to get out. The handle was right there on the right side of the slider but pulling it did nothing.

"Fucking bitch."

Emilia looked over her shoulder as she fumbled with a lock below the handle. The two cops were in the short hallway, coming at her fast. One of them had a big handgun with a silencer the size of a missile launcher.

She kicked the swivel chair at them, bottling up the hallway. The men tripped over each other.

The silenced gun spit again, but the shot went wide into the sliding door. Emilia leaped through shattering glass as shards rained down. Momentum carried her across the tiny yard and over the wooden fence.

She came off the top like a wild thing, landed hard, rolled, and was back on her feet in an instant, zigzagging across an expanse of grass toward a wooded area behind the row of townhouses, hardly aware of the cold air searing her lungs.

Every muscle that spent hours swimming with Kurt or hitting the heavy bag in the police gym turned into a unified machine with a single mission.

Go go go.

CHAPTER 32

She was alive and in one piece. The phone was still in her hand.

Emilia breathed in through her mouth, keeping as still as she could, listening for the footsteps of her pursuers amid the sound of not-too-distant traffic. There was a street ahead of her somewhere.

The wooded area wasn't big enough to get lost in.

Her heart was beating so hard her vision was blurring, but she heard the faint crackle of a radio. Then a branch cracked, accompanied by a low grunt. She could make out a dark shape and realized that just one cop had come after her. The other was probably in a car, cruising to get her when the one on foot flushed her out of the woods.

Speed was her savior. Emilia flitted from tree to tree until they ran out at the back of another row of townhouses, the reverse image of those on Links Drive. The rear of each house was hidden by a tall wooden privacy fence, exactly like the one at Campos's house. Once again, as well, the houses were staggered, making some of the fences protrude and others appear to recede.

The crackle of the radio was on her left, louder now, too. Emilia couldn't just stay in the trees.

Bending low, she ran to the nearest townhouse and found the handle to the fence gate. Locked.

Frantic momentum carried her to the next fence, but that gate was locked, too. She kept going, as fast as she could on the slippery, freezing grass. All of the gates set into the tall fences were locked.

Without warning, she came to the last house in the row, a corner unit just like Campos's place. A police car idled in front. She cringed, heart thundering, praying the cop in the car had not seen her. They'd done exactly what she expected, and now she was trapped in their pincer movement.

She couldn't go forward. She couldn't go back. She could only go up and over.

The spike of adrenaline had ebbed. Shaking from cold and fear, Emilia stuck the phone in her pocket and managed to pull herself up over the fence using brute force. She landed in an awkward sprawl on a child's red plastic pedal car. The toddler-sized vehicle trundled away from her, colliding with a big blue plastic bin that came up to her shoulder. The small yard was littered with children's toys, pots of dirt sprouting dead plants and a bucket of garden tools.

A sliding glass door led into the house. A curtain was drawn, blocking any view of the interior.

Something rattled along the fence line. The cop who'd followed her through the woods was pulling on gate handles, too. He wasn't doing much to conceal his approach. Leaves crunched under his feet. Emilia heard labored breathing. The cop was big, but not in good shape, or at least not in as good a shape as she was. Not even six feet from where she was crouching, the fence rattled and she saw the wood strain as he pulled on the gate handle. But it was locked and it held. He moved on.

Emilia began breathing again.

A minute later, a doorbell rang inside the house. A

woman's voice called out a response. Footsteps pattered from inside the house.

Just as she would have done chasing a fugitive suspect, the cops were going door to door. Voices carried through the glass door, although Emilia couldn't make out the words.

Without making a conscious decision, Emilia lifted the blue lid, used a pot of dirt as a stepstool and clambered into the bin. Smelling like vinegar and mold, it was empty apart from some plastic bottles. She closed the lid and was plunged into total, blue-tinged darkness.

She heard the squeal of the sliding glass door opening and heavy footfalls as someone walked around the little patio. A woman's voice kept up a steady stream in English, albeit with an accent Emilia didn't recognize.

Curled into a ball on the plastic bottles, Emilia breathed silently through her mouth, her lungs numb with cold. At any moment, she expected the lid to open. The cop would either haul her out or shoot her where she was. Surely he could hear her heart hammer through the plastic walls of the bin.

Finally, the footsteps moved away. The sliding glass door shut with the snick of a lock.

Emilia waited, her teeth chattering from the cold, wondering what her pursuers would do next. The answer came swiftly when she heard another sliding door open on the other side of the fence. They were evidently going through all the townhouses, peering into every yard.

She completely lost track of time, huddled in the bottom of the bin and shivering uncontrollably. Campos's phone was no help. There were no numbers listed under Contacts, no social media apps and no cellular service. Emilia scanned for available wifi and found that the connection feature was disabled. Apparently, Campos had managed to block any other use beyond his own video doorbell.

Her own phone was in her shoulder bag back at the townhouse on Links Drive. No doubt everything in the bag was now in the hands of the cops who'd killed Campos, including her wallet, the debit card Señora Mendez had given her, her hotel information and keys to the rental car. The letter from the *norteamericano* consulate signed by William Gifford.

Her passport.

The cops who killed Campos knew everything about her, which made her an easy target. They'd continue to hunt for her. They had to eliminate her as a witness.

Obviously, whoever wanted Campos dead knew he didn't die in Acapulco after all and had followed him to El Norte to finish the job. She was just at the wrong place at the wrong time.

Two hours passed before the line of townhouses was silent. Emilia lifted the lid of the bin and climbed out as quietly as she could.

She unlocked the gate from the inside and slipped out of the yard. She had no means of transportation, and no money. She couldn't go back to the hotel.

So stiff with fear she could barely bend her knees, Emilia started walking toward the sound of traffic.

CHAPTER 33

The huge outdoor shopping center was the perfect refuge, with shops lining several streets anchored by an elegant hotel. A big sign proclaimed it to be the Reston Town Center.

Colorful leaf decorations hung from lampposts and were festooned across rooflines. An ice rink was right in the middle of a giant plaza, bustling with mothers watching bundled-up children stumble on skates across the slick surface.

Emilia found the entrance to the hotel. A ground floor restroom was the perfect haven, with wooden doors on the toilet cubicles that extended all the way to the floor. It was warm in there, too. Gradually she stopped shaking and made a plan.

They were looking for a dark-haired woman in a gray suit. She needed a coat and hat, and probably a purse, too, just to look right. Once she had all that, she'd find her way to the Mexican Embassy in Washington DC and get help. Kurt had looked up the address for her as she was packing, and said it wasn't that far from Laura Campos's address in Virginia.

At the embassy, she'd find the right person and tell them everything. They'd have to believe her. She had the evidence of Campos's murder right on his phone.

Emilia forced herself to leave the warm restroom, her head on a swivel looking for cops in dark uniforms and hoping that her childhood pickpocketing skills were still sharp.

Thirty minutes later, Emilia slid a slim wallet up the sleeve of her suit jacket and went back to the hotel restroom. So far her efforts had resulted in a library card, a receipt for a store called Safeway, a folded 5-dollar bill, and a near-heart attack when a mother at the ice rink turned just as Emilia was sliding a hand into the woman's open purse.

This time, however, she struck gold. Sixty dollars in cash, plus four credit cards and a driver's license for a woman named Sandra Baxendale who also had dark hair and brown eyes.

Emilia's first purchase was a black cross-body bag to hide her new wallet and keep her hands free. The same store sold clothing, including coats, but she didn't want to charge too much at one time. In Mexico, stores were always wary about large purchases. which often required identification or a call to the credit card company before the charge would be put through. Emilia didn't know if the same practices obtained in El Norte but better to be safe than sorry.

But she had to act fast before Sandra Baxendale noticed that her wallet was missing.

So she took the purse and plunged back into the bright sunshine and freezing air and found another store where she bought a fuzzy black coat that came to her knees. A few stores down, a woman's sports outfitter was exactly the kind of place where she'd linger if this was Acapulco and life was normal. Emilia bought a pair of plain black yoga pants and a maroon knit cap and matching scarf.

Back to the hotel restroom yet again. From years chasing criminals, Emilia knew attitude was key to survival. Look scared and people noticed. Act like you belonged and they assumed you did.

Those were the rules in Mexico. *Por Dios*, let human nature be the same in El Norte.

The new and improved Sandra Baxendale walked out with false confidence, pretending to be just another *norteamericano* woman, doing what those women did during the day when *norteamericano* cops were busy killing Mexican *federales* who thought that a new name and a safe house protected them from their enemies.

CHAPTER 34

Embajada de Mexico.

The words on the modern façade, from which sprouted an angled glass tower, felt like a lifeline when Emilia saw it from three blocks away. She would find someone there who had half a brain, perhaps even a *federale* representative, and make them understand what had happened. Get them to call Acapulco and verify who she was and the letter she'd been given from the consulate. Above all, she'd explain about Campos and demand protection. She was a Mexican citizen. What else was the embassy for if not to help Mexican citizens?

It was mid-afternoon now and she had covered plenty of ground since the shooting and narrowly escaping the two cops. She'd discovered the local bus service because a stop served the Reston Town Center, anchored by a small shop selling an assortment of items like bottles of water and guidebook and candy bars. Emilia made the mistake of trying to buy a Spanish language guidebook and a bus ticket at the same time, to be met with a stream of incomprehensibly accented English from a turbaned clerk. In the end she paid the 24 dollars shown on the digital cash register for the book and left, confused and terrified that she was trapped in a nightmare.

Following the crowd, she realized that tickets were only available from an automated vending machine. The bus took her to a train station, where everyone had to get off. Emilia found herself swept along into a huge above-ground Metro train station, buffeted by commuters who knew where they were going.

Compounded by minimal signage and masses of people, the Metro service was hugely confusing. Another vending machine listed a bewildering variety of ticket prices. How did she know how much if she wasn't even sure where she was going?

"If you don't buy enough for the ride," a voice said at her shoulder, "it makes you go back and add money."

Emilia gave a start and swung around, still unaccustomed to being addressed in English. A young woman with a white earbud protruding from under her hat and a puffy coat with fake fur around the collar was staring at her impatiently.

"I don't understand." Emilia remembered to say it in English. The chart on the machine seemed to indicate that the cost of a single ride depended on both distance traveled and the time of day.

"Your ticket," the girl said petulantly. "If you don't buy enough, you have to add money at the end before you can get out."

"I see," Emilia said, although she really didn't. "So how much is a ticket?"

"Where are you going?"

"To the White House."

"Sure." The girl's eyes narrowed at the guidebook in Emilia's hand. "You protesting immigration? For or against?"

Emilia turned back to the machine. Sandra Baxendale's credit card bought 20 dollars worth of rides and spit out a single ticket.

A large map on a post helped get her bearings. This part of Virginia was due west of the city of Washington DC. All

Emilia needed to do was find the trains that would take her east. The White House would lead her to the embassy. They were both on Pennsylvania Avenue.

By a miracle, she got on the train going in the right direction. Once she was seated, hunched by a window, the train felt like a safe place. She was just another anonymous commuter intent on her phone. Appearances, not functionality, mattered today.

No one getting on or off the trains looked like either of the two cops. No one made eye contact with her. No one took any notice of her at all.

She thumbed through the guidebook, looking for directions to the White House. Luck was with her, along with the address, a Metro stop was given. Farragut West.

A disembodied voice called out the name of the stop and which side the doors opened before they got to each station. The various lines were named different colors but seemed to run in parallel. Rattled, she got off at a station called Roslyn, sure that she had to change to a different colored line.

Roslyn was huge and bewildering. Emilia was nearly in tears as she was buffeted by hundreds of bad-tempered commuters jostling to catch a train on any one of a number of platforms. There weren't enough signs. Odd words were painted on pillars and it took too long to understand that these were the last stop on the train line going in each direction when she thought that the lines were identified by color.

Anything left in her reservoir of internal optimism bled out onto the concrete as she fought her way through the crowds to puzzle out a map. A coffee shop beckoned, and she longed to get out of the madness for a few minutes, but getting to the embassy had to be her priority.

Eventually Emilia got on another train, found a seat and was drawing a breath of relief when the conductor announced the next stop and she realized she was going in the wrong direction. She tumbled off at the next stop, one called Courthouse. Emilia wanted to sob with confusion and terror that this horrible day was never going to end or that she'd get to the embassy long after it closed for the day. After a ten minute wait, she got on an Orange Line train that took her all the way into Washington.

By a miracle she turned the right way out of the Metro station, the tiny map in the guidebook leading her to Pennsylvania Avenue. Wind swept the sidewalks, litter, and leaves going past. Washington DC was as messy as Acapulco, although there were even fewer public trash bins. She spied a Smithsonian bag crumpled in one, lying on top of crushed fast food bags and threatening to blow away. She plucked it out, dropped in the guidebook and kept going. Ten steps later, she was just another museum-goer who'd overspent at the gift shop.

The embassy of Mexico was a unique-looking building with jutting tiers above the main entrance with its welcoming sign and a series of glassy angles zipping up the left side. The modern glass construction surrounded two historic townhouses. One was white painted brick and the other was natural brick. Both had four stories, two dormers, and a few narrow steps leading to the front door and an arch above the door.

They were out of place amid all the glass and steel, as if the old-fashioned frontages were giant stickers from a book of historic architecture someone had slapped on the modern building by mistake. Or maybe they were separate houses that didn't mind having a glass monstrosity built over them. Perhaps the embassy paid their owners rent for use of their roofs to support the embassy's upper floors.

Besides the strangely bifurcated architecture, Emilia was surprised by the number of people milling around the embassy. There were as many there as had been clustered around the El Norte consulate in Acapulco.

Were they visa seekers from other places trying to get into Mexico the legal way? People who'd gotten into El Norte illegally and now wanted help from their government?

She stayed on the other side of the street, pretending to make a phone call as she tried to figure out if the presence of so many other people would help or hinder her. With so many waiting to get past the guards to someone in charge, she'd only have a few moments to state her case and persuade them to take her seriously.

Something sticky on the Smithsonian bag provided the answer.

Fingerprints. All she had to do was get the people in the embassy to take her fingerprints and send them to Silvo. Every cop was fingerprinted as part of the job application process, and the prints were kept in perpetuity. Not only would her identity be verified but they'd be more likely to believe her account of Campos's murder.

The throng outside the embassy shifted as if having taken a collective breath. A man emerged from a break in the line and ambled casually toward the historic brickwork, fumbling to tap a cigarette out of a pack as he walked. After no more than half a dozen steps, he stopped and lit the cigarette with a disposable lighter, making a painfully slow production out of the simple act.

Watching him out of the corner of her eye, Emilia tapped at her phone as if making another call, glad for the camouflage afforded by the Smithsonian bag looped around one wrist. Was he looking at her? Was he waiting for her?

Whether he knew it or not, the man across the street made an easily seen target against the white painted bricks. He finally got his cigarette lit, sucked hard and exhaled a stream of smoke that hung in the bright, cold air. Definitely Mexican, wearing a dark blue puffer jacket unzipped over a brown suit. At least four inches of wool hem hung below the bulky nylon. The mismatch, along with a rumpled head of hair and the way he kept rocking on the balls of his feet, suggested that clothing choice wasn't high on his list of priorities right now.

His indifferent gaze passed over her and everyone else on that side of the broad avenue as traffic cruised between them.

A dark sedan slowed as it passed the main embassy entrance and the two historic façades. As it passed him, Puffer Jacket looked back in the direction the car came, as if wanting to avoid making eye contact with anyone inside.

The sedan continued down the street, showing Emilia a white license plate with black letters and numbers, with a red and yellow design along the bottom edge. Two men in dark uniforms and ball caps were in the front seat.

Emilia felt sick. The busy cityscape swung around her. Of course Campos's killers knew she'd go to the embassy for help. They had her identification, her passport, everything.

Puffer Jacket flicked away the half-smoked cigarette and

walked after the sedan. As he crossed the intersection, he slipped on a pair of sunglasses and picked up speed.

Still on the other side of the street, Emilia followed, keeping the man in sight, every instinct telling her that his cigarette had been a signal. Whoever he was, he knew the killers. Did Campos have a contact inside the embassy who'd turned on him? Did Diego Barrielos Luna's money and influence extend all the way to Washington?

Of course it did.

After three blocks, Puffer Jacket turned off Pennsylvania Avenue and went into a convenience store. Emilia slipped into a clothing boutique on the other side of the street and hurriedly picked out a muted floral shawl and a dark green hat with a brim, praying that Sandra Baxendale had yet to cancel her credit cards. The charge went through.

Puffer Jacket came out of the convenience store, looked both ways then continued north. No bag, nothing in his hands. Either he bought something small enough to fit in a pocket or he didn't find what he was looking for.

Or he went into the store as a surveillance detection exercise.

The area by the Farragut West Metro station was nice, but in Washington, much like Acapulco, the streets got seedier the farther they were from the tourist zone. Now the air carried the miasma of decline. Food wrappers and fast food cups stuck in sidewalk grates and lined the gutters. People lingered on corners as if they had nothing better to do and stared hard at those who passed. The air smelled like exhaust fumes.

Puffer Jacket led her another few blocks, then went into an electronics store advertising refurbished cameras and laptops.

Emilia hovered by a newsstand half a block away, pretending to study English-language newspapers weighted down with a stone so they wouldn't flap away in the wintry wind. Porn magazines wrapped in brown paper were heavier and stayed where they were. The vendor, an elderly man in a turban, said nothing when she bought a *People en Espanol* magazine, threw away the Smithsonian bag, and swapped the maroon cap for the green brimmed hat.

She left the newsstand carrying the fashion boutique bag, with the magazine, guidebook, scarf and cap stowed safely inside. Her crossbody bag was mostly hidden by the floral shawl. It wasn't a full disguise but hopefully made her look just different enough for Puffer Jacket not to recognize her as the woman who had been standing across from the embassy.

Once again, Puffer Jacket came out of the store empty-handed. As Emilia continued to trail him up the street, she was convinced that he was checking for surveillance. Had he seen her in the reflection of a store window? Did he recognize her despite her attempt at disguise. Was he setting a trap for her?

He abruptly yanked open the door of a fast food restaurant and disappeared. Trash cans on either side of the glass doors were overflowing with colorful detritus: waxed paper, ketchup-stained napkins and paper cups with straws still jammed in the lids.

The dark sedan was parked on the street half a block beyond.

Emilia froze on the sidewalk, buffeted by a group that surged into the restaurant as her instincts screamed. Whoever Puffer Jacket was, he was a Mexican from the embassy who was making contact with Campos's killers.

Her thoughts leaped around, too panicked to focus. If she found the Mexican with the cops, what would she do? Confront them? They'd hardly kill her in a fast food restaurant. No, they'd bundle her into the sedan and no one would ever see her again.

Yet she had to do something.

Without a shred of a plan, Emilia went inside the restaurant, both hands clutching the shopping bag. Sandra Baxendale needed something to eat.

Like pews dividing a center aisle, booths marched along the sides of the restaurant below enormous photographs of food presumably on offer. Posters urged her to get the child's meal complete with a giant fake diamond ring. It was a promotion for *Diamond Run 2*, Alejandra Messi's latest blockbuster movie which would be in theaters by Christmas, no doubt making the Mexican superstar and songstress a billion pesos.

All the booths were occupied. Neither Puffy Jacket nor the cops were in any of them.

A counter stretched across the back of the place with a lighted menu hanging from the ceiling above it. The menu choices were all combo meals. A handwritten notice taped on the glass read "No change. No subs." Two sturdier and more intentional signs dangled below. *Order Here. Pick Up Here.*

It was easy to mingle with the group ordering combos. Emilia paid for a Number Three with a credit card and received a foil-wrapped burger, fries and a cola on a plastic tray. She looked around for a seat and realized that the group ahead of her was mounting a flight of stairs to a second level.

At the top, she nearly dropped the tray. Puffy Jacket was sitting across from a beefy cop still wearing his ball cap. The other was sitting next to him, effectively trapping the Mexican against a window. Each had a plastic tray in front of them loaded with fast food.

Emilia calmly walked past and slid into the empty booth directly behind Puffer Jacket and his killer cop friend. She arranged her food with shaking hands and took out Campos's phone, pretending to tap and eat at the same time.

The upper level was full of sound. The murmur of conversations melded with piped-in music, the scuff of feet against tile floor, and the clatter of trays being stacked on top of a nearby trash bin.

The burger tasted like cardboard. The fries were rubbery. Not that taste mattered. Emilia was so tense she could barely swallow.

Her booth was sandwiched between Puffer Jacket and friends and a crowd of six loudly enjoying their meal. The group kept up a lively conversation, speaking so fast Emilia couldn't begin to translate their words into an identifiable language.

It wasn't until they heaved themselves out of the booth and noisily carried their trays to the trash can that she had any hope of hearing Puffer Jacket and friends.

Spoken in a low tone, the two words filtered through the ambient noise. Emilia held her breath, unable to believe she'd heard the name of a woman killed in Acapulco thousands of miles away from a dingy fast food restaurant in Washington DC.

"Who's that?" The sentence was delivered in heavily accented English by a hoarse, raspy voice. Puffer Jacket, Emilia thought.

She heard the slap of cardboard against the linoleum tabletop. "What do you make of this?"

"Looks real enough." His rasp was that of a heavy smoker.

"The passport is real. The visa is fake." This voice spoke in American English. The voice was a pleasant baritone, a nice voice no killer should be allowed to have.

"Looks real enough to me, but that's your business, not mine."

"Mexican passport makes it your business."

"So what do you want me to do about it?" A phlegm-filled cough from Puffer Jacket. Sounds of crinkling paper.

"Just giving you a friendly heads up before you get a call from the FBI." The other cop was speaking. His English was crisper and easier for Emilia to understand. "Some lowlife on the terror watch list was killed this morning. Female shooter. She was either his girlfriend or a partner or something."

"This is her passport?"

"She left the scene in a hurry."

"This is a genuine Mexican passport," Puffer Jacket said.

"The visa is fake," the American said.

"Fake? Must be a good one if it got her into the country."

The other cop spoke so quietly Emilia could barely hear him. "We think she'll show up at your embassy asking for a new passport."

"And if she does?"

"You detain her and call us."

"Not the FBI? Or the CIA?"

"You call us. We'll handle everyone else."

"I could get into trouble."

"Look, all we're asking for is ten minutes to find out who's making false visas," the American said. "Don't you want to know, too? It's a joint problem. After we get what we need, the FBI can have her."

"If they get her first, we'll never find out," the other cop added.

"All right. I should keep that."

Apparently, Puffer Jacket made to take the passport, because Emilia heard a slapping sound, then the skid of something moving across the table.

"No can do, *amigo*. It's evidence in a murder investigation."

"Who did the *chica* kill?"

"A Spanish terrorist. Went by the name of Mark Pardo. Basque separatist. Trained in Libya. Acted as a money agent for Hamas, moved around building his reputation as a trusted money mover. Was in Qatar a few weeks ago. Switzerland before that."

To keep from trembling, Emilia focused on the half-eaten burger on her tray.

"Maybe she had an accomplice waiting for her with a new identity and a new passport," Puffer Jacket said. "She could be far away by now along with the secret of how to get a fake visa into your country."

"We're just covering all the bases. She turns up, you detain her and call one of us. Got that?"

A raspy grunt of approval. *"Bueno."*

"Always nice doing business, *amigo*."

Emilia's seat jolted as the three men clambered out of theirs, the shift in balance rocking the framework that bolted all the booths together. Only when they were past her, did she dare to raise her eyes and watch them one by one descend the stairs to the ground floor. The stink of damp wool and cigarette smoke lingered in the Mexican's wake. Their trays and trash remained on the table in their booth.

Part of Emilia's brain shouted at her to follow the Mexican, to throw him against a wall and shout the truth to him. But the other part kept her glued to the seat.

Puffer Jacket's thanks had been for more than the price of lunch. They'd paid him, although she had no idea how much. Who was the man from the embassy more likely to believe? His *norteamericano* friends with deep pockets or a woman who the government of El Norte believed to be a terrorist and a killer?

Emilia ruefully congratulated herself for following her instincts and trailing the Mexican from the embassy. Her thoughts spun as she fiddled with the congealed fries in their cardboard sleeve. It was no surprise to hear that they had her passport but she wondered what they had already gleaned from Campos's array of electronics.

Her thoughts went to Rafa Gamboa. Did he rat out Campos? Was he ultimately responsible for her situation?

There was only one way to know.

CHAPTER 35

The Willard Hotel was on Pennsylvania Avenue, not all that far from the embassy. It was absolutely huge, with imposing classic architecture decorated with columns and moldings and a glass awning extending over the steps right to the street.

It was dark now, but the awning blazed with light. From where she was across the street, Emilia could easily read the words emblazoned across the glass front: *THE WILLARD INTER CONTINENTAL.*

A fleet of uniformed doormen waited to help people out of limousines and usher them up the sweeping steps, through double doors and into this palace of luxury.

Of course Rafa Gamboa, in his guise as movie producer Manolo Bernal, would choose a place like this to meet his handler.

The biggest gamble of her life was ahead, but Emilia was cold and tired. The temperature had dropped as the sun went down. She'd walked for hours, trying to blend into the scenery and find a wifi café with a computer at the same time, without success. An attempt to buy a latte revealed that Sandra Baxendale's credit cards had stopped working. All she had left was some cash and the Metro card.

The only luck she had was finding a pair of expensive sunglasses in the restroom of a museum. The find gave her an idea.

Since *Diamond Run,* more than one person had remarked

how much Emilia resembled the star. During her stint acting as the star's body double in Rafa Gamboa's movie, she'd been in the star's orbit long enough to know that she could mimic Messi's imperious attitude. Still, the idea was a huge risk. But without credit cards, her other choice was to linger in the freezing cold and hope to catch Gamboa before he went into the hotel.

If he showed up.

Exhaustion made the decision for her. For the past hour Emilia had reconnoitered the area around the Willard, using the guidebook to get her bearings and figure out the best way to approach the hotel. Few people arrived on foot, most came in the back of taxis or town cars with a uniformed driver at the wheel.

Opportunity came as she loitered half a block away from the edge of the glass awning. A long, sleek limousine pulled up in front of the hotel and disgorged a large group. Channeling not only Alejandra Messi but also every bitchy *gringa* who'd made life miserable for the staff of the Palacio Real, Emilia shook out her hair and caught up to the group, bringing up the rear without anyone noticing.

Shoulders square, coat buttoned against the cold, eyes hidden behind sunglasses despite the rapidly darkening evening, Emilia sailed past the doorman without acknowledging him.

But she faltered in the huge lobby, unable to keep herself from gawking. Chandeliers cast a buttery glow over yellow marble columns, dark paneling, red Persian rugs the size of Kurt's penthouse, and velvet seating Emilia wanted to sink into for a nap. Even the ceiling, bordered by ornate moldings, was a work of art.

"May I help you?" A young man in an impeccable dark suit approached. A discreet brass name tag informed her that he was Derek Corning, Assistant Concierge.

Heart hammering, Emilia tipped the sunglasses down on her nose in perfect imitation of Alejandra Messi.

"I'm meeting Señor Bernal in the bar," she announced in English and immediately corrected herself. "Mister Bernal. The movie producer. When he comes, make sure we're not disturbed."

Derek Corning hesitated, then his eyes grew wide.

"Oh my goodness, Miss Messi," he gushed. "We're delighted to have you here at the Willard. I'm so very sorry, but no one called ahead to let us know you'd be here."

"Or perhaps your staff made a mistake," Emilia said with a sniff.

"Let me escort you to the Round Robin bar and offer you a complimentary cocktail," Corning simpered. "When Mr. Bernal arrives, we'll direct him to you."

Emilia pushed the sunglasses up on her nose again, because of course that's what Alejandra Messi would do. "You know Señor Bernal?"

"Yes, he's been here before," Corning said with a smile that said he was accustomed to dealing with the famous and self-obsessed.

He led her across the lobby, past a sign saying *Round Robin Bar* and into a dimly lit space anchored by a huge round dark wood bar ringed by leather-backed barstools. The place was snug and intimate, nothing like the expansive light-filled Pasodoble Bar in the Palacio Real with its seemingly endless bar clad in blue mosaic tiles and two levels open to the ocean. Instead of the rhythm of the waves softening every conversation, jazz music muted the hum of mostly male voices and the clink of glasses.

"A private table?" Corning led her past the unique circular bar where a few men in business suits were watching two bartenders attired in white shirts and black vests craft their cocktails.

"Of course."

Hyper alert, Emilia was aware of a silent message passed between Corning and the bartenders as they skirted the bar. As in the Palacio Real, no doubt the staff had some proprietary signals to make each other aware of distinguished guests.

A waiter materialized, also clad in black and white. "Welcome to the Round Robin."

"Miss Messi would like privacy," Corning said. "She's expecting a guest shortly and does not want to be disturbed."

"Of course. It will be my pleasure." The waiter gave Emilia a nod, acknowledging that he was in the presence of an Important Person, and indicated a table for two in a corner, flanked by tall, upholstered armchairs. Emilia chose the chair facing the bar so she could see who came and went. Corning pulled out the seat for her and she dropped into it with lazy Alejandra Messi indifference.

"Miss Messi is our guest this evening," Corning said to the waiter.

Emilia wondered if Alejandra Messi would actually say the words *thank you*. Probably not. She gave an icy smile in lieu of thanks. "When he comes, Mister Bernal may ask for Mister Pardo. But I'm here instead. A surprise."

"Of course." Corning gave her a look of willing complicity. "We'll do our best to keep the secret."

He shimmered off and the waiter asked if she'd like to try one of the Round Robin's signature cocktails, perhaps the Paloma?

Emilia said fine, she'd try it. Two nerve-wracking minutes later, he was back with a glass rimmed in salt and embellished with a wedge of grapefruit, as well as a tray of assorted meats. "The Round Robin is pleased to host you, Miss Messi. A complimentary taste of our charcuterie specialty, compliments of our chef."

"Yes, well." Emilia bestowed a tight smile. "Please extend my appreciation."

"Of course." The waiter left. Emilia was alone.

Once again she pulled out Campos's useless phone and pretended to text and scroll. The wild card was how long she could pass herself off as Alejandra Messi. For all she knew, the actress could be on live television this very minute.

In between fake text messages, she prayed that she would recognize Rafa Gamboa because the man was a chameleon.

The first time she'd encountered him was during his role as El Acólito, a Santa Muerte priest holding forth in the middle of nowhere. Strutting, imploring and praying as hundreds of women chanted and swooned. His hair was long and he was shirtless, the better to show off the skull-faced black Santa Muerte tattoo inked across his chest.

He'd been mesmerizing, a larger-than-life character. Undercover to ascertain if the mysterious El Acólito was inciting the gang rivalry littering Acapulco with dead men and Santa Muerte artifacts, even Emilia wasn't exempt from the allure of the testosterone-fueled priest. She didn't learn until much later that the entire El Acólito act was a *federale* operation to get inside Diego Barrielos Luna's operation.

When Campos engineered their next encounter, Gamboa was undercover again. This time he was Manolo Bernal, actor and movie producer with bespoke suits, blonde Hollywood highlights in his hair, and a stash of passports in different names, presumably for other *federale* purposes.

No matter which persona Gamboa wore, his sense of morality was not so much limited as non-existent. Nothing mattered except for the rush he got from being the leading man in yet another danger-filled counterdrug operation.

As an undercover *federale*, he was a relentless and creative hunter.

But as a human, Rafa Gamboa was a tragic failure. Even when he knew who Emilia was and what he'd done to her, Gamboa never showed remorse, never apologized. Instead he mocked her weakness.

As far as Emilia knew, the one decent thing he'd ever done was to extricate a young girl from the fringes of the cartel where she was being used to mule drugs. It was one good deed in an ocean of sin committed in the cause of putting Barrielos Luna out of business.

A few more people came into the bar. Expensive suits. Designer dresses. Rolex watches and diamond rings. It was too warm for the coat, but Emilia kept it on. Alejandra Messi would hardly show up in public in a pink blouse and yoga pants.

As the minutes dragged, her stomach got progressively tighter and tighter, until Emilia could barely force down a sip of the tart Paloma. Any minute, Corning was going to come into the Round Robin and expose her as an imposter.

An hour crawled by. Emilia kept tapping the dead phone and registering haughty emotion because a famous star like Alejandra Messi would hardly sit alone and stare like a zombie at a doorway all night.

Maybe Rafa Gamboa wasn't going to show up. Maybe he knew that Campos was dead. Read about it on social media. Or maybe he had arranged the hit on Campos. He knew it took two tries but that the man was finally dead. There would be no need to make the meeting.

Even if Gamboa's hands were clean, he might have heard that either Vicente Campos or Mark Pardo was dead. Perhaps he was in touch with Ruiz. The more Emilia thought about it, the less probable it was that Gamboa would show up. She finished the Paloma and relaxed enough to start worrying about where she was going to sleep tonight.

A triumphant Derek Corning came into the bar, leading another man in a long overcoat.

There was no question that it was Gamboa. He was channeling his Manolo Bernal persona in gray cashmere that rippled over wide shoulders like water. His wavy hair was again anointed with blonde highlights.

He carried himself with just the right amount of muscular swagger, one shoulder slightly forward, chin high. Just like when he was El Acólito, his eyes traveled across the faces of women who instantly became his admirers.

Gamboa's glance fell on Emilia as Derek Corning pulled out the other chair at her table. He blinked but was a good enough actor not to react any more than that.

"Manolo," Emilia said. To her surprise, her voice didn't

shake. "Mark couldn't make it."

"What a surprise." Gamboa reached for Emilia's shoulders. "Drinks with Alejandra Messi."

She stiffened as he lightly kissed her on both cheeks.

Once seated, Gamboa ordered himself a Belvedere vodka martini with two blue cheese-stuffed olives. The waiter asked if he could bring Miss Messi another Paloma. Gamboa said yes before Emilia could respond.

"Where's Campos?" Gamboa asked softly as soon as the waiter was out of earshot.

"He's dead," Emilia whispered back. It was a relief to speak Spanish again.

Gamboa drew in his breath. "When?"

"This morning."

The waiter returned with their order and a silver dish of nuts. They waited to speak until he melted away again.

"This morning?" Gamboa maintained his outward composure. One knee was crossed over the other, a foot idly tapping the air. The charcoal wool of his suit was so fine, it was almost liquid. A starched white shirt and a burgundy tie turned him into just another power broker here at the center of the universe.

"At the villa in Reston." Emilia was surprised at the tangle of emotions his presence created. The old loathing and anger resurfaced, yet she also felt a childlike relief. Here was finally someone from her own world; a life preserver in an unfamiliar and stormy sea. "Two cops came in and shot him. Double tap with a silencer."

Gamboa froze even as he held the miniature sword and its burden of two speared green olives. "How do you know?"

"I was there." In a few terse sentences, Emilia told him about the attempt on Campos's life in Acapulco and Ruiz's plea that she come to El Norte to inform Campos's widow. Then she recounted discovering that Campos faked his own death, the shooting, her desperate escape and eavesdropping on the conversation in the fast food restaurant between Puffer Jacket and the two *norteamericano* cops.

Gamboa said nothing as she went on. When Emilia was done, he drained the martini.

Emilia finally sipped her second drink, the alcohol taking the edge off the panic that had kept her going all day. A few slices of sausage and wafer-thin ham kept the alcohol from going to her head. "They have my passport, my hotel key, my wallet. Everything."

"You've got a bigger problem than a missing passport." Gamboa exhaled, tension tightening his fine features. "Ruiz knows that Laura Campos doesn't live in Reston. It's a safe house for the unit."

"He told me--." Emilia trailed off.

Gamboa cut her off, the speed and urgency of his tone contrasting with his relaxed posture. "Either Ruiz knew Campos's death in Acapulco was fake and organized another try at the safe house. Or he truly believed Campos died in Acapulco but wanted you out of the picture, so he set you up because it was better to do it here than there."

Emilia closed her eyes for a moment, the better to recall Ruiz's trembling reaction to Campos's supposed death in Acapulco. "But he was all torn up. He really believed that Campos was dead and that Laura Campos needed to be told. He sat in Silvio's office and cried."

"We're all actors in this business. Hell, you have this whole bar convinced you're Alejandra Messi."

"The men who killed him wore cop uniforms. Why would they bother to lie about him being a terrorist." Emilia stiffened. "He wasn't, was he?"

"No, of course not." Gamboa slid his empty martini glass to the side. "You're missing the point here. Terrorists are about the only kind of criminal the *norteamericanos* can't abide. If you're branded a terrorist, their *federales* get involved. That way they can keep you from getting a new passport and leaving the country."

Emilia steadied herself with another swallow of her drink. Amid the rush of relief, she'd forgotten what a good actor Gamboa was. He'd never give himself away in an easily handled situation like chatting over drinks in a posh bar.

If Gamboa had set up Campos to be killed in either Acapulco or Reston, her presence as a witness wouldn't have been part of the plan.

Or maybe Ruiz knew Gamboa was planning to betray Campos in Reston and threw her into the mix to prevent it.

Or maybe Gamboa and Ruiz were partners in crime and hired the two assassins.

Yesterday she swore Ruiz truly believed Campos was dead in the Acapulco morgue. Then why send those two cops to the house in Reston?

He set you up because it was better to do it here than there.

But why would Ruiz want her dead?

Too many theories. None made sense.

She realized that Gamboa had asked her a question. "What?"

"What about the stuff in the safe house? Phones, laptops?"

"If it was in the house, they have it." Emilia produced Campos's useless phone. "This was his. He used it for the video doorbell but it's not connected to a network. I think it recorded the cops when they were at the door."

Gamboa took the phone, tapped the screen. "The battery's dead."

"I had to pretend to text all day." Emilia took the phone back.

He signaled for another martini. "Tell me about the man from the embassy who spoke to the two cops."

"Small. Slim. Mid to late thirties. A smoker. Had a voice like somebody who inhales three packs a day. He knows something about surveillance, too, because he walked a detection route before getting to the restaurant."

A fresh martini was delivered. The light jazz music was lively and lulling at the same time.

Gamboa thoughtfully ate an olive. "Did you say the Mexican was wearing a puffy blue jacket?"

"You know him?"

"I think it's Ruben Suarez, the CISEN rep in the embassy. Intel. Coordinates with FBI, CIA."

"He knew the two cops," Emilia told him. "It wasn't the first time they'd met. And it wasn't by accident either. It was a scheduled meet. The kind you have with a good street snitch. The ones who earn their keep."

"Did money change hands?"

"I think so." Emilia realized just how bad the situation was. "*Madre de Dios*, the CISEN rep is being paid off to cover up what happened to Campos and doesn't even know it."

"Let me get this straight." Gamboa held up both hands as if to stop her train of thought. "Are you saying they paid him off so that in case you showed up at the embassy asking for a new passport, he'd make sure you got handed over to them?"

"That's exactly what I'm saying. Haven't you been paying attention?"

He frowned. "How much money?"

"I don't know. Does it matter?"

"It does if it's more than I'm paying him."

A group of people went past, momentarily obscuring Emilia's view of the entrance. They paused to watch the bartenders do a flamboyant juggling and mixing act, forming an overdressed scrum by the big horseshoe. The performance was met by an appreciative round of applause.

As the group left, a blonde man in a green jacket came into the bar. Obviously alone, he climbed onto a stool fronting the horseshoe and made himself conspicuous by gazing around the room.

Emilia wasn't sure what drew her eye to him. Maybe it was because the place was far too elegant for casual pickups yet that's what he seemed to be looking for.

Her mouth went dry. "*Oye*," she whispered to Gamboa. "Do you see the man in green by the bar?"

Gamboa smiled as if she'd told a joke, slightly moving his head in the process. "Tasteless green coat?"

"He was there this morning."

"One of the cops?"

"No, the next-door neighbor. He's wearing the same jacket. I was standing on the porch, waiting for someone to answer the door. He came out of the house next door. We said hello to each other. He got into his car and drove away."

"And now he's here. Someone found Campos's calendar."

"*Madre de Dios*." It took all of Emilia's strength of will not to jump up and run. "What do we do?"

"Good question." Gamboa turned to her. "Is this a set up? Are you working for Barrielos Luna?"

The question was so unexpected that Emilia could only gape at him. "Me?"

Gamboa's eyes burned into hers. "Maybe you killed Campos and made up this story about killer cops. Kept me here talking until your baby-faced *halcone* showed up. Right how he's texting the real killers to pick me off on the street."

"Listen to me, you *pendejo*." Emilia's surprise bloomed into anger. "That guy is trouble for both of us. I don't know how or why but I don't believe in coincidences right now. So check your ego and help me figure out what to do."

"You know what, baby sister?" Gamboa snarled. "This feels like a set up to me. You're still in the revenge business. I think you killed Campos, just to be here instead of him. Hell, maybe he's not even dead. You just made sure he couldn't be here tonight."

"Oh no, you and Ruiz killed Campos," Emilia flashed back. She didn't know if she believed what she was saying or not. "Twice. Barrielos Luna got to you, didn't he? Promised to make you into a big movie star. That's what the stupid movie is about, isn't it? You, it's all about you. Who cares who gets hurt along the way? You never do."

The man in the green coat now had a glass of beer on the bar in front of him, yet he continued to tap on his phone.

A muscle in Gamboa's jaw pulsed. "You and I have a trust

problem, baby sister."

"Maybe because one of us is a rapist and a human trafficker," Emilia retorted. "Stop calling me 'baby sister.'"

"That's right, you have a name. Is it Emilia or Ester today, Alejandra?"

"What should I call you? Manolo? Rafa? Or just Fucking Liar?"

"I'd turn you over to Suarez right now," Gamboa whispered furiously. "Except that Campos was a friend. If you're telling me the truth, I swear to God I'll find out who killed him. If you're mixed up in it, then you'll go down too. They say that blood is thicker than water, but not in our family."

It was a worthy performance, especially if Gamboa had colluded to get rid of Campos and align with Barrielos Luna. "We're all actors in this business," Emilia mimicked.

Gamboa flagged down the waiter. "We have an issue," he said in English, emphasizing the last word. "Miss Messi specifically chose the Round Robin for privacy but we see that the paparazzi have descended upon us."

"On behalf of the Willard, I'm so sorry, Mr. Bernal." The waiter looked around discreetly. "What can we--."

"The man at the bar in the green coat," Gamboa cut him off. "He's been stalking Miss Messi for two days."

This time the waiter produced a cell phone. "I will notify hotel security immediately."

"Manolo, I want to go," Emilia pouted, slipping on her sunglasses again.

Gamboa casually slipped the waiter a 100-dollar bill. "Do you have a back way out of the bar?"

Having murmured into his phone, the waiter led them through a door just a couple of feet away. Almost invisible, it was just another length of wallpaper-topped wainscotting when closed. They slipped through and the waiter silently closed it behind them.

A short hallway brought them to the hotel kitchen, as large and spotless as the one in the Palacio Real's flagship restaurant. The noise level of banging pans and shouting chefs abruptly stopped.

The entire staff turned to look at the newcomers.

Emilia's cheeks flamed as all the chefs and dishwashers and busboys burst into applause. Obviously, the news that Alejandra Messi was in the hotel had spread. Shouts of "We loved *Diamond Run*!" and "Congratulations!" accompanied the clamor in both English and Spanish.

"Wave," Gamboa ordered into her ear.

Emilia complied, even as they kept walking. At the rear door, she impulsively turned and blew a kiss and was rewarded with more cheering and clapping.

Once outside, Gamboa put his hand under Emilia's elbow and steered her briskly around the hotel to a boxy black Lexus SUV parked on the street.

"Where are we going?" she asked once as Gamboa started the engine.

"We're not going anywhere," he replied. "We're going to wait and see what he does."

"So you believe me," Emilia challenged him.

"I'm testing a hypothesis."

"Fine." Emilia pulled up the collar of the black coat and settled in to wait.

Fifteen minutes later, the blonde man in the green coat came out of the front entrance of the hotel, cell phone pressed against one ear. He looked up and down the street, with jerky motions and erratic pacing that radiated tension.

"He's nervous," Gamboa remarked, breaking the silence inside the Lexus.

A car with an Uber sticker in the rear window stopped in front of the hotel. The blonde man dove inside and it pulled away from the curb.

"Show time," Gamboa said and shifted into gear.

They followed the Uber car through the darkened streets. Traffic was light and it was easy to keep the other car in sight. Emilia had to admit that Gamboa knew what he was doing, never getting too close but letting a car or sometimes two get between the Lexus and its prey. Emilia found herself actually admiring his surveillance skills.

They crossed over a long bridge, lights shimmering along the banks of the Potomac River. More lights glinted from a steeple high above.

"Georgetown University," Gamboa supplied as if she'd asked what was perched so high above the water.

The other side of the bridge was a maze of skyscrapers. Gamboa kept the Uber car's taillights in sight as they wound through the streets.

They passed the skyscrapers and came to a neighborhood of low brick cottages. A sign welcomed them to Shirlington Village. The Uber coasted to the curb in front of a row of brick townhouses, smaller and older than the townhouses in Reston. Half a block behind, Gamboa parked the Lexus and killed the headlights.

The blonde man got out of the Uber, trotted to a central door illuminated by a hanging lantern and let himself in with a key. Emilia caught a glimpse of a vestibule with white walls before the door closed. From the architecture, it looked as if the six townhouses shared that common entrance.

A light popped on in the last townhouse on the left. A small parking lot beyond the building housed three cars. One was a white SUV. "I think that's the same car he was driving this morning," she told Gamboa as she pointed it out.

"Go check if there's a name for that apartment," Gamboa said.

"You go check," Emilia said.

"I drove."

"It was your idea." Emilia was afraid he'd drive off without her. "You go."

Gamboa cut the engine, pointedly pocketed the key fob and got out of the vehicle. He walked up the path, the cashmere coat swirling around his calves. He'd taken the fob because he was just as afraid that she'd drive off and leave him stranded as she was about him leaving her.

The thought evened the playing field, but only a little. He knew the territory. She didn't.

He presumably had a place to sleep that night. She didn't.

He had a passport; probably several. She had none.

Gamboa climbed behind the wheel again and dropped two envelopes in Emilia's lap. "I got the license plate number of that SUV. Tomorrow we can see if it belongs to Steven P. O'Grady in Apartment 6. He was too busy to check his mail today."

Emilia tore open the first envelope. Inside was an electric

bill from a company called Dominion Power. "Electricity isn't very expensive here," she said.

"The apartment is probably the size of a shoe box."

Gamboa started the engine and they rolled away from the line of brick townhouses. The quaint neighborhood of Shirlington Village wasn't large and they were soon on a wide boulevard.

The second envelope contained a letter welcoming Mr. O'Grady to the State Department Federal Credit Union.

"State Department Federal Credit Union." Emilia read the words aloud in English. "Is that a bank?"

"Only for people who work at the State Department." Gamboa kept driving. "That's the foreign secretary's people. They run El Norte's embassies. Dish out money to the deserving poor around the world and throw Fourth of July parties."

The letter touted the many benefits Mr. O'Grady could expect including digital banking, low interest vehicle loans and safe deposit boxes in six different locations. As an employee of the Diplomatic Security Service, he was entitled to ten free cash withdrawals per month. Even fees levied by foreign ATMs were included.

Another turn and trees and houses went by in a blur as the road looped and twisted like rope coiled over rocky ground. Emilia caught sight of a street sign. *Kirby Road.*

Eventually they emerged onto another wide boulevard lit by ample streetlights but nearly deserted. They sped along, passing a dark guard shack. A complex of buildings lay off in the distance behind it while a grassy median formed a barrier between the entrance and the shack. Some sort of government installation.

More turns and the Lexus slowed. The houses on either side of the street were large and fronted by rolling lawn that was still green despite the temperature.

Gamboa pressed a button on the dashboard and the garage door of a huge house with a stone and painted brick façade began to rise.

"What is this place?" Emilia asked. She had no idea where they were, which meant that she was totally in Gamboa's power.

"Rental," Gamboa said and drove into the garage. An overhead light popped on as an articulated door rumbled into place behind the Lexus.

Emilia was trapped. Fear came at her like a bird of prey, pecking at her face, her heart, her defenseless hands. "So now what?" she asked.

To her surprise, Gamboa knuckled his eyes like an overtired child. "I don't hate you, you know."

"That's rich. If anyone is entitled to do the hating, it's me. You raped me."

"You got to grow up with her. With family." He spoke quietly.

Her. He meant Sophia, their mother.

Emilia was almost choked by a high tide of resentment. "Our family was so poor I slept on the kitchen table and sold candy to pay school fees. You had everything I never did. Good schools. College. An apartment in Mexico City."

The overhead light must have been on a timer because it clicked off, plunging them into darkness.

"And now you live in a luxury hotel. Yeah, Campos told

me all about you and your rich gringo months ago." Gamboa opened his car door. The car's interior light flicked on. "We can decide tomorrow which one of us betrayed him."

Emilia didn't open her door, belatedly realizing that they were to sleep under the same roof tonight.

Gamboa grimaced. "No need to get all prissy. I'm not going to touch you."

"You're never going to admit it, are you?" Emilia blazed. "What you did to me. What you did to those other women. Not a shred of fucking remorse when you should be on your knees for the rest of your life saying how sorry you are."

"You gave me a concussion," Gamboa said angrily. "Handcuffed me to a chair. Kept me a fucking prisoner in that house with your gorilla overseer. I'd say we're even."

"There is no *even*." Emilia made air quotes around the word. "We'll never be *even*."

"Right this fucking moment, I don't care. My priority is figuring out what happened to Campos. Sleep in the car if you want."

Gamboa snatched up the mail belonging to Steven P. O'Grady, making Emilia flinch at the sudden thrust of his arm. Then he left the vehicle and entered the house. A light went on. He left the door open.

Emilia was too tired to maintain her rage. She reluctantly went inside, swaying with exhaustion.

The garage led into a kitchen the size of the entire penthouse at the Palacio Real. A stone arch soared over a gas range decorated with brass straps. An entire wall of cabinets could easily contain every item Emilia owned with room to spare. The sink was a soapstone sculpture.

A marble island floated in the middle of the room, as big as the horseshoe-shaped bar in the Willard Hotel and surrounded by nearly as many stools. Silvery pendant lights cast a warm glow over the veined and polished surface.

"Who else is here?" Emilia asked.

"Nobody."

"You rented this place for yourself?"

"For Manolo Bernal," he corrected her. "He's a movie producer, not some local cop doing things on the cheap."

"Fair enough." Emilia pivoted, taking it all in.

"There are bedrooms upstairs," Gamboa said gracelessly. "Pick one."

"What about you?" Where will you sleep?

Gamboa gave her a look of outright pity. "I've got no interest in repeating the mistakes of the past," he said dryly. "I'm using the owner's suite on this floor."

He disappeared down a hallway.

It was nearly midnight. *A surreal end to a surreal day,* Emilia thought as she mounted the stairs. The first floor was so tall that the stairs turned in the middle, pivoting on a landing the size of a cathedral. From the top of the stairs she looked down on a vast foyer, with a carved wooden front door, a red Persian rug the size of a tennis court and a crystal chandelier dripping with loops of glass beads.

The first door she opened led into a bedroom with a king-sized bed and a plush sitting area, plus a television and an en suite bathroom. Emilia shucked off her coat, locked the door, crawled into the bed fully dressed, and fell asleep almost instantly.

CHAPTER 36

Lured downstairs by the scent of coffee, Emilia mistakenly detoured into a huge living room with a fireplace and acres of chairs and sofas before finding the kitchen.

Clad in a black tee and gray sweatpants, Gamboa was seated at the island with an open laptop. Three phones were arrayed next to it, the same arrangement as Campos used. In addition to the electronics, a newspaper was spread out to one side.

On the counter, a coffee maker promised warmth and caffeine. Emilia selected a mug from a row of hooks.

"Congratulations," Gamboa said. "you're officially a fugitive." He flipped the newspaper around.

Emilia fortified herself with a swallow of coffee and read the headline he indicated.

Murder, terror ties, rock Reston community

Mark Pardo, an independent importer of wine from Spain and Portugal, was shot and killed in his home in Reston yesterday. Pardo, 43, was under federal investigation for alleged ties to Middle East terror organizations. Neighbors report hearing shots fired in the early morning. A young woman was seen fleeing the scene shortly thereafter and is being sought as a person of interest.

She has been identified as Emily Encinos, a Mexican national assisting Pardo in his illicit financial dealings. Encinos is described as being of middle height, with long dark hair. At the time of her sighting, she was wearing a gray jacket and matching pants.

Her passport picture was captioned "Emily Encinos, Mexican national." The article briefly noted that she was assumed to be unarmed and provided a hotline number to call if spotted. Then it lapsed into a self-congratulatory paragraph all about how Reston had one of the lowest crime rates in the state of Virginia.

"This whole thing is an utter fabrication," Emilia sputtered.

"Whoever has your passport doesn't understand how Mexican names work," Gamboa observed. "They should have put it as Cruz Encinos."

"That's very comforting." Emilia abandoned the newspaper and slumped onto a stool. "How am I going to get home?"

"Answer me one question, first." Gamboa folded his arms. "Do you believe I had nothing to do with this?"

Emilia looked straight at him for the first time that morning. His eyes were red-rimmed. She realized with a jolt that he'd been crying. "Campos really was your friend, wasn't he?"

"Do you believe me?"

"Yes," Emilia heard herself say. She lifted her chin at the newspaper. "What about you?"

"I think somebody murdered Vicente and set you up to

take the fall." Gamboa didn't mince words.

"So where does this leave us?"

"Partners."

"Not hardly." Emilia turned around and stumbled back to the coffeemaker, barely able to breathe, let alone think. She poured herself another cup, her hand shaking so badly the coffee almost slopped out of the mug.

Congratulations, you're a fugitive. The words spun through her mind, blotting out everything else.

"Whatever's going on, you're the key. Why?" Gamboa's last word hit her between the shoulder blades.

Emilia spun around. "I told you. I have no idea why any of this is happening. It's crazy, just crazy."

"Ruiz is the only person who's got the connections here to make this terror story fly. *Federale* to *federale*."

"And I'm just some *chica* police detective." How was she going to get home to Kurt?

"Let me see that phone you took from the safehouse."

Emilia ran upstairs for the phone. Gamboa found a cord to recharge it. After an anxious few minutes, Emilia was able to show him the footage.

"Do you recognize either of them?" he asked and stopped the video to focus on the grainy faces.

"No." Emilia shook her head.

He played it again. Campos was never in the frame, but the beginning clearly showed the faces of the two cops. It ended as the dark uniforms passed into the house and the soft *thwip, thwip* of the silenced gun took the *federale's* life.

Gamboa tapped the screen to close the video. Emilia turned away to give him some privacy, struck by the raw grief on his face. She opened the refrigerator door and found the makings for a simple ham and cheese omelet.

Campos had been more than an agent handler for Gamboa. Friend, mentor and therapist, too. Campos had once told her that he'd contrived to throw her and Gamboa together in that abortive operation targeting Diego Barrielos Luna's distribution network because he knew they were brother and sister. Gamboa was on the edge and Campos gambled that rediscovering his sister would bring him back from the brink. The plan went awry but now she could feel gentler toward Campos about it.

Gamboa connected the phone to his laptop and downloaded the video. Finally he looked up. "There's got to be a reason why Ruiz set you up. What didn't you tell me last night?"

"I barely know Ruiz." Emilia leaned against the counter. She'd worn the same clothes for 24 hours and felt sticky and stupid, caught in some giant trap and unable to find her way out. "I've only spoken to him twice and I don't even remember the first time."

"What did you talk about?"

"A murder investigation I'm working on in Acapulco. A woman named Monica Montoya was killed in Casa de Plata, the apartment building where you used to leave money for your informant."

"The taxi driver," Gamboa supplied.

"Yes, him." Emilia stared at the ham and eggs as she swallowed more coffee, groping her way out of the fog of fear. "I talked to Campos and Ruiz in the Financial Crimes office. I asked if they knew anything about Monica, seeing as Financial

Crimes still owns the building. Neither had any idea what the mayor's sister was doing there. The place had been turned over to a realtor to sell and was locked up tight. They'd given the keys to the realtor but kept a second set until it sold. Ruiz went to get the extra set of keys and then I left."

"That's all?"

Emilia paused with both hands around the mug. "When Ruiz left the room, Campos told me that your movie is actually going to be released. My scenes and all. I wasn't happy about that and told him so."

"That's it? You didn't say anything else to Ruiz?"

"No, nothing."

"What about the murder investigation? Could Ruiz have killed the girl and Campos found out?"

That was a twist Emilia didn't see coming. "We've got a suspect. It's a domestic. Neither Ruiz nor Campos has anything to do with her murder."

"No links at all?"

"Except that yesterday, before . . . well, before the cops came, Campos admitted that he had talked to Monica a few weeks ago but didn't tell me because it would have compromised the cover for Financial Crimes."

Gamboa gave an odd laugh. "I can see how he'd do that."

It occurred to Emilia that he presented himself as the perfect morning-after lover. Tee shirt stretched tight across pectoral muscles, tousled highlighted hair, barefoot and attentive.

A lesson in how looks could be so deceiving.

She went on. "The dead woman worked for Carlota's re-election campaign. You know, mayor Carlota Montoya Perez.

Half sister to our victim Monica who wanted to know about finance laws. Campos told her he was the wrong person to ask and that she should go to the state attorney general's office."

"That's it?"

"That's it. Our prime suspect is an abusive boyfriend who claims he was with a hooker the night of her murder. She's dead, too. Hopefully he's under arrest for both murders right now."

"Did the boyfriend have access to Casa de Plata, too?"

"That's the only missing link." Emilia put her mug on the island. "I need to call Silvio. Get him to arrest Ruiz. Find out if he and Lima connect somehow."

"Lima's the suspect?"

"Yes." Emilia pointed to the row of cell phones by Gamboa's laptop. "Can I borrow a phone? I need to call Silvio. And Kurt. They'll both be wondering what's going on."

"You really think your gorilla can arrest Ruiz?" Gamboa gathered the cell phones toward himself. "On what grounds? You can't exactly waltz out of here and accuse him."

"Silvio needs to know what's going on. He can help."

"Really? What do you think Ruiz is doing right now?" Gamboa demanded. "He just found out that those two *norteamericano* goons fucked up. They're calling in reinforcements to find you. This is their country, remember, not yours. They've got your passport, put you on a terror watch list, and blocked you from getting help at the embassy. Basically, they've bottled you up. When they find you, they'll make up some resisting arrest bullshit so nobody is very upset that a terror suspect got wiped out."

Emilia gaped at him. She hadn't truly understood the

implications behind the short newspaper article.

Gamboa shook his head at her obvious naivete. "His friends here in El Norte have to get you before you figure out how to finger him and them, too. You have to assume he's watching everyone who's connected to you."

"What about you? Does Ruiz know where you are?"

"I'm not the one in trouble."

"I could call a newspaper." Emilia clenched her fists. "Go public. Show the video from Campos's phone."

"Don't you get it?" Gamboa exploded. "Poke your head above ground and they're going to kill you, same as Campos. And you won't even know why."

"So what am I supposed to do? Let them?"

"I propose a truce," Gamboa said, his voice strained. "You can go back to hating me after we find out who killed Campos and get you back to Acapulco."

Emilia found a frying pan in a cabinet near the giant gas stove, which bristled with knobs. It heated quickly, melting the lump of butter. She watched the eggs whisked with sour cream spread across the hot surface of the pan. "A truce," she repeated.

"Whatever the hell is going on, you're the key to why Campos was killed."

Emilia sprinkled roughly chopped cheese, tomato and ham across the stiffening egg mixture and covered the pan. "All right," she said. "A truce."

What real choice did she have? Gamboa was her only hope of survival right now. After what he'd done to her and other women in the name of a *federale* operation, the irony was almost painful.

"Good enough." Gamboa came to the stove and extended his hand. "Agreed?"

Emilia hesitated, then gave his hand a brief shake.

They ate her omelet and drank more coffee and made plans.

CHAPTER 37

To Emilia's surprise, although nothing should surprise her about him anymore, Gamboa produced a box of hair dye and a pair of glasses with plain lenses. Apparently, he carried a disguise kit in order to change his appearance depending on the requirements of the day.

The dye gave Emilia's hair a honey hue. Together with the big dark frames perched on her nose and a coat of very dark lipstick, she exuded an edgy vibe of Hollywood-meets-bookish-academic.

Moreover, the woman of the house that Gamboa was renting had impeccable taste. She was at least four inches taller than Emilia and her shoes were the size of boats, but her sweaters and underwear fit well, as did a short camel hair coat with rhinestone buttons.

Dressed in borrowed finery, with new hair and the glasses masking her face, Emilia looked nothing like the bland passport photograph in the newspaper or the terrified woman in a gray suit who fled Links Drive yesterday.

"Even I wouldn't recognize you." Gamboa thrust a portfolio and pen at her. "You can say that you schedule meetings with movie people and organize my email."

"Yes, Mr. Bernal," Emilia replied archly. Covered in dark green leather, the portfolio opened to show a pad of lined paper on the right and a clever plastic business card keeper on the left, loaded with cards from film stars and directors, all of whom were very recognizable. "Look, you've got Alejandra Messi's card."

"When you're done gushing, we can go." Gamboa had run clippers over his own head. The blonde highlights were gone, leaving him with a barely-there military haircut that called attention to a hard jaw and muscular neck. He was conservatively dressed in tan trousers and a black turtleneck sweater that fit his chest like a glove. He threw on a short black wool coat with a nautical look and tossed a black daypack into the back of the car. From the heft, Emilia could tell it was heavy.

"What's that?" she asked as she climbed into the passenger seat. "Burglar tools?"

"My go bag." Gamboa settled himself behind the wheel of the Lexus.

"Isn't the house safe?"

"The issue isn't where you sleep. It's making it back there."

"Oh." Emilia felt queasy. "What's in it?"

He called up the GPS app on a cellphone and started the engine. "The usual. Money, passports, alternate electronics."

Emilia digested this in silence, wondering how many phones he had and how he could keep their different purposes straight. More importantly, how many passports did he have? Truce or no truce, if things got sticky, would he disappear on her?

The Lexus purred past a line of huge houses. Immense edifices of sand-colored stone and chalky brick that proclaimed wealth and luxury, but no views beyond leafless trees and grass that looked artificially green. Unlike in Mexico, where houses this big would be concealed behind tall walls topped with razor wire. Here, in the suburb Gamboa said was called Great Falls, each house presented an open face to anyone who went by.

"Is crime very low here?" Emilia asked. "There aren't any walls. There's no privacy."

Gamboa laughed, as if she was ignorant. Emilia flushed.

The foreign landscape slid by. Then they were on a wide boulevard, passing the George Bush Center for Intelligence, which Gamboa told her was the headquarters of the CIA. A right turn and they were zigzagging along a road peppered with pretty houses.

The streets looked different in daylight. More cluttered with stores and signs of all shapes and sizes. The traffic was thick. At times they crawled along behind a line of cars, then everything would speed up with no explanation for the delay.

She knew they were back in the area around Shirlington Village when brick became more prevalent as a building material.

"Here we go." Following the phone's directions, delivered in English which Gamboa apparently spoke as well as he did Spanish, he turned onto O'Grady's street.

"Oh no." Emilia caught her breath as she saw flashing lights ahead.

Gamboa pulled over and cut the engine. "Let's see what's going on."

Frigid air chafed Emilia's cheeks and hands as they walked toward a knot of people on the sidewalk in front of the brick complex where O'Grady lived. An ambulance was there, along with a patrol car with Arlington Police stenciled on the side and the light bar on the roof sending out a distress pattern.

They joined the small group of onlookers who appeared to

be retired neighborhood watchers and two younger women with children bundled in strollers.

"Morning." One of the older men, hands jammed into the pockets of a canvas parka, nodded at Gamboa. "Not what you expect to see, is it? Not around here, anyway."

"What happened?"

"Fella who lived in the apartment there was robbed and killed last night." The man eyed Gamboa. "Did you know him? The police will want to talk to you."

"No, I didn't." Gamboa stepped closer to Emilia. "The wife and I are looking to buy some rental property here, thought we'd walk around."

The old man narrowed his eyes at them. "You people from California? Been coming out of the woodwork, buying up stuff around here, driving up property prices."

Gamboa lifted his chin at the open apartment door. "Was that where he was from? California?"

"New Jersey. Nice kid. Hadn't been here long."

Every muscle in Emilia's body said to run, but she stayed where she was as a cop came out of the apartment, went to the patrol car and extracted a roll of yellow crime scene tape. He talked into a microphone clipped to the collar of his jacket the entire time.

An emergency worker in an unfamiliar uniform came out of the apartment, walking backward as he guided a gurney topped with a black body bag down the steps. Another worker emerged at the head of the gurney and together they got the contraption and its hidden burden into the waiting ambulance.

The cops began stringing crime scene tape across the apartment door, now shut against the wind.

"Sorry to see this happen in your neighborhood," Gamboa said to the old man. "I think we'll keep looking."

Emilia needed no prodding to turn around and go back to the big SUV. "They killed him because he messed up, didn't they?"

"That would be my guess." Gamboa started the engine and made a U-turn. "O'Grady either didn't recognize you last night or did and lost his nerve. Either way, whoever sent him to the Willard decided he was a liability."

"Now what?" Emilia asked. Step 1 of their plan had already imploded.

Gamboa signaled and eased the SUV onto a broad highway. "Let's try out your disguise while I wait for Suarez to get in touch."

His notion of trying out her disguise was a bustling restaurant in Washington DC. Gamboa drove through the heavily congested midday traffic, giving Emilia new things to look at with every turn. When she asked if they were near the Mexican Embassy, Gamboa laughed and said no, they were well north of Pennsylvania Avenue. The place he had in mind was near Logan Square, which meant nothing to Emilia.

Finding a parking spot was almost laughable as Gamboa refused to leave the car with the valet services that commandeered cars in front of every restaurant and business, or so it seemed. They finally found an empty spot, he deftly dropped the Lexus into it, and they walked two blocks past brick mansions clustered together and adorned with spires and turrets and fanciful stonework, to a corner restaurant with flapping awnings called Le Diplomate.

"French bistro style food," Gamboa informed her as they

went in.

At his request, they sat in a booth where the banquette was a curve of red leather facing a round table. From this vantage point, they could both see the entire interior of the restaurant, including the marble faced bar with a tall, mirrored wall behind it.

The restaurant was grand and cozy at the same time. The ceiling was three stories tall, with paneling and pictures and historic memorabilia dotted around and huge cylindrical lights hanging over the dining area. It was a busy place, too, with counter height seating near the bar, regular tables pulled up to a red leather bench that effectively sliced the place in two, and more tables flanked by rattan chairs that Gamboa informed her were French classics. Almost all were filled, making it cheerfully noisy.

No one besides the waiter paid attention to them. Emilia felt shielded by her mannish glasses and *norteamericano* clothing. At the same time, she knew that she and Gamboa made an attractive couple.

"A man alone attracts attention," Gamboa said softly as they each studied a menu peppered with French language items. "A woman alone gets even more. But a couple? Invisible."

If Gamboa had chosen it to show off his polish or intimidate her, it didn't work. Thanks to Jacques, the chef at the Palacio Real, Emilia recognized everything on the menu that was written in French. She ordered the celeriac soup to start and the trout amandine as her entrée.

Gamboa didn't say so, but she knew he was surprised.

It was their second meal together, Emilia reflected.

Gamboa ate like a European, fork in the left hand, knife in the right, and a glass of white wine to go with his salmon and fava beans. Napkin on his lap, the glass of water next to the wine positioned just so.

He needed control over the small things, she decided, because the major parts of his life were wildly unpredictable. Even more so now without Campos tethering him to real life, as fragile and misguided as that thread had been.

Emilia didn't say much as they ate, being busy watching the lunch crowd and keeping Gamboa in her peripheral vision. Besides, what did they have to talk about that could risk being overhead by the foursome in the booth next to them?

Gamboa's pocket chimed when lunch was almost done. To Emilia's astonishment, he pulled out a different phone than the one he'd used for GPS navigation and tapped in a code. The screen transformed into a photograph of the cliffs at La Quebrada. More tapping and he glanced up with a look of satisfaction.

"Suarez will meet us for drinks at five o'clock."

They spent the next two hours shopping. Gamboa paid cash for Emilia's new clothes, including jeans, tops, and a pair of suede boots as soft as velvet. Gamboa bought himself two cashmere sweaters, alpaca wool socks, and a leather duffel bag just big enough for a trip to the gym.

This is ludicrous, Emilia thought as they returned to the Lexus laden with shopping bags. She was a fugitive, homeless without a passport, dependent on a man she once tried to kill, and having a ball spending his money. It occurred to her that the money was really from the bogus Financial Crimes unit and felt better.

They headed south through the endless traffic and ended up at a place called The Dubliner. Closer to the White House and the center of El Norte power now. Emilia felt the shift in the city's mood as if egos flew overhead in flocks like birds.

They were there well before Suarez and once again took a booth so that they both faced the door. The Dubliner was a big place, full of dark paneling with a bar that anchored an entire wall. It smelled both musty with age and yeasty with heavy beer and personal ambition. One part neighborhood bar, another part fabled corner in which to make deals and grease political wheels.

"From France to Ireland and we never even left El Norte," Gamboa said. Without asking, he ordered them both Guinness beer which came in tall glasses rimmed with foam.

Emilia thought it tasted like the gingerbread cake Jacques made for the Palacio Real at Christmas.

Given that Suarez knew that Gamboa was an undercover *federale*, although not the details of the operation against Barrielos Luna, a new identity was needed for Emilia besides Manolo Bernal's assistant. They agreed to say that she was a fellow *federale* sent out from Mexico City, named Ester Rubio. Gamboa would lead the conversation with a story sure to get the CISEN officer's attention.

"There he is." Emilia recognized the blue puffer jacket, this time topping a dark gray suit and a muted striped tie loosened at the neck.

Suarez greeted Gamboa, gave Emilia a lecherous look, and ordered a double Scotch. "Didn't know you were in town, Rafa," he said after the drink came and he'd swallowed half.

"Just passing through." Gamboa exuded relaxation.

"Thought you'd be interested in something I heard."

"What's that?"

"State Department is cleaning house. Cutting the Diplomatic Security Service."

Suarez took it big, sputtering out Scotch. "Where'd you hear that?" he rasped.

"Security chief in the El Norte embassy in Mexico City." Gamboa lifted his glass of Guiness, the creamy foam clinging to the glass above the brown beer, and took a leisurely sip. "Nothing's firm yet, but it looks like the job will go to Marine detachments that are already in embassies."

"No, that can't be right. I would have heard it from my sources here."

Gamboa spread a hand. "Maybe your sources aren't so good."

"Hey, I talked to DSS yesterday." Suarez leaned forward. "Two guys who practically run the place."

"Who?"

"Ted Harris and Clem Abbott."

"Harris and Abbott?" Gamboa shook his head as if he knew who they were and wasn't impressed. "What did they say?"

Suarez snorted. "They're worried about fake visas and the consulate in Acapulco."

"What's so special about Acapulco?"

"The place is a fucking shooting war. Did you hear that the mayor's sister was killed last week? Got the consulate all wound up. It's election season there, you know how it is. If the mayor's family is at risk, so is the El Norte consulate."

Emilia couldn't stay silent. "Did they catch whoever killed

the sister?"

"Arrested her boyfriend." Suarez eyed her with interest. "This your first time in Washington?"

"Yes," Emilia said. "Do those DSS types really know what they're talking about?"

Suarez gave a smoker's hack. "Believe me, they're real upset about that woman getting killed. Name's Montoya, same as the mayor. The cops in Acapulco are either amateurs or paid to look the other way. The guy will walk, like every other criminal there."

Emilia bit the inside of her mouth so hard it bled.

"You need to find some better sources," Gamboa said. "Harris and Abbott aren't plugged in."

"I got a feeling you're right. Can you believe they asked if I knew some fucking folk preacher?" Suarez rubbed his fingers together, an unconscious gesture that betrayed his need for a cigarette. "El Acólito. Ever heard of him?"

"Sorry." Gamboa shook his head. "Can't say I do."

Suarez shifted his attention to Emilia. "What about you? Ever hear of the guy? Runs around the countryside preaching about Santa Muerte."

Emilia managed a little laugh, trying to act amused rather than gutted. "No. What an odd thing."

"If you're going to be here for a few days," Suarez said. "I could show you around."

"She's busy," Gamboa said.

Suarez threw his hands up. Up close, his fingers were yellow from nicotine. "Didn't realize this was your territory."

"Gentlemen, excuse me." Emilia elbowed Gamboa to be let out of the booth. "You two can fight it out while I'm gone."

She felt eyes on her as she walked toward the restroom. Not only was she done with *estupidos* who referred to women as territory, but the knowledge that the cops who'd killed Campos were now looking through his operational history felt like a body blow. She needed a moment to collect herself.

When she came out of the restroom Suarez was gone.

Gamboa helped her on with the camel coat. Neither of them said a word.

Outside it was dark and beginning to rain. They walked rapidly through the cold and wet, dodging pedestrians heading for The Dubliner and its promise of beer, warmth, and noisy socializing.

When they got to the Lexus, Emilia was surprised to find that they'd been walking with her arm threaded through Gamboa's.

CHAPTER 38

Gamboa flipped a switch on the wall in the living room. The fireplace burst into life; flames conjured by magic. "It's gas," he said.

Few houses had fireplaces in Acapulco and Emilia had never heard of a gas-powered one. Where she came from, fire was for outdoor cooking grills. Like the big Regatta Night party when the hotel chefs had grilled shrimp and octopus and *robelo* fillets for the crowd on a grill that was as big as a bus.

Without asking, Gamboa handed her a heavy glass with an inch of amber liquid in it. "Hell of a day," he said.

Neither had been hungry for another meal, although the kitchen yielded an assortment of cheese and sausage that Emilia sliced and arranged, more to keep her hands busy than to actually eat anything. The platter was on the coffee table centered in front of the fire. Two huge leather club chairs faced each other across the low table, making for a separate conversation area. The rest of the living room was more formal, with a collection of plush sofas, low-slung chairs, upholstered ottomans and grand piano.

Emilia sank into a club chair. Gamboa folded himself into the one opposite and kicked off his shoes. His socks matched his tan trousers. Everything he wore looked brand new.

"You held it together pretty well today," Gamboa said, surprising her.

"So did you," Emilia admitted. "I guess those two fake cops found a gold mine of information in Campos's electronics." She couldn't bring herself to say *El Acólito*.

"We knew that already. It's how they knew to send O'Grady to the Willard." Gamboa lifted his glass, letting the firelight lick at the crystal. "He generally used a fingerprint to lock devices. They must have used his body to unlock whatever was at the house."

The fire threw shadows over the Persian rug and shimmered against the glass top of the coffee table. The kitchen light was on, warming the other end of the living room. In their corner, it was up to the fire to chase away the night.

The day had left Emilia despondent and exhausted. The drive back to Great Falls had been a nightmare of traffic and bad weather. Yes, they'd gained some information but nothing that helped them plan the next step.

It was still raining in steady sheets. Water ran down the windows in thick streaks.

"I feel like the clock is ticking against us," Emilia confessed and took a piece of cheese.

Gamboa took a healthy swallow of whiskey. "It's not going to be easy for Ruiz to trace me. His best hope is through credit card transactions. Best to be thinking that Manolo Bernal's got an expiration date. Four, maybe five days."

"But you paid cash for everything."

"Not for the house rental. I've been building a solid cover story for Manolo Bernal for months. No one does business in El Norte with somebody who doesn't have a financial past."

"Four or five days." Emilia absorbed this new detail. The forces against her grew more alarming by the minute. "Then what?"

Gamboa didn't immediately reply but sipped his drink.

The quiet house and the steady sound of the rain created a false sense of stability.

"Tell me about her," he said at length.

Emilia immediately knew that he was talking about their mother, Sophia.

In the past, this was a road Emilia refused to go down with him, especially after he stole Sophia's watch as some sort of twisted keepsake during the one and only time he'd met his real mother.

Tonight, Emilia decided he deserved to know. She didn't have the right to hide Sophia from him.

"She's kind," Emilia said. "A good cook. A good wife to her husband, Ernesto."

Gamboa swirled the whiskey in his heavy cut-glass tumbler. "I didn't expect her to be so young."

"She was 19 years old when her husband died. I was two. You were three."

"Has she always been like that?"

Again, Emilia knew what he meant. "Her husband was dead, she had no money, no place to live and her sister took her son. Her mind broke and she's been like that ever since. She's never had a job. Growing up, I was the adult. Mama was the child."

He didn't reply, just waited for her to go on.

In that moment, it was important to make him understand the past. "When I was little I thought I could fix her. Make her stop crying so much. Make her like other adults who did something to earn money and solve problems. But I never could."

"Did she ever ask about me?"

"No. No one ever said anything. Not my mother. Not my aunt and uncle. Or my cousins."

"Cousins?"

"The sons of Tío Raul and Tía Lourdes." Emilia hesitated. "Tío Raul is our father's older brother. Both of my cousins are cops. Alvaro is head of the evidence locker in Acapulco."

"Older or younger than me?"

"Both older."

She realized he had no idea that these relatives even existed. Part of her wanted to shield her family from him, but another part couldn't help but think that telling him was the right thing to do. In a way, she was paying tribute to Campos and his role as Gamboa's mentor, therapist, and sounding board.

Gamboa rested the glass of whiskey on his flat stomach. "Did you play with your cousins when you were little?"

"We were pretty wild." Emilia laughed. "Little pickpockets, to be honest. Ruben and Alvaro would cause a scene and I'd steal the goods while the shop owner was distracted. We'd sneak onto buses to go to the beach, swim where we weren't supposed to go. When we got older they took me drinking at the Sinfonia del Mar."

"How I envy you." Gamboa's voice was flat. "Karina made sure I had the best of everything and nothing that I wanted."

"I met Karina, you know." Emilia realized that she was treading on thin ice but also sensed she would not get another opportunity. "At first, I thought she was a lovely person. Sad, but refined and elegant. Later, I found out how cruel she was. To my mother." She hesitated. "And you."

"Cruel." Gamboa lifted the glass in an ironic salute to the woman who'd raised him. "Insane would be more a more comprehensive term."

"Growing up with Karina doesn't excuse the things you've done," Emilia said softly. This wasn't the time to pick a fight but neither could she let him use an unhappy childhood to justify his crimes.

He gave her a searching look, then sat upright, cradling the glass in his hands. "When I was four or five, I asked her what had happened to you and my mama. I knew my father had died, I understood that, but not you, not my mother. Karina said you were all dead and if I thought about you then you'd turn into ghosts and haunt me forever. I was terrified. Then she beat me for saying someone else was my mother and locked me in a closet for two days."

Emilia froze in horror.

As they sat by the fire, it was hard to reconcile the serious man in sober *norteamericano* clothing with El Acólito, the mesmerizing Santa Muerte priest who ran around a makeshift stage flaunting a bare chest tattooed with the saint of death. Nor was he Manolo Bernal, the swaggering movie producer making deals to promote a film based on the life of drug kingpin Diego Barrielos Luna. Or even the young Rafa Gamboa, *telenovela* heartthrob.

Who was this man across from her, firelight throwing shadows across his face? The hatred Emilia had carried for him for so long was ebbing, but she didn't know what would replace it. A new relationship with Manolo Bernal? With Rafael Gamboa Escobar? Or Ernesto Cruz Encinos, Junior? He was all of those persons, yet none of them completely.

Gamboa helped himself to more whiskey. "Tomorrow, we need to find ourselves some reinforcements. I know some people at DEA."

"The *norteamericano* Drug Enforcement Agency? But they're *federales*, too."

"Yes, but they're our kind of *federales*. We need to find out how your murder in Acapulco connects to Campos. If it didn't matter, Harris and Abbott would never have mentioned it to Suarez."

"The boyfriend we arrested is an investment banker." Emilia thought about Carlos Lima and wondered if Silvio had pulled a confession out of him yet. Would the *norteamericano* Diplomatic Security Service be mentioned?

"We need to talk to Silvio," she urged anew. "Maybe our suspect has even confessed by now. I know you said Ruiz might be tapping him, but maybe we have to take the chance."

"Did Campos ever meet Silvio? Would his information be in one of Campos's phones?"

"*Por Dios*." Emilia's heart sank. "Yes and yes."

"Still want to call?"

"No." As angry as she'd been at Silvio last week, she wasn't going to put him in Ruiz's crosshairs.

The rain slowed to a patter. Emilia finished her whiskey. It wasn't her drink of choice but given the cold rain and her new status as international fugitive, it was the perfect way to end the day.

"We'll figure it out," Gamboa said. "We've got Campos, Ruiz, State Department security, and your murder investigation in Acapulco. They all connect. We just have to figure out how and why."

Emilia closed her eyes as a wave of fatigue rolled over her. "If only it was so simple."

"What do you think our lives would be like if we'd grown up together?"

It was an unexpected question. Emilia stared at him through sleepy slits. "Probably still be cops."

"We could have started a business." Slouched in the big chair, Gamboa swirled the liquor around his glass. "What about a bookstore like El Pendulo in Mexico City?"

Emilia smiled at the notion. "I've been there. It has a café."

Gamboa lifted his glass to her in a toast to their imaginary success. "Books and coffee in the old part of Acapulco. We'd run it together. On Sunday we'd have big family dinners."

He went on, talking about the books they'd stock and events they'd host there, the store growing bigger and more prestigious with every word.

Emilia sank deeper into the big leather chair. She listened to her brother invent a life he'd never have.

That scared little boy in the dark closet became a man who always needed to escape, to be someone else.

CHAPTER 39

The two DEA agents weren't quite what Emilia was expecting, not that she'd ever met a DEA agent before. To begin with, they were both around her age, rather than steel-haired veterans. They both knew Gamboa, greeting him like an old friend.

The woman, Nora Torres, came across as attractive, toned and aggressive. Emilia knew she'd be good in a bar fight.

An oval face that needed no makeup beyond a well chosen shade of red lipstick. Long dark hair in a single braid down her back. Her leather motorcycle jacket was flung over a tunic-length hand knitted sweater, black leggings and knee-high leather boots.

The other agent's name was Rick Bowen. He was the type of man who could blend in anywhere. Indeterminate ethnicity, medium height, trim build, short curly brown hair, clean shaven, muted plaid coat with patch pockets. He was the first to react after Gamboa related the entire sequence of events. She'd been introduced as a cop from Acapulco working the Monica Montoya murder investigation and shown them Campos's phone so they could view the doorbell video for themselves.

The conversation was in Spanish. Nora spoke Spanish with a Cuban accent.

"Jesus, this is crazy," Bowen blurted. He spoke Castilian Spanish and Emilia guessed he learned it at school, not at home.

"Rafa, these are serious allegations." Nora tapped the

phone's screen to replay the video. "Two State Department officers from DSS shooting up a Mexican safehouse in Reston on orders from someone in your outfit? I mean, this is wild."

"Harris and Abbott," Gamboa supplied. "Can you find out more about them?"

"I don't know." Nora handed the phone back to Gamboa.

They were in the DEA agents' big black Suburban while a frosty wind swirled outside. The vehicle was parked nose out in a small lot fronting a park. No one else was there.

Damp leaves skittered across the lot and disappeared into the trees flanking a paved path. Even inside the Suburban, every lungful of air chilled Emilia to the bone.

"This smells like money laundering," Bowen said. "We'd have to pull in the folks at Treasury."

"No, this is your patch," Gamboa said. "I'm betting this connects back to Diego Barrielos Luna. Ruiz isn't doing this on his own."

"That's not proof of a drug connection," Bowen argued, referring to the phone.

Gamboa rubbed his jaw. "Who else has this kind of money and a very long reach?"

Emilia was next to him in the back seat of the Suburban, snuggled into the leather while he leaned into the space between the two front seats to carry on the discussions with the DEA agents.

Nora touched Gamboa's arm in an unmistakably familiar gesture. "Okay, if we go on the premise that it's not a Treasury issue, what do you need from us?"

"I need to find out who paid Harris and Abbott to hit Campos." Gamboa paused. "And a way to get Emilia back to

Acapulco."

"Given what's been in the newspaper," Nora said. "We'd need a federal judge and a miracle to get her out."

"Jesus," Bowen exclaimed. "We're here with an accused murderer. We could lose our jobs for not turning her in."

Emilia gasped.

"Rick," Nora started but Gamboa cut her off.

"Look, don't you think it's more than a coincidence that Campos is killed and Emilia is set up just when the operation against Barrielos Luna is coming to a head? The distribution deal is signed. The movie could be in theaters in a couple of months. Emilia was part of it."

Emilia was surprised that the two DEA agents were obviously well aware of the scheme to use a movie to lure the fugitive druglord out of hiding. If Gamboa had help from the DEA, it was no wonder that he'd been so successful in El Norte as Manolo Bernal. She wondered if the so-called distribution company was a DEA front.

Everyone in Mexico knew that El Norte's *federales* had unlimited resources.

Half turned toward Gamboa, Bowen bristled. "Money from Barrielos Luna? You think he bought off State Department people to stop the movie? I thought he wrote the damn screenplay."

"I'm saying someone else doesn't want the movie out there. Maybe your State Department doesn't want him out of business because certain people are making too much money allowing his drugs into your country."

Rick scowled, reminding Emilia of Silvio. "That's a baseless charge, Gamboa, and you know it."

"No, I don't," Gamboa said, his voice now quiet and persuasive. "How hard has it been for your organization to do your job? Thin funding. Not enough agents. Your hands tied by bureaucrats as drugs pour over an open border. How many in this country died of opioid overdoses last year? We both know the number is over a hundred thousand and the number will be even higher this year. How long before that number doubles? Whose fault is that?"

"We'll figure it out, Rafa," Nora said, her hand still attached to Gamboa's sleeve. "You're not alone in this."

"Jesus," Bowen swore again. He opened the driver's door. "I can't think. This car's like an oven."

They all spilled out of the big vehicle.

Emilia gasped as she was greeted by an Arctic blast. In ten seconds she'd never been so cold in her life, the moist, heavy air penetrating her new boots as well as the black wool coat and maroon knit cap bought with the unwitting Sandra Baxendale's help. Emilia's eyes watered, turning the greens and browns of the park into a pine-scented blur.

Heads close together, Nora and Gamboa struck out together along a path that led from the parking lot into the wooded area. The shoulder of her black motorcycle jacket pressed against the arm of his wool peacoat. Their strides were even and in sync.

Emilia lingered by the Suburban, sheltered by the wind. Bowen walked a few steps away before tapping a cigarette out of a pack of Camels. He hunched over his cupped hand in order to light it.

Far ahead, Gamboa and Nora strolled past a stand of twiggy bushes. Two minutes later, Emilia could no longer see them at all. She waited, intensely uncomfortable with the dynamics of the situation. Who knows what Gamboa was telling the female agent.

Despite their truce, Emilia couldn't totally rule out being used as a bargaining chip.

She walked over to Rick Bowen. He finished his cigarette and gave her a sideways glance.

"You care about that?" he asked, cocking his head toward the path.

It took Emilia a minute to catch his intent. "Why, what's going on?"

"Don't you know?"

"Tell me."

"Rafa and Nora. They're a thing." He jammed his hands into the pockets of his pea coat and gave Emilia a smirk. "You've got a lot to learn if you're going to keep up with him."

"Yeah, well, maybe I ought to do that." Emilia backed away, liking the situation less and less every second.

She turned on her heel and trotted up the path. The park was a pretty mix of soft snow on evergreens and low bushes wearing a light dusting, but no one else was there to admire the mix of green and white. In the open spaces, picnic tables waited for warmer weather.

The path dipped, a long slow decline that led to a children's play area. The swings dangling from a metal playset moved idly in the breeze, their chains squeaking rhythmically. The ground underneath the swings was slushy and uninviting.

Rafa and Nora stood several steps off the path, partially concealed by a slanted marker showing a laminated map and illustrations of local birds. Arms around each other, they were locked in a smoldering kiss worthy of Romeo and Juliet.

"What's going on here?" Emilia exclaimed.

They broke apart, startled at the interruption.

Emilia felt the other woman's surge of jealousy like an electric charge.

"None of your business, Emilia." Gamboa was quietly furious.

"Wait a minute." Nora took half a step away from him, one hand curled into a fist. "What is going on, Rafa? Is there something you want to tell me? Is she more than just a cop you're working with?"

"I'm his sister," Emilia said.

Nora's eyes whipped from Emilia to Gamboa. "Sister?"

"A friendly warning," Emilia heard herself say. "I found out he was my brother from a rape kit."

"What's she talking about, Rafa?"

"Stop it, Emilia," Gamboa said tersely. "This isn't the time."

"He's hard on women," Emilia went on. "Didn't he tell you about his turn as a Santa Muerte priest in the wilds of Guerrero? Another crazy *federale* operation to get inside the Barrielos Luna organization with a human trafficking scheme. Didn't he tell you about the women who ended up as collateral damage?"

Rafa's face was like thunder. "Shut up, Emilia."

"No, let her go on," Nora said shakily.

Emilia obliged. "I was undercover, investigating a Santa Muerte cult led by a character called El Acólito. Turns out the cult was a cover for a human smuggling operation servicing Diego Barrielos Luna's outfit with young women." Emilia lifted her chin at Rafa. "He was El Acólito and he got his pick before the women were shuttled off to their final destination. He picked me that night."

"Rafa." Nora pressed that clenched fist against her heart. "Is she telling the truth?"

"I told you about the El Acólito operation." Gamboa spoke to her with his eyes boring into Emilia. "Not everything, but almost."

"Rafa." Nora hesitated. "I need to go. Rick and I need to figure some stuff out."

"Nora." Gamboa didn't touch the DEA agent but his whole body pulled toward her. "Let's talk about this."

"Not now, Rafa." Nora stepped onto the path, moving swiftly.

As Emilia stepped aside to let her pass, Nora thumped her with an elbow.

"Bitch." The word was spoken so softly that by the time Emilia was sure she'd actually heard the insult, Nora had disappeared over the crest of the gentle rise.

Emilia took off after the other woman and caught Nora by the sleeve, spinning her around. "Listen, *bitch*," she said hotly. "I thought you might want to know that he's a rapist. One *chica* doing a favor for another. Sorry if it means you have to pull your head out of your ass and face the truth."

Nora shook off Emilia's grip. "Do you have any idea what it takes to survive undercover as long as Rafa has? He's spent years pretending to be one of them. Becoming one of them for as long as it took to survive. You don't know what it's cost him."

"Love must really be blind if you're defending a rapist."

Nora stepped back as if she'd been struck. "I don't think you care about saving some girlfriend you never met from a bad man. You just wanted to hurt him because he hurt you. Okay, mission accomplished."

Footsteps on the path made them both look. Gamboa was there, still seething.

"I've got to go," Nora said and rushed off.

Emilia and Gamboa stared at each other as the sounds of slamming car doors and the rumble of a big engine flowed through the trees.

When the sounds of the DEA agents' vehicle faded, Gamboa lifted his chin. "Let's go."

On the way back to the house in Great Falls, only the chirpy voice of his phone's GPS broke the silence.

CHAPTER 40

Once inside the house, Gamboa disappeared down the hall to the owner's suite.

Emilia collected some fruit and crackers and hustled upstairs to the bedroom. She locked the door and tried to eat but the exchange with Nora Torres had left her shaken and uncertain.

Certainly she had a duty to warn any woman getting involved with a man who had committed rape and sold women in order to ingratiate himself with criminals. The DEA agent should know what kind of a man she let into her bed.

Obviously Gamboa wasn't going to tell Nora that he'd taken advantage of the fringe benefits of the El Acólito operation. Power, women, freedom from basic morality.

Last night, her brother invented a "what if" scenario. What if they'd grown up together, what if Karina Escobar de la Vega had never spirited him away. What if he wasn't the child Karina wanted because he was so like her sister's husband, the man Karina had loved from afar.

He didn't know it, but Gamboa had only touched the tip of the iceberg. There were countless more "what if" scenarios waiting out there. What if Emilia had never volunteered to make that trek to El Acólito's event? What if that investigation never happened?

Emilia reckoned that she would have been just fine if she never knew Rafa Gamboa existed. That he was Ernesto Cruz Encinos, Junior, born a year before her own appearance in the world.

She would have continued to believe in her mother's state of childlike wonder. No painful moment of normalcy, when Sophia all but admitted that when her son was taken away, she no longer wanted to live in the real world. That she chose to live in a fantasy of her own making, choosing what to believe and what to hide from.

Emilia slumped onto the bench at the foot of the bed. Of course she did the right thing in telling Nora Torres the truth, even if the woman didn't appreciate it. Any woman would want to know if her lover had a murky past littered with sexual violence.

The bedroom was traditionally elegant in a very *norteamericano* way, with alabaster walls and a four-poster bed. Emilia's bare feet nestled into a plush carpet the same color as the wall paint. The puffy quilt on the bed was covered in a paisley patterned fabric, all rich red, mustard yellow and a quiet steel blue. The last color carried over to the silk draperies and even the towels in the adjoining bathroom. It was almost like a hotel, minus the helpful staff and Kurt.

She dropped her head into her hands and missed Kurt so hard it hurt. If he was there, she wouldn't feel so helpless. So trapped and dependent on Gamboa.

What if the DEA agents refused to help because of what she'd told Nora? Maybe the truth had shattered Gamboa's working relationship with DEA.

"You have no sense of self-preservation," Emilia muttered to herself.

Footsteps pounded up the stairs, then there was a knock on the bedroom door. "Emilia?"

Emilia leaped off the bench. "What do you want?"

"Open the door," Gamboa ordered.

"It's late. We can talk tomorrow."

Gamboa thumped on the door. "Open up."

"She deserved to know," Emilia declared.

"Open the door!" Gamboa shouted.

"Go away, Rafa!"

Gamboa applied fist to door hard enough to make the wood panel shiver. "Open up!"

Emilia looked around wildly for a weapon. The brass lamp on the bedside table was tall and hefty. She yanked it off the table, the cord popping out of the wall socket.

The locked door trembled under a tremendous blow, then another, and another as if Gamboa was using a battering ram. Emilia barely had time to leap out of the way before the door crashed open, the frame raining splinters. Gamboa stood in the opening, breathing hard.

"I'll be gone tomorrow," he said. Disgust swept across his face at the sight of Emilia holding the lamp like a club. "Don't leave the house."

"Where are you going?" she demanded.

Instead of answering, Gamboa threw the leather duffel from their Logan Square shopping spree into the room. It landed at her feet.

"Make a go bag," he said and disappeared down the stairs.

Emilia tried to slam the door shut but the latch was broken. The door yawned open again. She grabbed her few possessions and the duffel and went into the next room along the hall.

She lay in bed in the dark later, unable to calm down. The door to the new bedroom was locked but the heavy brass lamp was next to her in case of an attack.

Adding to the dreadfulness of the day was the growing realization that she was seeing a lot of herself in Gamboa and vice versa. Their similar physical characteristics were undeniable. They had the same slight curve to the lower lip, same even white teeth, the same hands with broad palms and strong fingers. She and Gamboa even walked the same way with long, forceful strides.

Then there were the less visible but even more acute characteristics. Brother and sister were both hot-tempered. Given to taking action first and asking for permission later. Suspicious of others and angry when those suspicions were proven right.

They were both survivors.

Emilia thought about the fight with Silvio. She'd reacted the same way that Gamboa did tonight. She hadn't apologized to Silvio, either.

Emilia's hand closed around the stout brass stock of the lamp. At least today had made one thing clear.

The truce was over.

CHAPTER 41

He was gone before Emilia came downstairs the next morning. The house was silent, her bare feet echoing on the wood floors.

The coffeemaker was empty, just as she'd left it yesterday. Emilia went down the short hallway to the owner's suite and pressed her ear against the door and heard only more silence. No running water or sounds of someone moving around.

She wondered if Gamboa had abandoned her. No, she decided. As angry as he was yesterday, he still needed her to catch Campos's killers.

Left to her own devices, Emilia inspected her gilded cage. No electronic devices besides a television in a snug den off the living room. No magazines or books in Spanish. The few that were in English were far above her skill level.

She tested all the exterior doors and found that they locked automatically when closed, just like in most houses in Mexico. If she left the house, she wouldn't be able to get back in.

Having organized her go bag, the television kept her company for a few hours. A home decorating show in English. A few slow-moving *telenovelas* that felt more Miami than Mexico City although that's where all the breakup drama and love triangles supposedly took place. The issues were juvenile compared to what she was living through. Emilia turned it off.

She periodically checked the front of the house, half expecting to see a dark sedan glide up to the curb. But there were few cars. It wasn't the sort of neighborhood where people walked anywhere, either. Nothing was very close by.

The kitchen was an island of last resort. Emilia wandered through, opening cupboards, investigating the stock of food and cookware. The amount of dry goods was seemingly endless.

She decided to make herself a batch of *buñuelos*.

The fried treats recalled childhood days. She and her cousins clamored for Sophia and Tía Lourdes to make *buñuelos* a thousand times.

The recipe was simple. Flour, baking powder, sugar and salt in a bowl, estimating the amount of each. That done, Emilia used her fingers to bore a well in the center of the dry mixture and added an egg and a spoonful of vanilla, plus a drizzle of butter melted in the microwave.

Turning it into coarse grains was therapy, anxiety driving her hands to make light work of this step. Next spoonfuls of warm water until the granular mixture turned into a proper dough she could knead on the surface of the island.

The hard part of making *buñuelos* was dividing the dough into balls and flattening each until it was paper thin. It was absorbing work to roll and stretch, then fry them one by one. The end result was a stack of light and crispy golden circles. She scattered sugar over them, made herself a pot of coffee and was just about to indulge in a carb coma when the door to the garage swung open. Gamboa strode in like a landlocked sailor in jeans and navy peacoat.

"What's this?" He looked around at the messy kitchen.

"I made *buñuelos*." Emilia pointed to the stack. "I had some time on my hands."

"You buy *buñuelos* in the store."

"Poor people make them at home."

"Christ, whatever." Gamboa plucked the one from the top of the stack and bit into it, sugar cascading down his front. "Get your coat and your go bag. We need you to listen to something."

It was another silent ride in the Lexus, heading southeast as twilight fell on a mix of highways and wide boulevards. No GPS this time; Gamboa obviously knew the way.

The streets narrowed until they were in a neighborhood of small apartment complexes, shabby shops and broken sidewalks. They passed restaurant after restaurant tagged with signs, some hand-lettered. Foods of every nationality vied for attention. Greek, Vietnamese, Chinese, Guatemalan.

These were the local versions of the neighborhood *taqueria*. Emilia guessed each was long on good food and short on sanitation.

Rafa parked in the lot behind a small brick apartment building. "We're in Arlington. This is Nora's place."

Emilia didn't reply.

They trotted up three flights to the top floor.

Nora waited in an open doorway, wearing red lipstick again in combination with a fleece shirt and more black leggings. "Hello," she said cooly.

Emilia matched the woman's glacial squint with one of her own.

The apartment was bigger than the exterior of the building suggested, with a row of iron-framed windows slicing the far wall of the living room into thirds. An armless red leather sofa would have fit the mid-century architecture of Casa de Plata, same for the surfboard-shaped walnut coffee table. Two vintage posters advertising movies starring aliens and astronauts provided humor and more pops of red.

Other than that, the apartment carried the lonely vibe of an occupant who wasn't there very much. No plants, no bowl of fruit, no photos of friends, family or lovers.

Rick Bowen was there, seated at a small table by the farthest window, tapping on a laptop. He raised his eyes and nodded at Emilia. "Nice to see you again, Detective."

When they were all seated around the small table with him, Bowen produced a flash drive and plugged it into the laptop. "This is a download from the hard drive of a man named Lennox--."

"Thomas Lennox?" Emilia cut him off.

Bowen paused, hands hovering over the keyboard. "Yes. How did you know?"

"I met him in Mexico City. He tried to scam me. Said he was the Legal Attaché."

The rush of memories hit her hard. Lennox had presented himself to Emilia as a trusted diplomat. His approach was a ruse to stop the federal task force from investigating the Amistad 43 mass kidnapping instigated by Diego Barrielos Luna.

"Lennox was a Foreign Service Officer for the State Department for fifteen years," Bowen said. "Disappeared off the radar screen for a couple of years, then resurfaced as part of Diego Barrielos Luna's inner circle. By the way, we're not supposed to be chasing fellow Americans. You can't tell anyone that we have this."

"Who would I tell?" Emilia almost laughed but then realized she knew something the others didn't. "Lennox was with the team that attacked the convoy taking Barrielos Luna to the border.”

Gamboa frowned. “Where did you hear that?”

“I was there.”

“You were there?” Gamboa made no attempt to hide his surprise. “You didn’t tell me that.”

“It didn’t exactly come up.”

“You two can argue later.” Nora threw down a pad of paper and some pens. “Lennox is apparently in Mexico. He makes calls with an app that simulates a cell phone and records them. Listen and jot down anything you think is relevant.”

Emilia eyed the little flash drive sticking out of the side of Bowen’s laptop with suspicion. “You really think this is the real thing and not a bunch of crap Barrielos Luna wants you to have so you run in the wrong direction? Where’d you get it?”

“It’s real,” Gamboa said shortly. “We’ve already listened to a few calls.”

Rick turned the laptop so they could all see the screen. Two icons were labeled *Friends* and *Travel.* “These two folders are empty. The Default folder has audio files in it.”

He clicked on the third icon and a list of files popped up. Similar to the opaque spreadsheet of Monica Montoya’s phone use, each entry was titled with an automatically-generated series of numbers capturing the date and time of the call. Emilia leaned in to see the column showing the size in kilobytes of each audio file.

“Chronological order or take up where we left off?” Rick said, the cursor hovering over a tiny triangle at the top of the list.

“Chronological order,” Gamboa said. “I want Emilia to

hear everything."

The view rippled, readjusting the order. Now the list was topped with a date from six months ago. Rick clicked on the first file.

Throaty male laughter filled the air.

Mi corazón, I've missed you.

It was Thomas Lennox all right, speaking excellent Spanish with a strong *norteamericano* accent that flattened all the vowels. Emilia gave an involuntary shiver. The last time she'd heard his voice was during a nightmare of fire and death. She could almost hear again the thudding cadence of the helicopter that led the attack on the convoy heading to the border. Lennox and his gang of cartel *sicarios* had blown the doors off the armored van carrying Barrielos Luna to prison in El Norte.

The other police officer guarding the prisoner had saved Emilia's life but lost his own. Lieutenant Leonel Cardenas had been a friend. A lump surged into her throat.

"You okay?" Gamboa was staring at her.

Emilia swallowed hard. "Sure."

Lennox and a woman conversed for five audio files. He only mentioned her name once, calling her Pilar. In between scripted comments about packages and vacations, they made arrangements to meet using more codewords. Lennox ended every conversation by telling Pilar to be careful. *Ten cuidado, mi corazón.*

"She's a mule," Emilia said. It was maddening to listen to the voices planning the movement of drugs but not know what or where or how much.

Gamboa blew out his breath. "Obviously. Do you

recognize her voice?"

"No, she's no one I know."

The next five audio files were much the same. Emilia hoped to find a pattern to the unseen Pilar's movements or a way to break the code but the conversations were too random.

At one point, Lennox referred to oranges, which was right out of Barrielos Luna's screenplay for *A Misunderstood Man*. Emilia stole a glance at Gamboa. He rolled his eyes in an unexpected moment of mutual dark humor.

"I can't do more of this without an adult beverage," Bowen grumbled after an hour.

Nora produced beer and ordered pizza. It was dark outside the trio of windows. Cold seeped through the glass. Gamboa made a pot of coffee, clearly knowing his way around Nora's tiny kitchen.

A short pause for food and then Bowen clicked to start the next audio file.

Lennox opened the conversation in a harsh, impatient tone. The voice that answered him was that of a young man who wavered between bravado and trepidation.

Did you do as your uncle asked?

Yes. How is he?

He is well, very well. He asks if you are ready for so much responsibility.

Of course I'm ready. I am my father's son. I am El Barracuda.

Your father is in jail. It's better to be your uncle's nephew. And my student.

I've been practicing, just like you said. I'm good, real

good. Soon, everyone will know El Barracuda.

Listen to me. The Cathay Constellation docks in two days. The trucks are ready. I'm sending you the papers. Do you remember what to do?

Yes.

Good. Take the papers to the Customs warehouse at six o'clock in the evening that day. Not five and not seven. Precisely at six. The trucks will be waiting. Make sure all the oranges get loaded.

Do I go with them?

No. Stay in Acapulco.

The call ended with Lennox's habitual *Ten cuidado.*

"I think it's safe to say that the oranges aren't real fruit," Gamboa said. He looked at Emilia. "You look like you've seen a ghost."

It's better to be your uncle's nephew. And my student.

Emilia pressed her hands together, more agitated by this phone call than any of the others. "Lennox was speaking to Barrielos Luna's nephew. He's a kid named Nestor Flores."

They all stared at her.

"His mother is Barrielos Luna's half-sister, Adelita Garay Luna." Emilia felt almost dizzy. "Her husband Erik Flores owned the bus company in Lindavista that was involved in the Amistad 43 kidnappings. Adelita and Erik are both in jail."

"Flores." Gamboa leaned forward. "Didn't they also own the property where the bodies were found?"

"What was left of the bodies, anyway." Nausea rose every time Emilia remembered the barrels of acid used to dissolve the bodies of the 43 students who'd been in the wrong place at the wrong time.

"Flores," Gamboa repeated, drawing out the word. "Parents in jail, uncle on the run. Now the kid's learning the business from his uncle's pet gringo."

Emilia nodded. Nestor Flores would be 17 years old now, casting himself in the Barrielos Luna mold and giving himself a bold moniker. *El Barracuda.*

Even more so than finding Monica Montoya's killer, catching young Flores and getting him to turn on his uncle would be a brilliant way to end her police career. And a sharp stick in Chief Salazar's eye.

"I need to get back to Acapulco," Emilia said.

CHAPTER 42

It was nearly midnight when Emilia and Gamboa headed back to Great Falls. The quartet had listened to about half of Lennox's conversations. Apart from discovering that Diego Barrielos Luna's nephew was trying to style himself as the next great *sicario*, Emilia was impressed with the DEA's obvious access to Lennox.

Proximity was everything, given Lennox's status as a criminal wanted in both Mexico and El Norte. Whoever the asset was who had the guts to get close enough to suck information out of Lennox's computer, they had her unbridled admiration. She wondered if they were still alive or had died smuggling the flash drive to the DEA.

A few snowflakes floated out of an inky sky to settle on the Lexus as Gamboa drove through the residential neighborhood. Despite everything, Emilia was entranced. Snow was marvelous.

Great Falls was tucked in for the night. No other cars, no one on the sidewalks.

Houses were dark except for lights over front doors, revealing decorative wreaths and front lawns glittering with frost.

As they turned toward the house, the headlights swept across the street, lighting up a sedan parked facing oncoming traffic.

"That's the car," Emilia gasped as they went past it. "I recognize the *placas*!"

As if on cue, the sedan's headlights flashed on, blinding the rearview mirror of the Lexus. At the same time, another set of headlights zoomed directly toward them.

"Hold on," Gamboa said tersely. Tires screaming in protest, the Lexus fishtailed to a halt. Emilia was flung forward against the safety harness so hard it cut off her breath. Gamboa shifted into reverse. Gravity pressed Emilia against her seat belt like a massive hand.

He stamped on the accelerator and they careened backward, Emilia gasping for air. They were suddenly retracing their route, rear end first, as the headlights coming at them lit up the windshield and revealed a mid-size SUV.

Gamboa hit a curb. One corner of the Lexus bounced up like a carnival ride. Emilia was momentarily weightless.

White light filled the windshield. Gamboa braked hard. The Lexus spun, the night careening past Emilia's window, then hurtled through the intersection and toward the main road.

Emilia instinctively ducked as Gamboa shouted at her to *stay down, stay down*. The window behind her made a terrifying popping sound but didn't shatter. Wind whistled through a hole the diameter of her thumb, dagger-like cracks wreathed around it.

Gamboa kept his foot down as they passed green signs overhead for something called a Beltway. It seemed to Emilia that they were flying through a dark chute, the SUV and sedan still with them. An enormous highway yawned at the end of the chute. Four lanes in each direction, the opposing lanes separated by an undulating line of concrete barriers topped with short green poles. Traffic moved fast.

The Lexus screamed onto the highway and jockeyed for

position, Gamboa weaving in and out of lanes, trying to shake the two other vehicles. More signs flashed overhead and were gone before Emilia could read them. Trees loomed on the right, a wavering wall of darkness every time they jinked into the far lane.

Emilia glimpsed a sign welcoming them to Maryland. A second later giant green signs rose ahead directing them to other numbered roads: 270 and 95.

"Do you know where we are?" Emilia quavered.

Gamboa split his concentration between the road ahead and the mirrors. "Right . . . where . . . I want."

He jerked the car into the lane second from the barriers, tapped the brake. The Lexus bucked and slowed. The SUV chasing them drew up beside them. Gamboa braked sharply again, then tucked in right behind the smaller SUV. Now they were both in the far left lane streaking past the concrete barriers.

Emilia could almost sense the other driver's desperation as the Lexus rammed his rear bumper, shooting the vehicle ahead. Both she and Gamboa were jolted badly but he didn't slacken his speed.

The SUV swerved into the next lane in an attempt to get away. The hunter was now the prey. Emilia caught Gamboa smiling as he maneuvered behind the other vehicle again, then cranked the wheel hard.

They hit the rear quarter of the SUV at full speed, pushing it into a spin. The SUV shot across two lanes and slammed into the concrete barrier with the rending sound of tearing metal and speed chewing rock.

The Lexus flew past. The wreck was instantly in the

rearview mirror. "Where's the other car?" Gamboa demanded.

Emilia's head was on a swivel, but she couldn't distinguish the headlights growing smaller behind them. "I don't know."

"Let's get off this." Gamboa eased into the right lane. He took the exit marked River Road.

Their speed bled off. Emilia couldn't tell what damage the heavy Lexus had sustained but the ride was considerably bumpier than before.

The drive was a blur of confusing roads until they got on the highway leading to the airport. "This road has cameras," Gamboa said. "Hopefully they'll think Manolo Bernal took a flight out."

"Do you think they know we're together?"

"I think that's a safe bet."

Keys on the driver's seat, they left the dented Lexus in a vast parking lot at Dulles Airport and shouldered their go bags. As they headed for the terminal, Emilia felt the adrenaline sing in her veins and knew she'd crash soon but the wild ride through the darkness had been beyond exhilarating.

There was a line of gray taxis outside the terminal, the words *Dulles Flyer* emblazoned on the side of each car. Gamboa asked the first driver in line for budget hotel suggestions and they were rewarded with a short trip to one in nearby Sterling, Virginia. Once there, he paid cash for a single room.

Emilia didn't complain. Couples were invisible.

"Well, it's cheap all right." Gamboa said, looking at the vinyl paneling and faded bedspread. He closed the curtains.

"Which one of us gets the bed?" Emilia asked.

"Be my guest." After a turn in the bathroom, Gamboa

grabbed a pillow, pulled the coverlet off the bed, wrapped himself in it and stretched out on the carpet.

Emilia climbed into the bed and covered herself with a thin cotton blanket and the black coat. She turned out the light and willed her heart rate to calm down.

She heard Gamboa shift position. "Would it help if I changed my name to Ernesto Cruz, Junior?" he asked quietly.

"Help what?" she murmured, eyes closed.

"Help us. You know, be a family."

Emilia's eyes flew open. "Be a family?" she squawked and sat bolt upright. "What would help is if you were actually sorry for what you did to me and all those other women whose lives were torn apart by your El Acólito act. Apologize and do something to help them. Until then it doesn't matter what your name is. Call yourself Button for all I care."

Breathing like she'd just run a marathon, Emilia waited for a reply.

All she got was the sound of Gamboa snoring evenly and peacefully.

CHAPTER 43

It took two hours and a taxi, a bus, and the Metro system to get to Nora's apartment the next morning. Along the way, Gamboa bought a copy of *The Washington Post* and scanned the newspaper for reports of a major accident on the Beltway, but there was nothing. Nor was there anything about the search for Emily Encinos, a person of interest in the murder of terror suspect Mark Pardo in Reston.

"People in El Norte get bored quickly," he observed.

Once they told Nora and Bowen about the car chase, the sense of urgency was palpable. The four wasted no time gathering around the laptop again. Bowen found where they'd left off and clicked on the next audio file.

Lennox and Pilar crooned at each other for the next twenty minutes. Nothing about El Barracuda, just cloying love talk, with a few snippets of coded talk about moving oranges.

The morning dragged on. Lennox talked to several unidentified men about ordinary things. Women, movies, tequila, video games. Neither Emilia nor Gamboa could say if Ruiz was one of them.

A coffee break helped. Gamboa and Bowen had a pushup contest. Gamboa won.

"How many more?" Emilia asked wearily when Lennox ended another conversation with his usual *ten cuidado*.

Rick peeled himself off the carpet and checked the laptop screen. "Forty-seven."

Nora pulled on a red sweater over her tee shirt and another

pair of black leggings. "I'll make more coffee."

The next audio began. Lennox offered an enthusiastic greeting.

Emilia caught her breath.

Gamboa scrambled back into his seat. Nora came out of the kitchen with a canister of coffee in her hand.

For the first time, Lennox was speaking English.

Settled in?

Yes, no problems at all.

Good, good. Time to get to work.

What we talked about . . . I know exactly how to make it happen with big amounts of cash every time. No questions asked.

I knew you would. Just do it like we discussed.

Okay.

Our friend likes the mayor there. It's important to keep the status quo. You catch my meaning?

I see billboards all over. She seems very popular.

Don't believe everything you hear. Our friend needs you to put your thumb on the scales. Find a way to funnel cash into the campaign. Three percent of what you move.

Three percent is a big chunk of change. Who's on the receiving end?

That's up to you.

Me?

You're an American. Doors will open. If not, knock them down.

Do I get paid extra for this, ah, side job?

Sure, if she gets reelected. More than you ever dreamed of.

Proximity to our friend is where the money is.

Yeah, I hear you.

Three percent. Make sure you keep track because he is.

Don't worry, I can count.

That's why I like you. Enjoy the sunshine. Ten cuidado, hombre.

"I know him," Emilia breathed. "The man talking to Lennox."

"Who is it?" Gamboa demanded.

"His name is William Gifford." Emilia closed her eyes, seeing his charming smile and tortoiseshell glasses. "He's in charge of something important at the new consulate in Acapulco."

Bowen leaned back and let out a long whistle. "This is not good."

"They're talking about laundering money through the consulate." Nora put the coffee can on the table, the measuring scoop in her hand.

"Play it again," Gamboa ordered.

One bit of the conversation stood out even more the second time Emilia heard it. *Our friend likes the mayor there. It's important to keep the status quo.* She looked across the table at Gamboa. "You realize who the friend is, don't you?"

Gamboa grimaced. "Lennox just bought Barrielos Luna a diplomat who's been tasked with funneling money so the mayor of Acapulco gets re-elected."

"Carlota," Emilia supplied. "Carlota Montoya Perez."

"This is not good," Bowen repeated. He got out of his seat and stretched. "Embassies and consulates are sovereign national entities, which is why it was such a big deal when Ecuador breached your embassy in Quito to grab the former vice president who was wanted for embezzling or fraud or whatever. All our consulates and embassies use American dollars. Somehow, this Gifford character is using the State Department system to launder drug money for the Barrielos Luna organization."

Emilia pressed both hands to her head. Until this minute, Gifford had been one of the good guys.

The next conversation was with Pilar, followed by a two-second exchange with an unknown man that revealed nothing.

Bowen clicked to the next audio file and suddenly Lennox was speaking English again.

CHAPTER 44

Is the arrangement working?

Smooth as silk. Three percent goes a long way here. Her half-sister knows how to get things done.

Emilia gasped aloud. Nora glared.

Rick paused the audio. "What?"

It took Emilia three tries to get the words out. "He's talking about Monica Montoya, the mayor of Acapulco's half-sister. I've been investigating her murder."

"Things are starting to fall into place," Gamboa said.

Rick restarted the audio.

We've gotten friendly. More than friendly.

You dog! Good in the sack?

Let's just say that three percent and a cheap diamond buys a lot of enthusiasm.

What is she doing?

The word influencer doesn't begin to describe the way this woman works. She's greased enough palms for this whole city to slide right into the mayor's lap.

Make sure you keep a low profile. I don't want to see you in the newspaper as her arm candy. Especially if she gets fingered for buying an election.

No worries. Our engagement is not public knowledge.

Engagement? Are you serious?

For as long as it takes. But it's a secret.

How'd you work that?

It was her idea. She has a rich boyfriend she wants to dump but mama likes him, thinks he's gonna solve all their family money problems. I'm just some desk jockey gringo, my pockets can't compete. I understand, I told her. We'll sit tight until after the election.

I knew you were a lucky bastard.

Yeah, she's more worried about upsetting mama than she is about where the money is coming from. More importantly, she'll do anything to get in good with the sister.

God, I love it. You're a hell of an operator.

Yeah, one thing. We got an issue with your courier.

What's that?

He's a kid with a temper.

You just do what you're supposed to do and he'll do what he's supposed to do. All good, see?

Sure.

Okay, then. Ten cuidado, hombre.

"Gifford set up Monica with a fake engagement," Emilia exclaimed when the audio ended. "The fucking bastard."

Nora looked up from her notes. "I thought you said she was dead."

"She is. The autopsy showed that the blood on her finger was smeared like someone had pulled off a ring post mortem. She had a ring box in her car, too. No one knew where it came from."

Emilia blinked furiously, appalled to be on the brink of tears. Poor Monica. Duped by Gifford into thinking that he loved her when he was merely using her to inject money into

Carlota's campaign.

The diplomat was such a smooth liar. Emilia wanted to kick herself for swallowing his explanation about the consulate phone number. He used that phone to communicate with Monica.

Of course, Gifford was the person Monica met at Café Romeo, too, because he was new to Acapulco and didn't know it was a tourist trap the locals avoided. If Telmex had provided the content of Monica's last text message, it would be something like, *I'm here. Where are you?*

"Twenty more to go." Rick rubbed his eyes with the heels of his hands. "Who needs a break?"

"What time is it?" Nora stood up and stretched. Her red sweater matched the armless sofa.

"Almost five o'clock." Gamboa showed his watch.

They all had more coffee, although Emilia was already queasy from drinking so much.

More nauseating conversations with Pilar didn't help.

They were on the second to last file when Lennox spoke English again.

You've got a problem. Your girlfriend went to the cops.

What? No, she didn't. It's all good.

I've got a source. Believe me, she went to the cops. Get rid of her.

No, no. I would know if she did.

Find someplace quiet and make sure she never leaves.

Wait a minute . . . you're not serious, are you?

Nobody's asking, I'm telling you. She just turned into a serious liability.

No, there's got to be another way. I'll talk to her.

You don't get it, do you? She talked to somebody who can really make trouble for us and he passed on the word. We've got serious trouble unless we shut her up fast.

She really told the cops?

What don't you understand? She told the wrong people. We're in full damage control mode.

Good lord, I've slept with her. We're engaged.

Our friend isn't giving you a choice. You understand?

Oh God, oh God. I can't.

It's her or her and you. Your choice.

Oh God, okay, okay.

Someone will contact you with a place and time. You just get her there.

It wasn't supposed to be like this. She never said anything to me about going to the cops.

That's good. Maybe our friend won't blame you.

Oh God, oh God.

Man up and keep your mouth shut, understand?

Yeah, sure.

Ten cuidado, hombre.

The very last conversation was in Spanish. It was brief. Lennox gave Nestor Flores the address of Casa de Plata in Acapulco's Colonia Progreso neighborhood.

CHAPTER 45

"We arrested the wrong man," Emilia said, swamped with guilt. "The boyfriend. He's a total shit. But he didn't kill her."

She got up and paced, too agitated by the mistake to stay in her chair at the table. "His alibi was paper thin. We had a character witness who said he hit Monica, that he was abusive. And the woman he was supposedly with the night of the murder turned up dead, too."

Nora gazed at her with eyes that matched her sweater.

Bowen's face was lined with exhaustion.

"Don't get stuck on that," Gamboa ordered. "Gifford took your murder victim to Casa de Plata because Ruiz knew she'd talked to Campos."

Nora frowned. "What's Casa de Plata?"

"It's an empty four-unit apartment building in Acapulco." Gamboa paused. "We used it for an operation, then Campos decided to get rid of it. It's been empty for years."

"Am I getting this right?" Nora looked around the table. "On Lennox's instructions, a Foreign Service Officer named Gifford from our consulate in Acapulco is laundering money through State Department channels. Not only that, but he greases an election campaign because Barrielos Luna likes the mayor and wants her to stay in charge. To do it, Gifford starts a relationship with the mayor's sister. Gives her three percent of whatever he's laundering to dump into her sister's re-election campaign. She talks to somebody who makes Lennox nervous, so he gets Gifford from the consulate to lure her to an empty apartment building where Barrielos Luna's nephew kills her."

"Yes," Emilia breathed, recalling the day she and Silvio heard Carlota's argument with Hector Placido about campaign spending. "That's exactly what happened. That's why Monica Montoya was killed. Because she talked to Lieutenant Campos, thinking he really was in charge of Financial Crimes. She made it sound like the other campaign was doing something fishy."

Nora threw up her hands. "Your murder victim was dumber than a box of rocks."

No dumber than you sleeping with El Acólito.

Emilia pushed the thought away. "Gifford took back the engagement ring after she was dead. He probably thinks no one can connect him to her murder because nobody knew they had a relationship."

"Without this audio file, probably no one would. You said yourself that you arrested the wrong guy."

The tiny living room was cluttered with pizza boxes, notebooks, glasses, mugs, and paper napkins. Outside, the cityscape was bathed in battleship gray, kept from true darkness by too many apartment windows, streetlights, and car headlights boring yellow holes through the gloom.

Emilia realized how all the pieces were slotting into place. "When I saw Campos on Monday, he said that Monica actually thought Financial Crimes was really Financial Crimes. He thought she was asking because another campaign was engaged in mismanagement or fraud or something like that. Not Carlota's. He brushed her off with some stock answers and she went away happy."

Nora caught on immediately. "She actually wanted to

know about campaign finance because she was funneling Barrielos Luna's money into the mayor's reelection campaign. After it got washed through the consulate."

"Ruiz must have been there when she came to see Campos," Gamboa said. "He thought she confessed to the arrangement to launder Barrielos Luna's money and he sold the news to Lennox."

Emilia cast her mind back to the day she had talked to Campos and Ruiz about Casa de Plata. "When I interviewed Campos and Ruiz about Monica's murder, for a few minutes Ruiz was out of the room."

"Ruiz must have figured that Campos told you." Gamboa passed a hand through his hair, looking more agitated than Emilia had ever seen him. "Okay, I think we're putting it all together. Lennox and Gifford set up the money laundering thing through the consulate for Barrielos Luna. Gifford gets a bonus for keeping Carlota in office in Acapulco. Does it the easy way with a honey trap. The sister agrees to take his cash because she wants Carlota to win, too."

"But she gets nervous at some point." Emilia took up the line of reasoning. "Monica goes to Campos because she thinks he's really Financial Crimes and makes up a story about her sister's rival doing something bad. But it's just a cover story." She paused, holding up a finger. "Ruiz knows Monica talked to Campos but not the details. So he assumes the worst, which is that Monica told Campos everything and that Campos told me."

"It explains why Ruiz set you up here," Gamboa said grimly. "And arranged for Campos to be killed."

"And how Monica got into Casa de Plata." Emilia wanted

to bury her head in her arms and howl. How many hours had been spent fruitlessly questioning would-be purchasers, cleaners, and landscapers? "Ruiz had access to the keys this whole time. He could have made extras any time and given them to anyone."

"Like the nephew," Bowen added. "This El Barracuda character."

"Obviously, Lennox and Ruiz know each other," Emilia pointed out. "But how?"

"We know Lennox worked at the embassy in Mexico City," Nora said. "Did this guy, this Ruiz, ever work in Mexico City, too?"

"Of course he did." Gamboa rubbed his eyes. "I'll bet if you dig you'll find out that Lennox, Gifford and Ruiz all worked on something together. Goodwill, partnerships, et cetera."

"The Merida Initiative," Emilia suggested. "Everybody was involved in that."

"We were all going to combat drug trafficking, transnational organized crime and money laundering." Gamboa gave a hard laugh. "All it did was teach everyone how to pocket gringo money without being caught."

"Wait a minute." Nora rapped on the table. "Why does Barrielos Luna want this mayor re-elected?"

"I don't know," Emilia admired the way the other woman picked through the chaff to spot a key point. "Nobody's accused her of taking bribes or money from him."

"Still." Nora raised her eyebrows. "I'd really like to meet her. Look her in the eye."

"First things first," Gamboa said. "How do we get this

Gifford to squeal?"

"Get me back to Acapulco," Emilia said. "I'll arrest him."

Bowen frowned. "Arrest Gifford?"

"Of course, arrest him. If not for murder, then as an accomplice."

"You can't arrest Gifford in Mexico." Bowen closed the laptop. "He's got diplomatic immunity."

"He arranged for the mayor's sister to be murdered!"

"Doesn't matter. He's still got diplomatic immunity."

Emilia threw herself back in her chair and looked in her coffee mug. It was empty. "So now what?"

"Do we have to decide now?" Bowen yawned.

Dawn had fully claimed the sky in shades of orange and purple and a red streak that matched Nora's sweater. The colors seemed to captivate Gamboa who remained with his back to the living room.

"There's a man in prison right now for a crime he didn't commit," Emilia said. "Carlos Lima might be a jerk, but he doesn't deserve the bull pen."

"The what?" Nora blinked at her.

"A prison that's basically a corral for killers," Gamboa said to the window. "How tough is he?"

"He's a banker who wears fancy suits and gold cufflinks."

"Then there's no rush. He's probably dead already."

"Rafa!" Nora jumped up. "Let's think, people. Mexican law enforcement can't arrest Gifford, but the Legal Attaché in Mexico City can. If the Con Gen in Acapulco hears that Gifford has been laundering money through the consulate she'll want to cooperate."

"Money laundering?" Emilia exclaimed. "I want him for

murder.”

“You need to arrest Nestor Flores for murder,” Gamboa said. “Not Gifford.”

Emilia stalked to the window and spun him around. “Campos was attacked in Acapulco. He won the fight and made us all believe that the dead man was him. Now that man is in the morgue. Who do you think he is?”

Gamboa swore, sounding oddly like Silvio. “Nestor Flores.”

“You win the prize.” Emilia sank onto the spare red sofa. “I never thought to ask the age of the body. I just assumed it was Campos.”

“We’ve got a support flight in two days,” Bowen said thoughtfully.

“Not to Acapulco,” Nora said.

“But it could.” Bowen snapped his fingers, more animated than he’d been all day. “We can come up with a reason to lay over in Acapulco, at least for one night. Gives us an opportunity to talk to the Con Gen.”

“Not without me!” Emilia flared.

Gamboa pointed at Emilia. “Could you get her on the flight?”

Nora rolled her eyes. “Without a passport? No way.”

In response, Gamboa went to the black daypack which he’d dropped by the door. He pulled out a Mexican passport.

Emilia gasped.

“It’s not yours,” he said shortly. “This is a passport for Alejandra Messi so she can take a very private charter flight from her place in California to do some voiceovers without ever having to explain the extra stamps in her personal passport."

He opened the passport and slapped it on the table. "Could Emilia pass for Alejandra Messi?"

The two DEA agents peered at the passport photo. Emilia rocketed off the sofa and squeezed between them.

"Jesus," Bowen murmured, transferring his gaze to Emilia. "It might work."

"The eyes and the chin are right." Nora picked up the passport and held it up to compare with Emilia's face. "The nose is different, though."

"What about the real Alejandra Messi?" Emilia quavered.

"I'll deal with her people."

Nora tilted the passport, still comparing it to Emilia. "Close but no cigar, as the saying goes. Somebody will notice the difference. Alejandra Messi's pictures are everywhere. Plus, what about the biometrics?"

Gamboa stepped back, running a critical eye over Emilia in a way she didn't like. "What if she was sick?" he asked. "They'd breeze her through Immigration."

"No, they wouldn't." Nora closed the passport, handed it back to him, and hugged her red sweater tighter. "She'd get put in quarantine. The publicity would be wild. 'Global superstar in Mexican quarantine.' Her story wouldn't hold up for two minutes and we'd all be in big trouble."

"Let me rephrase that. What if she'd had an accident on a movie set and looked pathetic? Or was barely conscious?"

"On a DEA support flight?" Nora demanded. "How would we explain that?"

Gamboa raised his eyebrows. "Like anybody expects DEA to explain anything."

Bowen drummed fingers on the table, frowning with concentration. "We could stick Emilia on the support flight as Messi and add a box of computer parts to the manifest to justify a layover in Acapulco. As soon as we unload, we talk to the Con Gen. Then Gifford gives up Lennox to avoid jail time and we get some glory."

Emilia broke into the little planning session the three of them were having without her. "Carlota has to know, too."

"Who?"

"The mayor of Acapulco," Emilia said impatiently. "She deserves to know what happened to her sister."

Nora frowned.

"That's fair," Bowen said.

Gamboa spread his hands in supplication.

"Fine," Nora said. "So how do we turn her into Alejandra Messi?"

"I could pretend to have a broken nose," Emilia suggested. "Lots of tape, a little makeup that looks like bruises and black eyes. We could say I had an accident doing a stunt for *Diamond Run 2*."

"Or you could have a real broken nose," Nora said archly.

Emilia never saw it coming. There was just a rushing sensation, then a blur of red in front of her face and the bridge of her nose gave way with a tremendous *crack* of breaking bone.

Fireworks of pain went off inside her skull. Tears blinded her. Blood gushed out of both nostrils.

She heard Gamboa laugh.

CHAPTER 46

"Lieutenant Franco Silvio? This is Agent Rick Bowen from the Drug Enforcement Agency in Washington DC. We have a situation here that requires your cooperation."

"How can the Acapulco police department assist you, Agent Bowen?"

Just hearing Silvio's growl coming through the speaker of Bowen's phone made Emilia so homesick she wanted to cry.

Her face was authentically bruised, with two eyes ringed in purple and a yellow stain across one cheek, hidden by a giant bandage across her nose and cheekbones. At least the nausea had faded, although it was still hard to eat and breathe at the same time.

She'd stayed in Nora's apartment the previous night on a little cot the DEA agent had conjured from a closet. She didn't know where Gamboa slept, but he was back less than eight hours later.

Seated next to Emilia on the little red sofa, Bowen continued the conversation. "The Mexican actress Alejandra Messi is coming to Acapulco on a private flight facilitated by my agency. She's suffered an accident and for various reasons does not want to make it public."

"Could you repeat that? Did you say the actress, Alejandra Messi?"

"That's correct. We'd like you to personally accompany an unmarked police escort to meet her on arrival at the executive terminal at the airport in Acapulco and escort her to the Palacio Real hotel. I understand she'll be staying in the penthouse."

For an uncomfortably long pause, Silvio did not reply. Emilia imagined him behind his cluttered desk, wondering if what wasn't being said was good news or bad.

"What kind of accident did she have?" he finally asked. "Does she need medical attention? An ambulance?"

"Not life threatening." Bowen flashed Emilia a grin. "An ambulance won't be necessary. The fewer people to meet her upon arrival, the better."

Another pause as Silvio digested his response. Then, "Does the hotel know she's coming?"

"We were hoping you could make that arrangement for us."

A rustle of paper came through the speaker. "Give me the flight details."

Eighteen hours later, an official at Andrews Air Force Base stamped the passport and wished Alejandra Messi a good flight. Leaning heavily on the arm of DEA agent Rick Bowen and accompanied by movie producer Manolo Bernal, the actress shuffled aboard a King Air jet. Sunglasses hid two black eyes and a surgical mask protected the bandages covering her nose.

It wasn't hard to appear injured and exhausted. Bowen gave her a painkiller. As soon as Gamboa parked her in a seat and fastened the belt, Emilia closed her eyes and nodded off.

They stopped somewhere in Texas. Emilia and Gamboa stayed aboard the aircraft while Nora and Bowen attended to whatever was supposed to happen, and then they were taxiing down the runway again. The plane lifted into the air, swung over a city that stretched into brown nothingness and then all Emilia could see was strings of cotton clouds cutting through a hard blue sky.

CHAPTER 47

Aeropuerto Internacional Quetzalcóatl, Nuevo Laredo.

The words emblazoned on the unlovely concrete building flashed by as they banked to land at the airport in Nuevo Laredo.

Huddled in her window seat, Emilia watched as the single runway rose to greet them. The jet's tires burped against the tarmac. She closed her eyes as the plane rolled along, still feeling the effects of Bowen's painkiller.

When the plane finally came to a stop, Gamboa jiggled her. With difficulty, Emilia pried open her eyes.

"It's showtime," he said. "We've let them know that Alejandra Messi is aboard."

Gamboa helped her down a few steps to the tarmac where Bowen waited with a wheelchair.

They weren't at the main terminal but parked by a small building of whitewashed cinder blocks topped with a corrugated metal roof.

The inside looked raw and unfinished, with wooden partitions topped with Plexiglas, a counter littered with paper forms, and a dozen uniformed Mexican immigration officials milling around. An air conditioning unit buzzed ineffectually. The place smelled strongly of body odor, frying onions, and jet fuel.

The process went far too easy. Gamboa filled out forms for her, Nora hit the official with a badge, paperwork and rocket-propelled officialdom. Passports were stamped and returned.

Back on board, Emilia sank gratefully into her seat, opened a bottle of water and sipped. So far so good, but she wouldn't feel safe until they'd taken off from this dry border city and were winging their way across the country to Acapulco.

Without the air conditioning going, the aircraft grew uncomfortably warm. Sweat trickled down Emilia's neck. The painkiller was wearing off and her face hurt. Without a straw, every sip of water was a race against needing to take her next breath.

Outside, workers plugged in a hose linked to a fuel truck. Nora and Bowen stood nearby talking to the pilot.

After what felt like forever, Nora returned to the cabin. The pilots climbed into the cockpit.

Bowen clanged the door shut. "Seatbelts," he said and took his seat.

The fuselage vibrated as the engines started up again.

Gamboa's seat next to Emilia remained empty. The black daypack was gone. "Where's Rafa?" she asked.

"He left," Bowen said shortly.

"What do you mean, left?"

"Left as in not going any further on this aircraft."

That wasn't the plan as Emilia understood it, although maybe it had been Gamboa's plan all along. "Is he going back to Washington?"

"Just shut up, okay?" Across the aisle, Nora put a hand to her eyes and averted her face.

Emilia realized she was crying.

The jet rolled along the taxiway, giving Emilia a view of flat brown land bordered by distant scrub and low cinder block houses. Stopped on the apron of the runway, the engines spooled up, whining at fever pitch, then abruptly shut down.

"What the--," Bowen started.

"We've been ordered to shut down our engines and stand by for further instructions." The metallic pilot's voice couldn't disguise a note of forced calm.

"Fuck," Nora said.

CHAPTER 48

They waited for what seemed like eternity, until the pilot came over the intercom again. "We're expecting visitors."

Emilia watched out the window as a four-wheeler with two uniformed immigration officers zoomed up beside the plane. One of them pounded on the door. Bowen opened it.

"We're here for Señora Messi."

Emilia fought to stay calm as Bowen unfolded the steps and the two officials charged into the aircraft cabin. Their name tags read Casillas and Olmeda. They were both hard-faced men who wore their authority like a badge of honor.

They crowded around Emilia. "Your passport, please, señora."

"Of course," Emilia murmured. She plucked it out of the leather duffle, wondering if Gamboa had set her up.

Casillas snatched the passport out of her hand and opened it to the information page. Olmeda whipped out a cell phone and took a picture.

"Is there a problem, señor?" Nora asked.

"My wife is never going to believe this." Casillas handed the passport back to Emilia along with a creased pocket notebook of the same size. "*Por favor*, señora. Your autograph for her."

Olmeda offered her a pen.

"Of course." Emilia produced a credible copy of Alejandra Messi's looping signature. "Here you are."

Casillas flipped the page. "And one for my daughter."

Emilia wrote another signature.

"And my niece."

Nora and Bowen were silent as the pen scratched across the paper.

"And my cousin."

Emilia signed Alejandra Messi's name twenty times, using all the remaining blank pages in the immigration officer's notebook. No doubt the signatures would be sold, the photo of the passport serving to verify their authenticity. It was anyone's guess what this would do to Gamboa's plans to have the real Alejandra Messi finish the Barrielos Luna biopic.

Finally, the two burly officials exited the aircraft. When they were finally airborne again, Nora unbuckled her belt and dropped into the seat next to Emilia.

"You kept your cool," she said.

"Thanks."

"I owe you an apology."

Emilia lightly touched the bandages across her nose. "No kidding."

"No, I'm sorry for calling you a bitch. And, well, for being a bitch to you."

"Kill the messenger? Something like that?"

"I didn't want to hear the truth about what Rafa did," Nora said, studying her sleeve, her nails, anything but Emilia's face. "I knew things had gone badly. That he did bad things. But if I didn't know, I wouldn't have to make a decision. Then you came along and now I've got to decide."

It didn't take a genius to know what decision Nora was facing. "To stay with him or not."

Nora finally met Emilia's eyes. "I've been in love with him

since the day we met."

"How did you meet?"

"We were in a training class together at Quantico a couple of years ago. He was one of three officers from Mexico."

"Before." Emilia rolled her hand as if turning back time. "Before he went undercover as El Acólito."

"I hated the whole concept of that operation." Nora swiped at her eyes. "It broke him, it really did. It broke everyone associated with it."

"Lieutenant Campos knew. He tried to help him."

"He was the only one." Nora made her disgust at the Mexican *federale* chain of command all too apparent. "They don't care as long as Rafa performs miracles for them."

Emilia thought that the other woman was right. "Rafa's going back to Washington, isn't he? To find the DSS men who killed Campos."

Nora nodded. "He didn't tell me, but it's possible."

Of course that's what Gamboa would do. "He and Campos were close."

"As close as Rafa lets anyone get."

"You're close," Emilia pointed out.

Nora gave Emilia a crooked smile. "We were close. Now I'm not so sure."

The conversation took a practical turn. How to present the facts to Katherine Singletary at the consulate without Gifford finding out. What Carlota was likely to do. What were the chances Gifford would give up Nestor Flores.

By the time the plane landed in Acapulco, they were talking like friends.

The first person Emilia saw as Bowen wheeled her into the

executive terminal building was Mercedes, half hidden behind a bouquet of flowers fit for a movie star. Silvio was there as well, flanked by four cops in uniforms, none of whom Emilia knew.

Kurt was with them, his face tightening with concern when he saw the wheelchair.

It was all Emilia could do to not leap up and fling herself into his arms.

"Welcome, señora," Silvio boomed, parting the throng of airport personnel like the Red Sea.

Emilia kept up the pretense of being haughty and helpless until she and Kurt were in the back of a black Suburban with tinted windows used for police escort services. As Silvio installed Mercedes in the front passenger seat and took the wheel, Emilia gave Nora a wave. The DEA agents had their own arrangements for getting to a hotel. They'd regroup the next day.

The uniforms Silvio had brought piled into another Suburban. The two vehicles peeled out of the airport and headed south through the night toward the Palacio Real.

"My god, Em," Kurt said and hugged her close. "What happened? I looked for you everywhere. You never went back to the hotel. They couldn't find your rental car. The Mexican embassy was clueless."

"You were looking for me? In El Norte?"

"Of course."

"When DEA called, I told him to come back," Silvio said over his shoulder.

Emilia's story spilled out, with Mercedes turned around and Silvio swearing softly. Kurt said nothing but he held her more and more tightly. The Pacific passed by in a haze of fast-moving darkness as she related everything, the other Suburban tucked behind them.

"You have to arrest Bruno Ruiz," Emilia said to Silvio when she finished. "He enabled Monica Montoya's murder, got Campos killed and set me up."

"Ruiz was killed three days ago." Silvio looked at her in the rearview mirror. "With the same gun that killed Monica Montoya."

CHAPTER 49

Wearing a much smaller bandage across her nose and enough makeup to disguise the fading bruises around her eyes, Emilia watched the faces around the reception room in the *alcaldía* as Nora finished the presentation.

The scratching of Enrique Santibañez's pen as he executed his chief of staff role with a flurry of note-taking was irritatingly loud.

Bowen had returned to El Norte with the support flight, leaving Nora to execute the plan. Wearing a severe black pantsuit and turquoise blouse that called attention to her sharp features, the DEA agent owned the room while still managing to be respectful to the power players in the room. Namely both Carlota and Katherine Singletary.

Carlota had been rapt throughout.

On the other side of the seating arrangement, Katherine Singletary sat like a hefty stone, her lips firmly pressed together. Compared to Carlota's elegant cobalt silk suit, Singletary's polyester dress could have come from any local street vendor.

To protect the still anonymous human source who had passed Lennox's conversations to DEA, Nora used oblique terms like "signals intelligence" and "technical means." As agreed, she didn't mention the possibility that Monica Montoya had been funneling cartel money into Carlota's re-election campaign. Emilia and Silvio would raise that issue with Carlota, in private.

Darren Hoover, the Legal Attaché who arrived from Mexico City that morning, kept shaking his head. It was hard to tell if he was there to refute Gifford's role in Monica Montoya's murder or work out a deal with Mexican law enforcement.

Emilia and Silvio were seated on a spindly settee. Nora finished the presentation and took her seat in a plush armchair.

It had been Silvio's idea to brief the mayor and the consul general at the same time. Given that they were up against the whole diplomatic immunity problem, he was convinced that something would shake loose when both women were in the same room hearing of the plot to kill Monica Montoya.

Carlota spoke first. "A diplomat from your consulate plotted my sister's murder, which occurred on Mexican soil," she said, speaking in English directly to Singletary and making no attempt to hide her anger. "Let us now discuss justice."

"A tragic situation." Singletary was clearly unhappy that DEA had done an end run around her. "I speak on behalf of the American people when I say we mourn the loss of your sister."

"How kind of you," Carlota said icily. "Will the American people dispense with Señor Gifford's diplomatic immunity?"

Hoover cleared his throat. "What we just heard allows him to be charged with conspiracy to commit murder in relation to Miss Montoya's death. But from the American perspective, he needs to face charges of intent to defraud the US government and money laundering."

Carlota bristled. "That's secondary."

"DEA will have additional charges pending a fuller investigation," Nora interjected, earning a stone-face from Hoover.

"He should face charges in Mexico," Carlota insisted. "Charged with murder. Conspiracy to murder. Associating with organized criminal organizations."

"Only if the United States decides to waive diplomatic immunity," Hoover said bluntly.

For a man with so much power, the Legal Attaché was singularly unimpressive. Nora had described him as a "soup sandwich," an odd expression that somehow perfectly described the lanky, rumpled man. His necktie was loose, his brown suit was wrinkled and his shoes were scuffed and dull.

"Good." Carlota waved imperiously. "Do that."

Hoover sighed. "Madam Mayor, that will require a long and involved negotiation between our two countries. As much as I believe that you are right to seek justice for the crime of killing your sister, given the circumstances I would not advise my government to waste time negotiating with you."

Carlota's eyes bulged at Hoover's temerity. Santibañez touched her sleeve as if to prevent her from exploding, as he addressed the other man. "In that case, the mayor's office is prepared to seek redress at a higher level."

"Please, please." Singletary raised both hands, obviously trying to play peacemaker. "Let us consider the facts. The charges here in Mexico would be conspiracy to commit murder. Correct?"

"Yes," Carlota said shortly. Her fists were clenched in her lap. "The very least."

"He also faces charges in the United States, where diplomatic immunity doesn't apply. Money laundering, associating with a felon, intent to defraud and so on. Charges Mexico cannot bring because they occurred in a diplomatic mission covered by the laws of that country, not the host country."

Emilia immediately understood. Mexican law didn't apply to any crime Gifford committed inside the consulate. The conversation was no longer about justice for Monica Montoya.

Singletary went on. "In fact, if it is proven that Gifford was inside the consulate when he participated in plans regarding your sister, Mexico cannot charge him at all."

"This is outrageous," Carlota shrilled.

"What the Consul General is saying," Hoover interjected, "is that Gifford would be charged with many more crimes in Washington, with a greater chance of spending the rest of his life in jail if found guilty, than if his diplomatic immunity was waived and he faced charges in Mexico."

"What about if Gifford confesses?" Silvio interjected.

Hoover dropped his patronizing expression for a look of consternation. One eye fluttered with a nervous tic.

"Let us consider an arrangement," Carlota said into the opening Silvio had created. "Gifford may be taken into custody by your legal apparatus after being questioned here first."

"Questioned by the police here in Acapulco?" Hoover licked his lips. "About the murder of Monica Montoya?"

"Yes," Carlota replied, staring at Emilia.

It was Singletary's turn to shift uncomfortably in her seat, which hugged her hips. "That would be a violation of diplomatic immunity."

"Not necessarily," Silvio replied. "Questioning and legal charges are two different things."

Hoover tapped his chin thoughtfully. "Gifford would have to voluntarily agree to be questioned. There would also have to be observers from our government to make sure his rights are not violated."

"I volunteer," Nora said immediately.

Emilia wondered why she'd ever thought of the DEA agent as anything other than a friend.

"And if Gifford confesses to the murder of my sister while being questioned?" Carlota demanded.

"Depending on circumstances," Hoover hedged. "That admission of guilt could be presented to a court in the United States in conjunction with the other charges against Mr. Gifford. Charges he can't face in Mexico."

"So it's agreed?" Silvio pressed. "We question Gifford here, with observers. Then you can take him to Washington."

"I would have to be there as well," Hoover replied.

"This has to be voluntary on Gifford's part," Singletary emphasized. The woman was obviously angry, possibly at Hoover but certainly at Nora. "If he doesn't agree, my hands are tied."

Carlota gave Singletary a look that would have made a lesser ego wilt. "I can see how you would like to avoid publicity, given that a trusted member of your staff used your consulate to launder drug money right under your nose."

The mayor paused and meditatively tapped her billboard-worthy pout with a forefinger as if trying to remember. "What's the correct term? Is it recall? Yes, recall. That's the term your government uses when a diplomat is sent home in disgrace."

Singletary left without saying another word.

Nora winked at Emilia.

CHAPTER 50

The same crowd was milling around the consulate as before.

Along with Nora, Emilia climbed out of the car, then ducked her head in the open passenger window. "Don't go away," she said to Silvio.

"Very funny," he growled from behind sunglasses. "I'm giving you ten minutes. In and out, fast and discreet."

"Ten minutes," Emilia echoed, although they both knew the process of collecting William Gifford wasn't up to either of them. Inside the consulate, Katherine Singletary was in charge and the drama would go on as long as she allowed it.

The simple plan included getting there at the opening of business. Emilia and Nora would go inside and collect Gifford. Together with Hoover, they'd escort him to the queue of unmarked police cars waiting on the circular drive inside the perimeter gate. Taking no chances, Silvio had insisted that both women wear ballistic vests under their clothing.

The consulate doors wouldn't open for another twenty minutes, but a noisy crowd had already formed on both sides of the iron fence bearing the huge seal of the United States of America. Inside the fence, waiting Mexicans carried folders stuffed with papers they thought would earn them a visa. They clustered in somber groups of hopeful applicants. At least a third of those waiting were *norteamericanos* who sobbed into cell phones or argued with each other about lost passports or traveling companions who'd been arrested. More nationalities wandered in and out of line, responding to text messages, phone calls, and the shouts of family members relegated to waiting on the street.

Outside the fence, vendors, pickpockets and would-be legal advisors jockeyed for position and pestered the would-be supplicants.

"Pencil?" a street seller shouted at Emilia and Nora through the fence. "Newspaper?"

Someone else plucked Emilia's sleeve. "Can you help us? My sister forgot to pay her visa fee."

Emilia ignored them both, jogging Nora's elbow as they threaded their way through the crowd.

In the lobby, a young woman with a clipboard stepped forward to greet them. "Detective Cruz? Agent Torres? I'm Mrs. Singletary's secretary," she said in English. "She asked that I escort you to her office."

Emilia recalled the young woman from her previous visit. The young woman's desk was positioned directly in front of Singletary's office door, like the bed of an underfed guard dog.

They went up the stairs in silence but for the muffled scuff of their shoes on the marble steps. Worn over her white blouse and skinny black jeans, Emilia's ballistic vest got heavier with each step.

Nora was similarly attired in vest, tee and jeans.

The secretary led them past the oddly placed desk and tapped on Singletary's half-open door. "Ma'am? Your visitors are here."

In response to the reply, she stepped aside and let Emilia and Nora enter.

Katherine Singletary was behind her desk, reading glasses

perched on her nose, her right hand toying nervously with a pen. Darren Hoover, the Legal Attaché from Mexico City was in one of the leather armchairs, one ankle resting on the opposite knee in an unsuccessful attempt to appear relaxed.

On the sofa, one arm resting along the back, Gifford was the picture of the professional diplomat in a gray suit and paisley tie. Gracious as ever, he swiftly rose to his feet when Emilia and Nora came in. "Detective Cruz, what a pleasure to see you again," he said without a hint of guile or sarcasm.

Singletary made the introductions as if neither woman had ever met Hoover. Nora had genuinely never met Gifford but her body language gave nothing away whereas Emilia had to force herself to shake his hand.

"The police in Acapulco have questions regarding the death of a woman named Monica Montoya," Hoover said to Gifford, launching into the subject at hand in a way that Silvio would appreciate. "After reviewing the circumstances, the Consul General and I would like you to cooperate."

"Of course." Gifford blinked a few times, as if processing his response. "Of course, I've already answered Detective Cruz's questions. I doubt I can be any more helpful than I've already been."

"Additional information has come to light," Emilia said. "Leading to a new line of inquiry."

"Such formality." Gifford gave a laugh and relaxed against the tufted sofa once more. "Well, fire away. I'm happy to help local law enforcement."

"If you'd come with us, then." Emilia made a gesture toward the office door.

"Of course." Gifford stood again. "My office is just around

the corner."

"We have a car waiting to take us to the police station."

"Police station?" Gifford folded his arms. "With DEA? Is this a joke?"

Hoover stood as well, rounded shoulders causing him to stoop. "I'll come along and make sure the niceties are observed."

Gifford spun to face Singletary. "Katherine--."

She cut him off, throwing down her reading glasses at the same time. "The host nation has questions. You need to answer them. It's one hour in the cause of better relations, with both Agent Torres and Darren along to make sure your rights are respected."

"I'm here to advise you that it's in the best interests of the United States that you answer their questions to the best of your ability," Hoover said quietly. In brown trousers and a muddy colored sport coat too large for his spare frame, the man resembled a walking clothes rack. He might have powers in this building that Emilia didn't, but he was not an impressive figure.

Gifford raised his eyebrows and gave a tight laugh. "Well in that case, I guess it won't hurt to help. Again."

Singletary's secretary materialized at the door and held it open.

"You know that this is just a formality, Will." Singletary said as they readied to follow the secretary out the office door. "A few loose ends, that's all."

Once in the lobby, Emilia was struck with a premonition that Gifford was going to flee. He could knock down both her and Nora and disappear into the crowd. Hoover would do nothing. She lifted her chin at Nora, who must have been thinking the same thing. They both closed in nice and tight on either side of the diplomat, letting Hoover bring up the rear as they left the lobby and started down the broad stairs. On his right, Emilia clutched Gifford's bicep. Nora had his other arm.

"This feels very cozy, Detective." Gifford gave her a conspiratorial smile as they proceeded down the first step. "No pirates."

The crowd had lessened but there was still a sizable number of people milling around the side door to the consulate. The sight of a gringo in a flashy suit being escorted by two women grabbed their attention. A squad of *norteamericano* hippie types shouted at Gifford, who smiled and bobbed his head at them. Emilia wasn't sure what they wanted; traffic noise and the general hum of the crowd made it impossible to hear them clearly.

She saw Silvio leaning against the unmarked police car, tapping his sunglasses against a thumb. They made eye contact and he headed across the drive toward the little parade.

A zinging whine went by Emilia's face. Behind them, Hoover grunted. Emilia glanced over her shoulder in time to see the lanky man collapse to his knees, half of his face gone. At the same time, Gifford jolted as if something had struck his chest.

"Shooter!" Emilia screamed but the word was lost in an instant melee. The crowd was in an uproar, people running like headless chickens. Nora shouted to get to the cars.

Blood bloomed across Gifford's shirt. Emilia let him go and whipped out her gun. The crowd was running amok across her line of vision. She had no clear idea where the shooter was, only that they had to be beyond the iron perimeter fence.

Gifford absorbed two more shots, his body shaking as if in a high wind. He collapsed, knocking into Emilia. She went down on one knee.

The din was impenetrable. Emilia never heard the next shots. Nora fell hard and awkwardly, spinning to land partway on Hoover's spread-eagled body. Blood pumped out of her neck to stain the consulate steps and the Legal Attaché's rumpled clothing. Emilia shoved aside the dead weight that was Gifford, screaming at Nora to *get up, get to the cars, let's go, go, go.*

Then Silvio was there, roaring at Emilia *get down, get down.* Emilia shouted at him to *get the car, now now now.*

Instead, he threw himself over her, shielding Emilia with his body.

The bullets meant for her ripped into him instead.

CHAPTER 51

Nora Torres was dead.

William Gifford was dead.

Darren Hoover was dead.

Franco Silvio was almost dead.

Twelve hours in surgery. Two days in a coma.

Sitting on a hard plastic chair in Silvio's room in the critical care unit of the Santa Lucia Hospital, Emilia idly flipped through a copy of *Boda*. The bridal magazine was full of wedding dresses. Should she get a mermaid or princess style? Strapless or lace sleeves? A creamy color or bright white?

It hardly mattered when the face of every model reminded her of Nora.

The glass door slid open. Mercedes walked in with two cups of ersatz coffee from the family waiting room.

"Did you bring me one?" Silvio croaked from the bed. He was swathed in bandages, with his left arm strapped to his chest.

Mercedes went to his side and kissed his forehead. "The doctor said no coffee for you. Maybe tomorrow."

Silvio's eyes closed.

The dancer handed a cup to Emilia. Even in jeans and a tee shirt, Mercedes exuded grace. But if she didn't start eating more, she would wither away to nothing. Mercedes had been constantly by Silvio's side even during the coma days, reading to him, feeding him ice chips, reminding him of their plans for the future.

Once upon a time, Emilia had done the same thing in the same hospital unit when Kurt was hit by a joy-riding couple on a jet ski.

A nurse came in. "How is our patient today?"

"I keep falling asleep," Silvio growled without opening his eyes.

"You're making very good progress." The nurse began checking the bank of monitors, each with their own unique bleat, green-hued screen, and enough wires and cords tethered to Silvio to rig a sailing ship. "Your body needs sleep to heal."

Since the shooting, Emilia had only been in the office once to send an email to Prade at the morgue, asking the estimated age of the body processed as Lieutenant Vicente Campos. The response was swift. The dead man was in his mid to late thirties.

Which meant that it was almost certain Nestor Flores was the sniper who'd caused such horrific damage at the consulate. The teenager was still out there, learning the ropes of the narco business and erasing his uncle's enemies as El Barracuda.

The glass door slid open again. Chief Salazar walked in, decked out in full uniform with gold braid, holding his hat against his heart. Obregon followed.

"Only two visitors at a time," the nurse caroled.

Silvio's eyes fluttered open.

"I'll go," Mercedes said. She pressed Silvio's hand and slipped away.

Obregon murmured something to the nurse, who stalked out.

Emilia didn't move.

"Glad to see you're looking so well, Lieutenant," Chief Salazar said, falsely hearty.

"*Mi jefe*," Silvio responded.

"Santa Lucia is an excellent hospital," the chief went on. "I'm sure you are getting top-notch care."

Dressed in black as always, Obregon looked around at the bleeping monitors and the copy of *Boda* on the small table beside Emilia but not at her. "Is there anything you need?"

Silvio regarded both men stonily. "No."

Chief Salazar gave a grimace-like smile. "As you no doubt expect, Lieutenant, you're on medical leave for as long as necessary. Captain Esteban Cardona Moya will take over the detectives unit."

Silvio's hand hit the button controlling the hospital bed. With an electronic whine, the head rose a few inches.

"Union guidelines for an officer wounded in the line of duty are clear." Obregon said. "A position of commensurate responsibility will be made available once you are cleared for duty."

Emilia wasn't sure if Silvio, packed full of painkillers, understood the situation. Salazar was there to deliver the message that Silvio was being booted out of his job as chief of detectives. Obregon's message was that the union was happy with the decision.

"What about Special Assignments?" Silvio asked hoarsely.

"Sadly, that position won't be available," Chief Salazar replied.

"I see."

Obregon and Chief Salazar didn't need any more

encouragement. Another round of insincere pleasantries and they departed. The glass door whooshed closed behind them.

"Fuck them both and the horse they rode in on," Silvio's chest rose and fell with the effort to speak such a long sentence.

"All you had to do was stay in the car," Emilia said. "I'd be out of everyone's hair and you'd get promoted."

"Should have told me before," Silvio said in a croak.

"Yeah, you really fucked up." Emilia couldn't help but smile. She got up and refilled his water pitcher at the tiny sink. "I'm sorry for giving you a hard time before. You know, punching you in the car and everything."

"I never told Salazar I'd force you out, you know."

"Still should have told me."

"Okay. True." Silvio gave a ragged cough.

Emilia poured water into his cup and slotted a fresh straw into the lid. "You would have been a disaster at Special Assignments, anyway. They need someone with experience."

Silvio's laugh was cut short by a clench of pain.

Mercedes came in, a slight frown knitting her eyebrows together. "I saw them get into the elevator. What was that all about?"

"Franco's on medical leave until further notice," Emilia said.

"Well, that's good, right?" Mercedes looked from Emilia to Silvio.

The head of the hospital bed rose higher. The machinery around Silvio emitted steady, reassuring beeps. "What did the guy from the tapas place say about the delivery to Casa de Plata?" he asked, his voice a little stronger than before.

"You mean Madrid?" Emilia mentally switched gears.

"Sure. Monica placed the order and was there to receive it."

"What if it wasn't her?"

"You mean, not Monica . . ." Emilia trailed off. "*Madre de Dios*! Pilar. Lennox's girlfriend, Pilar."

"Who?"

"Pilar." Emilia's thoughts cascaded. "Katherine Singletary's secretary is named Pilar."

"Does she have diplomatic immunity, too?"

"No." Emilia grinned. Silvio was barely alive and still the best investigator she knew.

"Who are you talking about?" Mercedes demanded.

"A Mexican woman who could be the key to everything." Emilia waved the copy of *Boda*. "She probably thinks that *gringo* is going to marry her."

A few brief details and Mercedes's eyes widened. "How can I help?" she asked.

CHAPTER 52

Emilia waited behind the wheel of the big, rented SUV, a ball cap shielding her eyes and her hair tucked inside. The idling engine was barely audible in the commercial parking garage, on the second floor where consulate employees had designed parking spots. Her driver's side window was open, delivering exhaust-scented air and the low drumming of city traffic.

She watched as Kurt emerged from between two parked cars and ambled over to the large concrete pillar by the stairwell. He was immaculate in a faintly pinstriped suit, a white shirt and a tie that matched his ocean-colored eyes. From the way he stood, the long stemmed red rose in his right hand was invisible to anyone walking up the stairs.

It was just after 6:00 pm. Consulate employees were coming up in groups of twos and threes, wishing each other good night and getting into their cars. Despite the recent tragedy, the consulate was still open for business.

They'd watched this particular level of the parking garage for three days, sifting through the consulate employees who were assigned parking, until they were able to establish Pilar's routine.

True to form, the secretary was one of the last to climb the stairs to the second floor. Tonight, as every other night, she was alone, as if the camaraderie enjoyed by others wasn't good enough for the person holding such an exalted role as secretary to the Consul General herself. Or maybe Pilar just wasn't good at making friends.

Or Lennox kept her from getting too close to anyone in case she slipped up and mentioned the so-called "oranges."

"Señora Pilar?" Kurt approached as Pilar gained the landing, forcing her to either step back down or acknowledge him. "I have a message from Señor Lennox for you."

"Who are you?" Pilar's voice was surprisingly non-confrontational.

If Emilia had been in her position, she would have belted the guy and run like hell.

"My name is Mike. I work for Señor Lennox." Kurt held out the rose.

As soon as Pilar took it, Kurt whipped out a cell phone and tapped the screen. "He has a message for you."

Emilia was too far away to hear the audio but she'd memorized the brief audio.

Mi amor, I am sending my good friend Mike to escort you to me. You are in very good hands; I trust him completely. I cannot wait to see you. Ten cuidado.

The deepfake voice was identical to Lennox's timbre, right down to the muffled snorting chuckle and the inflection in his signature *ten cuidado* sign-off.

Emilia held her breath as she watched Pilar. Kurt gave the secretary a slight bow, hands behind his back now, playing his role as Lennox's confidante to the hilt. His deferential body language was no doubt bolstering Pilar's role in her mind as the girlfriend of Mike's powerful *jefe*.

Their exchange was too quiet for Emilia to catch but whatever Kurt said worked. Pilar allowed him to escort her to the SUV. Kurt handed Pilar up into the back seat, making sure she saw the bottle of Prosecco and long stemmed glasses.

He took the seat next to her, slammed the door closed, then reached between the front seats and snapped his fingers at Emilia. "Drive," he ordered brusquely.

"Si, señor," Emilia murmured. In the cartel food chain, a mere driver was far below Lennox's hand-picked messenger.

She navigated traffic, listening to Kurt flatter Pilar, ply her with Prosecco, and deflect the few questions she asked. Every time Emilia glanced in the rearview mirror, the secretary was sipping her glass of bubbly. Pilar didn't appear apprehensive, making Emilia think Lennox had previously sent messengers to escort her to his mysterious whereabouts.

The journey to Colonia Progreso took less than fifteen minutes. When the battleship gray walls came into view, Emilia clicked the button on a brand new remote and the equally new vehicle gates opened with no more noise than a well-oiled sigh. She drove in. The gates immediately closed behind them.

Apart from the new gates, Casa de Plata looked the same as on the day they'd discovered Monica Montoya's body. The empty fountain with the bronze ship sailed across an empty basin. Weeds and dry palm fronds littered the grubby lawn. Broken windows, stucco pocked with missing bits, the remaining fragments of mosaic twinkling in the twilight.

Kurt helped Pilar out of the SUV. "Why are we here?" she asked.

"You'll have to ask el señor," Kurt said.

Pilar gave him a smile. "I thought we were going to the beach."

"Ah." Kurt matched her smile. "Maybe later. Right now we must go inside. El señor is waiting for you."

He snapped his fingers at Emilia who was leaning against the SUV and she hustled to open the massive front door.

They all went inside. Kurt led the way to the east side ground floor apartment. Emilia peeled off to find the kitchen. Kurt and Pilar went straight through to the dining room, where he helped her into a particular chair and said he would go fetch Lennox.

In the kitchen, Emilia swiftly changed clothes into a black skirt suit and high heels. Wearing a gray maid's uniform and white apron Mercedes carried a tray of small plates into the dining room. Spiced olives. Potato puffs. Almonds. Slices of chorizo sausage and manchego cheese.

"El señor is delayed for a few minutes by a phone call," she said to Pilar, setting down the tapas and pouring the woman a new glass of Prosecco from the freshly opened bottle on the end of the table. "Please enjoy with his compliments."

"Ooh, this is lovely." Pilar selected an olive and popped it into her mouth. A sip of wine, then a potato puff. A sliver of sausage. More wine.

"Hello, Pilar." Emilia came into the dining room at the same time Mercedes locked the doors to the living room.

Pilar sputtered wine and dropped the olive she'd been preparing to eat. "Who are you?"

"Detective Emilia Cruz of the Acapulco police department."

The reaction was right out of a *telenovela*. Pilar's eyes widened almost comically as she leaped up, tipping over her glass. "What is going on?"

"We're going to ask you some questions about Thomas Lennox," Mercedes replied, catching the glass before the wine spilled out.

Pilar looked wildly from Mercedes to Emilia and back again. "I . . . I don't know anyone by that name," she stuttered.

"It's too late to play that game," Emilia said and pushed Pilar back into her seat. "You got into the car because Señor Mike had a message from Lennox. Remember? Unless you want to go to jail for being an accessory to murder, you need to answer my questions."

"Murder?" Pilar's voice came out in a squeak. "I didn't murder anyone."

"Monica Montoya was murdered in this very room." Emilia walked around Pilar's chair. "She was drinking white wine and eating tapas with William Gifford. You know who he was, right? Gifford was laundering money through the consulate and passing some of it to her. When she got nervous about the arrangement, Thomas Lennox sent a man to kill her."

"I don't know what you're talking about."

"Put your hands up," Mercedes said.

"What?" Pilar gaped at the dancer in confusion.

"Put your hands up by your shoulders!"

It was the first time that Emilia had heard Mercedes raise her voice. The combination of graceful gestures and harsh tone was startling. Pilar raised both hands, palms out.

"That's just how Monica Montoya died," Mercedes told her. "Her killer shot through her hands into her chest. She died right in the chair you're sitting in. I was there, you see. I saw her sitting there, dead with holes in her hands like stigmata."

Pilar gave a squeal of distress and tried to bolt out of the chair.

Emilia kept her seated with a rough shove and showed

Pilar a tablet. "Check out the pictures."

She tapped the screen, bringing up a photograph of Monica Montoya as they'd found her that Sunday. "Bullet holes in her palms. Olive oil on her fingers. Gifford brought her here. Made it look like a celebration with a spread from Madrid, the tapas restaurant."

One by one, Emilia made Pilar look at a dozen photos. Close-ups of Monica in the dining room and on the table in the morgue. Even the autopsy report, including a list of the contents of her stomach, the text echoing everything that was on the tray in front of Pilar at that very moment.

"When she was dead, Gifford collected up the food and left her," Mercedes said. "Right here. In this room. Still sitting on your chair. Because that's what Lennox told him to do."

"This doesn't have anything to do with me," Pilar cried.

"You placed the order with Madrid, Pilar," Emilia said softly. "You came to the gate when the man from Madrid brought it that night. We showed him a picture. He remembered you."

Pilar pressed her hands to her mouth.

"That makes you an accessory to murder," Emilia went on. "Thomas Lennox organized Monica Montoya's murder. Who do you think arranged for Gifford to die before he could be questioned? How much longer do you think he's going to let you live? You help him move money. You know too much."

"Stop it!" Pilar screamed. "These are lies, all lies. Thomas works for an important bank, an international bank with the contract for all the consulates in Mexico and Central America. That's why the cash has to be bundled and sent in a certain way."

Emilia gave the woman a shake. "You're not stupid. You knew that's not how banks do business. Thomas Lennox works for Diego Barrielos Luna! The Barrel Bomber! Lennox killed the Amistad 43 for him."

Pilar covered her face with her hands. Sobs wracked her frame.

"I've heard your conversations with him," Emilia said. "We know how deeply you are involved. He calls the money packages oranges, doesn't he?"

Pilar looked up beseechingly. "I never met anyone like him before."

Emilia felt zero sympathy. "How did you meet him?"

"Señora Singletary introduced us." Pilar's voice was choked with tears. "I passed the test to work at the consulate and she interviewed me. He was there. Then she invited me to a dinner party at a restaurant and he was there, too."

"He was rich and handsome and paid you a lot of attention," Emilia guessed.

Pilar's eyes welled up again. "Yes," she whispered.

Emilia carefully phrased her next question. "What about Señora Singletary? Does she know about the so-called banking contract and the bundles of cash?"

"Only her and Señor Gifford," Pilar said.

"Now it's only her," Mercedes pointed out. "And you."

A shiver went through Pilar's body.

Emilia crouched next to the secretary. "Pilar, when we arrived you told Señor Mike that you thought we were going to the beach. Tell me about that."

Pilar wiped her eyes again. "Thomas has a place on the coast, near Zihuatanejo. He's there sometimes. Says it's too crowded in Acapulco.”

“How do you know when he’s going to be there?”

In response, Pilar burst into tears again, rocking back and forth on the chair.

“He sent you a message.”

“Yes,” Pilar choked out.

Emilia slowly straightened, understanding the gift that the secretary had just handed them. “That’s why you went with us in the first place. He’s there now.”

Later, when Pilar had been taken away and Kurt went back to the Palacio Real, Emilia and Mercedes sat in the dining room and finished the bottle of Prosecco.

“Can you feel it?” Mercedes asked, looking around. She’d taken off her apron and unknotted her hair. “It feels different in here. Like Casa de Plata can breathe again.”

Emilia looked around, too. She’d felt nothing the entire time they were there. No invisible cobwebs brushing by. No pleading voice whispering through her thoughts.

Despite the bare walls and grubby windows, the apartment felt clean and fresh and ready to be made new again.

“This place is ready to be happy again.” Mercedes said. “Does that sound crazy?”

“No.” Emilia raised her glass in a toast. “I was just thinking the same thing.”

CHAPTER 53

Emilia was in a windowless interrogation room located in the bowels of a Mexican military base she never knew existed. Rick Bowen had returned from Washington and was with her. The DEA agent was silent and brooding with arms folded.

The interrogation room was sterile. Dun-colored concrete block walls, pierced on two sides with large glass insets that appeared dark to those inside. Both Mexican military and federal marshals from El Norte waited to view the proceedings from the other side.

Giving Emilia ten minutes to grill Thomas Lennox was all the thanks she could expect for the tip-off. Bowen was there to protect the DEA's source by making sure Emilia didn't mention Lennox's audio files.

In a few hours, the prisoner would be in El Norte and out of reach. Emilia wasn't told the particulars of the deal between Washington and Mexico City but he was being charged as accessory to murder for the deaths of Gifford, Hoover, and Nora Torres. A laundry list of other indictments awaited him as well, for money laundering, drug crimes, and even impersonating a State Department official long after he'd left that office.

Katherine Singletary had confessed to complicity in the money laundering operation and was already in Washington.

There was no evidence linking either Lennox or Singletary to the murders of Lieutenant Vicente Campos or Financial Crimes officer Bruno Ruiz Ramirez.

Lennox could be traced to the murder of Monica Montoya, but only through the audio files. Without Gifford's testimony there was no other evidence.

Emilia wanted to believe it didn't matter if Lennox was punished for Monica's murder because he'd be in jail for a long time anyway. The public outcry in El Norte was loud and angry, with calls to punish the mastermind behind the deaths of three citizens on its own diplomatic property. Perhaps he'd even face the death penalty in El Norte where that was still practiced.

In Acapulco, thanks to near-hysterical media coverage, public debate had shifted from the horrors of Mexican organized crime to the impact of bad foreign actors. Everyone was shaking a fist at the *norteamericanos* who had the arrogance to import their violence as if the city had no other kind.

Both Carlota and her rival Vallejo Loy made the distinction between crooked gringos and tourists whose wallets were always welcome in Acapulco, but were also reveling in the delicious sensation of holding the moral high ground atop a pile of actual diplomats from El Norte. Conveniently omitted from the media hysteria was the notion that the sniper who killed the three officials might be Mexican.

The door opened. Lennox shuffled in, chains running from his cuffed hands to shackles around his ankles. A guard in undecorated navy blue fatigues and a face-covering balaclava planted the prisoner in the chair opposite Emilia.

"Ten minutes," the guard said and took up a position by the door. Bowen nodded thanks.

Lennox looked the same as when Emilia encountered him

in Mexico City so long ago. Wavy light brown hair, thoughtful smile, friendly eyes. He and Gifford were two of a kind.

Emilia remembered meeting Lennox in the Starbucks next to the U.S. Embassy on Paseo de la Reforma. He'd been looking for a place to sit in the crowded coffee shop and asked to share her table, introducing himself as Tom Lennox, the Legal Attaché. That first impression was of a gracious and well-dressed man in his mid-thirties. He'd won her confidence with a beautifully embossed business card with his name and title on it.

Of course, it was all an elaborate swindle to derail the Amistad 43 task force and spring Diego Barrielos Luna out of prison, a situation Emilia didn't understand until too late.

"Well, if it isn't the woman who lived." Lennox sat with his cuffed and clasped hands on the table as if they were there for a business meeting. He completely ignored Bowen. "I told Diego that leaving you alive was a bad decision."

"I'm not here for a trip down memory lane," Emilia said, although just the mention of that horrible day sent her blood pressure soaring. "You sent a *sicario* to kill a woman named Monica Montoya. She was dating your pal William Gifford."

"Cut to the chase, my dear." Lennox showed zero remorse for his friend's death. "You're here to find out if Carlota Montoya Perez was witting. If she knew her campaign was being funded by Diego Barrielos Luna. Was she in on it from the start and did she use her sister as a go-between." Lennox rolled his eyes dramatically. "Is she Diego's creature? Is that what you want to know?"

"No, but you want to tell me." Emilia was amazed at the steadiness of her own voice.

Lennox smiled. "No idea. You'll have to ask them."

"Did Carlota have her sister killed?" Emilia asked softly.

"What a question." Lennox shook his head and settled back in his chair. "You're fishing, Detective."

Emilia was conscious of the minutes ticking away and of the evil seeping out of the man. She straightened her spine. "Tell me about a narco junior named Nestor Flores. His parents are in jail for their role in the Amistad 43 murders."

"No, never heard that name." Lennox's cheek twitched, causing one eye to squint for a brief, barely discernible moment.

"We have his DNA from Monica Montoya's crime scene," Emilia lied. "He killed her as well as the three in front of the consulate. Wounded my lieutenant, too. Tell me where to find him and I'll put in a good word for you with the *norteamericanos*."

Lennox laughed outright, a big hearty guffaw. "You have no leverage with Washington."

"Nestor Flores," Emilia repeated doggedly.

"Have you found El Acólito yet?"

If he'd abruptly slapped her, Emilia could not have been more stunned. Diego Barrielos Luna's last words to her, as the whole military convoy burned and the life drained out of her wounded partner, crashed through her brain.

El Acólito. I know where he is and I'll find him before you do . . . When it's time, I'll bring you El Acólito. In return, you'll do me a favor.

"Well?" Lennox cut through her memory.

Heart jumping in her chest, Emilia looked past him at the guard who held up two fingers, indicating how many minutes left. Bowen remained silent.

Campos had said that he and Gamboa were meeting at the Willard Hotel because Gamboa had something important to pass on. That thing could only be the flash drive filled with content downloaded from Lennox's laptop.

When Campos died, Gamboa gave the flash drive to Nora, the only other person he could trust. She invented a cover story about anonymous DEA assets to protect him.

Did Lennox and Barrielos Luna know that the same man who was producing the Barrielos Luna biopic starring Alejandra Messi was the same man who procured women as El Acólito? Did they suspect him of being a *federale*? Of stealing information from Lennox's private communications?

Gamboa's personas were so mixed up by now she had no idea how much danger he could be in.

As too many thoughts crashed through her head, one stood out. She had to protect her brother.

"I'm no longer interested in El Acólito," Emilia managed.

Lennox clicked his tongue. "I think you're lying."

The guard pointed to the clock and then to the door.

"Time's up," Emilia said.

The door opened and Lennox was taken out.

"What a monster," Emilia said shakily after a long minute.

Bowen rolled both hands into fists atop the table. "I'm staying," he said.

"In Mexico?"

"In Acapulco. They've made a position for me at the consulate in Acapulco." He paused. "In my spare time I'll be looking for El Barracuda."

Emilia had thought of him as nondescript before; now she

realized that she'd only seen Rick Bowen in the shadow of Nora's intensity. On his own, Bowen was a quiet, tough fighter. He wouldn't have her depth of local knowledge yet could draw upon DEA's considerable assets. Aircraft, technology, informants, a network of other agents throughout Mexico.

"About Nora," she ventured. "While you were in Washington, did you see . . . uh . . . see my brother?"

"No," Bowen replied. He took a deep breath. "But he has to know about Nora. It's been all over the news."

"He'll be looking for El Barracuda, too."

"Good." Bowen shoved his chair away from the table and stood. "I can use all the help I can get."

"His methods aren't your methods," Emilia said.

CHAPTER 54

Election day was cooler than the norm, leading Emilia to wear a cream cotton sweater under her navy blazer. Trousers with a faint cream and navy windowpane pattern and polished loafers completed the outfit. Plus her engagement ring, which she had worn nonstop since she got back to Acapulco. If work took her to a bad neighborhood, she'd slip it into a pocket.

Not that it promised to be that sort of day.

Traffic was unusually light at the ungodly hour she left the Palacio Real complex and turned left onto the Carretera Escénica. For once the highway was devoid of tourist vans and buses. The billboards lining the highway still looked fresh and new, the candidates rising above the previous week's tragedies both literally and figuratively.

Several tour companies had announced shutdowns for the day due to the expected violence at polling places. Kurt and the Palacio Real staff had extra activities planned to keep guests on site and avoid downtown hotspots. Cooking classes with Jacques, mixology lessons in the Pasodoble Bar, a lecture series about Mexican history, plus excursions to the hotel's private island and all manner of water sports.

Santibañez ushered her into the familiar reception room, indicated coffee and pastries on an antique sideboard and said he'd let Carlota know she was there.

The double doors closed behind him, leaving her alone in the opulent space.

Emilia paced and wondered what Nora Torres would do if

she was there. Probably have three cups of coffee, then arrest Carlota.

Yesterday's interview with Lennox had provoked uncomfortable questions. Was Carlota a woman whose campaign money had been managed by others without knowing where the cash came from? Or a woman who ruthlessly manipulated another into being a conduit for drug money to advance her own political ambitions? Was she brazen enough to order a murder when her half-sister got nervous about money matters?

Emilia drifted to the window. Scattered groups of people were coming toward the *alcaldía*, some carrying placards. She couldn't tell if they were for or against Carlota.

Not that it mattered. In a month or two, all this would be someone else's problem. Emilia was going to quit. The choice was hers to make and she chose Kurt, a man who'd raced into danger to search for her.

The double doors opened and Carlota breezed through, stiletto heels clicking on the marble until muffled by the huge Persian rug anchoring the furniture. Santibañez jogged along at her elbow.

"A minute before I cast my vote." Carlota was dressed in a pink tweed skirt suit with a wide portrait collar. A small gold cross nestled in the hollow of her neck, her hair was pulled away from her face, and her nails were the exact same shade as the outfit. Brown alligator pumps completed the look.

The combination of soft color and severe style proclaimed her as both feminine and powerful at the same time.

"First things first." Carlota swept onto the edge of a chair. "How is Lieutenant Silvio?"

"Thank you for asking, señora," Emilia said. "He's recovering, but it will take some time."

"Please pass on my regards when you see him."

"I'm sure he'll appreciate it."

Carlota tapped manicured fingers on the arm of her chair. "On to immediate issues. What did you find out yesterday?"

"Lennox didn't tell us anything about Nestor Flores, the *sicario* who styles himself as El Barracuda." Emilia paused. "But the DEA is stationing one of its agents here in Acapulco with orders to find him."

"Is this El Barracuda here?" Carlota asked.

"He was once," Emilia replied. "But it's impossible to know where he is now."

Carlota got out of her chair and went to the window. The sound of the crowd outside was getting louder. Chants of *CAR-LO-TAH, CAR-LO-TAH* had a drumbeat cadence.

Emilia squeezed her hands together, wondering what was going on in Carlota's head. Sadness? Guilt? Ways to cover up her involvement? Satisfaction at the growing size of the crowd outside?

Santibañez cleared his throat. "What are the chances that Lennox will tell our friends in El Norte where El Barracuda is?"

"Zero." Emilia didn't mince words. "Lennox knows his life is over if he betrays Barrielos Luna in any way. Even if he's in prison in El Norte."

Which is why A Misunderstood Man starring Alejandra Messi is going to be in a theater near you soon.

"Does Lennox's extradition to El Norte weaken Barrielos Luna?" Carlota demanded. "Is the fugitive more vulnerable now?"

It was an interesting question and even more interesting that Carlota was the one to voice it.

Emilia considered. "Possibly."

"If you find his nephew he'll be weakened even more." Carlota turned away from the window and pointed at Emilia. "What about this DEA officer? Competent?"

"I believe so, señora. He'll have tremendous resources at his disposal."

Carlota tossed her head, earrings catching the light and bouncing pindots around the room. "Work with him, Detective. Use him. I want you to catch this El Barracuda and bring him to justice. Mexican justice for my sister's murder."

"I appreciate your confidence, señora, but this is clearly a *federale* responsibility." Emilia pressed a finger against the ruby in her engagement ring, feeling the facets and the gold rim around the stone. It was time to make her declaration out loud. She took a deep breath. "In fact, I'm leaving the police department in order to get married."

Carlota went to the sideboard and poured herself a cup of coffee. "Enrique, can you step outside for a moment."

It wasn't a question.

Emilia sat very still. It was election day. No doubt Carlota had a full schedule of sticking pins in Vallejo Loy's voodoo doll. Instead she was lingering over the pastry tray.

"Are you leaving the police department of your own free will?" Carlota resumed her seat, with a cup of coffee in hand. "Or is this a decision someone else made for you?"

Emilia was torn between blaming Chief Salazar and wondering what the repercussions might be for Silvio if she did. "Señora--."

"Never mind, Detective," Carlota cut her off. "I know the answer to that question and you are too aware of the consequences to answer with the truth. The fact is that I owe you a debt. You brought me closure. Victoria Alvarez, too. The risk to yourself was very great, I know. As a politician I take risks, but it's not the same. I greatly admire your courage."

"Thank you, señora," Emilia murmured in surprise.

"I spoke to Victor Obregon about Chief Salazar's decision regarding your marriage and informed him that the outcome is not acceptable. We cannot afford to lose experienced police officers because of a ridiculous prejudice. Chief Salazar will be retracting his decision."

Emilia felt her jaw drop. "With respect, señora. How did you find out?"

"Lieutenant Silvio spoke to me while you were out of the country. He felt that you'd been very unfairly treated, especially given your record of achievements."

Speechless, Emilia could only nod.

Placing her cup and saucer on a nearby table, Carlota reached out and gripped Emilia's wrist. "Only you can find the man who killed my sister. The *federales* can't. They're less than useless and riddled with informants. The *norteamericanos* play in Mexico like a big sandbox. If they find him first, they will dictate the terms of his punishment. I won't have that. Find El Barracuda. I'll give you anything within my power to grant if it helps you find him. Afterward, you can name whatever job you want in my city. Anything. Do we understand each other?"

Emilia was captivated by Carlota's iron grip and piercing stare. "Yes, señora, I'll find him," she murmured.

"Good, then that's settled." Carlota let go, breaking the spell.

The double doors opened. Santibañez stood in the entrance with his ever-present clipboard. "It's getting late, señora," he announced.

Carlota stood, smoothing her skirt. "Good luck with the hunt, Detective. Keep me apprised."

"You, too," Emilia blurted like an *idiota,* her head still swimming. "I mean, good luck with the election today."

"Can I count on your vote?"

"Of course," Emilia said.

CHAPTER 55

The house where Rafa Gamboa grew up wasn't far from the down-on-its-luck pink apartment building, but Emilia would leave Las Brisas without stopping there.

Carrying the package, she climbed the stairs to the Alvarez apartment.

"Detective Cruz." Victoria Alvarez answered the knock. "How can I help you?"

"Good morning, señora." Emilia stepped into the foyer. "I'm here to return your picture."

Belinda Alvarez appeared next to her sister. "I hope you replaced the glass."

"Yes, and again, I apologize for having broken it."

"Won't you stay for coffee?" Victoria inquired.

"Yes, please stay." Belinda Alvarez sounded like she and Emilia were new best friends as she took the framed picture and set it on the hall table. "We owe you such a debt of gratitude for finding out what happened to Monica. The least we can do is offer you a cup of coffee."

"Yes, thank you." Burning with curiosity at Belinda's shift in attitude, Emilia readily accepted the invitation.

The family had been told everything, although the question of money laundering had been glossed over. Without an explanation from Gifford, there was no hard proof that Monica knew where the money for her sister's campaign originated. Likewise, the fiction that Financial Crimes was a police unit was maintained.

But coffee with the Alvarez sisters was little more than a courtesy. The three sipped coffee and nibbled sugar cookies in the dining room. The conversation avoided dicey subjects like the funeral, Sergio Alvarez's failed business with Felix Montoya, and if they were going to vote later today.

Victoria complimented Emilia's ring. Emilia thanked her and said she planned to get married next year.

The conversation died after that.

"I'll walk you downstairs," Belinda said when Emilia was ready to go. "I want to show Emilia the garden."

"Of course." Victoria embraced Emilia. "Thank you so much for everything."

Belinda chattered away as she ushered Emilia down the stairs. Had Emilia chosen a dress yet? Planned a honeymoon?

Emilia barely needed to reply. The other woman clearly was just filling time until they were someplace private.

That place was apparently a sagging sofa in the dimly lit lobby.

"I didn't want Victoria to relive all of this again," Belinda said by way of explanation. She looked younger than ever in a starched white blouse and cobalt blue silk trousers, with dangling lapis earrings and her hair tumbling over one shoulder. "Was Monica really engaged to that gringo? William Gifford from the consulate?"

"Yes." Emilia nodded. "He was a very charming man. I expect he made her very happy right until the end."

"What about Carlos?"

"Carlos Lima?" Events had relegated him to the role of minor player in the drama of the last few weeks, especially given that Macias and Sandor had tracked down the dealer who sold Beso Sanchez the pills that led to her death. "He acted in a suspicious manner but was released and all charges dropped. The poor girl who could have confirmed his alibi died of an accidental drug overdose. He had nothing to do with it besides giving her enough money to buy pills laced with fentanyl."

"Yes, well." Belinda gave a small, rueful laugh. "I'm sure you understand. I'd like you to expunge his record. His fingerprints, interview, arrest. Everything."

"Expunge his record," Emilia repeated.

"Yes, make sure Carlos's moment as a person of interest gets lost." Belinda's fingers climbed an imaginary career ladder. "A police record might be problematic in future, if you know what I mean."

"And why would you care about Carlos Lima's future?"

"Carlos and I have been in a relationship for some time." This time, Belinda's laugh was a nervous whinny. "Of course, Victoria doesn't know. He was never happy with Monica, she was too immature for him, but I could hardly tell my sister that I'd taken up with her daughter's boyfriend."

Emilia had already showered that morning, but knew she'd need another after this conversation.

"I'm eight years older than Carlos, but the sex is incredible," Belinda lowered her voice. "I was with him that night, you know."

"What night?" Emilia asked, although the answer was obvious.

"The night that Monica died." More nervous whinnies. "The Viejo Dorado suite at the Boulevard is our sanctuary. We meet there every few weeks. Carlos pays for the girl, then gives her something extra so she'll leave but claim to have stayed.

That way no one else who uses the suite will be suspicious that Carlos isn't using it like the rest of them."

Pays for the girl, then gives her something extra. Emilia wanted to shake the other woman for her callow attitude toward the late Beso Sanchez.

But it was more than that. Belinda's official statement said that she was home the night of Monica's murder. If she'd told the truth, it would have saved the police from wasting countless hours on Carlos Lima.

"I could arrest both you and Carlos for lying to the police," Emilia said. "But it's not worth the paperwork."

Belinda swallowed nervously. "What about Carlos's arrest record? Can you fix it?"

"I hope your sister never finds out what a *puta* you are." It was Emilia's turn to laugh, albeit with grimly ironic humor. "You know that he likes them young, don't you?"

She walked out without saying another word.

CHAPTER 56

Carlota's main rival Nadio Vallejo Loy conceded the election in the early evening. The mayor's supporters poured into downtown streets in jubilation.

The violence had been minimal. No one gunned down. Only a few trash fires and beatings. Even the cheering crowds did little damage.

Emilia wasn't sure if the relative peace was because an army of cops from across the state of Guerrero were at every polling place or if local gangs had decided to take a break while media pundits crowed about imported violence from El Norte.

Or perhaps Barrielos Luna paid criminals to swig tequila and stay home for a couple of days. Then everyone could feel good about his chosen results of the election right away. *See, Carlota really is tough on crime.*

Silvio and Mercedes came to the Palacio Real to watch the victory fireworks with Emilia and Kurt from the penthouse balcony. It was Silvio's first outing since being released from the hospital.

Emilia tried to disguise her alarm when she saw him using a cane and taking slow, careful steps. His face was slimmer, reflecting how much weight he'd lost.

Yet he was on the mend, with Mercedes's help. The dancer seemed to know instinctively when he would accept help and when he could manage on his own.

The velvety sky above the gently rolling Pacific was dotted with stars. Kurt lit several lanterns and hung streamers of *papel picado*, creating an exclusive, festive atmosphere. Huge pots of red geraniums scattered around the balcony scented the air. Steel drum music drifted up from the Pasodoble Bar.

They had a late supper on the balcony on the living room side of the penthouse, starting with ceviche that Emilia made herself and served with thin slices of avocado and a sprinkling of fresh cilantro. She followed up the spicy fish cocktail with a roast chicken basted with an ancho chili plum sauce, courtesy of the restaurant kitchen. Rice, beans, pickled vegetables and warm tortillas completed the entree. Flan for dessert, also from the restaurant.

The conversation ranged from Silvio's new physical therapy regime to Emilia's bizarre conversation with Belinda Alvarez to the sweet deal that Metro Properties had given them for Casa de Plata.

Emilia decided to tell Kurt later about the whole business with Chief Salazar and Carlota's intervention. She'd thank Silvio later, too.

Mercedes helped Emilia carry the dishes into the kitchen. When they returned to the balcony, Kurt poured them all a glass of post-dinner brandy. "Almost time," he said.

They converged on the wall to view the show. Silvio and Mercedes stood close together. He draped his good arm over the dancer's shoulders and she leaned into him. Held her close and they kissed. It was a quiet moment of intimacy that Emilia never expected to see.

The two couples had just enough time to toast each other before the first rocket soared up from Isla la Roqueta out in the middle of the bay. The projectile howled into the darkness before exploding into a cascade of red, white, and green streamers to celebrate Carlota's victory. More fireworks followed. Rocket after rocket burst into sizzling color against the arc of the night sky.

"The more I think about it," Silvio said during a lull. "The more I think Carlota was in on it."

"I said the same thing to Em earlier." Kurt tipped his glass in a salute to the like-minded. "Her campaign needed the money. Vallejo Loy put up a good fight."

"We never raised the issue of her campaign getting laundered money," Silvio said. "I think we both know why."

"No." After the moment earlier with Carlota in the *alcaldía*, Emilia was sure. "No, I don't think Carlota knew that Barrielos Luna was involved. I'm not even sure Monica did. Monica wanted to do Carlota a favor. Create a bond with her sister. That's why she took the job when her whole family was against it. I think she really, really wanted to be part of Carlota's life and not just because she was politically ambitious herself."

"So nobody asked questions where the money was coming from?" Kurt asked.

"Not the point," Silvio responded with a touch of his old gruffness. "Monica Montoya gave Barrielos Luna a way to get to her sister. His money helped Carlota win. She's in his pocket forever."

"What about El Barracuda?" Emilia asked. "He's the man's nephew yet she wants his head on a plate."

Silvio shrugged. "So she says."

"If Barrielos Luna wants her to stay as mayor," Kurt said. "There's got to be a good reason."

"I know," Emilia admitted. It was the question she'd been

wrestling with ever since Nora Torres had pointed it out.

"Whether she knows it or not, Carlota is playing a very dangerous game." Silvio raised his glass. "Well, here's to the devil you know."

They all touched glasses.

"And to cheap real estate," Kurt said.

"I'll drink to that." Mercedes rested her head on Silvio's shoulder. "We live in such crazy times; you never know what's going to happen. Casa de Plata is going to be our shelter from the storm. I can't wait until we can move in."

The house phone, which was Kurt's direct connection to the hotel's front desk, trilled from the living room. As more fireworks arced into the sky, Kurt disengaged from Emilia and went to answer it. He was back a moment later, eyebrows raised.

"Em, there's a package for you downstairs. The concierge said a man named Bernal dropped it off."

The brandy glass nearly slipped out of Emilia's hand. "Is he still here?"

"Who? Bernal?"

But Emilia was on the move. She left her glass on the top of the balcony wall, flew through the penthouse into the elevator and sprinted through the doors as soon as they opened at the lobby level.

"Where's the package from Señor Bernal?" she breathlessly asked the night concierge.

The young man behind the desk passed her a padded envelope the size of a paperback book.

Emilia snatched it up. Her name was scrawled across the front, along with the name of the hotel.

She didn't open it but ran to the entrance where the doorman and valet were chatting. Both were pleasant young men she'd spoken to many times since moving into the penthouse with Kurt. "Señor Bernal," she said, looking from one to the other. "Where is he?"

The valet answered first. "He just handed me the package, señora, and drove off."

Of course he did.

Emilia carried the package to a secluded seat on the perimeter of the lobby. She found the little tab saying *Tear Here* and opened the envelope to find a Mexican passport, a folded page of newsprint, and a sealed white envelope.

The passport was her original, complete with visa and the stamp showing the date she'd entered El Norte. It bore a new exit stamp, purporting to show that she had departed the country 48 hours later.

The newspaper page was from the *Washington Post*. Emilia immediately saw the relevant article.

Diplomatic Security Service officers killed in DUI accident

Theodore F. Harris, 42, and Clement Abbott, 38, were both killed when the car they were in failed to make a turn on Kirby Road in Arlington, Virginia. According to Arlington police, the blood alcohol level of both men exceeded the legal limit. They were pronounced dead at the scene.

Harris and Abbott were both employed by the Department of State's Diplomatic Security Service and had served overseas with that agency.

Rafa had gotten his revenge, just like Nora knew he would.

Emilia set the newspaper aside and slid her finger under the flap of the white envelope, breaking the seal. She drew out a greeting card decorated with a Picasso line drawing of a hand holding a bunch of flowers.

It was blank inside except for two scrawled words.

I'm sorry.

A shadow fell across her lap. Kurt stood by her side.

"Want to tell me what's going on?" he asked softly.

Emilia swiped at her cheek with the back of one hand, surprised to feel tears. "I'm okay," she said and smiled up at him. "Better than I've been in a long time."

El Fin

Acknowledgments

My late mother Jean, to whom this book is dedicated, was my first and best cheerleader.

She read everything I wrote and had no reservations about telling everyone she knew about my books. Long after dementia prevented her from reading, she kept a dog-eared copy of *Cliff Diver* with her.

The world is a little quieter without my mother, but I still hear her encouragement every day.

Special thanks go to my siblings for their strength and support as our mother slipped away, as well as to my husband and children.

Thanks also go to editor Kerry Watson, whose knowledge of Mexico and technical editing are the perfect combination, and to proofreader extraordinaire Shelby Robinson.

CARMEN AMATO

You're invited

Thank you for being a part of Detective Emilia Cruz's world. Stay connected and informed about what's next by joining my Mystery Ahead newsletter and get free access to the Detective Emilia Cruz Starter Library, lost chapters and more.

Every other Sunday, the newsletter gives you insider updates, sneak peeks at upcoming books, and book reviews of must-read mysteries.

Go to mysteryahead.substack.com or scan the QR code below.

Meanwhile, enjoy the recipe on the next page and the list of Spanish words used in Detective Emilia Cruz books.

All the best, Carmen Amato

Taqueria Shrimp Tacos with Seasoned Slaw

Ingredients

1/2 cup plain Greek yogurt

1/4 cup minced fresh cilantro

2 tablespoons freshly-squeezed lime juice

1/4 teaspoon ground cumin

14 teaspoon fine sea salt

1/4 teaspoon freshly-cracked black pepper

3 finely chopped green onions

2 finely chopped garlic cloves

4 cups shredded cabbage (ok to use a bagged mix)

1 pound large shrimp, peeled and deveined

Dash of salt and pepper

3 tablespoons packaged taco seasoning (any brand)

2 tablespoons avocado or olive oil

8–10 flour tortillas (or corn tortillas)

1 avocado, peeled, pitted and thinly-sliced

Optional toppings: chopped fresh cilantro, chopped red or white onion, crumbled cotija cheese, and/or lime wedges

Directions

Whisk first 8 ingredients together to make a creamy dressing. Pour over cabbage, mix well. Set aside.

In another bowl, toss shrimp with taco seasoning, salt and pepper. Heat oil in large frying pan. Cook the shrimp for 3 to 4 minutes, flipping once, until they are opaque and cooked through.

Assemble tacos by filling flour tortillas with generous helping of slaw, then layer on shrimp, avocado and toppings as desired.

Excellent with a cold beer!

Spanish words commonly used in the Detective Emilia Cruz series

Abarrotes: snacks

Agua de jamaica: cold tea made with dried hibiscus

Alcaldia: town hall and/or mayor's offices

Amigo: friend, buddy

Barrio: neighborhood

Bayos blancos: white beans

Cabrón: slang meaning dumbass

Campesino: subsistence farmers, country dwellers

Casita: little house

Cédula: identity card

Cerrado: closed

Chatarra: junk

Chica: girl

Comida: the main meal of the day, usually eaten in early afternoon

Conchas: sweet rolls topped with sugar and shaped like a conch shell

Coyote: guides who take people over the US-Mexican border illegally for a price

Dios mio: my god, an exclamation

El Norte: the United States

Falta: lack of

Federales: slang for the Policía Federal Preventiva, federal law enforcement agency

Guayabera: men's button-down shirt with a straight hem and multiple pockets

Halcone: word meaning falcon, used to mean a person acting as a lookout
Hojalateria: brake shop for cars
Hombres: men
Jefe: chief, person in charge
Jitomate: tomato
Las Brisas: upscale neighborhood on the eastern side of Acapulco Bay
Libraría: bookstore
Libro: book
Llantas: tires
Loco: crazy
Lotéria: lottery
Madre de Dios: Mother of God, used as exclamation
Maldita: damn, damned
Mercado: market
Mujeres: women
Muertos: papier maché skeleton figures used to decorate Day of the Dead altars
Narcomanta: banner bearing a message from a gang or cartel
Norteamericano: North American
Ofrenda: altar
Palapa: traditional Mexican shelter roofed with palm leaves or branches
Papel picado: streamers of tissue paper cut into silhouette designs
Parrilla: grill for food, usually assumed to be for meat
Pastelería: pastry shop
Patrón: boss
Pendejo: asshole, jerk

Permiso: excuse me

Peso: Mexican monetary unit, roughly equivalent to $0.10.

Placas: license plates

Por dedazo: expression meaning "by the finger" to indicate patronage

Por favor: please

Prima/primo: female or male cousin

Privada: enclosed subdivision and/or the gate to the property

Prohibido el paso: "Keep out" warning

Queso fresco: soft cheese common in Mexican recipes

Rayos: exclamation, similar to "oh hell"

Reina: queen

Salsa verde: tart green salsa usually made with tomatillos

Sicario: cartel henchman or assassin

Talavera: hand painted pottery from Puebla

Taqueria: taco restaurant

Telenovela: television soap opera

Ten cuidado: be careful, take care

Tiendita: little store

Tío/Tía: uncle/aunt

Tumbadore: person who steals drug shipments

Zocalo: town square

About the Author

Carmen Amato is the author of the Detective Emilia Cruz mystery series pitting the first female police detective in Acapulco against Mexico's cartels, corruption, and social inequality. Starting with *Cliff Diver*, the series is a 2-time winner of the Outstanding Series award from CrimeMasters of America and was hailed by National Public Radio as "A thrilling series."

Inspired by the real-life exploits of her grandfather Joseph Sestito, who was a deputy sheriff in upstate New York during Prohibition, Carmen is also the author of the award-winning Galliano Club historical fiction series.

Her standalone thrillers include *The Hidden Light of Mexico City*, which was longlisted for the 2020 Millennium Book Award.

A 30-year veteran of the CIA where she focused on technical collection and counterdrug efforts, Carmen is a recipient of both the National Intelligence Award and the Career Intelligence Medal.

A judge for the BookLife Prize and Killer Nashville's Claymore Award, her work has appeared in *Huffpost, Criminal Element, Publishers Weekly,* and other national publications.

Join her popular Mystery Ahead newsletter for updates and great book reviews: *mysteryahead.substack.com.*

9 798989 140374